DOMINO RUN

by

ANDREW IYER

LONDON
MADISON PUBLISHING
1995

Published in 1995 by
Madison Publishing of
83, Albert Palace Mansions
Lurline Gardens
London SW11 4DH

Printed in Great Britain by
City Print Services, London

Front cover designed by
Artifex Design, Covent Garden
London

ISBN 0 9526373 0 8

British Library Cataloguing in Publication Data.
A catalogue record for this book is available
from the British Library.

AUTHOR'S NOTE

This book is dedicated to Bobby Moore OBE, a truly dignified and courageous man, who I had the privilege of knowing.

I would like to thank the following people in particular for helping to make this book a reality, and in so doing for supporting the Cancer Research Campaign so generously: Martin Gebbie of Artifex Design for designing the front cover of the book, Andrew Boxall of City Print Services for printing this edition, Nick Gould of Ince & Co. for his advice and Louise for her support and patience throughout.

Above all, I thank everyone who buys a copy of Domino Run. By doing so you are contributing to what I believe is a very worthwhile cause.

Andrew Iyer

The Cancer Research Campaign

Cancer can strike without warning at any time, devastating entire families when it does.

300,000 people will be diagnosed with cancer this year and 1 in 3 of us will develop the disease.

For over 70 years the Cancer Research Campaign has been fighting cancer on all fronts. The charity is now the leader in the development of new anti-cancer drugs and the supporter of one third of all cancer research in the United Kingdom, including some 700 scientists in the country's universities and research institutions.

By supporting the Cancer Research Campaign, you will be helping to enable vital research to continue in the search for an absolute cure to the cruellest of diseases.

All of the author's royalties and all profits made by the publisher from sales of this book are being donated to the Cancer Research Campaign.

CHAPTER 1

Brussels. Friday, 18th November 1994.

Chancellor Schmidt, head of the recently unified German Republic voted "Yes" on behalf of his country. The seventeenth "Yes" vote of the afternoon. All of the Member States had now voted except Great Britain.

The meeting hall in the magnificent Eighteenth Century villa in the southern part of Brussels, which was housing the session of meetings of the Council of the European Communities was bursting with people. In the centre of the hall stood a huge oval table at which sat the leaders of the eighteen Member States. Immediately behind each of the leaders' blue leather chairs were slightly less ornate chairs for european advisers and permanent representatives. Further chairs were grouped behind these, in which sat junior Community officials and more advisers. In all, there were over three hundred men and women crammed into the room.

The press gallery above the hall was also packed. Representatives from most of the World's major newspapers and television stations were there. Large television cameras dominated the front of the gallery. In between the television cameras were dozens of smaller telescopic lenses recording every expression on the face of each politician.

As soon as the German Chancellor had cast his vote there were loud cheers from the floor of the meeting hall. Permanent representatives, the civil servants of the European Community, congratulated one another and foreign ministers smiled and nodded their approval for the benefit of the cameras.

The office of President of the Council is held for a term of six months and rotates among the Member States. The Presidency was currently with Italy. The Italian President repeatedly demanded silence until the hall became absolutely quiet. Attention focused on the British Prime Minister, the last leader to vote on behalf of his country.

The Council of the European Communities is the body where the interests of the Member States finds direct expression. It is made up of delegates of the Member States, each state being represented by a member of its government. When general matters are discussed Member States are usually represented by their foreign ministers. For more important matters, political leaders will attend in person.

The Council was voting to admit The Romanian People's Republic into the European Community as a Protected Member. For most matters the Council makes decisions in accordance with the majority of votes cast. However, there are a few matters, including the admission of new Community members, which must be decided unanimously.

The British Prime Minister had two buttons on the table in front of him. One would signal that Great Britain voted "Yes", the other that the vote cast was "No". The ancient room and the press gallery were totally silent. All eyes were focused on the British leader.

The British Prime Minister leant forward, being careful not to catch the eye of anyone at the table and pressed the "No" button.

The hall erupted. Permanent representatives from across the table shouted at their British counterparts and the various foreign ministers looked over at the British Prime Minister and shook their heads dramatically.

Flashes of light illuminated the press gallery as photographers shot reel after reel of film for the morning newspapers. The television cameras rolled collecting footage of the British Prime Minister for the evening news shows.

The Italian President attempted to regain control of the meeting to formally announce the outcome of the vote, but it was useless. The shouting continued. Everyone knew what the British vote meant. For the second time, Romania had been denied Protected Membership of the European Community by Great Britain.

The British Prime Minister ignored the shouting around him. He turned sideways slightly in his chair, looked behind him and nodded in the direction of the chairs at the back of the room reserved for British officials. His nod was discreetly returned by His Royal Highness Prince Richard, the Prince of Wales.

CHAPTER 2

London. Monday, 21st November 1994.

"Everyone's been looking for you. I've been trying you on your mobile 'phone for the last hour," said Elizabeth as David stuck his head around the door of her tiny office. "I've about a dozen messages for you and Mike Henderson has asked me twice to let him know the moment you get in. How did the meeting with Metalex go?"

"Not bad," replied David. "They're beginning to recognise they have a problem that's not going to go away by itself, but you know some clients. They're so worried about what they think we're costing them they tend to keep us out of things for too long, usually to their peril later. What does Henderson want and who's called the most times?"

Elizabeth referred to the pad of messages on her desk before answering her boss. "Peter Marshall at Maxoil has called twice. He, as usual, wouldn't tell me what he wanted, but he says he needs to speak to you urgently. Dr. Mollini called from Italy..." She was about to continue reading from her list of names when David cut in.

"Peter Marshall called twice." David sounded surprised. "Why didn't you give him my mobile number or call me yourself?"

"That's what I said. I've been trying to get hold of you for the last hour," replied Elizabeth. "I called Metalex, they told me you'd left them and were on your way back to the office. Whenever I called your mobile all I got was you message service saying your 'phone wasn't in use."

"Yes, that's right," said David apologetically as he realised that he would not have been contactable underground. "I got fed up waiting for a taxi so I got on the tube. My 'phone wouldn't have been working. I'll call Marshall now. Can you bring the other messages into my office in a moment with a mug of steaming hot coffee please? It's raining out there and I'm soaked through." David took the message slip with Peter Marshall's name and number from Elizabeth and walked into his own office at the far end of the corridor.

He was anxious to call Marshall. He looked at the times scribbled down on the piece of paper recording when Elizabeth had taken the calls. The last one was over an hour ago. Marshall was the Deputy Director of Technical Services at Maxoil International Marine Limited, the most significant British company in the Maxoil petroleum group, the third largest oil corporation in the World. He was a Texan by birth and in character. David had met Marshall at a conference at the end of the summer, organised by the Baltic Exchange from its temporary home in the Lloyd's Building in the City of London. The Baltic Exchange's building in St. Mary's Axe had been destroyed by an IRA bomb two years earlier and the task of finding new permanent accommodation for the Baltic was proving to be a difficult one. The conference had been on various aspects of shipping and marine insurance law and David had delivered a paper entitled, "The Consequences of Material Non Disclosure by Insurance Brokers", a topic of significant interest to the City at a time when insurance brokers were regularly being accused of placing risks in the market negligently.

During one of the coffee breaks, Marshall had introduced himself to David and they had discussed the consequences of a recent decision of the House of Lords in a case known as "Pine Top", concerning the principles of material non disclosure in insurance. David had been surprised to learn that someone involved with technical services for Maxoil clearly knew some law and was well informed on current developments affecting the marine and insurance sectors of the City. Marshall had explained to David that his job included the coordination of legal services. He was one of Maxoil's many in-house lawyers, only more senior than any David had ever met before. He had been sent to London to streamline the group's legal services in the U.K.

Marshall had met David for drinks since the conference at Lloyd's a few times and on one occasion for lunch. He was convinced that the Texan liked him and hoped that the in-house lawyer was impressed with his knowledge of international trade law.

Solicitors are always anxious to cultivate potential new clients for their firms. The 1980s had seen the emergence of many new law firms in the United Kingdom legal market and the long standing links that many companies had with particular law firms which had helped to guarantee the loyalty of clients had been eroded. For the first time ever, law firms found themselves having to openly compete with one another in order to attract new business and keep existing clients. Competition was rife and no more so than amongst the top City law firms.

David Bowstead was a Senior Litigation Assistant in the firm of Holland Chapman & Co., one of the City's oldest and most respected law firms. Holland Chapman & Co., like the vast majority of City law firms, practised commercial law, a phrase that was sufficiently wide to enable it to take on any potentially lucrative case of a commercial nature it was offered, in comparison with criminal or ordinary civil cases, whilst being sufficiently imposing to allow the firm to avoid acting for companies that had need of solicitors but could not pay the high fees that City firms charged. However, in some respects Holland Chapman & Co. was unique amongst major City practices. The firm only handled litigation and generally only international trade litigation, in particular shipping, insurance, construction and commodity trading disputes. These areas are regarded as the Rolls Royce disciplines of litigation. Holland Chapman & Co. did not act for banks, divorce celebrities or handle property transactions. The firm acted for companies that traded all sorts of goods around the World, ship owners, oil majors, construction companies and the largest insurance organisations on the planet. Holland Chapman & Co. was the best in its chosen fields. The firm knew it and so did the competition.

Traditionally, City law firms make up new partners annually at the beginning of May. David Bowstead was up for partnership the following year. He knew that when the partners of Holland Chapman & Co. were deciding whether he should be invited to join them, his potential earning capacity for the firm would be one of the most important considerations. In order to achieve partnership at a firm like Holland Chapman & Co. David would have to demonstrate an ability to attract new clients to the firm, of the type that could regularly afford the fees of a top City law firm.

David knew that solicitors did not make it as far as senior assistants in top City firms without being very good lawyers. By the time an assistant was senior enough to be considered for partnership at Holland Chapman & Co., the assistant's legal ability was not usually in question. What really mattered was what he had to offer to the fabric of the firm and whether he would be able to carry the prestigious flag of Holland Chapman & Co. into the future. In other words, could he earn big money for the firm?

Typically, assistant solicitors in the City can expect to work anything up to ten years after qualification before being considered for partnership. Most firms only make up a handful of new partners each year and on average seventy five per cent of assistants will be disappointed. For those that do become partners in the country's largest law firms, the rewards are considerable. Senior partners can expect to earn in the region of half a million pounds a year and some will make over a million pounds a year. It is this prospect that keeps most young solicitors going month after month when they are having to work a six day, ninety hour week.

Holland Chapman & Co. did not act for Maxoil. The firm had never acted for the oil major. David had asked the firm's librarians to check the number of cases in which Maxoil had been involved in the Commercial Court from the beginning of 1984 until the end of the previous year, 1993. A convenient ten year period. One Maxoil company or other had been named as either Plaintiffs or Defendants in a total of one hundred and twenty four writs issued during the period. Of these one hundred and twenty four cases that had been commenced in the Commercial Court, thirty two of them had proceeded to trial. This was a lot of disputes for any company to be involved in and did not include commercial arbitrations which by their very nature are confidential.

David estimated that Maxoil had probably been involved in fifty to sixty arbitrations during the period he was considering, in addition to the cases in the Commercial Court. Maxoil were, David had decided, one of the most litigious players in the international trade arena.

His research had identified three law firms that regularly acted for the oil corporation in cases in which they were involved in the Commercial Court. David had no reason to think that these firms did not also handle between them Maxoil's arbitrations. It had not come as a surprise to David that the oil company employed the services of three law firms rather than just one. The cases in which Maxoil had been involved during the previous ten years fell into three distinct categories. Shipping disputes involving everything from run of the mill charter party and bill of lading disputes to more dramatic collisions at sea; insurance disputes concerned mainly with spills and hull insurance involving Maxoil vessels and commodity trading disputes concerning Maxoil's various oil trading companies. Each of the law firms Maxoil used were regarded as leaders in one of these fields. David had been attempting to persuade Marshall that the interests of the his employer would be best served if one law firm handled all of Maxoil's litigation and arbitrations. As well as Maxoil benefitting from one team of lawyers knowing all about the organisation's business, this would inevitably reduce Maxoil's overall legal bill, which David estimated at being in the region of five million pounds a year.

It had been this revelation by David during his recent lunch with Marshall that had seemed to have the most impact. David had explained that Holland Chapman & Co. was a leader in all of the areas of the law in which Maxoil were repeatedly involved. Marshall had been aware of the firm's reputation and indicated to David that he was under pressure to cut his company's annual legal budget.

David knew that Maxoil would not transfer their business to Holland Chapman & Co. without first trying the firm out, irrespective of the firm's first class reputation. If Marshall was genuinely impressed with David and the firm, David could expect Maxoil to instruct him on a small case first of all, but on one that was difficult. If Marshall was happy with the way in which the case was handled, David could expect more cases of a larger nature. Eventually, if the relationship was working Maxoil would ask to meet a team of partners and other assistants from the firm with a view to retaining Holland Chapman & Co. on a permanent basis, subject of course to reaching agreement on fees. The Partnership was aware that David was cultivating Maxoil as a potential client and was impressed with how he was conducting things. If the relationship did move up a gear, partners specialising in areas of the law which concerned Maxoil would form the basis of any team offered to handle the oil company's litigation. At that stage these partners would "run" Maxoil as a client, but David knew that he would be closely involved and that the inclusion of Maxoil amongst the firm's clients would almost certainly put his partnership the following year beyond doubt.

As soon as David got to his office he pressed the buttons on his telephone that in turn activated the speaker and automatically dialled Marshall's number from the telephone's memory. As the number was being dialled David took off his damp overcoat and threw it into one of the two chairs that stood opposite his desk. He had a file in his hand entitled "MAXOIL -MARKETING" by the time the voice on the other end of the line answered his call.

"Maxoil International, how may I help you?"

"Peter Marshall please. This is David Bowstead returning his call." It only took a few seconds for David to be put through.

"Dave, Pete here, glad I finally caught up with you. Your secretary tells me you've been running around a bit this morning."

"Yes," replied David "sorry I wasn't here when you called. I was out at a meeting with clients."

"No problem. Can you spare me a couple of minutes?" David smiled to himself. Marshall knew that David had plenty of time for him.

"I'm all ears, what can I do for you, my secretary said it was urgent?"

"I'd like to instruct you on a new case. We recently chartered a tub called the "Oil Star 2" from an outfit in Greece to carry crude oil from Kharg Island to Corpus Christi. Well, it turns out that the Greeks only had the damn vessel on time charter, not the owners you see. They've gone bust and the actual owners, some Panamanian company are saying that they haven't been paid hire for the vessel in full by the Greeks. Sounds like the Greeks screwed them, but that's their problem right? They want to know whether we will contribute to the ongoing costs of the voyage, the vessel's about half way to Corpus Christi. We paid freight in full to the Greeks and can prove it, but I'm concerned that the Panamanians will suspend the voyage when they get to Corpus Christi and lien the cargo unless we give them some more money. Can you have a look at the contracts for me and let me know if we are legally obliged to pay anything to the Panamanians, which I certainly don't want to? I'd also like your views on what steps we can take in the English Courts to force them to deliver the cargo at Corpus Christi if they try and blackmail us when the ship gets to the States. If they pull a Forty Five on me Dave, I want a Magnum in my pocket to shoot them in the ass with. Is all this clear?"

David was too experienced a solicitor to interrupt a client when he was explaining a problem. Whilst Marshall had been talking, David had been noting everything down on a legal pad. "Yes, crystal clear," he replied. "I have a few questions and I'll need to see all the documents you have."

"Shoot," said Marshall. David asked him a number of provisional questions concerning the voyage and the exchanges that had already taken place between Maxoil and the Panamanian owners of the vessel. Once he was satisfied that Marshall had told him everything, he told his new client what specific documents he would need to see to be able to answer the questions Marshall had asked.

"I'll courier my entire file over to your office within the hour," replied Marshall. "When do you think you can let me have an answer?"

David remembered his trip to Miami. In the excitement of getting his first case from Maxoil he had completely forgotten about the Cuban and his coffee. "I have to go to Miami on business this evening," he said quickly. "If you can get the papers to me before I leave for the airport, I'll read them on the 'plane and 'phone you tomorrow with answers."

"That'll be fine. The "Oil Star 2" will be at sea either way for another week. I'll expect your call tomorrow. See ya Dave." With that Marshall hung up.

The door to David's office opened and Elizabeth came in carrying a mug of steaming coffee which she put down on his desk. She picked up his dripping overcoat and hung it on a peg behind the door.

"Marshall just instructed me on what looks like a potential economic duress case," said David. "All those evenings drinking Bourbon listening to him explain why he loves Texas so much might just pay off after all. I'll dictate up the minutes from my meeting with Metalex this morning. We better get them on the file in case something happens on that one whilst I'm in Miami and Martin Mcdonald has to advise them. They're his clients after all. Good news about Marshall though. He said he'd be sending the papers over within the hour. Could you look out for them? I need to take them with me to Miami."

"I'll make sure the post room knows to send them straight up as soon as they arrive," she replied. Although Elizabeth did not congratulate David on getting instructions from Maxoil she was pleased for him. Elizabeth was thirty nine years old. She had worked for Holland Chapman & Co. for fourteen years and had been David's secretary for the last five years. When she had first started working for him she had also worked for another assistant in the firm, but it had soon become apparent that David would keep her very busy by himself. They had become a team and before long the other assistant for whom she worked was allocated a new secretary and she was left working just for David.

She enjoyed working for him. Some of the other secretaries

complained that they would not like to work for David because of the long hours he asked Elizabeth to keep, but she did not mind this. David was very good at what he did. She had worked for enough solicitors over the years to be able to recognise ability. Whilst David and Elizabeth would never discuss such things, she knew he was up for partnership the following year and hoped he got it. The case from Peter Marshall would be a feather in her boss's cap.

"Don't forget Mike Henderson wanted to see you as soon as you got in," said Elizabeth as she left David's office.

Mike Henderson was one of the firm's oldest partners. Holland Chapman & Co. had sixty four partners. Henderson was the most senior after the Senior Partner Robert Metcalf. Three years earlier Henderson had been invited by the Partnership to become Senior Partner. He had declined. Senior Partners of City law firms have little time to handle cases. They are charged with ensuring that their firms strive forwards as strongly as possible. Henderson was a litigator and he intended to continue being a litigator. The Senior Partnership had not been for him. He was sixty eight years old, one of the oldest solicitors still practising in the City. He was also one of the most respected. A more colourful story about him concerned an incident a few years earlier when the Judge in charge of the Commercial Court, faced with a young lawyer from Holland Chapman & Co. on an application being heard in the Friday summons list, considering that the young lawyer was not as familiar with the case in question as he should have been, ordered the lawyer to either go away and acquaint himself fully with the case or send the partner from his firm who was responsible for the case to Court the following Friday. The following week when the Judge's Clerk announced the application again, the Judge looked up not to see the young lawyer bowing to him before addressing the bench, but Henderson. On seeing the veteran solicitor and knowing his reputation, the Judge politely stood up, bowed back to Henderson and granted the application without hearing any submissions.

Henderson's many years in the City had not lessened his enthusiasm for what he did. Whenever he was asked if he was thinking of retiring he would reply that he would continue to practice law at Holland Chapman & Co. until his clients did not want him any more or until he died. There was little prospect of his clients abandoning him. He was a tenacious litigator who had been known to literally intimidate lesser opponents into

11

accepting settlement terms which were overly generous to his clients. There was however a real prospect that his heart might give out because of his weakness for cigars.

David had worked for Henderson for the last three years. Henderson acted for a number of wealthy commodity traders who preferred to trade in their own names rather than through companies. Holland Chapman & Co. did not act for many private individuals, preferring to act for major corporations instead. Contrary to the impression many people have of the law, the most money is generally not to be made acting for wealthy individuals. The problems of the rich can produce big fees for solicitors, but private individuals, even wealthy ones, do not find themselves in nearly as many disputes as corporations do. From a law firm's point of view, the greater the number of problems a client has the more money the firm will earn in the long run. Henderson did not entirely agree with this approach. As a result he had a number of private clients all of whom were heavily involved in international trade in one way or another. One such client was a Cuban coffee trader who lived in Miami who David was going to see the following day.

David had a pretty good idea what Henderson wanted to talk to him about and decided the other messages could wait until after he had seen his boss. He managed one long gulp of coffee before he headed out of his office for the sixth floor of Holland Chapman & Co.'s building.

Unlike many City firms, Holland Chapman & Co. was not organised into departments. The firm's philosophy was that it was essentially a litigation firm and encouraged its lawyers to become competent in all areas of the firm's practice. One of the consequences of not having departments was that the layout of the office was not organised in a conventional way, with partners and assistants who worked together sitting in offices which were located near to each other. Henderson's office was on the top floor of the building and it took David almost five minutes to walk through the firm's corridors before he reached his boss's office.

The old lawyer's door was never closed. He did not rely upon his secretary to prevent unwanted employees from seeing him. If he did not want to see you he told you so in no uncertain terms. If he did, he welcomed you into his office with a smile. David was pleased to see Henderson smile as he walked into his room. No sooner had David walked in through the door than Henderson replaced the cigar he was holding into his mouth and drew on it passionately.

"You wanted to see me Mike?" David asked, as he conditioned himself to the familiar smell of cigar smoke that always surrounded Henderson. David did not smoke himself, but did not find the smell of cigars unpleasant. Nevertheless, he always had to breathe slowly for the first minute or so on entering Henderson's smoky office.

"That's right David, I wanted to talk to you about our outstanding invoices to Garces before you go and see him. Your flying out tonight aren't you?"

"Yes," replied David. He had hoped that he might have an opportunity to mention the new instructions from Marshall, but could see that his boss had other things on his mind.

Henderson continued. "I see from the account ledger on Marcel Coffee - V - Garces, that our Cuban friend is being a little slack about paying our bills. Is there a problem with the case which I should be aware of? As you know, I've been happy to leave you pretty much alone on this one, but we aren't bankers David and are not in the business of giving clients endless credit." David felt as if he was being lectured to by his former headmaster. "Garces hasn't paid our last two bills and currently owes us eighty thousand pounds."

"I know," replied David. "Whenever I bring up the question of the outstanding bills with him on the 'phone he apologises and says he will arrange to transfer funds to us without further delay. He always has an excuse when the money doesn't arrive."

"That may be, but he hasn't paid us a penny for over nine months and you've incurred a lot of costs one way and the other getting ready for the trial next month," said Henderson. David was uncomfortable with Henderson's reference to him having spent money rather than the firm.

"I've told him that if he wants us to proceed and defend him at the trial next month he must give me a bankers' draft for the eighty thousand when I see him tomorrow, plus another fifty thousand as a payment on account for the likely costs of the hearing," he replied. "I haven't briefed Counsel yet and won't until I get money from Garces. Garces's needs our help Mike, more than ever at the moment what with the trial about to begin. I'm confident he realises that he has stalled us for as long as he can and will give me the money when I see him."

Henderson looked at David for a moment.

"You're right, he does need us and would be stupid to try and stick it to us now. Just make sure you come back with the money David. I get enough criticism from my partners for acting for guys like Garces without having to explain why he's not paying his bills on time."

"He's always paid in the past I believe," said David "and since I've worked for him at least has never questioned the amount of a bill."

"I should think not," replied Henderson. "He's always received and continues to receive first class advice." This made David feel a little less uncomfortable as the advice Garces had been getting for the last three years had all been given by him. "Make sure he pays us David. Let me know what happened when you get back."

As David walked back to his office he cursed himself over the Garces's bills. He should have known better. Garces was a trader. Although very wealthy his money was always tied up in one deal or another, or was deposited with brokers around the World who would buy and sell coffee for him on one of the international coffee exchanges, usually in London or New York. He should have pressed Garces for payment of the outstanding bills before he ran up so many fees getting ready for the trial. David knew that Garces could not afford to loose the case that was due to begin in the Commercial Court in January and was confident that the coffee trader would pay up if it was made clear that without the money the firm would abandon his case. Nevertheless, Henderson had reprimanded him and David knew that his boss was right.

"Damn you Garces," he said under his breath. David was determined to return from his trip with the money Garces owed the firm.

David spent the rest of the afternoon before he left for the airport at his desk returning his calls and dictating letters and faxes to clients and opposing solicitors on a variety of cases. He had one hundred and seventeen open cases. Not all of these were active on a daily basis, but nevertheless this was considerably more than most other assistants in the firm. David was very much a product of the Holland Chapman & Co. philosophy. He had cases covering almost every aspect of the firm's international trade practice, but the area of the law that most interested him was insurance.

When he had first joined the firm as an articled clerk nine years earlier, the London insurance market that is known as Lloyd's had existed for centuries without any major problems. Even as a young lawyer, as he learnt how the market operated, David like many other lawyers in the City had feared that Lloyd's was on the verge of suffering a severe crisis as a result of the way in which insurance cover was organised, which would undermine the very existence of the ancient institution. During the late 1980s he witnessed Lloyd's almost collapse with some Names, the people who invest in the Market, losing everything as a direct result of how their money was managed on their behalf.

He had been involved in a number of the important cases that had arisen out of the heavily publicised collapse of the LMX spiral. The problem of the LMX spiral was simple in outline but horribly complicated in detail. During the late 1980s, the practice that existed at Lloyd's whereby syndicates reinsured one another began to grow out of control, in the sense that some of the syndicates involved lost track of the size of the liabilities they were in fact underwriting. There then occurred five catastrophes which gave rise to extremely large claims; Piper Alpha, Exxon Valdez, Hurricane Hugo, Phillips Petroleum and Windstorm Daira. The Names on some of the less cautious syndicates, most notably a series managed by Gooda Walker Ltd., found themselves faced with ruinously high losses. When the Gooda Walker case eventually found itself in the Commercial Court, it was decided by the presiding Judge that the underwriters for various syndicates involved had been negligent in the way in which they had carried on business, in particular that they had not given adequate consideration to the nature of the risks inherent in the LMX spiral.

David's expertise in insurance law and his detailed understanding of how the Market functioned was widely recognised in the firm and was one of the reasons why he was up for partnership a year early.

He had always wanted to be a lawyer. At first he had wanted to be a barrister like his father, practising criminal law. As a boy he had watched his father prosecute a murderer in Birmingham. His father's picture had appeared on the front page of the Birmingham Gazette after the accused had been sentenced to life in prison. David had decided that his father had the most exciting job in the World.

He had been educated at a small boarding school in South Wales before going up to Oxford University where he had read law. It was during his first year at Oxford that his interest in commercial law was born. He had been fascinated by the concept of English law which allows for the most part business men to almost entirely govern their relationships with one another by contract, subject only to a few statutory guidelines in certain areas. For the most part business men he had discovered were free to contract with one another as they chose, no matter how incredible their agreement might appear to a third party. He soon formed the opinion that the area where a lawyer could most use his skills and imagination was in interpreting such contracts. A lawyer could expect to earn a good living from commercial work and his ambition to become a commercial litigator was born.

After university and the mandatory year at law school when law graduates who are already destined for careers in specialised areas of the law, nevertheless, must pass endless exams in everything from conveyancing to divorce law, he joined Holland Chapman & Co. as an articled clerk. He had been with the firm ever since. In the seven years since David had qualified as a solicitor he had occasionally been approached by recruitment firms keen for him to go and work for rivals of Holland Chapman & Co. He had turned all offers down flat. He intended to make it into the Partnership and see his career out with the firm.

David was thirty years old, six feet tall, well built with broad shoulders on an athletic frame. He had a dark complexion, as if he had been in the sun. This, with his wavy jet black hair and bright blue eyes gave him a striking appearance. He was handsome. Not in a temporary fashionable way, but in a classic way that women have found irresistible throughout the centuries. As well as being blessed with good looks, David was dynamic. He had a passion for what he did that was infectious. People who had no interest whatsoever in the law would become intoxicated over dinner by David's accounts of his latest cases. Like many successful lawyers he could at times be a little over confident even arrogant occasionally, but most of the women who knew him found this characteristic attractive in itself.

Nevertheless, he was single, very single as his friends often reminded him. He told himself that this was part and parcel of climbing the corporate ladder. If he was going to get a partnership at all, let alone a year early, he had no time for a serious relationship. There would be plenty of time for love and romance once his name was on the firm's letterhead.

The truth was that David had a broken heart. An old fashioned broken heart. Three years earlier he had been engaged to Helen. He had fallen in love with her when he was a junior assistant at the firm. She had been young and full of life. David fell in love with her almost as soon as they met. Eventually they had started living together in a flat that David rented in Fulham. As David's career progressed and he began to earn more money he bought a bigger flat in Chelsea and a ring, took Helen to Venice for the weekend and proposed to her. She accepted immediately and they planned the wedding for the following summer.

Six months later Helen had called David at work one afternoon and asked him to go home early because she wanted to talk to him urgently. Sensing that something was wrong David had hurried to their flat in Chelsea. Helen had announced that she was not happy any more and had decided to leave him. She had told David that it was not him, but her. She needed to find herself. That was the only explanation she offered him. She had spent the night at a friend's house and David had spent the night in tears.

The following evening he had returned from the City to discover that Helen had removed all of her belongings from the flat. Her keys had been pushed through the letter box, the only remains of David's first love. He had not seen or spoken to her since. He had heard that she had gone to live in New York, but was not sure.

Helen leaving affected David in two ways. The first was that he threw himself into his work with such force that Holland Chapman & Co. decided to consider him for early partnership. The second was that although he regularly dated women, he had closed his mind to the idea of having a loving relationship with someone again. On a day to day basis this did not really bother him, but he knew that something he had once had with Helen was missing from his life. He was no longer able to trust a woman.

"You'd better get going if you want to catch your 'plane," said Elizabeth who had walked back into David's office. "The file from Peter Marshall has arrived." She handed the file to David.

It was five o'clock. Time that he got going. As Elizabeth left the room, he packed his flight case with the papers he needed for his trip. Like most solicitors he had two briefcases. One was small, made of leather and served as little more than a cosmetic item for Court applications or meetings with new clients. The second was a sturdy, black flight case, the type that pilots have carried on to aeroplanes for over fifty years, and which every self respecting lawyer with a heavy case load uses for long trips. As well as placing into this case papers necessary for his trip to Miami, David put his lap top computer inside the case. He was proud of the fact that he was one of the few lawyers in the firm who was computer literate and could type at a decent rate of knots. Some years earlier the firm had provided him with a state of the art Compaq lap top computer which as David put it, had all of the bolt on extras.

As David left his office he shouted goodbye to Elizabeth through the open door of her office and headed for the firm's car park. Holland Chapman & Co. had a private car park beneath its building which could accommodate up to thirty three cars. An office block in the middle of the City that had parking facilities was a luxury, a luxury that Holland Chapman & Co. paid its landlords four thousand pounds per parking space each year for. The firm was not short of money and would have rented even more spaces had they been available. Unfortunately they were not. This was a problem because although the firm had thirty three spaces it had sixty four partners.

David always preferred to drive to the airport. It took a little longer in the rush hour than taking the tube, but it meant that he did not have to lug his luggage to and from his office and across the street on to the Underground. The firm had a policy of allowing assistants who were travelling on business to have priority to park in any parking spaces that became available. David had been in luck that morning.

He put his flight case in the trunk of the Golf next to his lightweight suit carrier. He only expected to be away for a few days.

David was driving a 1989 Golf GTI. A car he found entirely practical for the winter in London. Quick, relatively sporty, but most of all small enough to park on the streets of Chelsea where he lived without too much trouble. He always felt sensible when he drove the Golf. He had different feelings when he drove his second car. Three years earlier, when David had received his first substantial bonus from Holland Chapman & Co., he had blown the lot on a red 1971, 350 SL Mercedes sports convertible. A long name for a very stylish car. He loved to drive the Mercedes. He had spent a lot of money over the last three years restoring the car so that he was confident that there was not a better example of an early SL on the road. He drove the Mercedes from April until the end of the summer each year. During the winter he garaged the car in Shropshire at his parents' house. His flat in Chelsea did not have a garage and renting one in London was difficult and extremely expensive.

As David drove towards Heathrow he was pleased that it was the Golf he would be leaving parked outside in the rain for possibly three days and not the Mercedes.

He parked the Golf in the long term car park at Heathrow Airport and took the courtesy bus to Terminal Four. It was 6:15 pm. He had over two hours before his flight left for Miami. After checking in and clearing customs he wandered through the duty free area of the terminal before going to the British Airways Executive Lounge. David helped himself to a beer in the lounge. It was early for a drink but it was going to be a long flight and he hoped that a couple of beers and a glass of wine with dinner would help him sleep. He picked up a copy of the Times and sat down to read. He had driven to the office that morning and had not read a paper all day.

The Times like most of the serious newspapers was still full of articles about the British Government's decision to block Romania's application for Protected Membership of the European Community. It was the second time in the three years since the Community had opened its doors to former soviet satellite states that Romania's application had been rejected. On both occasions it had been Great Britain which alone amongst the Member States of the Community had exercised its veto to block Romania's application for membership.

There were two pictures on the front page of the Times. One was of a group of Romanian protesters standing outside 10 Downing Street waving banners demanding that the Prime Minister withdraw his opposition to Romania's application. The other was of the Prince of Wales boarding his private jet before leaving Brussels. David wondered what the Prime Minister had against Romania.

"Sir, your flight is boarding now. If you would go to gate fifteen," said the British Airways representative. David put the copy of the Times down. He could take it with him on to the aeroplane but wanted to clear his mind. There were problems in the World, but right now he had problems of his own in the form of a bankers' draft he hoped to see on Garces's desk when he met him the following day.

David boarded the aeroplane quickly. The early evening flight to Miami was not the most popular flight to Florida, but it suited him. He found that he could sleep well in his executive class seat and was more or less ready for business when he arrived. Anyway, he had little choice with flights as he could not afford to spend any more time than was absolutely necessary away from London with the Garces's trial so close.

He sat back in his seat, kicked off his shoes and made himself comfortable whilst he waited for the pilot to taxi the Boeing on to the runway.

CHAPTER 3

Bucharest. Monday, 21st November 1994.

    The President of the Republic looked down from the window of his office on to the large courtyard which occupied the distance between the re-named Presidential Palace and the bland, military gates that had been erected by the communists to keep protesters out of the building, in the days when the Palace had been at the heart of Nicolae Ceausescu's Romania. When Romania had a king, this had been the Royal Palace. Whilst the political character of Romania had swung from one extreme to the other over the decades of the Twentieth Century, all of the country's leaders during that century had chosen to rule from this ancient building.

    The President was in his late fifties. He had the rugged, worn out features of a labourer and wore a cheap suit that did not fit his body well. The shoulders of the suit were lightly sprinkled with dandruff and the cuffs were slightly frayed. His face was drawn and the sparkle in his eyes had deserted him years ago.

    It had been raining for most of the day and the President regretted that his country looked and felt so miserable whenever it rained. The parliamentary guards at the gate in the courtyard appeared to share the President's disappointment. They sheltered from the rain in their weather worn station box waiting for their shift to end.

    The President walked back to his desk and for the third time that afternoon picked up the crinkled telex that lay ominously on his blotting pad. It had passed through many sets of hands before it had arrived at the President's office. The telex was not very long but it meant nothing but trouble for him. He ran his fingers through his hair feeling the cheap hair grease he had used since he was a young man. His hair was too long for a leader his advisers were always telling him.

The telex had been sent to the Romanian Foreign Minister only forty eight hours earlier and already every newspaper in Europe was running some kind of story as a result of what it said. His tiny press office was struggling to deal with the requests for comments that were pouring in from Europe's television stations and newspapers. The press office had not been so busy since a similar telex had arrived on the Foreign Minister's desk the previous year.

Both telexes had been sent by the Office of the President of the Council of the European Communities and both telexes had confirmed that Romania's applications for Protected Membership of the European Community had been blocked by the British veto.

The President sat back in his chair and pondered the telex he was holding. He had been in office since May 1990, over four years. Romania's first freely elected President after the end of communism and the overthrow of Ceausescu.

During the years Ceausescu ruled Romania, the President had worked as a floor manager in a factory in Buzau, a town north of Bucharest. He had been an obedient Party member and had not been unhappy with his lot in life. By local standards he had been well paid and the position he had held in the factory allowed him to acquire light manufacturing components cheaply which he sold for a profit on the black market. He was not a greedy man and had been content to supplement his income from his job at the factory by making only one or two ventures on to the black market each month. He never found out how his employer had discovered that he was stealing items from the factory store house and selling them on the black market.

When he was eventually confronted by his employer he had been terrified. In those days the penalty for supporting the black market was life imprisonment. Surprisingly, however, his employer had not reported him to the Communist Party and he did not lose his job. He had been told to stop taking risks on the black market and within a month had been promoted to office manager, moved off the factory floor and given a pay rise which although modest, had made up in part for the income he had lost from his illegal activities on the street of Buzau.

It had been the time of the Revolution and the executions of Nicolae and Elena Ceausescu on 22nd and 25th December 1989. The appalling conditions that persisted under communism finally became intolerable. A new mood developed in Romania and that mood was rapidly organised into the Social Democracy Party of Romania, known simply as the PSDR. The Party's roots were in the factories of the big cities. Under Ceausescu, males between the ages of fifteen and seventy were required to work six days a week in one of the country's five thousand state factories if they were unable to find an alternative job. It was his proud boast that unlike capitalist countries in Western Europe, Romanian had full employment.

Ceausescu invested uncontrollably in energy intensive heavy industry, neglecting agriculture although the Wallachia, Moldavia and Transylvania regions of the country are some of the most fertile areas in Europe. There were few agricultural jobs left in Ceausescu's Romania by the end of the 1960s and most young men were forced into the factories on leaving school. This might not have been too bad, but Romania's policy of full employment was not carried out in the same way as many socialist countries have carried out similar policies. Romanian factory life under Ceausescu was hard. Pay for anyone who was not in a position of authority as most were not was low, conditions were depressing and the chances of ever leaving the factories before the state declared that you were no longer fit to work at the grand old age of seventy, were slight.

Surprisingly, it was not these Victorian conditions which resulted in the birth of the democratic movement in Romania. Europeans have endured hardship for many centuries in certain countries without positive protest. It seems to be a characteristic of Europeans, particularly those from the East, to endure appalling conditions for generations without real complaint. What finally destroyed the Communist Party in Romania at the end 1989, was corruption in Ceausescu's Government and in the factories he had built.

Romania has one of the World's most substantial deposits of iron ore. The vast majority of the state factories were involved in one way or another in the mining or processing of ore. The methods of extraction and processing used in the country were old fashioned being massively over labour intensive. However, Romania had plenty of available labour and Ceausescu's policy of compulsory employment guaranteed the workforce. Whilst vast quantities of ore were mined and processed in Romania and sold to the West in one form or another, Romania under the communists was not a wealthy country. Almost as soon as Ceausescu became President in 1967 Romania's economy began to suffer. By the late 1970s the country was heavily in debt. Ceausescu borrowed from whoever would lend money to Romanian in order to finance his building spree. His official policy was to restrict free trade with the West. Free enterprise was outlawed in Romania. All areas of international trade, including ore exports were conducted through the Communist Party's Office of Trade for the People of Romania. The Office was not very good at exploiting the country's ore resources and the factories, year after year, reported little if any profits.

Ceausescu justified this to the Romanian people by insisting that although Romania was blessed with large deposits of valuable minerals, the mining and processing methods used were very expensive. He would not abandon the Communist Party's founding principal of "individual industry for the benefit of all, by all", which was set out as Article 1 in the Party's Handbook, in favour of more efficient methods of extraction and production. Ceausescu controlled the country's media so effectively that most Romanians before the Revolution were grateful to the Office of Trade for the People of Romania, for getting what they were told was a good price for their country's ore on the international markets.

The truth was very different. Even by mining and processing ore using the outdated methods preferred by the state factories, revenue from ore sales had in fact become colossal by the late 1980s. What the average Romanian was not told was that during the mid 1980s the price of ore increased rapidly as other traditional producer nations were forced to restrict their own mining, as easily accessible deposits began to run short for the first time in two hundred years. Romania did not have supply problems and Romanian ore increased in value on the World markets by seven hundred per cent in less than a year as the available supply of ore in the World shrank.

This new revenue was not used by the Romanian Communist Government for the good of the people. Ceausescu did not use the new revenue to reduce the country's national debt, or to improve the quality of life for the average Romanian. Some of the money was used by Ceausescu and Party officials to feather their own nests, but the vast majority of it found its way into the hands of the men who ran Romania's state factories. Men who before the ore boom had driven second hand Russian built cars, imported new Mercedes and BMWs into the country and built vast mansions along the country's picturesque lakes in which to live. Some even arrived at their offices each day by helicopter. The newly established wealthy of the country strengthened their links with Ceausescu in order to protect their positions. Corruption amongst Party officials became rife.

The government passed new mining laws collectively known as the Mining Regulations which did not regulate mining, but rather allowed the men who ran the factory towns, who were given the title of guardians, to have absolute autonomy over the income earned by the factories in each of the towns they were responsible for. These men were called guardians because under the new laws they were charged with distributing the money their factories earned to the communities which served the factories. The problem with the system was that it was policed by the Communist Party. Factories did not have to keep accounts and anyone who was a potential threat to a guardian's authority was either paid off handsomely or removed. Most of the time violence was not necessary. The guardians were stealing such huge amounts of money that they were able to buy off even the most committed reformist.

Ceausescu embarked on a building spree on a colossal scale. People were starving throughout Romania, but Ceausescu built factories, office blocks and apartments for high ranking officials to live in. To him a developed country was judged by the number of factories and large office blocks built, even if there was no use for the buildings once they were completed.

Neither the Mining Regulations nor the inflated price of Romanian ore survived for very long. Within three years of the cut backs in World ore production, new highly efficient methods of mining ore were developed by the West which resulted in much higher yields of product from each tonnage of ore mined. Certain central European countries also discovered deposits of ore at depth deeper than had been mined before, but which could be extracted cost efficiently as a result of developments in mining techniques. World producers began mining heavily again and the price of ore fell sharply. It was the end of the huge revenues that had been enjoyed by Ceausescu and the guardians and within two years resulted in the end of the Communist Party in Romania. If corruption in the factories and in the government began the process of change, the collapse of communism in the Soviet Union put democracy in Romania beyond doubt.

When most people in Romania had been poor, the restrictions of communism had been tolerated by the populous. People were never exposed to an alternative way of life. The rise of the guardians and the leaders of the Communist Party and the blatant decadence of these officials infuriated the factory workers. However, it was the outrageous grandeur in which the Ceausescus lived that disgusted Romanians the most. Once it was discovered that the government had misused the revenues earned from the country's ore and the Ceausescu's corruption had become shockingly visible, revolution in Romania was imminent.

By the beginning of December 1989, the price of ore was falling fast and Ceausescu had nothing with which to pacify an angry country. When the Revolution arrived it did so rapidly. The communists had been in power for so long that they had become complacent. Their army was not well drilled and the Generals did not have an appetite for civil unrest. What is more, the one important element of Romanian society that Ceausescu and the guardians had not bribed in order to ensure compliance was the military. This was probably because Ceausescu did not think that he would require the Generals' services. Ceausescu did not see himself as a dictator. He was mistaken on both points. He was a dictator and when civil unrest broke out he needed an army to protect him. The Revolution could have been stopped in its infancy if Ceausescu had been able to deal with the initial revolutionaries in Timisoara. However, when he looked to the army he was confronted by soldiers as outraged with the careless spending and decadence of the ruling classes as the rest of the people of Romania were.

The military was of little assistance to the communists who had no alternative other than to let democracy take its course. This was true of the entire country with the exception of the Banat region in the west of Romania. Banat had always been the power base of the communists and the new democrats made little progress in that region of Romania at first. Even after Ceausescu was executed on Christmas day 1989, much of Banat remained loyal to the Communist Party.

As well as Nicolae and Elena Ceausescu, the managers of the factories and most of the guardians became victims of the Revolution. A few guardians escaped with parts of their rapidly acquired personal fortunes safely deposited in Swiss banks. The man who had discovered the

President stealing from his factory was one of these men. He had realised before the price of ore began to fall that the decadence of Ceausescu would eventually bring down the communist government. He watched the growth of the democratic movement and when he was convinced that the end of communism was in sight, secretly helped to establish the PSDR as a political force in the industrial centre and north of the country.

He rapidly pushed the man he had promoted after catching him stealing into the fore front of the political debate. The President had been a reluctant politician at first, but he had gone along with his employer's wishes without objection. After the execution of Ceausescu a provisional government was formed that was forced to abolish the leading role of the Communist Party and the country held free elections in May 1990. It had been the Guardian who had persuaded the PSDR to elect as one of its early leaders a man from the factory floor who had progressed not by bribery but by ability. A true Romanian. It had been the Guardian who had arranged for the Democratic Assembly to unanimously elect the President as the first leader of the new Party.

In May 1990, a man who had once sold shoddy industrial equipment from the back of a twenty five year old car on the black market was elected President of the Romanian Republic, promising improved human rights and a market economy.

The President looked down at the telex in his hand again. Its consequences were of monumental significance to the country he governed. The financial security offered to emerging democratic European countries by Protected Membership of the Community had been denied to Romania for the second time in succession. This was a disaster for his country. The years since the Revolution had not been good for the people of Romania. The revolutionaries had promised a great deal, but by early 1994, inflation had reached three hundred per cent annually and unemployment ten per cent. Romania was on its knees and the European Community had seemed to offer a way out.

In spite of the seriousness of the situation caused to Romania by the telex the President was holding it was not this that immediately concerned him. It had not been his idea to apply for membership of the Community and after the first rejection he had not wanted to apply again. Applying for membership had been the idea of the Guardian and the President's old employer had been certain that the second application would be successful. It was not the continuing hardship of the people that worried him on that gloomy afternoon, it was the Guardian's inevitable anger.

The President was not a fool. After he had been elected into office he had expected the Guardian who had played such a crucial part in his elevation to want to be rewarded. The President had offered him a position in the country's new Cabinet. The Guardian was not interested in government, or in high office. He was only interested in himself. The President knew this and it made him all the more afraid of his former employer. But what could he do? The President was tired of office. The four years he had held office had been the worst of his life. He was not cut out to forge a new country as his Party's slogan boldly announced he was doing. If it had not been for the Guardian he would have been overthrown almost immediately after he took office.

It had been the Guardian who had quietened his early opponents. It had been the Guardian who had arranged for the remnants of the Communist Party in Bucharest to close down their headquarters and it had been the Guardian who had taken care of that business in the Banat region during the elections.

The Guardian had explained to the President that membership of the European Community was what the people of Romania wanted and what the economy of the country needed. Even with no more than an elementary understanding of economics the President had seen the force of this. His country's two main difficulties were a lack of revenue now that the price of ore was at an all time low and political isolation in Europe. Membership of the Community offered a solution to these problems. After the Guardian had arranged for Romania to apply a second time for Protected Membership of the Community, the President had found himself pushed into a three month tour of the European capitals. He had met most of the European leaders, an experience he had hated. If the President was uncomfortable with politics in his homeland he was even more uncomfortable playing the international statesman.

The President loved Romania, but he could not help feeling that the country he governed was a second rate European power. His tour of the European capitals had only reinforced this view. The culture of Paris had left him speechless, the sophistication of Rome had left him in awe and the energy of London had made him realise that even if Romania was allowed into Europe, she would be joining a league that she was not yet equipped to compete in. He had hated touring Europe. The worst thing of all had been the realisation that the leaders he met did not take either him or the

27

country he led seriously. It was not because Romania was struggling economically. The former Soviet Union countries by all accounts had even more financial difficulties than Romania. The problem was that Romania was not considered by Western Europe to be a potential military threat. The country had an army that it could not pay for which was ill equipped. Whereas Western Europe was concerned that if democracy in Russia failed, that country's mighty arsenal might fall into the hands of a dictator, thereby threatening World peace, no one was concerned that the Romanian army might run rampage across Europe if democracy collapsed.

The President had been embarrassed by the tour, especially by the British leg when the British Prime Minister had refused to meet him. The President had met the leader of the Labour Party, but not the Prime Minister or members of his government.

The President knew that in spite of the shame of Romania having been rejected twice, when he met with the Guardian later that afternoon the Guardian would insist that Romania apply for membership a third time. He suspected that his old employer had already laid the ground work for another European tour, something that the President wanted to avoid at all costs. The Guardian was so determined that Romanian should achieve Protected Membership that if the President had not known better he would have thought that the Guardian had become the country's greatest patriot overnight. The President did know better and although he did not understand why exactly, he firmly suspected that the Guardian's determination to see Romania in the European Community was in some way linked to the man's own fortunes.

The first rejection had made the Guardian so angry that the President had feared for his own life should the Guardian blame him for the British veto. News of the second rejection would have reached the Guardian even before the President. The Guardian was always better informed than the President.

He checked that the door to his office was closed and took a flask from the bottom drawer of his desk. At first, after he had been elected he had kept the drawer locked, but recently he had been having to open it so frequently that he did not bother with the key any longer. It was the same old coffee flask the President had carried with him when he had peddled components on the black market in Buzau. In spite of the emergence of a market economy in Romania there was still a black market of sorts. He knew that his kitchen staff bought food from black marketers when supplies in conventional shops ran out.

The flask did not contain coffee, it contained something stronger. Whisky had become the President's friend. Too good a friend of late. When the burdens of office became too much he retreated into whisky. Usually cheap American whisky which was readily available throughout Romania. He poured a large measure of the rusty coloured liquid into the cup of the flask and emptied the cup in a single gulp. He poured another and drank with enthusiasm. He tasted the whisky in his mouth and felt its effects inside him. For a moment he forgot about his problems and the telex on his desk. He took another drink from the cup until it was almost drained. The warming effect of the liquid felt good on such a cold day. He finished the cup and poured himself another full measure. He always felt better when he was with his friend.

He was tired of the demands of the Guardian. He was after all the President. He would tell the Guardian that Romania would not be applying for Protected Membership again. If the rest of Europe did not want his country, then the rest of Europe could go to hell. Whisky always made the President confident. He would tell the Guardian that he was not going to tour Europe again. He would solve the problems of Romania without the help of the West and without the interference of the Guardian. The President took a final drink of whisky from the cup before picking the telex up one more time. He did not need Europe or the Guardian.

The button on the telephone on the President's desk shone red for a moment and then went dull before shinning red again. The President put the cup down and picked up the receiver.

"Mr. President, your visitor has arrived. I'll show him in." His secretary did not wait for the President to ask her to send the visitor into his office. This visitor was never asked to wait. The President looked at his watch as he let the receiver clumsily find its own way back to the telephone. The Guardian was two hours early. The telex that only moments earlier he had been able to ignore was suddenly all that he could think of. He heard heavy footsteps approaching his office and saw the handle of the office door turn without even the announcement of a polite knock.

CHAPTER 4

The Guardian sat in the back of a jet black Mercedes with heavily tinted windows. The handmade Italian suit he was wearing fitted perfectly. His hair was short.

People noticed the big car as it hurried along the roads from the northern part of Bucharest where the Guardian chose to live on its way to the Presidential Palace in the centre of the city. The Guardian paid no attention to the curious eyes that followed his car along the road. Although the car was noticeable, the tinted windows prevented onlookers from seeing who was inside. He preferred it that way. He was a cautious man when it came to his own security. The car was fitted with the best bullet proof panels available anywhere in the World and the driver, a six foot five inch giant, was an ex-special forces sergeant. Nevertheless, the Guardian believed that keeping as far away from public scrutiny as possible was still the best form of security.

It was difficult to fault the Guardian's reasoning. After all, the way he did things had kept him alive when the revolutionaries had first assumed power in the factories and had enabled him to keep almost all of the money he had stolen from the community he had once headed, when Ceausescu was finally overthrown.

The Guardian was not a big man physically, in fact you could be forgiven for dismissing him out of hand if you were ever to come across him. He had small, cold eyes. His mouth was also small, nothing more that a line across his face really. He rarely smiled.

He had been born into a very poor family in a small farming village outside Oradea in the west of Romania in 1932, when King Carol ruled the country. He had been the youngest by a few minutes of twin boys, both premature by two months and considered by the old ladies of the village to be too small and weak to survive the winter. His elder brother died seven days after the two boys were born and the Guardian had not been expected to live for much longer. The odds were against him. He was premature, his mother's milk suffered from the malnutrition that haunted the families of the village and his father, on seeing how small and frail his son was, did not want him to survive to be a further burden in his already difficult life.

But the boy did survive, protected in all things by his mother. At the age of three he was struck by polio which distorted and twisted his body. It seemed to his mother that her only son was destined not to reach manhood. For most of his childhood the Guardian was ill. The effects of polio stunted his growth, making him appear younger than he was. His father was continually angry with the small boy because he was not strong enough to work in the fields with the other young boys of the village. From the day he was born, his father never made love to his mother again.

As the years passed and the Guardian's health did not improve his father's anger and frustration grew into hatred. By the time the Guardian had reached fifteen years of age, he had overcome polio but was left permanently stunted.

On his fifteenth birthday his father came home from working in the fields more angry with his son than usual and stinking of the wheat beer brewed in the village. He had always beaten the boy for no reason, but on that day the beatings were more savage than ever before. Trying to protect her son from his father, the Guardian's mother had thrown herself in front of the big man only to receive blows across the side of her face which she could not withstand. The Guardian had watched helplessly as his father hit his mother eleven times. The boy had counted each blow as it was delivered, praying that each would be the last. As she slumped to the floor, into a pool of her own blood, the Guardian had known his mother was dead. He ran from the shack that had been his home for fifteen years chased by his father. In spite of his crippled body the Guardian found a strength that day which had carried him beyond the murderous reach of his father's fists. He ran and ran until the sight of his father standing in the road waving his arms in the air and shouting at him was long gone. He knew then that he would never live in the village of his birth again. He also knew that some day he would see his father again and that when he did he would kill the man who he had watched hammer his mother to death.

Years later, the boy who had grown a little taller and was by then a man did return to the village. He found his father leaning over an old plough in the field behind the shack that had once been his mother's home, complaining to a young woman beside him that the plough had broken again. The Guardian did not stop to greet his father or the woman. He took a club fashioned from the branch of a tree from inside the bag he carried and viciously struck his father about the head exactly eleven times. He counted the number of each blow out loud. He did not stop counting when, after the third blow his father was lying dead at his feet. He stopped only after he had delivered the eleventh blow.

He discovered from the woman who had screamed at him not to hit her husband that soon after his mother's death his father had remarried. Finding nothing in the old shack of any value, the Guardian had taken his inheritance by raping and then strangling to death his father's second wife.

The years that followed saw the Guardian leave Romania and eventually end up in West Germany. It was the West Germany of the late 1950s and opportunities for non German nationals to prosper were plentiful. He soon had a good business trading ink on the black market in Bonn. He stole the ink each week from a depot controlled by the British Army and sold it to the newspapers at a huge profit. He became one of the most reliable black marketeers in Bonn. He would stop at nothing to get what his customers needed, killing whenever necessary.

Above all the Guardian was clever. He soon realised that he was not blessed with the natural attributes of an assassin. He was too small and his body too weak. Whenever he needed to eliminate an individual during those early years, he would employ someone better equipped for the task than he was, who, for the right price would carry out the Guardian's instructions without question.

By the late 1960s the opportunities to exploit the situation in West Germany in ways the Guardian was good at had almost entirely vanished. The West German economy had become so strong that black marketers were no longer in demand. In 1968, one year after Ceausescu became the second post war leader of Romania, the Guardian returned to the country of his birth and set up business in Bucharest. He quickly learnt how Romania functioned and in no time at all had an operation which was profitable enough to give him the funds he needed to bribe his way into the factories. The Guardian witnessed Ceausescu embark on his megalomaniac building spree, constructing factory after factory. He knew from his experience in West Germany that the state factories of Romania could not be as unprofitable as the people of Romania were told they were, especially after they had been championed by Ceausescu. The Guardian suspected that Romania already had a developed layer of corruption centred around the country's ore mining and production industries and he wanted to benefit from this corruption. His idea was simple. If Ceausescu was stealing from the country through the factories, he would steal from Ceausescu by controlling the output and revenues of as many factories as possible; not because he had ideas of robbing the rich to feed the poor, the only person the Guardian was interested in feeding was himself and he had a huge appetite. Unlike most Romanians at that time, he did not fear Ceausescu, believing he was cleverer than the dictator. Working within Ceausescu's system was going to make the Guardian a small fortune.

His ambitions were achieved even faster than he had thought possible. Within four years of returning to his homeland, he was appointed chief of a small factory in the Moldavian region of Romania. Moldavia is a fertile region that traditionally had hundreds of small farms which raised mainly sheep and cattle. Under Ceausescu, all but a few of these farms were replaced by factories and the farmers left with nowhere to work other than on the factory floors.

The Guardian's first factory was a desperate place. After ore has been processed it leaves a residue of a thick dust like substance which has certain low priority uses. The Guardian's factory worked with this black powder. Most of the workers by the time they reached their late thirties were half dead as a result of a life time of breathing in the dust. Few ever reached retirement age. Under the Guardian the factory prospered at the expense of the workers. He drove the men so hard that the factory actually began to make a profit; not because sales went up, but because factory operators were paid by the communists with reference to the volume of product they pumped out of their factories each year. The Guardian increased the production volume of the factory by twenty five per cent in three years and received more money from the communists as a result. Almost all of the extra money the factory earned found its way into the Guardian's pocket.

By the middle of the 1970s the Guardian was running thirty five state factories. He ruled his empire savagely. During those years when the communists were content to leave him alone he had over fifty men killed for a variety of reasons. Remembering the lessons he had learnt in West Germany in the 1950s, he employed professional assassins to carry out the murders.

He developed interests in other European countries and built up a chain of contacts in most of the capital cities of Western Europe. During the years that Ceausescu outlawed foreign travel by ordinary Romanian nationals the Guardian was able to travel regularly. He was both a friend of the Communist Party, dining with Ceausescu occasionally and secretly a friend of those who opposed the dictator. He watched the communist governments of the World slowly become outdated and anticipated that eventually the Romanian Communist Party would be toppled.

When the ore boom of the 1980s arrived, he was appointed Guardian to the largest group of factory towns in the country. He stole millions, far more than anyone in the Communist Party realised because unlike the other guardians and government officials, he was not extravagant with the money he stole. He also preferred to use fear as a way of controlling people rather than bribery.

When the new feeling of democracy in Romania had taken hold to such an extent that Ceausescu's future was doomed, the Guardian began to secretly donate money to the new democratic movement. When the Revolution came, he had enough new friends to ensure that his wealth was not threatened. He even managed to get one of his puppets elected leader of the infant Social Democracy Party of Romania soon after the communists were forced to recognise the democrats at the beginning of 1990.

He had survived the changes in Romania and was now more powerful than ever. In spite of this his ambition had grown over the years and he wanted more: more he realised than Romania had in her coffers to steal without the intervention of the European Community.

The Mercedes turned a sharp corner and swerved to avoid a pot hole in the road. The jolt brought the Guardian back to the matter at hand. He had received notice of the Council's decision to reject Romania's application before the President had been officially informed. He had a network of people on his payroll in Brussels who provided him with top level information very quickly. This asset had often helped him to make money. On this occasion however, the news of Romania's second rejection had been altogether too public.

The first rejection had been a disappointment and the Guardian had cursed and shouted at the President. After he had calmed down he had recognised that democracy in Romania was in its infancy. The leaders of Europe had not even met the new head of Romania and it had not surprised the Guardian on reflection that the British were reluctant to open the door of the Community even wider than it had already become. The second rejection however, had come as a complete surprise to the Guardian. The President of his country had been on a visible tour of Europe and had been received well by most of the nations' leaders. The Guardian had arranged for hundreds of foreign trade delegations to visit Romania since 1990, to see for themselves how the country had embraced democracy and market economics and he had spent hundreds of thousands of dollars during the last twelve months bribing every European Community official he could into promoting Romania's interests in Brussels. He had been sure that this time Romania would be awarded the prize he sought of Protected Membership of the European Community.

In 1991, the Member States of the European Community created a new class of Community membership. Europe had changed. The Soviet block had crumbled, slowly at first and then with such speed that politicians and business men had suddenly been confronted with their new style Eastern European neighbours. New markets opened up across Eastern Europe and Western businesses fell over themselves to establish footholds in the new democratic countries.

The USA and Japan were as quick to take advantage of the collapse of communism in Eastern Europe as Germany and Great Britain were. It soon became obvious that unless steps were taken to stop the advance into Eastern Europe of the Americans and the Japanese, before long a new trading block would emerge in Europe, financed by the Dollar and the Yen, to the detriment of the European Community. Because of this, Brussels announced that former Soviet satellite countries that had successfully established democratic governments, respected human rights and operated free markets were eligible to apply for membership of the European Community in return for complying with the Community's restrictions on importing into the Community non Member States'

35

products. In other words these new democracies were told to choose between economic union with the USA and Japan or with the European Community. Most chose Europe.

The leaders of the European Community also realised that unless steps were taken to protect new members, these countries would be exploited by the West because their economies were not sufficiently developed to enable their businesses to compete on the European markets. Therefore Protected Membership was created.

If a country was made a Protected Member of the European Community, it benefitted from the advantages of Community membership without having to put up with some of the restrictions. Its currency was not linked to the other European currencies and export regulations into other European States such as they were, did not apply to exports from Protected Member countries. At first the most lucrative benefit given to Protected Member States was the creation of the Protected Member States Export Bonus. Protected Members were paid a bonus for all goods they exported equal to twenty five per cent of the value of the goods sold. This was intended to enable developing economies to undercut other European exporters on the World markets and earn income for their economies.

It resulted in a huge rush by Western European companies to establish factories and operations in Protected Member States, in order to benefit from the bonus scheme, which applied to all exports from such countries as long as fifty per cent of the exporting company's share capital was beneficially owned by nationals of the Protected Member State.

The Protected Membership scheme was a success. However, by its second year it had become apparent that still not enough capital was being attracted into the Protected Member States for them to catch up with the rest of Europe. A second method of financing industrial growth in these developing democratic economies was devised. A loan scheme was offered during the first five years of membership of the Community to all new Protected Member States. This loan scheme was administered by the European Fund.

The European Fund would lend a Protected Member up to one billion dollars for "industrial development". European economists agreed that if the economies of Eastern Europe were to survive, Eastern European countries needed to develop strong industrial bases. How much money a Protected Member State could borrow was directly associated to the number of "industrial units" of sufficient size it had. One medium size factory was regarded as a single industrial unit for example. The conditions of the loan were simple; lending was unsecured, repayments were deferred for five years which coincided with Protected Membership coming to an end and the funds borrowed, whilst having to be repaid by the governments of the Protected Member States, had to be made freely available to operators of industrial units so that they could spend the money on the equipment and machinery they needed quickly, without having to channel purchase orders through their governments.

The money had to be spent on equipment produced within the European Community, unless equipment was not available, or identical equipment could be purchased outside the Community for at least thirty per cent less than within the Community, which was considered to be unlikely. All that an operator of a factory had to do to qualify for money, up to the limit he was entitled to dependant upon the size and number of his industrial units, was produce an order form certified by the seller that he was purchasing industrial equipment worth a stated amount. His government then had to hand over the money to him within fourteen days. The driving philosophy behind the scheme was to allow the economies of the Protected Member States to become viable by the time Protected Membership ceased after five years, when new Community Members would have the same advantages and disadvantages in the Community as the traditional Member States. Getting the money into the hands of the people who actually needed it to build their businesses up quickly was, therefore, considered to be vital.

The Guardian had calculated that Romania had more than enough factories of sufficient size to qualify for the country's maximum loan of one billion dollars. In fact money given to just sixty per cent of the country's ore factories would exhaust Romania's one billion dollar entitlement. Either directly or indirectly, by 1993 the Guardian controlled just over thirty per cent of Romania's larger state factories. The Guardian had spent the last three years setting up hundreds of shell companies throughout Europe which on paper were involved in the business of manufacturing or selling industrial machinery. None of these companies were genuine. They all had nominal share capitals and no assets whatsoever.

Through complicated chains of directorships innocently operated by a host of law firms scattered throughout Europe, ownership of these companies could be traced, with considerable patience only, to the Guardian. Confirmed sales on the order forms of these companies showing orders from factories in Romania for industrial equipment would obligate the Romanian Government to pay the purchaser identified on the order form the entire value of the apparent purchase within fourteen days.

If Romania could get into Europe and if he moved fast enough, the Guardian estimated that he could collect half a billion dollars from the Romanian treasury within six months.

The money would be paid to his own European companies which on paper would be selling the factories he controlled industrial equipment. By the time it was discovered that the equipment had never been shipped to Romania, which could take years, the Guardian would have retired to a country where a multi-millionaire is able to enjoy the fruits of his labours properly. The Romanian Government would be left with the problem of repaying the half a billion dollars to the European Community when the country's five years of Protected Membership expired.

The Guardian considered the work ahead of him. He had not even thought of abandoning his ambitious scheme after the second rejection. The delay was annoying but he was confident that Romania would be accepted as a Protected Member of the Community on a third application. All he had to do was persuade the President to sanction a third application and make sure that the British did not use their veto again. The first of these obstacles would not be difficult to overcome. His former employee was a weak, unsophisticated man who was easily manipulated by the Guardian. The President would do what he was told. He would go on another high profile tour of Europe after the application had been filed.

The second obstacle had at first appeared difficult for even a man of the Guardian's resourcefulness to overcome. Shortly after the second application for Protected Membership had been filed on behalf of the President of Romania, the Guardian had commissioned a fall back plan to be drawn up, intended to provide a series of alternative ways of guaranteeing Romanian acceptance in Europe if the second application was blocked. The Guardian was a thorough man and although he had fully expected the second application to succeed he had nevertheless paid one hundred and fifty thousand dollars for Operation Domino to be planned and prepared. He was now glad that he had.

The Operation although straightforward was daring, but the Guardian had taken daring steps before. Upon learning that Romania's second application for Protected Membership had been rejected he had decided to put the Operation in motion at once. The next thing he had to do was persuade the Planner to travel to Bucharest.

As the black Mercedes slowed down to approach the gates leading to the Presidential Palace, the two guards who had been sheltering from the rain in their hut ran up to the gates as they heard the sound of the car's engine. The President did not receive many visitors for a head of state and any activity on such a cold day was welcomed by the guards. They had a procedure to follow in the tradition of all men who protect others.

The Revolution was only four years old and the President's security advisers were constantly concerned that he might be attacked, particularly as his policies for economic recovery were not working. The guards were under orders to visually identify all occupants of a car and inspect the papers of each individual. If their names appeared on the daily list of people with appointments to see the President they were to be let into the Palace grounds without further question. At the entrance to the Palace they would be searched by hand for concealed weapons and required to walk through a metal detector of the kind used at most airports.

The guards saw the Mercedes and paused as the car came to a stop in front of the gates. They saluted the tinted windows of the car before pushing the gates open for the car to drive through. The guards recognised the car as belonging to the Guardian. He was not a man who was accustomed to being asked to stop and show papers to soldiers and the guards were not going to risk his anger by asking him to do so today. Besides, he was a regular visitor to the Presidential Palace. An old friend of the President they assumed.

As the Guardian watched the guards salute his car through the window of the Mercedes he nodded his approval. It was quite proper in his opinion that Romanian soldiers should salute the man who ran their country.

CHAPTER 5

The President was able to replace the coffee flask in the bottom drawer of his desk before the Guardian entered his office. As he slowly pushed the drawer shut, trying not to make a noise the President noticed that he had forgotten to replace the cup on top of the flask, which stood empty on his blotter pad. The two men looked at the cup at the same time. The President was embarrassed. He knew the Guardian disapproved of his drinking, regarding the need for alcohol as a weakness. The Guardian was about to chastise his country's leader for drinking so early in the afternoon, but checked his temper. On this occasion he needed the President's cooperation and was prepared to overlook the man's indiscretion for once.

"You've heard the news then?" asked the Guardian deliberately. He never addressed his former employee as Mr. President or Sir when they were alone and it was not his practice to make small talk with people who worked for him. He went straight to the issue at hand.

The President was relieved that the Guardian had not referred to the cup on his desk. He had been expecting a rebuke. As he replied he pushed the cup into the top left hand drawer of his desk out of sight. The President hoped the Guardian had not noticed. He had.

"Yes, disappointing news, taking up a lot of my time. I think my press office must have been called by almost every newspaper in Europe since the news of the rejection was released."

"I presume you've told the press that we will be applying again as soon as possible," said the Guardian. The President waited for a moment before he answered. Only minutes before he had convinced himself that he was going to tell the Guardian that he had decided that it was not in Romania's interests to re-apply, but as he heard the tone in the Guardian's voice he remembered why he feared this man so much. He avoided giving a direct answer.

"But surely it's too soon for us to have to make a decision whether to apply for a third time? It must be too soon," he said anxiously. He looked at the Guardian hopefully.

"My people are drawing up the papers at the moment, they should be ready by tomorrow evening," replied the Guardian. "All you have to do is sign them and I'll arrange for them to be hand delivered to Brussels immediately. The next membership vote is not until the end of May next year. You'll have to give a press conference when the application is filed to explain that we are not deterred in our ambitions in Europe by this rejection, the usual stuff. Don't worry. I'll get someone good to write it. Just remember to read the cue screen we bought for you."

The Guardian helped himself to the chair opposite the President's desk and stared at the President. "And under no circumstances do I want to see you drinking again until membership is secure, is that clear?" The President looked away from the Guardian as he mumbled "Yes."

"We need to cultivate as much support as we can in Europe to put pressure on the British to accept us next time around. We will have to get you into see the British Prime Minister this time and as many of his Ministers as possible," explained the Guardian.

"Another tour?" asked the President in terror.

"Of course. Can you think of a better way for the rest of Europe to inspect their newest neighbour. We've only got until next spring to get the British on our side before the Council votes again."

"I won't tour again, not after the way I was treated last time," complained the President. "Apply again if you must, but I won't tour Europe."

The Guardian got up slowly from the chair and walked to a large portrait that hung on the wall opposite the President's desk. It was a painting of Romania's first freely elected government which had been presented to the President by the leaders of the PSDR on the day that he had been sworn into office. In the centre of the painting sat the President above the inscription ".. Our dreams are charged to you..". The

Guardian ran the palm of his right hand over the painting feeling the texture of the paint on the canvas.

Suddenly, the President heard a tearing sound. The Guardian had turned his hand over and the sharp point of the diamond ring he wore on his index finger was brutally slicing through the President's body.

"You will do exactly as you are told," said the Guardian without turning from the canvas to look at the President. "You will attend the meetings I tell you to attend, you will address the European representatives I tell you to address, you will deliver the speeches I give you to deliver and you will, without question, tour Europe again. Is that absolutely clear?" The Guardian walked up to the President's desk and leant across it peering down on the seated head of state.

The President was determined not to give in without a fight, the prospect of touring Europe again distressed him so much, but he did not want to make the Guardian any angrier than he already was. He rose to his feet hoping that the confidence he had felt earlier would return if he was standing up. It did not. He was desperate for a drink.

"I must insist," he said a little too formally for a man of action, "that you leave that decision to me. I always welcome your advice as you know, but I'm the elected leader of this country and on a matter as serious as this the ultimate decision has to be mine. I think it's too soon for Romania to apply for membership again, in the circumstances."

The Guardian smashed both of his fists on to the President's desk. "Listen to me you little shit," he shouted doing nothing to disguise his anger. "I don't give a monkey's ass what you think. If you don't do what is expected of you completely, I'll crush you like the worthless puppet you are."

"I run this country not you," shouted back the President. "Get out of my office before I call the guards." The President had never been so forceful with the Guardian before. He trembled as he ordered the Guardian from the room. In that split second he decided that he had had enough of the Guardian dictating to him. He was not going to be paraded around Europe by this man again.

The Guardian was surprised. He could not remember the President ever having disagreed with him let alone defy him and order him to leave. It was time to get rid of this idiotic man he thought, but not before Romania was in the Community. He was not going to let his former employee stand in the way of half a billion dollars and the retirement he planned for himself.

The Guardian did not shout back at the President in spite of wanting to strangle him at that moment. He turned towards the door and started to walk, slowly.

"Of course, you've left me with no alternative in the circumstances," he said after he had taken a few steps. "It's clear that you no longer have the best interests of our country in mind. Protected Membership of the Community is what this country needs. God knows that the policies of your government are not addressing the crippling economic condition that Romania is in. If you won't do the best for the country and refuse to sanction another application for membership, I will personally make sure that the electorate knows that you're no longer the best man to lead our fine nation. I have no choice now but to divulge to some of my contacts in the press your involvement in the vote counting in Banat during the election. Do you really think the Romania people will tolerate your indifference to European membership when they learn how their leader got elected?"

The Guardian would use the argument that Protected Membership of the European Community would benefit the Romanian economy when it suited him. The President had heard this justification for the Guardian's enthusiasm for Europe before. However, he slumped into his chair on hearing the reference to Banat. Like many leaders in the World, whilst ascending to power he had broken rules along the way. The rule he had broken in Banat during the elections would certainly bring him down if word of it ever got out. He could not ignore the Guardian's threat.

After the PSDR had been officially recognised at the beginning of 1990 and Romania's first free elections announced, it had rapidly become obvious that the elections would be a formality. The PSDR was so popular that victory was inevitable. However, Romania was breaking free from years of communism and the leaders of the PSDR wanted the support of the entire country. If the new order was to survive and if the death of communism was to be permanent, it was important that the PSDR won all electorate regions in the country. Support for communism by the time of the elections had collapsed almost completely throughout Romania except in Banat. There, communism held its attraction to the local people.

As a result of this, before the votes cast in Banat had been counted in full on the day following the general election, it became obvious that the communists were going to win a significant number of seats. This would have meant that the country's new Parliament would include eight communist representatives; enough to cause problems for the new leadership. The President had been informed of the inevitable outcome of the count in Banat and had been persuaded by his closest advisers that steps must be taken to force a recount which had to be won by the PSDR candidates standing for the seats. The President had agreed that such steps should be taken for the good of the country and one of his advisers had been charged with ensuring that a recount took place which would secure power overwhelmingly in Banat for the PSDR. The adviser had been the Guardian.

As soon as the results of the first count were declared, the Guardian arranged for the Chief Counting Officer to be presented with evidence that indicated that the count had been tampered with to the benefit of the communists. Two of the counting officers were blackmailed by the Guardian to say that they had been paid by the communists to fix the count. A second count took place, this time supervised by the Guardian's own men and the eight seats were won by the PSDR candidates. The communists shouted conspiracy but no one listened. The result that the majority of people in Romania wanted had been achieved.

Before long the communists who had been accused of attempting to fix the count were imprisoned. The Guardian did not trust the prisons to keep the two counting officers he had blackmailed silent. They both had fatal car accidents within three months of the elections. The official reports put their deaths down to drunk driving as it had been noticed that since being accused of fixing the count both men had taken to drinking heavily. The President had only discovered some time after the elections when he was in office what had actually happened in Banat. The Guardian had let him find out, but had never before mentioned it to him personally.

The President considered his position as the Guardian slowly walked to the door of the office. He did not understand why the Guardian was so keen for Romania to become a Protected Member of the European Community. He was not an expert himself on the European Community but did know that even if Romania was admitted, Protected Membership would only last for the first five years. After that the country would be vulnerable to Western European marketeers. Romanian would be a second class Member State. The President had no doubt that the

Guardian really wanted Romania to join the European Community for his own personal advantage, but he could not detect why exactly.

If he did not agree to cooperate, the President knew that the Guardian would bring him down. He was tired of high office and had already decided not to run for re-election the following year but he did not want to be remembered as the man who had fixed Romania's first free elections. The humiliation of such a revelation would destroy him. He had experienced how ruthless the Guardian was and believed that if the events that had taken place in Banat during the last elections came out into the open, the Guardian would find a way to distance himself from the scandal and lay the blame for the entire incident at his feet. The President caught sight of the torn painting hanging on the wall in front of him.

"My dear friend, there is no need to do that. Perhaps I'm being a little hasty. Perhaps you're right, we should try again for the good of the country. I will sign the documents as usual as soon as you have them ready and do whatever you think necessary to assist the application."

As the President spoke he felt as if he still worked for the Guardian on the floor of one of the man's factories. He wondered if he would ever be allowed to retire from the Guardian's service.

CHAPTER 6

Miami. Wednesday, 23rd November 1994.

"Come on Garces, where the hell are you?" said David to the large glass doors. David had spent two difficult days in Miami. He was standing at the British Airways desk at Miami Airport waiting to check in and catch the evening flight to London.

He had spent most of the flight out from London two days earlier reading the documents Peter Marshall had sent over to his office. By the time he arrived in Miami David had analyzed Maxoil's new shipping problem, considered the oil company's legal position and had been ready to advise his new client. David was sufficiently senior at Chapman Holland & Co. to be able to give advice to clients without discussing it first with one of the firm's partners.

The first thing David had done after checking into the Sonesta Hotel on Key Biscayne on the outskirts of Miami, had been to prepare a fax to Marshall advising him of the position concerning the "Oil Star 2", which it was suspected, would refuse to deliver her cargo at Corpus Christi without an additional payment being made. David always carried a supply of the firm's headed notepaper with him whenever he travelled on business and preparing written advice and sending it from Miami had been straightforward. He had realised that Marshall would be impressed to find written advice waiting for him when he went into his office in

London the following morning. On this occasion the time difference between London and Miami had worked in David's favour.

Once Marshall had been dealt with, David slept. The following morning he turned his attentions to Garces. David was determined to leave Miami with the money the coffee trader owed his firm. He had gone out to Garces's home on the far side of Key Biscayne. Garces had been expecting him. David had met Garces many time before but never in Miami on Garces's home turf. The coffee business had been good to Garces David had decided when he had seen the man's house. A huge, tastefully decorated mansion set in its own grounds with tennis courts and a secluded private beach. He had guessed that it must be worth close to three million dollars. This had encouraged David. A man of such wealth should have no difficulty paying his legal bills.

David had raised the matter of the outstanding eighty thousand pounds and the additional fifty thousand pounds as soon as he had seen Garces. He had considered on the flight over how best to ask Garces for the money he owed the firm and had decided that the professional thing to do was to bring the matter up as soon as possible by making it clear that he was under instructions not to do any further work on Garces's case until a bankers' draft was presented to him. Garces's reaction to the request for payment had been to invite David to play him at golf. In fact he had insisted that David play him and had even teased that they should play double or quits for the outstanding fees. David had not known whether to take Garces seriously, but not wanting to have to explain this one to Henderson had played the round of his life, leaving Garces trailing in his wake.

Over a late lunch of fresh stone crabs back at Garces's house, the coffee trader had told David that he would arrange for a bankers' draft for the entire one hundred and thirty thousand pounds to be delivered to the house that evening. He also made it clear that he expected David to get down to work without further discussion of the outstanding bills.

David had spent the rest of the day and most of the evening preparing a lengthy statement for Garces to sign. He found Garces a patient interviewee which had surprised him. As Garces had given his account of how he had persuaded one of the World's largest coffee houses to back his idea of cornering both the New York and London coffee markets, David had not been able to help admire Garces's courage. Here was a man who was not afraid to take risks. Risks on such a scale that most men could not

47

even comprehend the potential exposure Garces had faced.

David finally completed the statement at 11:30 pm, and Garces had signed it after carefully reading it through twice. David had been shown to the door without mention of the bankers' draft he had been promised. When he asked Garces about the money, the Cuban explained that he had not had time to arrange for a bankers' draft to be obtained that afternoon after all. He promised to have a draft delivered to David's hotel the following morning. With that he had left David with one of the servants who escorted him to a taxi that was already waiting to take him back to the Sonesta Hotel.

David had been booked on to an early flight to London the following morning. He cancelled his booking when he got back to his hotel and resigned himself to a night in Miami. Under different circumstances this would not have been an unpleasant prospect. He was sufficiently familiar with Miami to know where to go for a friendly drink and a good meal. However, he was not able to relax at all. He had a feeling that Garces had outmanoeuvred him and that he would be going back to London not only without the money the coffee trader owed the firm, but with even more chargeable time to be billed to Garces. David had eaten alone in his hotel room that evening and had a very bad nights sleep.

The bankers' draft did not arrive at the Sonesta Hotel the following morning. By lunch time David had become intolerably impatient. He had changed his return flight and was booked on to the overnight flight to London. He had called Garces at his home and had been told by his client that the bankers' draft was not ready, but should be available later that afternoon. Garces had suggested that he meet David at the airport with the draft. David had agreed.

So David was waiting at Miami Airport for Garces. He could only afford to wait for a further thirty minutes before he would have to check in and clear immigration if he was going to make his flight. He was scouring the airport entrances for Garces wondering if his client would turn up with the money, or whether he would have to explain to Henderson why it was that he had returned to London empty handed. Garces had already caused David to spend an extra day in Miami at a time when he was too busy to be away from London unnecessarily.

"David, here you are." It was Garces, at last. "Sorry if I've kept you waiting. The price of coffee in New York rallied and I've been selling part of my long position. Did you find things to do last night?" Garces smiled as he asked David this question.

"Yes," answered David, hoping that he did not look too relieved to see Garces. "I had a very pleasant dinner in my room and caught up on some other business. I need to be going though, to catch my flight. The office would not be pleased if I had to stay another night in Miami. Were you able to get the bankers' draft from your bank?" David expected another excuse.

"Of course. You didn't think I'd let you go back to London without the money did you? Mike Henderson would string you up by the balls if you went back empty handed. Here you are." With that Garces handed over a bankers' draft for one hundred and thirty thousand pounds.

"Thank you," said David. He was so relieved to have the money in his hands that he could not think of anything else to say.

"Next time you're here we'll play golf again and next time I'll beat you," joked Garces. David just smiled.

The two men said their goodbyes and Garces left. David checked in and walked off towards the departure lounge. It was 6.00 pm. He had about forty five minutes before his flight would board. He wanted a drink but did not have time to search out the British Airways Executive Lounge. He found a bar in the main lounge and ordered a cold beer. Finally, he began to relax.

David took the bankers' draft from his pocket and examined it. He noticed the date. It was dated Monday 21st November, two days earlier. Garces must have had it all the time, he realised. "Damn you Garces," he said out loud.

He carefully folded the bankers' draft in half and slipped it into the outside breast pocket of his jacket. He sipped his beer and smiled to himself. Garces's game had delayed his return to London, but at least he had the money. David decided that if he did play Garces at golf again, next time he would let his client win.

CHAPTER 7

The Planner sat in the British Airways Executive Lounge at Miami Airport thinking about his daughter and about the man who had summoned him to leave Miami. The Planner was sixty one years old with messy grey hair and drawn, almost gaunt features. A Pole by birth who had fled Poland for the United States of America as a child with his parents shortly before the outbreak of the Second World War. He had lived with his parents in Washington before they had died when he was in his early twenties. Although his parents had died young, in their mid forties, they lived long enough to see their only son graduate from Washington University with a double first in Mathematics and Advanced Pure Engineering.

   Their son had been a modest genius. On graduation the Planner had joined PETCO Engineering, one of America's largest and most respected engineering companies. PETCO Engineering specialised in designing and manufacturing very complicated pieces of machinery and equipment for use in the aviation industry. The Planner had spent seven years at PETCO before being recruited by the Civilian Division of the US Airforce Aircraft Analyst Unit in Philadelphia. The AAU, as it is referred to has a number of functions. The most important of which is analysing weaknesses or potential weaknesses in US military aircraft. All domestic aeroplane manufactures have teams of investigators who analyse aeroplane wrecks and tell their employers what went wrong. The AAU does this for the US Airforce, and more.

The Planner became the AAU's most effective analyst. He was not only able to detect after a crash involving a US military aeroplane what had gone wrong, but could identify from the plans of a prototype where an aeroplane that was still on the drawing board was potentially vulnerable and what needed to be done to minimise the intended aircraft's weaknesses. He had spent most of his working life analysing drawings, plans, equations and calculations for some of the most sophisticated and complicated machines ever developed by man.

His recommendations resulted in the F-14A Tomcat's manoeuvrability limitations being detected and resolved whilst the aircraft was still on the drawing board, by the moveable wing design, saving the US Airforce millions of dollars in research costs and preventing the introduction of the Tomcat being delayed.

When US naval experts had been puzzling over how to built fighter aeroplanes that could take off from and land on aircraft carriers, whilst at the same time still being large enough to carry sufficient arsenals to be effective fighting machines, it had been the Planner, on temporary secondment to the US Navy, who had designed a take off and landing system that achieved these goals, which resulted in modifications being made to aircraft carriers rather than to the fighters themselves. The Planner had spent six months watching videos of fighters taking off and landing on every conceivable surface before understanding precisely the restrictions that were unique to operating a large fighter from an aircraft carrier. He designed a simple system which resulted in a fighter's up thrust being multiplied during take off giving accelerated lift and its down force being harnessed on landing, slowing a large fighter jet down almost immediately.

The Planner was running his own analysis unit by the time he was thirty five. He worked for the AAU until 1980. In July 1980, his wife was killed in their home by Arab fanatics who had discovered that the Planner was a US Airforce civilian officer, which technically he was although he had always considered himself to be a civilian engineer. The AAU is a secretive division of the US Airforce and the government was anxious not to draw attention to the unit through the killing. There was a cover up by the US Airforce on instructions from the Pentagon. The official story circulated by the US Airforce was that the Planner's wife had been killed by burglars. Everyone was sympathetic but no one would recognise officially that terrorists had killed the Planner's wife. This meant that there was no official enquiry and no prospect of the terrorists being caught. The Planner became disillusioned with the airforce as a result of this. He tried telling a journalist who he knew well the truth, but the following day the newspaper man was run over. The official explanation was that the journalist had walked out in front of a car. This had been the final straw for the Planner. He was offered and had taken early retirement. He would never forgive the airforce for abandoning his family after all that he had done for the United States military over the years.

The Planner had retired to Miami and the sun. He had been only fifty two years old. He found that the pension he was paid by the airforce was inadequate. After the death of his wife he had struggled at first to bring up his only daughter. He had spent what money he had sending her to a private girls school in England. Although he missed her terribly he believed that sending his daughter to England was the best thing he could do for her. She did well at school and after finishing her "A" Level examinations stayed on in England. She moved to London where she set up her own company.

The Planner's frustration with the United States authorities grew into hatred after he moved to Florida. He had problems holding down a job. Whilst the US Airforce had suited him well, industry did not. He was constantly asked to compromise his findings to keep within budget. He worked for a speed boat design company for awhile, but discovered so many flaws in the boats the company built that he was asked to leave. He was told that the company built straightforward boats that ordinary people could afford to buy, on finance, which would never do more than pull overweight water skiers across still bays.

The Planner had first met the Guardian ten years earlier in New York. The Planner had been working at the time for a family firm that designed and built hang gliders. The company was taking part in an exhibition in New York and the Planner had been sent to New York as part of the exhibiting team. It had not been an accident that the Guardian was at the exhibition buying equipment on behalf of the Romanian Sports Federation. The Guardian had learnt of the Planner a few years after he had left the AAU from a contact in the Pentagon. He had no interest in the military, either in Romania or in the United States. He was however, interested in a man who could analyse and detect the most obscure problems from piles of plans and sketches.

It had not taken the Guardian very long to persuade the Planner to carry out a job for him. At first the Planner had not been interested, but his hatred for the United States and his acute lack of money had convinced him that he should do what the Guardian asked. He had intended to do just one job for the Guardian.

He was paid fifty thousand dollars to review the plans of a twelve year old oil tanker and devise a way for her to be sunk without the possibility of a court or investigation detecting foul play. This had been child's play for the Planner. It had taken him just three weeks to come up with a plan which he had proudly told the Guardian was fool proof. The Planner had enjoyed the analytical challenge even if straightforward for a man of his expertise and he had been pleased with the money he was paid. However, during his time with the AAU the Planner's work had always been harmless, that is his recommendations would improve an aeroplane or system on an aircraft carrier. His particular genius had never before directly caused something to be destroyed.

The following winter at precisely the time the Planner had recommended that the operation to sink the vessel should take place, a nine year old tanker called the "Osprey" went down in rough waters twenty five miles outside New York Harbour. Three of the vessel's crew were drowned. The public enquiry and court case that followed could find no evidence to support the underwriters' allegations that the vessel had been deliberately sunk. The underwriters were ordered by the High Court in London to pay out on the vessel's insurance policy and the owner of the "Osprey" collected ten million dollars. The Planner had watched in horror television pictures of the search for the three missing crewmen shortly after the "Osprey" went down. The vessel belonged to a Liberian company which was secretly beneficially owned by the Guardian.

The Planner heard nothing further from the Guardian for over two years. When the Guardian contacted him again the fifty thousand dollars had been spent, most of it on educating his daughter. At first he had refused to plan the Guardian's next operation. He continued to refuse to cooperate until the Guardian had shown him a series of photographs of his daughter at school in England playing with her friends. The Guardian had not needed to openly threaten the Planner. The only thing left in the World that the Planner loved was his daughter and he had understood what the photographs meant. Obediently, he planned the Guardian's next operation, the theft of diamonds from a vault in a South African mine.

The difficulty had not been finding a way of getting into the vault. The Planner had been provided with detailed plans of the safe and of the mine and had detected a potential weakness in the automatic locking system of the vault's doors. Whatever information the Planner needed he had been told to ask for and the Guardian provided it. How, the Planner did not known. The difficulty had been working out how to get away with the diamonds once the vault had been cleared out. The mine was in the middle of nowhere and the alarm system used was one of the best in the World, having been specifically designed for the vault a few years earlier.

When the Planner had called the Guardian on the scrambled satellite telephone line the Guardian had insisted he use for emergencies only and had told the Guardian that the alarm system was impregnable, the Guardian had exploded into a rage. The Planner had been terrified for his daughter and had told the Guardian that he would work something out within twenty four hours. He had. He applied his considerable genius to the problem and logically went over each of the alternatives until he had devised a plan that would work.

He decided that the alarm to the vault could not be breached, but calculated that the sound of the alarm would not be heard at the far side of the quarry, which was over half a mile away from the building in which the vault was housed. Exact details of the mine and the surrounding area had been sent to him by the Guardian.

His plan involved an explosion at the far side of the quarry before the thieves made their escape. He researched every mining accident that had occurred in South Africa during the previous fifteen years and discovered that the way in which mines across the country dealt with quarry explosions was uniform. He concluded that everyone, including the guards in the building where the vault was housed would have been called to the far side of the quarry by the time the vault's alarm bells sounded.

The operation had been a success. The Guardian's men got away with over ten million dollars of uncut diamonds. Not as valuable by any means as they would have been had the diamonds been stolen after they had been cut, but completely untraceable. After that the Planner's ability in the eyes of the Guardian was assured. He planned three further operations for the Guardian, not as ambitious as the first two, but illegal and difficult to put together, requiring the Planner to develop skills beyond the parameters of mathematics and engineering. All three of the operations were a success and although the Planner would have obeyed the Guardian's instructions because of his daughter come what may, he was always paid well by the Guardian for the work he did.

Over the years the Guardian became more and more obsessed that the Planner should take steps to ensure that total secrecy was maintained whilst he was planning an operation. The Planner purchased a powerful computer on which he made his calculations, stored information, noted his considerations and drafted detailed operational reports for his employer. The Guardian always insisted on a written report explaining every aspect of each operation the Planner devised. The computer system provided the security that the Guardian demanded.

All of the Planner's work was protected by a series of passwords that he was confident not even the most accomplished decoders at the CIA could break. The Guardian for his part obtained a sophisticated document scanner which could copy exactly any document on to a computer disk. It was the only one in Romanian and was housed in a guarded room in the basement of the Guardian's office in Bucharest. Whenever the Planner requested information or documentation which he was unable to get himself, the Guardian would arrange for the necessary information to be obtained and if it was in documentary form, copied on to a computer disk. The disk would then be delivered by courier to the Planner rather than the document itself.

Had anyone actually taken the trouble to try and access the information on the computer disks that passed between the Guardian and the Planner they would not have been able to do so. The computer disks were encoded with passwords. Without the correct passwords the files on a disk could not be accessed. When the Planner finished an operational report it was sent to the Guardian in Romania on computer disk in the same way. Security was achieved.

Occasionally, the Guardian could not avoid providing the Planner with an original document or with some other vital piece of material he requested, but this was rare and the Guardian was satisfied that the system was secure. The Guardian had never questioned a request from the Planner for information. He judged the Planner by results. Every operation planned by the Planner had gone exactly as anticipated. If the Planner said he needed certain information to put together a plan, the Guardian simply obtained the information irrespective of how difficult it was to get hold of. Only twice over the years had he not been able to get hold of certain highly confidential information the Planner had requested.

This system meant that the two men had not actually seen one another for over five years. This suited the Planner. He was scared of the Guardian and was not exactly proud of his new profession. He found it easier to block out what he was doing as long as he did not have to see the man who paid him.

Operation Domino, the most recent operation the Guardian had instructed the Planner to devise was the most frightening of all. The Planner could not believe that even the Guardian would do such a terrible thing. He had not questioned his instructions however, ever concerned for his daughter. He knew that if he crossed the Guardian there would be nowhere in the World for his daughter to hide.

He had been instructed to come up with a sound operational scheme just under a year ago. He had spent one month first of all thinking of as many ways as possible of achieving the goal the Guardian had set him. Satisfied that he had thought of every possibility, he then spent a further two months identifying where each method he had discovered for carrying out the Operation was potentially vulnerable before selecting the method he considered was the most likely to succeed. He then carefully built up a fool proof operational plan so that nothing could go wrong.

He considered that the Operation could only be carried out successfully on one of three days before the end of the year. It had not been possible to plan the operation beyond the end of the year because information the Planner would have needed to be able to do this had not existed at the time. The Guardian had been provided with complete details of Operation Domino over four months ago in the usual way on computer disk and the first two of the three selected dates on which the Planner had intended the Operation to be carried out had passed without incident. With some relief, the Planner had concluded that the Guardian must have decided not to carry out the Operation after all.

Then, a few days ago, out of the blue he had been contacted by the Guardian and told that there was a slight modification required to the plan before Operation Domino could go ahead, a modification that the Guardian had insisted could only be made in Romania. The last of the three selected dates for the Operation had been only a week away when the Guardian had contacted him.

The Guardian had told the Planner to make sure that he was in Romania by the last possible date on which the Operation could be carried out. The changes that were anticipated only effected the latter stages of the Operation and the Planner had been told that he only needed to arrive in Bucharest a few hours before the start of the Operation. He was to be met at the airport in Bucharest by one of the Guardian's men and would be the Guardian's guest until after the Operation had been carried out. The Guardian had forbidden the Planner from making copies of any of the plans he had devised over the years. However, satisfied that the Planner's computer could not be accessed by any one other than the Planner himself, he had instructed the Planner to store all information relating to a particular operation he was working on, on his computer until he was instructed to delete it, which the Guardian told him to do after each of the operations had been successfully carried out.

The Planner complied with the Guardian's instructions in full. Once he had considered keeping copies of the details of each of the plans, but had not done so. He had realised that if the Guardian ever discovered his treachery his daughter would be dead within hours. As he had done at the AAU, the Planner always followed his instructions to the letter.

However, on this occasion the usual procedure was not being followed. The Guardian had instructed the Planner to copy all of the details of Operation Domino on to a computer disk, delete the information from his computer's hard drive and bring the disk with him to Romania. The Guardian's explanation for this uncharacteristic departure from the customary procedure had been that the Planner would need the information and document images he had stored on his computer in order to be able to make necessary modifications to the Operation. The Planner had done as he had been told, protecting the information on the disk with a password in the usual way.

The Planner sat in the airport lounge drinking brandy, scared out of his wits. He was drinking too much he knew. His doctor had told him that he had a weak heart and must stop drinking and smoking. He lit another cigarette, the sixth he had lit since sitting down fifteen minutes earlier. The Guardian's instructions had made the Planner very suspicious. He had no choice other than to go to Romania, but could not come up with a rational explanation to explain why the Guardian wanted to see him. The Guardian had never asked to see him in the past on the eve of an operation he had planned. And why did he only need to see him a few hours before the start of the Operation if changes were really required? Although the Planner considered the Guardian to be totally ruthless, he had never before feared for his own life. He had always considered that the Guardian would not kill him whilst he was of use. Now however, he was worried. Perhaps the Guardian had decided that he knew too much and the time had come to dispose of him? He was leaving for Romania unsure if he would ever return. Because of this the Planner had decided to fly to Romania via London. He wanted to visit his daughter. He was going to surprise her. He had not seen her for over a year.

The Planner was most afraid for his daughter. He was old and tired and feared for his daughter should he be killed by the Guardian. If the Guardian did kill him would he go after her? She knew nothing of her father's activities for the Guardian. She thought the money her father gave her now and then and the money he had spent on her schooling had been given to him by a grateful United States Government. He had never been able to tell his daughter how her mother had really died, or why he had left the AAU. She thought he had been given a golden handshake and a large pension by a grateful Uncle Sam.

The Planner had decided to put in place a kind of insurance for his daughter should the Guardian ever bother her. He had made an appointment to see a solicitor whilst in London. The same solicitor who had assisted him with school arrangements for his daughter over the years. The Planner intended to copy the details of Operation Domino from his own disk on to a disk compatible with the solicitor's word processing system and tell his lawyer the password needed to access the information on the disk. The solicitor would be instructed to only ever access the information on the disk in the event that the Planner's daughter vanished, or died.

The disk he carried with him contained more than just the details of the Operation. The Planner had included a separate file with as much information about his employer's past as he knew. He had summarised the Guardian's crimes in which he himself had been involved. The sinking of the "Osprey", the diamond theft in South Africa and the others. Finally, the Planner had included a profile of the Guardian, recording the contact details he had for him and a comprehensive description of the Romanian. Whilst the Planner had not seen the Guardian for over five years, there had been a time when the Guardian had not been so illusive. The Planner suspected that the name the Guardian used when dealing with him was an alias, but he had addresses in Romania and in Europe where he had in the past sent operational reports and he had telephone numbers. The Planner had no doubt that this information about his employer would make it easy for the international police agencies to track him down.

The Planner would tell his daughter that if anyone from Romania ever showed up to bother her in the future, she was to divulge that if anything happened to her, complete details of Operation Domino and of the Guardian would be passed to the police immediately. The Planner knew that his daughter would ask a lot of questions which he would not answer. However, he also knew that she was sensible enough to remember what she would be told and to act on her father's instructions should the Guardian or his henchmen ever show up.

He finished his drink and looked at his watch. There was still fifteen minutes before his flight began boarding. He looked around for a waitresses and signalled for another brandy.

CHAPTER 8

The British Airways flight to London was finally called. David finished his beer and walked to the departure gate. He grimaced when he saw how full the flight was going to be. Because he had only booked on the flight late the previous evening, there had been no non-smoking seats left in executive class and economy had been full. He had hoped there might nevertheless be a spare non-smoking seat on the aeroplane when he actually boarded, but the number of people queuing to board made this seem unlikely. However, it was still worth a try he decided.

David waited until everyone queuing for executive class had boarded before boarding himself. He asked one of the stewardesses if there were any spare non-smoking seats in executive and was told that the entire flight was full. As David was shown to his allocated seat in the smoking section of the cabin he thought of Garces delaying him in Miami for an extra day and hoped that his neighbour for the flight was not a heavy smoker. The Boeing 747s used by British Airways for flights to and from Miami only have two seats on either side of the aisle in executive class, so that if your neighbour does smoke during the flight there is no unoccupied centre seat to dilute the effects of his cigarette.

David stowed his flight case in the overhead locker and sat down in seat number 24C, an aisle seat on the left hand side of the cabin. He was wearing a jacket in spite of the Miami sunshine because he knew that it would be cold when the aeroplane touched down at Heathrow. He felt a slight chill from the cabin's air conditioning unit and decided to keep his jacket on for the time being.

The man in the seat next to him was sitting quietly and did not acknowledge David's presence at all. David thought he looked a little nervous and suspected that the old man next to him did not have much experience of aeroplanes. This probably meant that he would smoke heavily during the flight, David feared. David and the old man sat silently whilst the crew sealed the outer door of the aircraft and the seat belt sign was illuminated by the Captain. A stewardess went through the emergency escape drill in case of a crash and the old man seemed as uninterested in it as David was. The aeroplane began to taxi towards the runway and within minutes was airborne, climbing to its designated thirty three thousand feet corridor for the journey to London.

"Miss. Miss, can I have a large brandy straight away," barked the Planner as soon as the aeroplane was airborne. The Planner took a packet of cigarettes from the inside pocket of his jacket and lit one almost by remote control. For the first time he seemed to notice David. "Would you like one?" he asked, offering the newly opened pack to David. "I only just remembered to get a new packet before I got on, but I can spare one if you fancy a smoke. Would've been a disaster if I'd have run out of smokes half way over the pond don't you think?" David did not agree. The Planner was already exhaling tobacco all over him.

"No thanks, I don't smoke," said David.

"Is that a fact. Can't get through a waking hour myself without a smoke," replied the Planner. "My doctor has told me to give up, but that's easier said than done. I've just been smoking for too long now." The stewardess returned with the Planner's brandy and David felt the aeroplane begin to level out as it arrived at its corridor.

"And can I get you anything Sir?" asked the stewardess to David. David thought that another beer might help disguise the taste of the Planner's cigarette that had infiltrated the air around him.

"I'll have a beer please," he replied. David watched as the Planner sipped his brandy. He had deep yellow stains around the ends of his fingers. He had smoked a lot of cigarettes in his time. David guessed that his travelling companion was in his sixties. He was quite well dressed and had an old leather briefcase wedged between his thin legs which David thought must be uncomfortable for him. "Would you like me to put that in the overhead locker to give you a little more room?" he asked, pointing to the briefcase. The Planner looked at the case and his legs tightened around it.

"I prefer to keep it down here with me, but thanks anyway."

"Is it full of national secrets," joked David, "or do you keep you travellers cheques in there?"

"Nothing like that. I just prefer to have it where I can see it that's all. You never know on these long flights, I might dose off and never see it again." This amused David. The idea of someone stealing the old man's case. Then he thought of his own case in the overhead locker containing about two thousand pounds worth of computer equipment and he looked over at the Planner.

"You're not serious are you?" he asked. The Planner just smiled at David and continued to drink his brandy.

David felt himself staring at the right side of the Planner's face. The blood vessels around the man's eyes had burst and he had red streaks across his cheeks that betrayed his appetite for alcohol.

"What's the matter?" The Planner had caught David staring at him and did not much care for it.

"Nothing," replied David feeling guilty. "My name is David Bowstead," he said quickly, trying to change the subject.

"Is it?" replied the Planner without giving his name in return. "And what was Mr. Bowstead doing in Miami?"

"Oh, just business. Had to see a client and sweat a bit," answered David, recalling for a second the saga with Garces's bankers' draft. "How about you. Do you live in Miami?"

"Yes. The good weather makes up for the lousy fucking government." David was surprise by the Planner's sudden outburst. He wondered what the United States Government had done to annoy this old man so much. David noticed the Planner tense up and clutch his briefcase between his knees.

"There's no need to worry," David told the Planner trying to sound reassuring. "These 747s have the best safety record of any 'plane, so I understand. Flying really is the safest way to travel. Hardly any crashes."

"Maybe, but if there is a crash that seat belt won't help you," said the Planner looking down at the seat belt still tightly strapped across David's waist.

"Guess your right, but I wouldn't worry if I was you. When you gotta go you gotta go."

The Planner grunted at David.

"What do you do in Miami?" David asked.

"I'm retired now. But I used to test 'planes for defects. Not these albatrosses. Mainly military 'planes." David was impressed. Like most men who watched Tom Cruise hammer across the sky in the movie "Top Gun" in the mid 1980s, David had a fascination for jets and admired anyone that had anything to do with them. David recalled that travelling upside down at Mach One was supposed to be better than sex.

"Did you ever fly in any of the fast ones?" David was displaying his ignorance of aviation without even realising it.

"No. I stayed on the ground most of the time. When you've seen what I've seen on the drawing board you tend to develop a healthy respect for gravity." The Planner smiled for the first time as he said this. "You're right though. These 747s are pretty safe. A lot of people thought that they would fall out of the sky when they first came along, but Boeing got it right more or less."

"More or less?" asked David.

"Yes," replied the Planner. "You see the safety problem with 'planes, all planes but especially big passenger jets is not so much the 'planes themselves, but the fuel they carry."

"There's something wrong with the fuel?" David felt uncomfortable.

"No. The fuel is fine as fuel goes. The problem is that the damn stuff is carried in the wings." The Planner pointed out of the window to his left and David looked out at a section of the wing. "See that huge Rolls Royce engine. That's what's keeping us in the sky basically. The space in the wing around the engine is full of aviation fuel. One spark in the engine and Boom!"

"Shit," said David.

"I'd say shit all right," replied the Planner. "They've tried for years to develop a non flammable fuel without luck. All they can do is insulate the engine to keep the fuel away from it in case there is a fire, and keep their fingers crossed."

"Keep their fingers crossed," repeated David.

"That's right. Pretty silly really to surround a great big engine with highly flammable liquid but the only alternative at the moment is to carry the fuel in the main cabin which means less space for seats which means less money for Mr. United States Airline or whoever." David was beginning to wish that he had never brought the subject up.

"Well you certainly seem to know a lot about 'planes," he said. The

Planner grunted again.

"Actually, these days I spend more time thinking about oil tankers," he replied. Since the Guardian had contacted him a few days earlier, the Planner had been having nightmares about the "Osprey" and the three crew men that had been killed.

"Ships," said David. "Now you're talking my language. I work for a law firm in London that specialises in maritime law. Don't tell me you know all about scuttling ships as well as building jets." The Planner looked at David and decided to change the subject.

"I'm on my way to London to visit my daughter. She lives in London. Clapham. Do you know it?"

"Yes. I live in Chelsea. Clapham is practically down the road. What does you're daughter do in London? Is she at university?"

"No. She runs her own catering company in the West End." David thought this sounded pretty boring but smiled and nodded his head as if he was impressed.

The Planner had finished his brandy and the cigarette he had been smoking. He lit another cigarette, called the stewardess over and asked for another drink. David declined the stewardess's invitation for another beer. The Planner sucked hard on his cigarette and coughed. He had the cough of a marathon smoker. A sharp almost piecing cough. This man was in bad shape, David thought.

David had not noticed that in fact he had not been the last person to board the aeroplane. As he had been making himself comfortable in his seat, a man in his late thirties had walked passed him unnoticed and sat down in the aisle seat two rows behind David on the other side of the aircraft. The man was about average height and build for a man in his late thirties with rather nondescript short, dark hair. His complexion was on the dark side as well, but not so dark that his face was striking in any way. The man wore a plain grey jacket. He carried no hand luggage only a dark raincoat which he had rolled up and placed on the floor under his seat. He was not a man that you would look at twice or remember having seen. With the exception of his small piercing eyes, nothing about him was distinctive. To some men this might have been a considerable handicap. To the Mechanic his neutral appearance was a positive advantage. The Mechanic was in the killing business: being able to disappear largely unremembered into a crowd of people had helped him ply his trade for over fifteen years without ever having been caught. He was good; too good to be travelling from Miami to London on the same flight as the Planner by chance.

The Mechanic took the copy of the Miami Herald offered to him by the stewardess. From behind the newspaper's open pages he observed the Planner and David.

The Mechanic did not like this hit. Why the Guardian had not simply allowed him to kill the Planner in Miami he did not know. The Guardian had been adamant. The Planner was to be strangled in the back seat of a taxi that would be waiting to take him from the airport in Bucharest to meet the Guardian. The taxi driver would be one of the Guardian's men. The Mechanic's instructions were clear. He was to take the Planner's briefcase and replace it with a similar case he would find in the trunk of the taxi. The replacement case would contain papers and documents explaining that the Planner had been invited by the University of Bucharest to give a series of lectures on Advanced Aviation Engineering. The necessary officials at the university had been bribed by the Guardian to confirm this story. The Romanian authorities would conclude that the Planner had been killed by airport attackers, an increasing problem in Bucharest. The hit could not have been more straightforward and the Mechanic wondered why the Guardian was not using one of his own men: killing the Planner hardly presented any difficulties. However, the Guardian had insisted that the hit must be carried out by the Mechanic himself. The Mechanic was being paid five hundred thousand dollars, his usual fee, to follow the Planner for two days before he left Miami to make sure he was making arrangements to travel to Romania, tail him to Romania and kill him in the manner prescribed: easy money in the Mechanic's opinion. He had been told not to contact the Guardian other than to confirm that the Planner had been killed, unless something went wrong.

Whilst he had been observing the Planner during the previous two days, the Mechanic had broken into the old man's house undetected one afternoon when the Planner had been dozing in the Floridian sun on his porch and had inspected the airline ticket he had witnessed the Planner collect from a travel agency that morning. The ticket was for a flight to Bucharest with a stop over in London. The ticket was supposed to be for a direct flight to Romania and so the Mechanic had contacted the Guardian. The Guardian had asked the arrival time of the flight from

London to Bucharest. The Mechanic had confirmed that the Planner was due to arrive in London on the morning of Thursday 24th November and was booked on the first flight to Romanian from Heathrow the following morning which arrived in Bucharest at 9:30 am local time. The Guardian had been satisfied.

The Mechanic had carried out three hits for the Guardian in the past. All of the people he had previously killed for the Guardian had been fairly prominent. An American industrialist who had been involved in Easter European politics before the collapse of the Soviet Union, a well known French newspaper reporter who had been covering the elections in Romania in May 1990 and a South African junior minister who had been responsible for approving the country's diamond excavations. All three killings had been made to look like accidents and on each occasion the authorities had been fooled. Why the Guardian was prepared to pay half a million dollars to have a seemingly insignificant old man killed the Mechanic could not figure out. Nevertheless, he was being paid to kill the Planner and kill him he would, exactly according to the plan.

In the Mechanic's business reliability was the most important thing and the Guardian was a very good customer. The Mechanic was paid half of his fee two days before he carried out a hit and the balance after the hit had been successfully concluded. His Swiss bank account was very healthy and the Mechanic intended to keep it that way. He looked over at the Planner and David again. They were still talking. He wondered who the young man was who was taking such an interest in the Planner. The Mechanic made it a rule never to engage in small talk with anyone, particularly during a long flight. It did not matter who the young man was. He would not be in the way in Bucharest.

"How long will you be staying in London?" David asked the Planner.

"Just overnight. I have to fly to Romania early the following morning," he replied.

"Romania. What on earth could drag you from the Miami sunshine to Romania?" David joked.

The Planner regretted that he had mentioned Romania. He did not know what lay ahead of him in the Guardian's country but his instinct was not to make it known that he was heading there. He wished he had not told David this. The Planner thought for a second, taking a slow drink of brandy to give himself a few more seconds thinking time before he answered.

"I have an old friend from my time with the airforce who lives in Bucharest," the Planner lied. "He's ill. Might not see out the year. I want to see him one last time." The Planner hoped that this sounded convincing.

"I'm sorry." David asked nothing further, but he was surprised that an ex-US Airforce man should had a good friend in a former communist country. David was dragged from this thought by the stewardess.

"Sir, would you like the chicken or the beef?" He had not had time to read the menu to see what was offered by the galley. The menu was stuffed into the seat pocket in front of him with the usual assortment of in-flight magazines. The stewardess was waiting for a reply.

"I'll have the beef and a glass of Bordeaux please," he replied without bothering to check the menu. He guessed that the galley had Bordeaux. In his experience all executive class menus offered that particular wine. He was right. The stewardess nodded her approval and David smiled to himself knowing that she would have nodded her approval in the same way if he had ordered the chicken and a class of Chardonnay or the vegetarian dish and mineral water.

"And for you Sir?" she asked looking at the Planner.

"No food for me, just a large brandy please," he replied. The stewardess was smiling and nodding as she moved on to the passenger sitting behind David.

"Tell me a little more about your time with the airforce. It sounds fascinating," David said. The Planner was relieved that the conversation had moved on from Romania and was happy to talk about something else.

"Well, as I mentioned I basically spent my career analysing data." The Planner launched into an explanation of how he had been recruited to the AAU and how for the first few years he had spent his time analysing military aircraft crashes to try and discover what had gone wrong. He went on to explain that he had eventually moved into weakness evaluation and headed up a team which resolved the manoeuvrability problems of the Tomcat and which a few years later, redesigned the take off and landing systems used on US aircraft carriers. He recounted his career with enthusiasm and David could detect nothing to explain the Planner's earlier disparaging remark about the United States Government.

David was transfixed by the Planner's stories. All of his childhood questions about aeroplanes were being answered by a man who was clearly an expert in the field of aviation. A lot of what the Planner was telling David was highly confidential, but the Planner had given up worrying about the Official Military Secrets Regulations to which he was still subject the day the airforce had told him there would be no investigation into his wife's death. He was enjoying the attention he was getting from David. No one had asked him to talk about his career for years and he found that he still had a passion for what he used to do. Neither David nor the Planner noticed when the main cabin lights were dimmed after dinner to allow those passengers that wanted to sleep to do so. David had intended to get at least a few hours sleep before arriving in London, but was so captivated by the Planner's account of aviation that he forgot all about this. The Planner talked and talked and smoked and drank. He repeatedly called the stewardess over to re-fill his brandy balloon. The more he talked the more he drank and smoked.

The Planner had exhausted the topic of US military aircraft by the time the 747 was three quarters of the way over the Atlantic Ocean. Next, the conversation moved on to civil aviation, a subject David found just as fascinating. David was flabbergasted at the Planner's detailed knowledge of apparently every aspect of civil aviation. The Planner was well acquainted with the development of every passenger aeroplane ever built. David decided that the US Airforce had been crazy to let his man retire.

By the time the 747 was flying over Ireland heading for the final stage of the flight into South East London the Planner was explaining to David what the future of aviation offered. The Planner described aviation in a way that made it seem the most glamorous pursuit in the World. As the 747 approached Heathrow David envied the pilot in the cockpit.

The Planner had been talking more or less continuously for over five hours. In that time he had given David a comprehensive history of both military and civil aviation as well as an insight into what David could expect from the airlines of the World during the following ten years. The Planner seemed exhausted. He coughed loudly as he had done throughout the flight and his face was red from the vast amount of brandy he had consumed.

"Ladies and Gentleman, this is your Captain speaking. We are about to begin our descent into London Heathrow Airport. Please return to your seats and fasten you seat belts. The local time is a little after six in the morning and the temperature in London is forty degrees, a little colder than the weather we left behind in Miami." David felt the 747 bank slightly to the left and wished he was in the cockpit with the flight crew for the landing.

The pilot positioned the 747 for the approach and the whine of the landing gear being lowered could be heard. David looked over at the Planner.

"Nearly there now," he said. The Planner nodded at him and David thought he looked a little ill. The Planner loosened the collar of his shirt and pulled the knot of his tie free.

"Please put your seats in the upright position and extinguish all cigarettes, we will be landing in three minutes," announced the senior stewardess over the intercom. The Planner clumsily stubbed his half smoked cigarette out in the ashtray in the arm of his chair. He coughed again. David looked at him. He really did not look too good, David thought.

"Are you alright?" he asked.

"Yes. I think I must have had too much brandy. I never know when to stop my doctor keeps telling me. I'll be fine." David was not so sure. He wished the aircraft would hurry up and land. David tried to look past the Planner out of the window to see how far away the runway was but could not see clearly. The Planner coughed again and David noticed that the old man's right hand was twitching slightly.

David felt the 747 drop further and thought the runway could only be seconds away. He looked across at the Planner again. The Planner had started to sweat and his face was turning a bright red. David looked around for a stewardess, but they were all seated at the front of the cabin in anticipation of the 747 landing.

"Hang on, we'll be on the ground any second now," he told the Planner. Suddenly, David felt a thud and heard the screech of the aeroplane's tyres hitting the tarmac as the 747 touched down. The Planner started to cough even louder and more aggressively than he had been doing, as if he was desperately trying to clear his throat. The twitch in his right hand had developed into a violent shake. David stared at the Planner not knowing what to do. He looked again for a stewardess. The 747 was hurtling down the runway gradually loosing speed and the cabin crew were still all seated.

The Planner turned and looked at David and tried to lift himself up from his seat. His breathing was strained and he was now coughing continuously. He tried to talk but could not. He gripped his chest as he tried to stand up, half out of his seat and then without warning went into convulsions before collapsing on to David's lap. David tried to lift him up but could not. As the 747 slowed down David realised that the Planner must have had some kind of attack, probably a heart attack.

"Please, help me," he shouted to the cabin crew who were beginning to unbuckle their seat belts. "This man needs help. He's collapsed." Within seconds two stewardesses were at David's side. They turned the Planner on to his side as much as possible so that his head was facing in the direction of the seat in front of David.

"What happened?" asked the more senior of the two stewardesses.

"He started to cough, went red and looked like he was choking. Then he grabbed his chest and fell on top of me," David explained. The stewardess turned to her colleague.

"Go tell the Captain we have a possible heart attack victim back here and we need an ambulance and priority disembarkation." The second stewardess ran off in the direction of the cockpit. The 747 came to a complete stop and the senior stewardess started to give the Planner mouth to mouth. David held the Planner's head and followed the instructions he was given by the stewardess. He heard someone announce over the intercom that all passengers should stay seated even thought the aeroplane had stopped as there was an ill man on board who needed to be helped off the aeroplane quickly. It seemed to David that he was cradling the Planner's head in his arms for an eternity. In fact it was only a few minutes before the sound of the ambulance's siren could be heard as it pulled up alongside the 747.

David saw two paramedics rush into the cabin and come to his side. One fitted an oxygen mask over the Planner's face and loosened the buttons of his shirt. The other paramedic hoisted the Planner's upper body from David's lap and pulled him from the seat. The first paramedic held the oxygen mask in place over the Planner's nose and mouth with one hand and carried an oxygen bottle with his other hand whilst the Planner's lifeless body was dragged across David's lap. As the Planner was lifted into the aisle the paramedic who had hold of the Planner's torso told David to lift the old man's waist and legs as they were pulled from the seat and help carry him off the aeroplane. David tried to manoeuvre himself out of his seat whilst at the same time lifting the Planner but the Planner's right leg got caught between the back of the seat and his briefcase. David felt down by the Planner's legs and got hold of the case. He pulled it up from the floor freeing the Planner's leg but there was nowhere to drop it other than back where it had come from. The paramedic told David to hurry. He swung the case over the Planner's body and gently brought it down on the Planner's upper legs.

The paramedic and David carried the Planner along the aisle to the door at the front of the 747, down a set of rolling stairs that had been wheeled up against the side of the aeroplane and into the back of the waiting ambulance. Before David had a chance to realise what was going on he was sitting in the back of the ambulance with his hands around the head of the Planner as the ambulance sped away from the 747 towards the terminal building.

The Mechanic had not been able to see the Planner fall across David's lap from where he was sitting. He did not know that something was wrong until David shouted for help and the stewardesses ran to David's side. He had sat quietly watching the Planner being carried from the aircraft. He saw David swing the Planner's case on to the old man's upper legs and carry it off the aeroplane. As the Planner was carried down the stairs to the ambulance the Mechanic got up from his seat and headed in the direction of the open door. He was stopped by one of the stewardesses who told him that the 747 would taxi to its scheduled arrival gate where the rest of the passengers would be able to get off. He asked the stewardess where the old man would be taken and she reassured him that the airport had a fully equipped Medical Centre in Terminal Four.

The Mechanic did not return to his own seat. Instead he sat down in the seat that David had occupied. After making sure that no one was watching him the Mechanic skilfully checked the area around the two seats which had been occupied by David and the Planner for anything belonging to the Planner. Finding nothing he looked out of the window and saw the ambulance heading for what he guessed must be Terminal Four. Certain that the ambulance was in fact heading for the Medical Centre he returned to his own seat and waited for the aeroplane to arrive at the disembarkation gate.

As soon as the doors of the 747 were opened the Mechanic picked up his raincoat and dashed off the aeroplane, knocking over a stewardess who was standing by the open door preparing to say goodbye to the passengers as they left the aeroplane.

CHAPTER 9

Heathrow. Thursday 24th November 1994.

David felt the ambulance rush across the tarmac away from the 747. He was still disorientated and was not quite sure where the ambulance was going. The Planner had gone into convulsions less than ten minutes ago, but it seemed to David that hours had passed since he had been discussing aviation with his flight companion.

The Planner lay on a stretcher with the oxygen mask over his face. David was still dazed but he heard one of the paramedics say that the Planner was still alive. The Planner's eyes were closed and he made no sound or movement. The small monitor screen to his side showed an intermittent bleep which David knew indicated that the Planner was still alive. In spite of the stretcher and the tubes that were protruding from his body the Planner maintained a light grip around David's left hand. Not a tight grip, but strong enough for David to know that it was intentional. David thought the Planner must be terrified and tightened his own grip around the old man's hand.

Gradually David began to calm down and take stock of where he was. He realised that the Planner must have had some kind of seizure possibly a heart attack and remembered how much brandy the old man had drunk during the flight and how red his face had become at times during his account of life with the AAU. David hoped the Planner did not die. He wondered again where the ambulance was going. He was about to ask one of the paramedics when the ambulance screeched to a halt and the back doors of the vehicle were pulled open as vigorously as they had been closed. Three men in hospital uniforms appeared. Quickly, they lifted the stretcher out of the ambulance. The Planner was still gripping David's hand. As the stretcher headed towards the doors of the Medical Centre inside Terminal Four so did David. None of the medical staff rushing around the stretcher seemed interested in freeing David from the Planner's grip which had tightened slightly as the stretcher had been lifted out of the ambulance.

Unsure of what he should be doing, David gripped the Planner's hand even tighter and went with the stretcher through two sets of rubber doors in the direction of a room that had its doors held open by more men in hospital uniforms. As the stretcher was pushed into the room David expected someone to remove the Planner's hand from his and take him away. No one did. David stood next to the Planner as medical staff rushed around the old man fitting drips and shouting instructions to one another that David was unable to comprehend.

"Let him go now. We'll look after him," said a young nurse to David. David had been holding the Planner's hand for so long that he did not release it immediately when asked to do so. "We will look after your father now," said the nurse. The nurse put her hand on to David's hand and tried to separate him and the Planner. David realised what she was saying and tried to release the Planner's hand. As David loosened his grip the Planner tightened his own grip around David's hand as much as he could. David stared at the old man lying on the stretcher, tubes running from his body and remembered his own father who had died two years earlier. Then he thought of the daughter the Planner had proudly boasted of during the flight.

"He's not my father," David said to the nurse as she tried again to separate the two men's hands. "I don't even know his name." David felt guilty that he did not know the Planner's name. He had stayed up all night discussing aviation with him, but the old man had not once given David his name. All of a sudden the nurse was called out of the room by a doctor and David was left holding the Planner's hand.

He felt the Planner feebly move his hand up towards his face, dragging David's hand with him. The Planner was struggling to pull David down to his face and David realised that the old man wanted to speak to him.

For a moment David froze, not sure if he should bend down over the Planner or turn away. He looked behind him and saw the nurse talking to the doctor in the doorway. David could feel the Planner's frail attempts to pull him closer. The Planner was now so weak. David bent over the old man and put his ear close to the Planner's mouth. He was still holding the Planner's hand.

"My daughter." The Planner mumbled these words into David's ear and then began to cough again. The sound of his coughing alerted the nurse in the doorway. She looked across at the monitor screen by the side of the Planner's bed and checked his vital signs. They had not changed. The doctor was giving her instructions and she was having to concentrate hard.

"What about your daughter?" David replied, not entirely sure if he had heard the Planner correctly. It was difficult to understand him with the oxygen mask strapped over his face. The old man tried to clear his throat and reached up to his face for the mask. The Planner's eyes cried out to David for help. His frail hand reached the left side of the mask and he tried to pull it from his face. David watched, wishing the Planner would leave the mask where it was, but he recognised the look in the Planner's eyes. It was the look of someone who knew he was dying and had something important to say. David's own father had looked at him in the same way from his hospital bed moments before he had told David that he had always loved him. His father had died moments after saying those words. He had never before told his son that he loved him and David would never forget his father's dying words or how relieved he had seemed to have said them.

David looked at the Planner's eyes again. The man was dying and he had no family there to say his farewells to. Just a stranger he had met on an aeroplane who shared his interest in aviation. David leant a little further over the Planner and pulled the oxygen mask to one side of the old man's face. He hoped the nurse had not seen him. He thought how old and tired the Planner's face seemed. The old man looked into David's eyes.

"My daughter. The Romanian will come for her. Tell her she is safe from him if she uses the disk. Give her the disk. Tell her to use her real name. Her real name. My case. In my briefcase."

The Planner whispered these words to David not from fear of being overheard, but because his breath was leaving his body. His eyes slowly closed and David heard a loud bleep and the nurse and the doctor who had been standing in the doorway were at the Planner's side shouting and massaging his chest. David was pushed back and watched the explosion of activity. He knew the Planner had died: not because the monitor which recorded the old man's vital signs was bleeping loudly, but because the Planner had let go of his hand.

Another nurse put her arm around David's shoulder and told him to leave the room. David turned to go and saw the Planner's battered briefcase on the chair by the door. He remembered how the Planner had not wanted to let the case be put into the overhead locker on the 747 at Miami and thought of what the Planner had just said. As he followed the nurse out of the room, David bent down and picked up the case and walked out of the room with it in his hand. No one noticed him. Everyone else in the room was too busy trying to revive the Planner. It was no use. The Planner was dead.

David sat in a chair in the corridor outside the Planner's room. The doctors were still in there, but the bleeping noise had stopped. The doctors had turned the machine off, but David did not know this.

He considered the case at his feet. It was on old brown case with a single latch holding the strap in place. The type of briefcase that is popular with academics the World over. David tried the latch. It was locked. He tried again, this time with a little more force. The latch was old and in places rusty. It came free on the third attempt and the strap that held the case shut loosened. He open the case and examined the contents inside without removing anything. A few papers and a ruler, what looked like a large scientific calculator and tucked inside one of the sleeves, a thin blue computer disk.

David took the disk out of the Planner's briefcase. He had heard what the Planner had said although the old man had not made much sense. Something about his daughter, a Romanian and a disk. David examined the computer disk he held in his hand. It was a standard Sony three inch floppy disk that could be loaded into just about any computer available on the market. The disk had a label on one side of it on to which someone, David presumed the Planner, had written the letters "O D" in red ink. David had seen hundreds of disks just like this one. He had about a dozen strewn across his desk at Holland Chapman & Co.

Thinking about computers and his office reminded David that he had left his own flight case on the aeroplane in the locker above his seat. His lap top computer and portable printer were in the case. Actually, he thought to himself, the firm's lap top computer and portable printer are in the case. He hoped he had not lost them.

"Are you the old man's son?" asked the doctor who had walked out of the Planner's room. The doctor looked at David, getting ready to break the news to him that his father had a second heart attack and had died moments earlier.

"No, he was not my father," answered David, making it clear that he already knew the Planner was dead. "We sat next to one another on the 'plane and I came here with him in the ambulance." The doctor looked at the disk David was holding in his hand. David felt like a grave robber all of a sudden. He instinctively stuffed the disk into the right side pocket of his jacket and quickly fumbled to close the case. He hoped that he had not broken the latch beyond repair. One of the nurses came forward and handed David a cup of tea.

"Did you know the man's name or if he has any family? Is he English?" asked the doctor.

"No. I mean I don't know, I mean I didn't know his name. He didn't tell me." David realised how strange this must sound. "He was an American from Miami. Flew to London to visit his daughter on the BA flight I was on." As David said this he remembered that the Planner had told him that he was flying on to Romania to visit an old friend. Did this have something to do with a Romanian visiting his daughter, David wondered?

"He has a daughter in London. That's something. Do you know her name?" asked the doctor.

"No," replied David.

The doctor considered David for a moment. He had had quite a shock. No need to detain him any longer than necessary, the doctor decided.

"You'd better go to the Airport Security Office. They'll want to talk to you. Get some details, that sort of thing. Are you feeling up to that?"

"Yes, I'm fine," replied David. "But I left my bag and coat on the 'plane. How do I get them back?"

"Don't know, but the guys in security will be able to help you," the doctor answered. "Nurse, can you show him the way?" The nurse nodded and the doctor turned and walked away. David was pleased that he had read law at university rather than medicine. He would not have liked the doctor's job.

"This way please," the nurse said to David. "The Security Office is just through those swing doors over there." The nurse pointed down the corridor to a set of swing doors under a sign that read "NO ENTRY". David stood up and carrying the Planner's case followed the nurse to the Security Office in the adjoining building.

David had recovered almost completely by now and was feeling a little stupid for having taken the Planner's case out of the medical room. He wondered how he was going to get his own belongings from the 747. He knew that after the rest of the passengers had disembarked, the aeroplane would be routinely checked and his case and coat would be discovered, but he was not sure where they would be taken. He would ask the Security Officer he decided.

The nurse showed David into a small room that had "SECURITY" etched across the door. He sat down at the desk in the room and within a few moments an Airport Security Officer in a uniform that resembled a policeman's uniform came into the room and sat down opposite him.

"Good morning Sir," he said to David. "I'm the Desk Officer. I understand you accompanied the old gentleman who died off the aircraft earlier this morning." David had left the 747 less than half an hour ago, but already he felt like he had been in the terminal building for hours.

"Yes," he replied. He glanced at his watch. It was just past 7:00 am.

"Did you know the old man well?" asked the Officer.

"No," replied David.

"Heart attack. Probably had too much to drink on the 'plane. I'm told his mouth smelt of strong alcohol," the Officer informed David. "Tragic, but we see a lot of deaths here these days I'm afraid. I'll need to get some details from you Sir."

"Fine, whatever," said David. "But I left some valuable belongings on the 'plane when I came off with the old man. Will they be alright?"

"Should be taken to lost and found by your airline. You'll be able to collect them from the baggage collection lounge as soon as you're done here," replied the Officer. "I just need to take some details from you. What's your name and address?" David proceeded to answer the Officer's questions. He gave his name and address, his occupation and details of his flight. He was not able to recall the exact number of his flight. The Officer asked him to explain exactly what had happened on the aeroplane. David gave as full an account as possible. He was

77

beginning to feel tired. No sleep at all during the flight combined with the events of the last half an hour had worn him out. He was anxious to finish with the Officer as quickly as possible, particularly as he suspected that he would have to go over the same ground again with the police eventually anyway.

Nevertheless, David explained that the Planner had been drinking heavily during the flight and had not got any sleep. How that whilst the 747 was landing the Planner had an attack of some sort and had collapsed on to his lap. How he had somehow been bundled into the ambulance with the Planner and then into the room in the Medical Centre before explaining to one of the medical staff that he was not the Planner's son.

David was tired and did not tell the Officer that the Planner had mumbled something about his daughter, a Romanian and a disk just before he had died. He wanted to get out of there and thought that this would only complicate things unnecessarily. Anyway, David had decided that the Planner had been rambling and that he must have misunderstood the old man in any event. The Officer made a detailed note of everything that David said. When David had finished his account the Officer noticed the case on the floor by David's feet.

"I thought you said you left your hand luggage on the 'plane when the deceased was carried off," he said.

"I did," replied David, realising that his earlier explanation did not account for the case by his feet. "This is not my case Officer." The Officer looked at David for a moment before speaking again. David felt uncomfortable.

"Is that the old man's case you told me about?" the Officer asked. David had explained that he had first started talking to the Planner when he had offered to stow the old man's briefcase in the overhead locker. He realised that the Officer was more observant than he had given him credit for.

"Yes. It came off the 'plane with him." David was a little flustered and hurriedly put the case on the desk as if offering it to the Officer.

"Have you looked inside it?" asked the Officer. David instinctively said that he had not looked inside the case. He was beginning to feel like he was being questioned by his old headmaster. How could he explain that he had poked around in the case only moments after the old man had died? He was beginning to feel that he was being accused of some kind of crime and was more anxious than ever to get out of the terminal building.

David had forgotten all about the computer disk he had hurriedly stuffed into his jacket pocket.

"I had better keep the case Sir," said the Officer in a matter of fact manner. "In due course it will find its way to the deceased's next of kin." David just nodded.

The Officer asked David a few more questions, including details of where he could be contacted in case the police wanted to talk to him. He gave his office telephone number as he still intended going to Holland Chapman & Co. straight from the airport.

"So where do I get my bags from?" David asked once the Officer had completed his questions.

"Have you cleared immigration yet?" asked the Officer.

"No," replied David. I told you, I was taken off the 'plane with the old man."

"Do you have your passport with you?"

"Yes I do." With that David took his passport from the inside pocket of his jacket and handed it to the Officer.

"This appears to be in order Sir," said the Officer, "but you will have to clear immigration in the usual way." The Officer gave David directions out of the security building back to the arrivals section of the airport. David was surprised at first that the Officer let him wander off unaccompanied. However, he discovered that the only way to get out of that part of the building, other than by doors that were either guarded or locked, was through the arrivals lounge. David walked at a brisk pace anxious to retrieve his case and coat and be on his way.

CHAPTER 10

The Mechanic estimated that it would take the ambulance only a few minutes to reach the Medical Centre inside the terminal building. The Mechanic usual never ran. It only drew attention to him which was to be avoided. However, as he left the aeroplane he accelerated up to a full sprint as he ran from the arrival gate into the airport. He had no choice, time had become too valuable for him to dawdle.

The Mechanic was not very familiar with Heathrow Airport and did not know exactly where the Medical Centre was in relation to the arrival gate he had just left. He calculated that a passenger would not be able to gain access to the Medical Centre before he had cleared immigration. The aeroplane had eventually pulled up at gate twenty four, some distance from the immigration desks, but at the speed the Mechanic was moving he was at immigration within a matter of minutes. The Mechanic was in good shape. He regarded fitness and agility as crucial assets in his chosen profession. It was early morning at Heathrow and there were no queues of people waiting in line to clear immigration. The Mechanic handed over the false passport he was travelling under and was cleared after a few customary questions about the nature of his business in London.

Once through immigration, the Mechanic found an airport porter and lied to him that his friend had fallen ill on the British Airways flight from Miami and had been taken to the Medical Centre. He explained that he wanted to know how to get to the centre to see if his friend was all right. The porter took the Mechanic into the baggage collection area on the ground floor of the airport and up to a door marked "NO ENTRY", which was patrolled by a security guard. The Mechanic repeated his story to the guard and was allowed through the door into a passageway that linked the Security Centre to the Medical Centre in a part of the terminal building that was not accessible to the general public. He followed the signs for the Medical Centre, this time walking rather than running, looking anxious as if he was worried about someone close to him. The corridor was not very long and the Mechanic was soon in the heart of the airport's Medical Centre.

The Medical Centre at Heathrow is well equipped, with a full surgery for emergency operations as well as a number of smaller consulting and treatment rooms. Nevertheless, the centre is deliberately compact with the main surgery and other rooms all built off a single corridor which contains a waiting area.

The Mechanic walked up to the desk in the waiting area and asked the nurse at the desk if an old man from the British Airways flight from Miami had been brought in earlier that morning. The nurse confirmed that the Planner had been brought directly to the Medical Centre from the 747 shortly after the aeroplane had landed. The Mechanic told the nurse that he had sat next to the Planner during the flight and had seen him collapse. He wanted to know how the old man was doing. The nurse thought how kind it was of the Mechanic to enquire about a fellow passenger and made a telephone call whilst the Mechanic waited, trying his best to look genuinely concerned.

"I'm very sorry to have to tell you Sir, but the old gentleman you asked about died shortly after he was brought in this morning," said the nurse after she had finished on the telephone. "He had a second heart attack which was just too much for him so I understand. I'm very sorry."

"He's dead?"

"That's right Sir. As I said, a second heart attack," the nurse repeated. The Mechanic thought for a moment.

"I would like to pay my respects," he said. "May I sit by his body, just for a few minutes?"

"I'm afraid that will not be possible," answered the nurse. "The doctors would not permit it. Did you know the gentleman well?"

"Well enough," said the Mechanic sharply, turning away from the nurse. He preferred to ask the questions and considered that his conversation with the nurse should be kept as short as possible. The longer he spoke to her the more likely it was that she would take note of what he looked like. This possibility always made the Mechanic uncomfortable. "I have information about the old man which the authorities will need concerning his next of kin and business in London. Who should I talk to?"

"Security is probably the best place to go. Through those doors over there." The nurse pointed in the direction of the large swing doors that led back to the corridor from which the Mechanic had emerged moments earlier, but the Mechanic had already moved away from the desk. He had no reason to doubt the nurse was correct and the Planner was dead, but he was a professional and these things had to be verified. If the nurse was mistaken and the old man was not dead the Mechanic would need to give nature a helping hand. He bent over a water fountain and pretended to drink. As he did he thoroughly reviewed the lay out of the Medical Centre. In addition to the corridor that linked the Security Centre to the Medical Centre, a single corridor led from the waiting area for about fifty yards to a set of rubber swing doors. These were propped open. Beyond the doors the Mechanic could see a further set of doors that led out to the tarmac where ambulances could pull up.

Off the corridor were five doors. The one nearest the swing doors that were propped open read "SURGERY". One of the other four doors had a sign that read "PRIVATE". The remaining doors did not have signs, only numbers "1" to "3" respectively. The Mechanic dismissed the door marked "PRIVATE". It was the door to the doctors' offices and nurses' rest room. He also dismissed the room marked "SURGERY". The Planner had died of a heart attack and a heart attack patient would not have been taken into surgery on arrival at the Medical Centre. The Mechanic decided that the Planner's body was in one of the other three rooms. It was only forty five minutes since the 747 had landed and the Mechanic guessed that if the Planner was dead his body would not have been moved yet.

He considered which room to try first. His instincts told him to check the room nearest the swing doors first on the basis that it was the first room that the ambulance staff would have reached when they wheeled the Planner's stretcher into the Medical Centre. At that moment the door of room number "2" was opened and a doctor walked out followed by a lady and a child. The Mechanic heard the lady thank the doctor and told the boy not to play around the baggage carousels again. The boy's left knee was bandaged. The Mechanic smiled to himself. There were only two rooms left.

There were three other people in the waiting area in addition to the Mechanic and the nurse behind the desk. They sat in chairs reading, uninterested in the nondescript man drinking from the fountain. The Mechanic waited for the nurse at the desk to turn away and then in total silence slipped across the corridor, opened the door of the room nearest the swing doors and stepped inside, closing the door behind him as he entered. He moved so quickly that no one in the waiting area even noticed him leave the water fountain.

The Mechanic did not move as he closed the door behind himself. The lights in the room were off. The room was completely dark. He held the handle of the door tightly closed as he waited for his eyes to familiarise themselves with the darkness. He did not search for the main light switch by the door. He had already checked the rim around the door from the vantage point of the water fountain and had noted that a line of light would be visible around the frame of the door if the lights inside the room were turned on. He did not want to advertise what he was doing. As his eyes became accustomed to the dark he saw the outline of a bed and a lamp to the side of the bed. Slowly he edged towards the lamp, being careful not to bump into anything as he moved. He found the lamp and felt for a switch. As he switched the lamp on he directed the beam of light towards the floor away from the door behind him. He could see.

Within seconds he had surveyed the Planner's room. His eyes fixed upon the bed and the outline of a body covered by a white sheet. The Mechanic pulled back the sheet and checked to make sure that the Planner was dead. The old man's body was still dressed. His shirt had been unbuttoned, but his jacket was still on as were his trousers. The Mechanic systematically checked the pockets of the Planner's jacket and trousers twice, occasionally turning to check the door to the room. The Planner's pockets had not yet been emptied by the medical staff. He found a few coins, a handkerchief, the stub of the Planner's boarding pass and a small bottle of brandy, wrapped in a Miami Airport duty free bag. Once he was satisfied that he had not missed anything the Mechanic pulled the sheet back over the Planner's body and lifted the lamp from the table by the side of the bed. He directed the beam of light from the lamp around the room searching for the Planner's briefcase. He could not see it. He checked under the bed and inside a tall wardrobe, the only piece of storage furniture in the room. The case was not in the room.

The fact that the contents of the Planner's pockets had not been removed indicated to the Mechanic that the police and airport security had not been in the room yet. If this was the case the Mechanic was surprised not to find the briefcase. The only logical explanation that occurred to him was that one of the medical staff must have taken the case to security after the Planner had died. He remembered the two signs he had seen in the corridor linking the Medical Centre and the Security Centre. As silently as he had entered the room the Mechanic left.

The Guardian's plans for the old man had not turned out as arranged, thought the Mechanic as he walked back down the corridor towards the security section of the building. However, the old man was dead there was no doubt of that, albeit if not by his own hands and had not died in Bucharest as the Guardian had wanted. Surely the Guardian would be satisfied. From one point of view things could not have turned out better so far as the old man was concerned. The Mechanic preferred people to die or be killed in such a way that it appeared they had died of natural causes or as a result of an accident. Blatant assassins advertised too much to survive in his world for long. His customers however, often wanting to leave a message did not always agree.

Even with the Planner dead there was still the matter of the old man's case. The Guardian had instructed the Mechanic to switch cases after he killed the Planner in Bucharest. His instructions had been quite clear on this, although he had not been told why the old man's case was so important. The Mechanic did not know what was in the Planner's case that interested the Guardian so much, but killing the old man was only half the job. He also had to get hold of the case and deliver it to a hotel in Bucharest. The only sensible reason the Mechanic could think of to explain why the briefcase was not in the room with the Planner's body, was that one of the medical staff must have taken the case to airport security.

He reached the door that announced "SECURITY CENTRE" at the far end of the corridor and walked through. The first door he saw in the Security Centre was labelled "SECURITY OFFICER". He was not comfortable knocking on the door. Men in the Mechanic's profession do not often voluntarily walk into police stations or airport security offices. Although he had never been caught and was frequently disguised existing under a variety of aliases he knew that Interpol had a number of photographs of him in various guises which were available to the security departments of international airports. There was a risk that an officer in the Security Centre of the airport might recognise the Mechanic if the guard had seen a photograph of him recently, but the Guardian considered this very unlikely and was prepared to take the risk in order to establish whether or not the Planner's case had been taken to the authorities.

The Mechanic had not carried out any hits in England since arranging for the son of a drugs dealer to be killed in a helicopter crash two years earlier. The son had stolen fifteen million pounds worth of cocaine from his father, a powerful Hong Kong drugs dealer and the father had hired the Mechanic to kill his son in a dramatic fashion as a warning to others around him that he would tolerate disobedience from no one, not even his own family. The Mechanic had not been to England since that hit. England was too cold for his liking and was a country he did not visit unless he was being well paid to do so.

As he knocked on the door the Mechanic began formulating a series of questions in his mind to ask one of the security officers which would reveal where the case was without alerting the officer to his interest in it. The Mechanic heard a voice tell him to come in and he pushed open the door. The first thing he saw as the door swung back into the room was the Planner's case on the desk in front of him. Behind the desk sat a middle aged man in a dark uniform. He was filling out forms.

"Yes. What can I do for you?" the Officer asked in a tone which made it clear that he was not happy at being interrupted. The Mechanic dismissed the idea of killing the Officer and taking the case. He needed the case but had no way of knowing how long it would be before the Officer's body would be discovered and the airport's security put on full alert. Stealing the case would result in a low level search of the airport. Killing the Security Officer would result in the airport being sealed, possibly before he had a chance to escape.

The Mechanic was an accomplished mimic. He was able to carry off accents and the mannerism of a variety of different nationalities with considerable ease. This talent helped to make him an effective killer allowing his disguises to be truly convincing. He thought of the Planner before answering the Officer.

"Howdy Officer," said the Mechanic in a perfect Texan accent. "The little ole nurse at the desk back there told me I should come an'talk to you about ma poor ole friend who died in your hospital awhile back."

"The old man on the BA flight from Miami?" asked the Officer, putting the pen he was holding down and forgetting about the forms on his desk for a moment.

"That's the man, God rest his soul," said the Mechanic. "Damn fine guy. Been a business associate an'a friend o'mine for a few years now. Real shame. Real shame."

"Were you on the 'plane with him?" asked the Officer.

"Sure was. We flew over from the States together."

"That's strange," replied the Officer, "the young man who came off the 'plane with the deceased said nothing about anyone accompanying him on the flight." The Mechanic thought fast and moved towards the chair in front of the desk. He should have realised that the Officer would have spoken to David by now. The Mechanic recalled how they had talked and talked through the night. He cursed himself silently.

"May I?" he asked indicating to the Officer that he would like to sit down. The Officer nodded and waited for the Mechanic to answer.

"Well ya see, Officer, I was in the non-smoking section of the cabin. I don't like to smoke and my friend, a real smoker, was up in the smoking section puffing away like a Mississippi steam boat. They got him off the 'plane before I even knew what was going on. I think he did 'ave some young guy sitt'n next to him now that you mention it."

"I see," said the Officer. "And what was the deceased name?"

The Mechanic knew the Planner's name. He knew a lot about the old man. He had spent two days in Miami following his every move. He suspected that the Officer did not entirely believe him. He also calculated that security had by now discovered from the airline's passenger list the name of the dead old man. The Mechanic told the Officer the Planner's name and even gave him the Planner's address in Miami. The Officer relaxed and smiled at the killer.

"I'm very sorry about your friend. It seems that he had too much too drink during the flight and his heart gave out just as the 'plane was touching down. Are you able to help me with some of the details? We know his name and address, but not much more at the moment. We will need to contact his family and anyone he was going to see whilst he was hear in England."

"Sure. I can tell you all that," replied the Mechanic, who glanced at the case on the side of the desk. "But is there any chance of a large coffee before we get started? Jet lag is start'n to kick in a bit."

"Of course," said the Officer. "If you would kindly wait here I'll get us both one. We have a machine in the canteen, but it will take a few minutes."

"Fine. I'll just wait here for you," replied the Mechanic loosening his tie as if he was making himself comfortable for a long interview.

The Mechanic remained seated listening to the sound of the Officer's feet on the tiled floor of the corridor. When the noise of the footsteps had faded almost completely he picked up the case from the desk and walked out of the room back down the corridor in the direction of the Medical Centre. When he came to the door marked "NO EXIT" through which he had entered the corridor fifteen minutes earlier, he knocked on the door and when it was opened told the same guard that he had been informed by the staff in the Medical Centre that his friend had died. The guard thought that in the circumstances it would cause no harm for the Mechanic to re-enter the baggage collection area through the door he was patrolling rather than through the arrivals section of the airport and he let the Mechanic back into the lounge. The guard did not notice that the Mechanic was now carrying an old brown briefcase which he had not had with him before.

The Mechanic knew that he did not have much time before the Security Officer would return to his office and discover that both he and the case were missing. He needed to speak to the Guardian before leaving the airport to ensure that whatever it was the Guardian wanted was in fact inside the case. He walked casually with the skill of a professional to a bay of telephones. The Mechanic did not usually contact his employer during an operation. He received his instructions along with a photograph of his target in an envelope, which was pushed under the door of a hotel room. Arrangements were made with one of the Guardian's men by telephone and after a hit had been carried out the Guardian would always verify it himself and credit the Mechanic's numbered Swiss bank account with the balance of his fee. All that the Mechanic knew was that the money came from different banks each time. He suspected that his sometimes employer lived in Romania and was a German by birth but he did not know for sure, nor did he care.

On this occasion the Mechanic had been provided with a telephone number which he had been instructed to call only if there was a deviation in the plan. He had already called the Guardian once, but considered the premature death of the Planner to amount to a deviation.

The Mechanic recognised the number was that of a satellite telephone. His call would be routed through a series of decoders and be channelled across four different countries before he spoke to someone: that was the surest way of avoiding detection and the Guardian was paranoid about secrecy. His instructions were to call the number, give a series of passwords when the line was answered and the number of the telephone he was calling from then hang up. He would be called back within two minutes. All he had to do was find a telephone that would accept incoming calls.

He found a telephone in the corner of the baggage collection lounge from where he had a good view of the main entrances into the large room and dialled the number. It took a few minutes before he heard a voice on the other end of the line say "Yes." He gave the series of passwords and then the number of the telephone he was calling from. He pushed and held down the receiver brace of the telephone with his left arm, effectively hanging up the telephone but still allowing him to hold the receiver to his ear as if he was talking. Experience had taught him that a man standing in a telephone booth not talking on the telephone was very suspicious. The conversation he had with his imaginary girl-friend was well rehearsed and would last for ten minutes before he would have to start repeating what he was saying.

The Mechanic only had to wait a minute and a half before the telephone rang. He removed his arm from the receiver brace immediately answering the call and waited for the person on the other end of the line to speak.

"What's happened?" asked the Guardian from his mansion in Bucharest. It was two hours later in Bucharest than at Heathrow. The Guardian had left an early morning meeting to take the Mechanic's call. After speaking to the Mechanic in Miami, he had not expected to hear from the assassin again until after the Planner had been murdered. The call from Heathrow had, as the Mechanic suspected, been routed across four different countries on two different continents before the link was made to the satellite telephone in the secret basement bunker of the Guardian's mansion. The passwords had identified the caller as the Mechanic and the telephone number he had given identified his location as Heathrow, England. The Guardian's men had wasted no time interrupting the Guardian's meeting. A call on the satellite telephone could only mean a complication with the hit. The Guardian was in the bunker and speaking into the receiver within two minutes of the call having first been received.

There were two reasons why the Guardian required the Mechanic to leave the number of the telephone he was calling from and wait to be called back. The first was so that the Guardian's sophisticated computer system would have the thirty seconds it needed to identify the voice on the other end of the line and confirm that it was the voice of the Mechanic. The second reason was that by calling the number back the return call could be protected by a scrambler that could only be operated for calls made from the satellite telephone. The technology that made these precautions possible was expensive, but the Guardian never once doubted that the cost was worthwhile. Stories in the international press of amateur telephone tappers not to mention professional tappers could not be ignored in his opinion. His system was guaranteed to keep all of his important calls absolutely confidential.

The Guardian waited for the Mechanic to answer him.

"I'm at the airport in London," he replied calmly. "The old man had a heart attack on the 'plane and then another in the airport hospital. He's dead. His body will probably be returned to Miami. No one is suspicious. He just had a heart attack and died."

"And his briefcase. What has become of the man's case?" asked the Guardian nervously.

"I have it in my hand now, but I need to dump it fast and leave the airport before it's missed," he replied.

The Guardian relaxed. The Mechanic was always thorough. The Planner had died, not as he had intended in Romania in the back seat of a taxi, but silenced forever nevertheless, and the Mechanic had the case and the computer disk.

The Guardian had been uncomfortable with the thought of the Planner carrying a disk with him to Romania which contained complete details of Operation Domino, but he had needed some sort of realistic bait with which to persuade the Planner to leave Miami and travel to Romania. The Guardian had not watched the Planner that closely over the years and consequently had become concerned that the Planner might not have been as careful as he should have. He had decided to terminate his involvement with the Planner once and for all. After Operation Domino had been executed, he would have no further need of the Planner's particular skills. He could not be sure that an investigation in the United States into the Planner's death would not link the Planner to himself. He knew however, that he could control any investigation in Romania and that if the Planner died in his country in apparently unsuspicious circumstances there would be no investigation at all in the United States.

The Guardian could have threatened the Planner to ensure that he travelled to Romania but he had not known for certain how the old man would have reacted. There was too much money at stake for the Planner to become suspicious of the Guardian's motives in asking him to travel to Romania, so the Guardian had fabricated a story that the details of the Operation needed fine tuning as a result of new information the Guardian had obtained. The Guardian had lied to the Planner that he had not kept copies of the information and documentation the Planner would need and had told him to bring everything to Romania with him on computer disk in the usual way, so that he could modify the Operation.

The need for the Operation to be slightly altered and for the information that was stored on the disk to be brought to Romania had been the bait to get the Planner out of the United States and it had worked. The Planner had followed his instructions to the letter with the exception of the deviation through London. This had not concerned the Guardian. He knew that the Planner rarely left the United States and would not pass up the chance of seeing his daughter in London if he could.

As soon as the 747 had taken off from Miami the Guardian's men had broken into the Planner's house and had stolen the old man's computer. It was now on the sea bed about two miles south of Miami Beach. The only record remaining of Operation Domino and the material the Planner had relied upon to formulate the Operation were stored on the disk in the Planner's briefcase which the Mechanic was holding.

"You can get rid of the old man's case, I have no interest in that. I only want the computer disk he was carrying, which is inside the case," said the Guardian quickly. The Mechanic undid the old clip that held the case closed and rummaged around for the disk. On finding nothing he told the Guardian to wait for a moment. He bent down and holding the receiver in his left hand emptied the contents of the case on to the floor by the telephone booth and searched amongst them. He could not see a computer disk of any kind.

"There's no disk in the case. I've just checked through all of the contents and there's nothing."

"Are you sure?" asked the Guardian, not quite believing what he was hearing.

"Yes, quite sure," answered the Mechanic who was not accustomed to being second questioned and did not like it. "What would you like me to do?" he asked. "I can't walk around with this case for much longer." The Guardian stood up and tightly gripped the receiver of the satellite telephone. He could not understand where the disk could be. The Guardian had insisted that the Planner carry the disk in his briefcase rather than in his luggage or about his person so that there could be no chance of the disk being misplaced or damaged.

"He must have been carrying it on him," said the Guardian half to himself and half into the receiver.

"No," replied the Mechanic who was expecting an answer. "I checked the old man's clothes twice before the police got to the body and there was no computer disk."

"What?" shouted the Guardian, throwing his free hand up to his forehead.

The Guardian was thinking. So was the Mechanic who was conscious that he was still holding the case he had stolen from the Security Officer's desk more than ten minutes ago. It would not be long before the theft was discovered. The airport was not busy enough for it to take the authorities very long to spot him holding the case if he stayed where he was. The Mechanic waited for the voice on the other end of the line to speak. As he did he watched a lady struggling to retrieve a large suitcase from one of the baggage carousels in the centre of the room.

"When he checked in at Miami he had a suitcase. He checked it in as non hand luggage," said the Mechanic suddenly.

"His suitcase," repeated the Guardian thinking aloud. Without waiting for a fuller reaction to this information the Mechanic told the Guardian he would call back in a few minutes and hung up.

The Mechanic walked over to the lady who was struggling with the oversized suitcase and helped her drag the case off the carousel and on to a trolley. The lady thanked him and pushed the trolley off towards Customs. Her suitcase was extremely large and tilted slightly from side to side as it lay on the trolley. As she pushed the trolley through the "NOTHING TO DECLARE" exit thinking about the long drive back to

Colchester that lay ahead of her, she did not notice the old brown briefcase squashed underneath her own suitcase. Neither did the customs officials.

The Mechanic located the carousel on which luggage from the British Airways flight from Miami was circulating. Most of the other passengers from the flight had already collected their luggage and only a few cases were still on the carousel. The Mechanic recognised the Planner's suitcase and lifted it on to a trolley. He pushed the trolley in the direction of the men's toilet. The toilet was empty. The Mechanic carried the Planner's case into one of the cubicles and searched every inch of it and the contents inside. The disk was not there. He tore the case apart, systematically checking the lining inch by inch, but did not find the computer disk. When he was sure that the disk was not in the case he put the assortment of clothes back inside and carried it out of the toilet. The Mechanic dumped the Planner's case on a carousel that was full of suitcases from a flight just in from Stockholm and walked back to the telephone booth.

"Do you have the disk?" asked the Guardian. This time the Mechanic had to wait only thirty seconds before the Guardian called him back on the secure line.

"No. It wasn't in the suitcase," he replied.

"Are sure? Did you double check?" demanded the Guardian. The Mechanic did not appreciate being questioned like this, but held his tongue. After all the man he was speaking to was paying him a great deal on money.

"Absolutely sure," he replied. "I checked the contents of the case thoroughly as well as the lining. The disk is not there."

"Check again. It must be hidden in there somewhere," insisted the Guardian frantically.

"It's not," answered the Mechanic firmly. "I know how to search a suitcase".

"Then where the hell is it?" The Guardian was becoming angry. Angry at himself. He should not have told the Planner to take the disk with him. It was always too risky. The entire Operation would be ruined and he would spend the rest of his life in prison if the information on the Planner's disk fell into the wrong hands. Not exactly what he had planned for his retirement.

"You must find that disk and bring it to Romania," he told the Mechanic in a calmer tone.

The Mechanic had decided that he had already spent too long hanging around the airport without appearing suspicious. However, he was a professional and his reputation was important to him. He wanted to find the disk not least because he had not been paid in full yet.

As the Mechanic stood talking to the Guardian on the telephone he watched the baggage collection area for security guards: being ever alert was conditioned into him. He noticed David who he recognised from the 747, talking to an official at the British Airways customer service desk. As he watched the young man he remembered how he and the Planner had talked all through the night, how the Planner had collapsed on to David's lap shortly before the aeroplane had landed and how he had seen David place the Planner's briefcase on the stretcher and help carry the old man off the aeroplane. The Security Officer had remarked that a young man had been in the Medical Centre and had talked to the Officer. The Mechanic had been puzzled that the Planner's clothes had apparently not been checked, but that nevertheless, his briefcase was not in the room with his body. The Mechanic watched David and smiled to himself.

"I know where the disk is," he told the Guardian. Quickly, the Mechanic explained David's involvement to the Guardian. The Mechanic was convinced that David must have been given the disk by the Planner before he had died. It was the only explanation.

"Get the disk back my friend and I will double your fee," said the Guardian. "Make sure you kill this young man. The old man might not have told him anything, but I can't risk that. He's insignificant to me. Just kill him and bring the disk to me as arranged. Keep in contact on this number."

The Guardian hung up. The Mechanic was the most reliable assassin he had ever known. He was confident that David would be dead in less than an hour and he would have the disk back under his control again.

CHAPTER 11

David had walked back to the arrivals lounge as quickly as his tired legs would carry him. He was fed up and wanted to leave the airport. The events of the morning had worn him out. He passed through immigration and collected his suit carrier from the baggage carousel used for the British Airways flight from Miami. The Security Officer had told him he would be able to collect his own briefcase and coat from the lost and found office in the baggage collection area. As he looked around the large room he could not see a lost and found office, only customer service desks for various airlines. He went over to the British Airways customer service desk and explained that he had left hand luggage on the flight in from Miami. He was told by the lady behind the desk that nothing had been handed in. After making three telephone calls she told David that the aircraft had not yet been checked for forgotten luggage. There was a shortage of cabin assistants and all cabin checks were delayed that morning. He was told that the aeroplane would be checked in about an hour and that he was free to wait. Alternatively, the airline would arrange for the items he had described to be delivered to him anywhere in the country with their compliments.

The prospect of waiting in the baggage collection area for an hour did not appeal to David. He handed the representative his business card and asked her to have his flight case and overcoat delivered to his office as soon as possible. A little over an hour after carrying the Planner off the aeroplane into the waiting ambulance, David walked out of the terminal building in the direction of the courtesy bus stand to catch an airport bus to the long term car park where his car was parked.

The airport bus pulled up outside the terminal building and David sighed with relief. As he boarded the bus he checked his watch. It was 8:10 am. The morning air was cold and he was missing his overcoat already. As he sat down he pulled the collar of his jacket up around his neck and folded his arms across his chest. 8:10 am he thought. In the morning traffic it would take about an hour for him to drive to the City. This morning he did not have the luxury of a parking space in the Holland Chapman & Co. private car park. He would have to park in the public car park near the office. This was expensive, but David did not care. He wanted to hand Garces's bankers' draft to Mike Henderson as soon as possible. With luck and the traffic lights with him, David was confident he could be in Henderson's office by 9:30 am.

The bus moved slowly through the airport. The bus David was on and others like it spend all day and night picking up and dropping off passengers between the long term car park outside the main airport complex and the four terminal buildings. In the early mornings the airport is at its quietest. There were only three other people on the bus with David. An old couple who David overheard had enjoyed their three week trip to Vancouver to visit their daughter and her family and a man who appeared to David to be in his late thirties who sat at the front of the bus by himself. The man had boarded the bus with David. There was nothing remarkable about this other than David had noticed that the man had no luggage with him at all.

Almost all of the flights in and out of Terminal Four are international flights and David wondered how it was that the man had no luggage, not even an overnight case or a lightweight suit carrier. Perhaps his luggage has been lost as well, he thought as the bus circled the island at the end of the tunnel by the entrance to the airport which is dominated by the model British Airways Concorde. David admired the model Concorde as he always did whenever he passed it. The Planner had told him that British Airways and Air France, the two operators of Concorde, were winding down their Concorde schedules and would be abandoning the supersonic passenger aeroplane within five years. David had always considered Concorde to be a remarkable machine. He hoped that he had an opportunity to take a flight on one of the remaining supersonic passenger jets before they were all taken out of service.

The bus proceeded along the road that ran parallel with the airport perimeter, passing aeroplanes parked in hangers and waiting on the tarmac. Even at this early hour there was a lot of aircraft traffic scattered about the runway area. David decided that the job of coordinating the movements of so many large jets must be a difficult one.

On the bus went. Past the car rental depots with their rows and rows of new Ford Escorts and Vauxhall Cavaliers, past the private parking and car valeting companies until it eventually reached the airport's long term car park. The car park had been almost full when David had parked his Golf GTI a few days before and it was still almost full. He could not recall ever having seen the car park even only half empty. It seemed that the airport's boast of being one of the busiest in the World was not an exaggeration. His car was parked in bay 10 G. The nearest drop point was bus stop Three. The bus driver stopped the bus at bus stop One and waited for a few seconds to see if any of his passengers wanted to get off. No one did. At the second bus stop the elderly couple got off the bus and David helped them with their luggage of which they had plenty. The bus driver drove the bus around to the far side of the car park and stopped at bus stop Three.

David swung his suit carrier on to his shoulder and climbed down from the bus. He alighted from the doors in the centre of the bus and noticed through the corner of his eye that the man who had been sitting at the front of the bus by himself got off after him by the doors at the front of the bus. The doors closed with a burst of hydraulic energy and the bus trundled away. Within seconds it had turned the corner of the car park and was accelerating into the distance.

It was not a very nice morning. There was a slight wind and the sky was grey. David could see that it had been raining and was beginning to wish that he had been able to stay an extra day in the Miami sunshine. He looked up at a sign that indicated he had to walk back through eight rows of cars to find parking bay 10 G. As he walked he could hear heavy footsteps behind him on the damp tarmac. He sensed that he was being followed and without stopping glanced over his left shoulder. About ten yards behind him David saw the man from the bus walking towards him. The man had a raincoat and gloves on. Again it struck David that the man was not carrying any luggage. David began to walk a little faster. Not too fast, he told himself. The man had probably parked his car near to David's Golf and there was no need to over-react.

The footsteps were getting closer and David glanced over his shoulder again. The man was not looking around the car park as if searching for his car. The collar of his raincoat was turned up around his neck and David could not see the man's face that well. From the little he could see however, David considered the man to be suspicious. He had brown hair and darkish skin. David anxiously searched the mass of cars for the Golf. At first he could not see it. Then he spotted it two rows in front of him over to the right. He turned right and glanced behind him. The man from the bus also turned right and was now less than five yards behind him. David fumbled in his trouser pockets until he found his car keys. He approached the Golf and was conscious that the man was close behind him. David reached the trunk of the Golf and turned around sharply. His pursuer stood right in front of him.

Instinctively, David took a step backwards putting three feet in all between the man and himself. The man said nothing. He just looked around the car park.

"May I help you?" David asked, unsure what else he should say. The man said nothing. He took a step forward moving closer to David. "What do you want?" demanded David. The man looked around the deserted car park. Oh God, thought David. He's a mugger.

"Did you accompany the old man who died on the British Airways flight from Miami this morning?" asked the Mechanic. His accent was not familiar to David but it was clear that he was not a European. David was momentarily relieved. This was not a question a mugger would ask a victim before he attacked.

"Yes. I sat next to him," he replied.

"I have some questions that I would like to ask you about the old man's death," continued the Mechanic.

"I've already been through it all with airport security," said David.

"I'm with the airline not with airport security. We're concerned that all of the old man's belongings are returned to his next of kin." This surprised David. He could understand the airline wanting to know what happened to the old man, but why would they follow him to the car park to ask questions? Anyway, he had told the lady at the customer service desk all about the old man when he tried to get his flight case and coat back.

"You were on the bus with me a few moments ago weren't you," replied David. "Why didn't you ask me about the old man then? Why wait 'till I'm by my car?" The Mechanic did not reply immediately.

"About the old man's personal possessions. Do you have anything that belonged to him?" The Mechanic looked around the car park again and inched a little closer to David.

"No," replied David. He did not like this man and was not happy with the Mechanic's explanation of what he wanted. "Can I see your airline pass please?"

"Did the old man give you anything on the 'plane or in the Medical Centre?" asked the Mechanic quickly, ignoring David's request for production of credentials. David had had enough of this nonsense.

"Your pass," he demanded firmly. His instincts were telling him to get out of there, but he stood his ground. The Mechanic was not as tall or as well built as David, and the lawyer was no coward. All in all he thought the Mechanic looked fairly ordinary, but there was something about the stranger that worried him. Something that he could not quite put his finger on. David pushed one of the keys he was holding into the lock of the trunk handle. He wanted to get in his car and get going. He lifted the trunk and threw his suit carrier into the back of the Golf as casually as he could, as if he was expecting the Mechanic to produce his credentials before he would talk to him any further.

"Did he give you a computer disk?" asked the Mechanic as David slammed the trunk of the Golf shut.

"A disk?" repeated David. "What disk?"

"A computer disk that stores information. That sort of disk," said the Mechanic. At the second mention of the disk David remembered the thin blue Sony disk he had stuffed into his jacket pocket when he had been sitting in the Medical Centre over an hour earlier. He had forgotten all about it. His right hand instinctively dropped to the side of his jacket and he felt the outline of the disk through the fabric. Realising what he was doing, he quickly moved his hand on to the trunk of the Golf.

What does this man want with the old man's disk, thought David? Why would he follow me all the way to the car park just for an old computer disk? It made no sense to David. He recalled the Planner's confused dying words and his reference to a disk and to a Romanian. Was the man standing in front of him from Romania? His accent was certainly muddled. David had first thought the Mechanic was South American, but now he was not sure. He was about to deny that he had the disk as he did not believe that his questioner was genuine, but it was too late.

The Mechanic had seen David's hand drop to his jacket pocket when the disk was mentioned a second time. He knew at once where the disk was.

The sudden explosion of pain across the left side of his face knocked David back sideways against the Golf. The second blow, this time to his left side bent him over slightly. David had not been punched since his days on the rugby fields of Oxford and he had not been expecting the attack. His face ached and his side pounded from the blows.

The Mechanic had become tired of questioning David. Once David revealed the location of the disk there was no need for the conversation to continue any longer. The Mechanic had delivered the two blows to David with some force and had it not have been for the Golf, David would have been knocked to the ground.

The Mechanic seized his advantage and tried to turn David in order to get a hand into the right side pocket of his jacket. David had fallen on to his right side and the Mechanic was struggling to manoeuvre him around when he felt a solid blow to his chest. David had not targeted the Mechanic's chest. As he regained his senses he simply punched at the body of the Mechanic who was mauling him and landed a blow to his attacker's chest. The blow momentarily winded the Mechanic who loosened his grip on David and stumbled backwards. David felt the weight of the Mechanic move off him a little and he pulled himself up, pushing the Mechanic away from him as he did so. The Mechanic was already off balance as a result of the blow to his chest and David's push knocked the killer over.

Although he had freed himself, David's movements were slow and clumsy. His side hurt and he could not stand up straight. He moved around to the side of the Golf trying to get hold of the driver's door handle. He pulled the handle and the door came ajar. The pain in his side was passing and he was able to stand a little straighter. He had almost recovered when his left leg was pulled from under him by the Mechanic and he crashed to the ground by the door of the Golf, falling on to the left side of his body. The Mechanic had only been immobilised by the blow to his chest for a matter of seconds and David had not moved fast enough. As soon as he began to recover, the Mechanic lunged at David from the floor and caught his left leg bringing him down in a heap on the ground.

The Mechanic was angry now. David had hit him, pushed him off balance and knocked him to the floor. As he stood up he kicked David in the stomach causing him to cough and yell out in pain. He pushed David over on to his front on the tarmac and knelt on David's upper back, pinning him firmly to the spot with his right knee. The Mechanic unbuckled his trouser belt and pulled it free of the trouser loops. With his left hand he grabbed David's hair and pulled him up on to his knees, whilst throwing the belt around David's neck with his right hand. Letting go of David's hair the Mechanic stood up pulling the belt tight around David's neck.

The jolt of the belt tightening around his neck made David cough again and he put his hands up to his neck and felt the belt under his chin. The pain was becoming worse. David searched with his fingers for a gap between the belt and his neck into which he could slip a finger to pull the belt away from his throat, but it was no use. The Mechanic stood above him pulling the belt tighter. David tried to move from side to side but the Mechanic was over him, preventing him from wriggling free of the noose. He could hear the sound of the leather belt smacking against the skin of his neck as the Mechanic slowly strangled him.

"Bloody hell. What's going on mate?" asked the voice. David was not able to see where the voice had come from. "You're killing him". The Mechanic looked up. Over to his left he saw a man with his son and wife standing about fifteen yards away from the Golf, holding two bright green suitcases. The family had been walking to the bus stop nearest to where they had parked their car and had heard David coughing and had seen the two men brawling on the ground. As they came closer they saw the Mechanic strangling David. He ignored them. He could feel David's strength slipping away. Just a few moment more, he thought to himself as he pulled the belt even tighter around David's neck.

"I said you're killing him mate. I'll call the cops," shouted the man nervously. The man's wife looked at David kneeling on the ground and began to scream.

"Die, die," shouted the Mechanic as he pulled the belt tight in one last attempt to kill David.

The woman's screams filled the morning and the Mechanic became aware that he was in the middle of a car park being watched as he strangled a man. He let go of one end of the belt and it dropped to the ground in front of David. Suddenly David could breath again and he gulped in the cold, damp air. As the belt loosened around his neck David slumped forward putting a hand out to stop himself from collapsing on to his face. The woman's screams were getting louder. The Mechanic turned to the man and his family and shouted at them aggressively in a language none of them understood. As he shouted at them he felt around for the opening of the right side pocket of David's jacket. David was not fighting any more and the Mechanic had released his grip on him completely. He would have another opportunity to kill David he knew, in a less public place. For the moment he would retrieve the disk and escape his audience over the fence into the airport complex.

As the Mechanic shouted at the family and fumbled for the disk David lifted his head and looked out across the car park. In the distance he saw another airport bus pulling away from bus stop Four. He observed from the route of the road that although the bus was gaining speed having visited all of its stops in the car park for that particular run, it would have to slow down considerably to negotiate a sharp bend before accelerating towards the exit junction. The bend was about fifty yards directly ahead of where David was kneeling. He felt the Mechanic's grip on him loosen and felt his attacker's body turn to the left as he shouted at the man and his wife who stood in the car park. David mustered what strength he had left and in a mighty effort scrambled to his feet and began to run towards the bend in the road before the Mechanic realised what was happening. David was dizzy and short of breath, but he nevertheless managed to run in and out of the cars away from the Mechanic.

His escape caught the Mechanic by surprise. He felt David jump free as he turned his head to shout at the screaming woman. As the Mechanic got to his feet David was about ten yards away and accelerating. The Mechanic wasted no time. He was up, running after David gaining speed within seconds of David's departure.

David was fit but the ordeal he had just survived had exhausted him and as he ran he found it difficult to take deep breaths. He could hear the Mechanic behind him but was afraid to look around in case he tripped over or crashed into a parked car. The two men ran in and out of the cars knocking wing mirrors and car doors, the Mechanic gaining on David all the time.

David was now about fifteen yards away from the bend in the road ahead of him and he could see the bus approaching the bend from the other end of the car park. The Mechanic was so close behind him that David could hear his panting. David dug deep for the remaining morsel of energy he had and ran out from the last row of parked cars on to the edge of the road just past the bend, vaulting a small steel barrier fence as he did so. The Mechanic was practically on top of David and would have reached him by the time they got to the last row of parked cars had it not been for the barrier fence. He did not see the fence until the last moment and had to check his stride in order to clear it, causing him to slow down.

As David landed in the road the bus passed him as it came around the bend. It had slowed to ten miles an hour to negotiate the sharp turn and had started to accelerate again when David, who was chasing the rear of the bus, got hold of the emergency window handle that hung down from the back of the bus and pulled himself up on to the large rear bumper. He held on to the handle as tightly as he could, wedging his feet into the small gap between the bumper and the bus in order to secure himself as the bus gained speed.

The Mechanic chased after the bus. David prayed for the driver to go faster. At first the distance between David on the bumper of the bus and the Mechanic did not increase and David was afraid that the bus was not going to accelerate. It did, and David watched the Mechanic fall further and further behind. Despite this the Mechanic did not slow down. He kept chasing the bus. David did not understand why. Surely this man realises he cannot out run a bus, he thought. Even though he was getting away the sight of the Mechanic chasing him terrified David.

"Stop running, stop running," David said over and over again. Still the Mechanic ran after the bus. David was having difficulty holding on. The emergency handle was not very big and he was only able to hold on to it with one hand. Only the front parts of his shoes were pushed into the gap behind the bumper and the heels kept slipping as the bus followed the contours of the road. He was afraid he might fall off and buried the fronts of his shoes deeper into the gap.

David's heart almost stopped beating when he felt the bus start to slow down. He tried to lean out sideways to see why, but almost fell back off the bumper. The bus continued to slow down and the Mechanic got closer and closer. The bus slowed to about four miles an hour and David finally managed to lean out sideways. He saw that the bus had approached the barrier at the exit gate to the car park and had been forced to slow down. David realised that although it would only take a matter of seconds for the barrier to lift, by the time the bus had got up speed again his pursuer would be upon him.

Jump off, he told himself. As David tried to move to the side of the bumper to jump clear and start running again, he was unable to move his feet. The fronts of his shoes were firmly wedged into the tight space between the back of the bus and the bumper. He pulled his legs and tried to move his shoes sideways to dislodge them. He could not use his hands to help. The only thing stopping him from toppling over backwards was his hand on the emergency window handle and he was not able to hold on to the handle and reach his shoes at the same time.

The bus was now at a complete standstill and the Mechanic was less than ten yards away. Desperately David wriggled his feet and pulled with his legs.

The barrier lifted and the bus began to pull out slowly into the main road. The Mechanic was now running faster than the bus was moving. Three yards, two yards. The Mechanic was up behind the bus which was just beginning to accelerate. David gripped the emergency handle and pulled his legs with all his strength. He felt his left shoe come loose. The Mechanic grabbed at David's legs but could not get a good grip. He moved his hand higher and grabbed out at David's jacket trying to get hold of the pocket which the disk was in. He got his hand on to the bottom corner of the jacket as David finally managed to get his left foot free. Gripping the emergency handle tightly, he kicked his left leg back with all the force he could muster in such a precarious position and caught the Mechanic square in the jaw with the heel of his shoe.

The blow was not very powerful compared with a blow to the chin by a fist, but it disorientated the Mechanic who stumbled and fell to the ground, pulling on David's jacket until the fabric had slipped through his hand. David managed to hold on despite the Mechanic's attempt to drag him from the bumper.

The Mechanic was soon on his feet again but this time chasing the bus was futile. The bus was on the perimeter road and was soon travelling at forty miles an hour. David and the Mechanic watched one another get further and further apart until David saw the Mechanic turn and run back towards the car park. He said a prayer and held on.

David regained his composure within a few minutes of the Mechanic giving up the chase. The horrible reality could not be ignored. The Mechanic had tried to kill him. Had it not been for the screaming lady, he realised that he would now be lying dead by his car in the airport car park. The Mechanic had tried to kill him in order to get the disk. He felt for the outline of the disk in his pocket. It was still there. What was so important that a man would kill someone for a computer disk, David wondered desperately?

The bus turned a corner and David saw that he was returning to the airport. He decided to get off at the first terminal the bus stopped at and find a policeman or security guard. As the bus passed over a bridge on the way to Terminal Two, he thought about the Planner again and what he had said just before he died.

"What the hell is on this disk?" David shouted, as he hung on tightly to the back of the bus.

CHAPTER 12

The chase had tired the Mechanic. It was not the Mechanic's exhaustion however that made him curse out loud in Spanish as he watched the bus accelerate along the airport perimeter road away from him. There was no point continuing with the chase. He could not catch the bus now.

The Mechanic cursed because he was angry with himself. He had broken all of his own rules in the car park and now David and the computer disk were racing away from him back towards the airport. The Mechanic had intended to kill David quickly and quietly, recover the disk and vanish into the morning mist within a matter of minutes. However, he had rushed, conscious that he was in a very open space unable to detect whether anyone was approaching. The car park was not the ideal place for a killing, but the Mechanic had nevertheless expected to eliminate David without difficulty. The blow he had received to his chest had taken him by surprise throwing him back into a momentary daze. David had been escaping to the safety of his car and the Mechanic had lunged for his legs without thinking and before he had rechecked the area of the car park they were in. Strangling David however had been his most serious mistake.

The Mechanic knew nine different ways to kill a man with his bare hands. Each very fast and silent other than for the sound of a man's throat being ripped out, or his neck snapping as it was twisted one hundred and eighty degrees on his shoulders. The Mechanic had been angry. He had not just wanted to kill David who had put him to so much trouble on what should have been a straightforward hit. After being punched in the stomach, the Mechanic had wanted to hurt him.

Strangulation, the Mechanic knew is not a pleasant way to die. The pain of the neck being squeezed and the increasing shortage of breath are almost unbearable. The realisation that death is imminent is the worst thing though. People who have narrowly survived strangulation have recounted that although they fought the rope around their neck until their strength ran out or their breath was gone, they believed from the moment that the noose was put around their necks that their life would be at an end in a matter of moments.

The Mechanic had been enjoying wringing the life from his prey so much that he had not noticed the family unloading luggage for their holiday from the trunk of their car, or that their car was parked close to the bus stop behind David's car which meant that they would walk right passed the Mechanic and David. Had the Mechanic done his job properly he would have twisted David's neck snapping it like a twig in autumn, removed the disk from his coat pocket and have rolled the body under the Golf long before the family had walked up to the car. All they should have seen was a man kneeling on the floor with his back to them, apparently tying his shoe laces. Instead they had seen the Mechanic strangling the life out of David. Slowly, enjoying his work at first and then, when the Mechanic had seen them, much faster anxious to finish.

When the woman had started to scream the Mechanic had decided to forget about killing David for the moment and get the disk. David's neck was strong and the Mechanic had found strangling him quickly difficult. He had expected David to be half dead as he let the belt fall free from his neck. He had not expected him to bolt. At first the Mechanic froze as David ran ahead of him, but his instincts took over. In one movement he was on his feet chasing his victim. The Mechanic was older than the man he chased, but he had not just been half strangled to death. David had not been able to run as fast as the Mechanic and the killer had expected to narrow the gap probably catching up with David by the time they got to the road ahead. He had not seen the small fence at the edge of the road until it had almost been too late and had to check his stride so as not to crash into it and tumble through the air.

This had given David the valuable seconds he needed to get up on to the bumper of the bus before being caught by the killer. The Mechanic had surveyed the road the bus had been on and had seen that the bus had to pass through the barrier at the exit before it could leave the car park. He had guessed that the bus driver would slow the bus down, possibly even bringing the vehicle to a complete stop before the barrier was lifted. So he had chased the bus. His guess had been right. As the bus slowed he had gained on David. The Mechanic had expected David to jump from the bus at any moment as the speed of the vehicle decreased, but he had not. He had managed to get a hand to David's coat and was all set to hurl himself around the lower body of his prey and pull David to the ground when he had felt a sudden pain in the bottom of his jaw, had lost his balance, falling to the ground, turning his head in the direction of the bus in time to see smoke puff out of it's exhaust pipe as the driver changed gear and accelerated away.

The Mechanic was very angry and wanted to kill David. He did not usually want to kill the people he was paid to assassinate any more than he did not want to kill them. They were just targets to him and it was his job to kill them. He had never killed anyone for personal reasons, only for money. As the Mechanic got to his feet and wiped the blood from his chin he wanted to kill the young man hanging on to the back of the bus, not because it was his job, but because David had got the better of him and that infuriated the Mechanic more than anything else.

His desire to kill David was strong, but he was a professional and knew that his immediate problem was the disk. The Guardian wanted the disk back and the Mechanic wanted to get paid and not lose one of his best customers. He walked quickly back to the car park. He did not run as he did not want to draw further attention to himself. As he walked he saw the woman who had screamed standing in a bus shelter with her husband and son waiting for a courtesy bus to take them to the airport. It was unlikely they would report what they had seen to a security guard at the airport. People, especially the British, preferred to stay uninvolved in the Mechanic's experience. Nevertheless, he thought to himself, he needed to get out of the car park as fast as he could.

He walked back to David's Golf. The ignition keys were still in the driver's door lock. He looked around and satisfied that he was not being watched opened the driver's door, got in and started the engine. He drove in the direction of the exit barrier. The Mechanic drove quickly. His prey already had a head start and he had no time to waste.

It was still early morning and the car park was not busy. The Golf was at the barrier in less than two minutes. As the car screeched to a halt the

Mechanic saw that the barrier would only open if a parking ticket was inserted into the appropriate slot. He looked around the inside of the car and found the ticket. He stuffed it into the slot, but the barrier did not open. The ticket emerged from the slot and a red light reading "UNPAID" flashed at the Mechanic. He had no time to waste paying the parking fee. He reversed the Golf back from the barrier some thirty feet, moved the gear lever into first and revved the engine a little. As he slipped the clutch the Golf hurtled forward, smashing through the barrier at thirty miles an hour. The Mechanic swung the car around to the right, out on to the airport boundary road. As he accelerated in the same direction as the bus, he could hear alarm bells ringing at the barrier behind him. The Mechanic changed gear and pushed the accelerator pedal to the floor.

He knew that the bus was heading back to the airport, but did not know which terminal David would get off at. The bus would stop at each of the terminal buildings in turn to drop off and pick up passengers. He could think of no logical reason why the bus would not stop at the nearest terminal first. The Mechanic knew that David would be unable to hang on to the back of the bus for very long and would almost certainly get off at the first terminal the bus stopped at. As the Golf emerged from the tunnel into the airport complex the Mechanic checked the road signs. The nearest terminal was Terminal Two. There was hardly any traffic inside the airport complex and the Mechanic was pulling up in the unloading bay of Terminal Two less than ten minutes after he had first started the Golf's engine in the airport car park.

David had jumped from the bus as it slowed down to stop in front of the first terminal building it came to. He had not cared which terminal the bus stopped at first. His arms were aching and it was becoming increasingly difficult for him to hang on to the emergency handle. By the time the bus had emerged from the tunnel into the airport complex, David had freed his second shoe from behind the bumper.

He was relieved that he had survived the journey from the car park to the terminal without falling off the bumper. As he jumped down from the back of the bus and walked in the direction of the electronic doors that led into the terminal building, he did not notice that he was entering Terminal Two. He had other things on his mind. He needed to find a policeman or an airport security guard as quickly as he could and explain what had happened in the car park.

As David entered the terminal building he repeatedly looked around him. He was looking for the Mechanic. He did not know if the Mechanic would try and attack him again. He hoped that even if the killer figured out where he had gone, the Mechanic was some way behind him. Nevertheless, David kept seeing in his mind the look of sheer determination that he had seen on the Mechanic's face as the killer had chased the bus through the car park. David feared that such a man would not give up easily and this thought frightened him. He looked over his shoulder again searching for a darkish man in a raincoat. For the moment at least he was safe.

Heathrow Airport is very well guarded. Armed policemen assigned to the Airport Police patrol the terminal buildings as both a visible deterrent and to be on hand in case of an incident of any kind. Plain clothes detectives also constantly patrol the various lounges, mainly on the look out for smugglers, in particular drug carriers. As a result Heathrow has impressive security figures and is able to cope with a colossal number of passengers each year. Early morning on a week day in November is not however, the busiest time of year at the airport. Early evenings in December and the spring and summer months are by far the busiest times. Nevertheless, armed policemen were patrolling the departures area of the terminal as David walked in.

He wasted no time approaching an officer and explaining how he had been attacked in the car park by the Mechanic. David was a mess. His hair was ruffled his jacket ripped and he was unshaved. What is more, he had deep bruise marks around his neck from where the Mechanic's belt had pressed against his skin. The policeman he approached was not sure what to make of David's rather garbled story, but was convinced that something untoward had happened to him. David was taken to the Police Centre at the far end of the terminal.

The Police Centre is different in size and function from the Security Centre David had seen earlier that morning inside Terminal Four. The airport's main security offices are located in Terminal Four, but each of the four terminals have small Police Centres operated by the Airport Police which deal with security inside the individual terminals rather than with the security of the airport as a whole, which is coordinated from the main Security Centre inside Terminal Four.

David was beginning to feel safe. He was taken to a small interview room and asked to wait for a detective who he was told would take his statement. Although he could not help feeling that he was back where he had started he did not mind waiting. The official atmosphere of the room he was in, with crime prevention posters on the walls reminding him he was in a police station of sorts, reassured him. He sat patiently waiting for the promised detective to arrive and take his statement. David noticed the fronts of his shoes. The leather was bent forwards and both soles had cracked from the strain of being wedged behind the bumper of the bus. Blood dripped from his left shoe. His neck was aching considerably now and he just wanted to lie down with an ice pack and rest.

Again he thought of the Planner and what he had said before he died. The old man had mentioned a disk and his daughter. The man who had chased him in the car park had first asked about the disk then had almost killed him for it. David took the disk out of his pocket. He was afraid that it would be crushed after the events of the morning, but it was still intact. There was nothing on the cover of the disk that gave David any clue as to what information was stored on it. Only the letters "O D". Whatever secrets or information were stored on the disk, David had decided to give the disk to the first police official he spoke to. The disk was dangerous and he did not want any more to do with it. At the same time he was curious to know what was stored on the disk that could be so important.

The Planner had explained that he was retired from the AAU. David had appeared suitably impressed when the Planner had revealed this. Seven years of commercial litigation had taught him how to appear impressed when he needed to, but in actual fact he had not had a clue what the AAU did before the Planner had explained something of his past. Yet the old man had been retired, David reminded himself, on his way to visit a dying friend in Bucharest. What could he possibly have that was of such interest that someone was prepared to kill for it?

David looked at the disk again. It seemed so ordinary, so everyday. It meant something, he was sure of that.

His neck throbbed and he put his hand to it. He slipped the disk back inside his jacket pocket and stood up. His throat was very sore. He wanted a drink of water and if possible something to cool the burning on his neck.

"Where the hell is this detective?" he said out loud in frustration. "Come on will you." David was not prepared to wait any longer. The dryness in his throat was acute by now. He was desperate for a drink of water. He opened the door of the small room and walked out into the corridor. The entrance to the Police Centre was at the end of the corridor to his right. There was another door opposite the room he had been in, but he could not see what he was looking for. He turned to the left and walked down the corridor away from the main entrance to the centre. He followed the corridor around to the right. As he turned the corner he saw ahead of him what he was looking for. David quickened his step slightly and in moments was drinking enthusiastically from a water fountain mounted on the left hand wall of the corridor.

The water fountain was in need of repair. A thin, constant line of water dribbled from the base of the fountain block into a red plastic bucket that caught the drips. The fountain had been leaking for some time and the bucket was almost full.

The sign announced "WAITING PERMITTED FOR FIVE MINUTES ONLY". The Mechanic parked the Golf right under the sign as near to the main electronic doors as he could get. He turned the engine off, opened the door and leapt from the car. He pulled the collar of his raincoat up around his head to hide from any prying eyes and walked quickly towards the doors. The unloading area was scattered with cars and people. A father wheeling a trolley to his car to carry his daughter's luggage; a girl hugging a young man as if she did not want to let go and a black cab dropping off a man in a suit who carried a briefcase and a compact overnight bag. None of them had any interest in the electronic doors of Terminal Two opening automatically for the Mechanic.

The Mechanic stopped once he was inside the terminal building and expertly reconnoitred the scene. He saw armed policemen strategically placed throughout the check in lounge wearing blue bullet proof vests and carrying semi-automatic machine guns strapped across their chests on quick release frames. Heathrow airport is the nearest place outside of Belfast that the UK has to a military zone.

The terminal was busier than Terminal Four had been earlier that morning and the Mechanic was pleased that there were now more people about. Crowds provide cover. He calculated that David would probably have approached the nearest police officer and explained that he had been attacked in the car park. He would have been taken away by the authorities and asked to give a statement and in due course provide a description of his attacker. Checks would then be made by the police and it would soon be discovered that the Golf was no longer in the car park and that the barrier gates had been smashed. He did not have long before the airport security net would begin to close around him. He needed to establish where his target was. He was certain that David was still in the airport somewhere, but he could not be sure that he was in Terminal Two. If he was not in the terminal, the Mechanic needed to establish this as quickly as he could and begin searching the other terminal buildings. The longer it took him to establish exactly David's whereabouts, the less likely it was that he would recover the Planner's disk.

The Mechanic concluded that if David had approached one of the armed policemen patrolling the terminal area with his story he would have been quickly taken to the nearest security facility. Ideally, the quickest way to locate the nearest Police Centre would be for him to ask one of the armed policemen where it was. He was not prepared to risk this, however. It was possible that his face might be remembered. The less contact he had with people in the airport the better.

There were no offices or doors in the central area of the terminal building. Just check in desks and information kiosks. All doors from the central area of the terminal were around the perimeter of the building. The check in lounge was vast and even with his perfect vision the Mechanic could not read the signs above all of the doors from where he was standing.

Without wasting any time he began walking around the edge of the lounge checking each of the doors in turn, trying not to appear suspicious. By the time he had walked around two sides of the building he had passed fifteen doors, most locked without signs. The first door he came to as he turned to walk along the third side of the building was a large frosted glass door with the words "POLICE CENTRE" etched across it. He pushed open the door and walked into the room. He found himself in a small waiting room, that had a counter which ran the entire width of the room. At one end of the counter the counter hatch square was resting up against the wall allowing access from the waiting room to the area behind the counter. At the left hand corner of the area behind the counter the Mechanic could see part of a corridor through an open door. The waiting room was empty. There was no one behind the desk. The Mechanic considered his options for a moment before ringing the bell on the counter. A policewoman appeared a few moments later and smiled at the Mechanic. She was in her early twenties.

"May I help you Sir?" she asked, waiting for the Mechanic to explain why he had rung the bell.

"Oh thank heavens me dear child, thank heavens I found your office," replied the Mechanic in a perfect Southern Irish accent. "It's me wallet you see. Gone. Vanished from me pocket without even a trace." The Mechanic did not have time for an elaborate disguise. Sounding as if he was from Ireland would have to do. His Irish accent was extremely convincing.

"I see," replied the policewoman. "Your wallet has been stolen?"

"That's right me dear."

"Did you see who took it?" asked the young officer.

"No. One minute it was there the next it was gone. As if the little people took a fancy to it, I dare say." The Mechanic shrugged his shoulders as he told the policewoman this and she could not help a small smile at the colourful Irish man. She had in fact only been with the Airport Police for three months, but prided herself on her knowledge of police procedure. There was a form for everything she had been taught and she would need a Theft Form completed by this passenger before she could process his details. She searched under the counter for the appropriate form and handed the Mechanic a pen.

"I'm afraid we have a lot of pick pockets operating in the terminal and I think you've fallen prey to one of them. There's not much chance of recovering your wallet I'm sorry to have to say. If you fill in this form as fully as you can I will give you an incident number for your insurance claim and we will let you know if your wallet or any of the contents are found." She handed the Mechanic a four page Theft Form.

"I have to fill all of this in do I?" asked the Mechanic trying to sound surprised as he considered the length of the form. "I've had me wallet nicked me dear, not the entire contents of me house." This time the policewoman could not prevent a large smile from appearing across her face.

"I'm sorry Sir. Regulations are regulations. I'll leave you in peace to complete the form. Just ring the bell when you've finished and I'll check it." She watched the Mechanic pick up the pen and begin to read the first question on the form before she walked from behind the counter through the door into the corridor.

The Mechanic waited for thirty seconds. From what he could see of the corridor no one was about and he could not hear any voices on the other side of the wall. He turned the Theft Form over and wrote on the back of it "TEMPORARILY CLOSED". He walked back to the glass door that led out of the waiting room and stuck the form to the glass using his saliva as an adhesive, so that the make shift sign was displayed to any one who might want to enter the Police Centre. Quickly and without making a sound he slipped behind the counter, through the open door at the rear of the counter and into the corridor. The Mechanic was taking a considerable risk. He did not know the lay out of the Police Centre and could not even be sure that David was there. If he was stopped now he would almost certainly be arrested as the area behind the counter was strictly off limits to the general public. He would say that he was looking for the young policewoman, but his presence in the corridor would arouse suspicion in any one he encountered.

The corridor was deserted and he walked further away from the open door being careful not to make a sound. He moved skilfully as if his life depended on complete silence. As he moved further down the corridor he heard voices and laughter. In the next room he had to walk passed policemen were drinking coffee in between shifts. The Mechanic was lucky that it was still early. Full time cover at the Police Centre began at 9:00 am. Before then only a skeleton staff ran the small office. The day shift were getting ready to begin at 9:00 am as the Mechanic approached the open door to the Staff Room. There was no other way to proceed down the corridor. The Mechanic would have to walk past the open door.

He moved his head close to the side of the doorway, pushing his face up against the door frame. Gradually, as he looked in through the open door the Staff Room came into view. The Mechanic could see three male officers drinking coffee, talking loudly to one another about a football match they had watched the previous evening. One of them was strapping a hand gun holster around his waist. The young policewoman who had spoken to the Mechanic in the waiting room was sitting on the edge of an old, slightly battered arm chair sipping coffee, reading a newspaper. No one in the room appeared to be taking any notice of the doorway. The Mechanic took one large step across the open space and was on the other side in the blink of an eye. He had not made a sound. He stood pressed up against the wall for a moment before he continued to walk along the corridor.

There were no other doors leading from the corridor before the right hand bend he could see ahead of him. The Mechanic followed the corridor around to the right. This part of the Police Centre had two doors on either side of the corridor. They were labelled "INTERVIEW ROOM 1" and "INTERVIEW ROOM 2". The Mechanic tried the first door which was unlocked and saw that the light inside was off. There was no one in the room. He walked across the corridor and tried the door to room Two. Again the door was unlocked and it swung open easily as he turned the handle and pushed. The lights in the room were switched on, but the room was empty. The Mechanic saw a dirty shoe print on the floor by the chair nearest the door and at the front of the print a small red smudge of blood. He smiled to himself like a hunter who knows he is closing on his prey.

He backed out of the room, pulling the door shut as he retreated. He looked at the floor and noticed tiny drops of blood leading away from the room he had just inspected. The corridor again turned to the right about twenty yards ahead of him. The Mechanic followed the corridor along and to the right moving quickly but in complete silence. He made no sound as he approached David who was bent over the water fountain drinking in the ice cold water.

David was twisted to one side as he drank, unable to see the shape of his attacker approaching him. The Mechanic moved across the corridor, opposite the water fountain so that David could not catch even a glimpse of him until it was too late. The Mechanic quickened his pace slightly. He was no more than fifteen feet away from David. As he approached David was still huddled over the water fountain. The Mechanic straightened his right hand so that his fingers were lined up tightly with one another, bending back a little as he tensed his hand. One blow to the back of David's neck and it would all be over. The Mechanic got closer. The only sounds in the corridor were the noise of the water spewing from the drinking spout and David swallowing. Ten feet. The Mechanic could sense the impending attack. Killing always excited him. He raised his right hand as he advanced towards David ready to strike as soon as he was in range. Eight feet. Seven. This time David would not escape, he thought.

At that moment the sound of the water running into the basin stopped. David had had his fill. The water was so cold on his teeth that he could not drink any more. He stood up and heard the faint sound of someone behind him. The sense of being approached from behind was familiar.

Familiar from the car park earlier that morning. Terrified, he swung around and came face to face with the Mechanic.

David saw in front of him the steely eyes he had not been able to put out of his mind since he had escaped on the bumper of the bus. He saw that the Mechanic's hand was raised and that his attacker was about to strike him. David stumbled back a few steps. There was not enough time for him to turn and run. The Mechanic was as good as on him moving fast now having accelerated as David had spun around.

Five feet. The Mechanic raised his hand higher as he prepared to strike, never taking his eyes off David. David dropped his head instinctively to protect himself from the blow he was about to receive. As his eyes looked down at the floor he saw the red bucket underneath the water fountain full of water. Without hesitation David kicked the bucket from under the fountain out towards the Mechanic. The bucket was heavy and did not travel very far, but it tipped over and the water it was holding spilled out across the floor into the Mechanic's path. The floor of the corridor was tiled. As the Mechanic stepped down on to the tiles he slipped on the water as it gushed out of the bucket and began to lose his balance. The momentum of his body threw his legs into the air and he crashed to the floor, landing in a puddle of water on his back. David watched in disbelief as his attacker flew through the air and came to ground with a thud.

"Run," David's brain told his body. "Run." At first David's legs would not move. He just stood there watching the Mechanic recover from his fall. It was the sight of the Mechanic's steely eyes as the killer turned and looked up at him that made David run. The two men stared at one another for a moment, then David bolted, not with difficulty as he had done when he had escaped in the car park, but like a gazelle running for his life.

David dashed down the corridor, flying around the bend. He ran in the direction of the waiting room as fast as he could. The Mechanic was right behind him. As David took off the Mechanic leaped to his feet and was in pursuit. He was only ten or twelve feet behind as David approached the Staff Room. David found his voice.

"Help. Help me," he shouted as he ran past the entrance to the Staff Room. The sound of running in the corridor had already alerted the policemen in the room and they were moving towards the doorway as David ran past. The young policewoman was closest to the doorway and was in the corridor first. As she hurried into the corridor she saw the Irish man she had spoken with not five minutes earlier tearing down the corridor in her direction.

"Stop," she shouted as she went for the gun by her side. She unclipped the safety strap and began to pull her revolver from its holster as the Mechanic got to her, put his arm out and spun her around to the side. He pulled her to his chest with his left arm, his momentum carrying both of them along the corridor and tightened his grip by pulling his arm up across his shoulder. He jerked the woman's neck upwards in a clean, effortless movement as he skid along the tiles. He heard her neck break, felt her body go slack under him and dropped her. He continued down the corridor towards the door that led to the waiting area. One of the policemen managed to get a shot off before the Mechanic was through the door and behind the counter in the waiting area, but the bullet missed the Mechanic completely, embedding itself in the door frame.

The Mechanic leapt over the counter and hurled himself at the glass door which flew open under his weight. He fell out into the departure lounge and looked for David. He saw him about forty feet in the distance. David was tearing across the open room, occasionally dodging in and out of baggage trolleys, in the direction of the Underground escalators. He ran faster than he could ever remember having run since he gave up athletics at school. The Mechanic also ran. He had never given up running and he soon began to catch up with David. Two policemen ran out of the Police Centre waving guns looking for the man who had just killed their colleague. One of them was talking on a hand held radio.

David could see the tops of the escalators ahead of him. Although he was afraid to look over his shoulder in case he stumbled, he knew the Mechanic was chasing him. He vaulted a baggage trolley that was in his way and landed with a thud. He lost his footing for an instant but regained his balance and ran up to the nearest escalator that led down to the Underground. He jumped on to the escalator. It was loaded with people and they were standing on both sides preventing David from running down. He had to stop. The slow pace of the escalator compared to the speed he had been running at was agonizing. He looked up at the top of the escalator and saw his pursuer get on. There was only about twenty five feet between then now.

The Mechanic did not stop when he got on the escalator. He began pushing people out of his way, moving down the steps getting ever closer to David.

David looked down. Come on, he thought. It was no good. He realised that the Mechanic would reach him before he got to ground level unless he got moving. He pushed forward, moving in and out of people as he tried to get past them, elbowing them out of the way when necessary.

The Mechanic saw the commotion below him and spotted David amongst the crowd on the escalator. He pushed more aggressively and moved faster. He was only ten feet away from David as David reached the bottom of the escalator and ran into the Underground station. David ran up to one of the automatic ticket gates, put his hands down on the barriers on either side of the gate and swung his body over. He landed badly, falling to the floor. Expecting the Mechanic to jump on him any second, he scrambled to his feet and ran in the direction of the nearest platform. The Mechanic had gained on David whilst they had both been on the escalator. As he reached the bottom and ran off the escalator he saw David vault the gate, fall and scramble to his feet. The Mechanic hurdled the gate in a single stride and ran after David. He was less than ten feet behind David now. The two men ran towards the nearest platform. David was not sure where he was going. He ran through a subterranean archway and out on to a platform. A train was at the platform about to pull away. David heard a familiar bleeping sound that indicated people should stand back from the train as the doors were about to close. He saw the black rubber trims on the carriage doors in front of him getting closer to one another as the doors slowly closed.

David realised this was his only chance of escape. He dived for the gap between the doors, crashing on to the footplate of the carriage as the doors slammed together. He felt a pain in his ankle and looked behind him. His right foot was caught between the doors. He pulled at his foot in desperation and watched through the gap the Mechanic reach the train. The Mechanic banged the doors and stuffed his arm through the narrow gap to try and force the doors apart. David watched in horror. If the doors opened the Mechanic would have him. He knew that the train driver would not be able to move the train without all of the doors being tightly closed. If the instruments in the driver's cabin indicated that one of the doors was not properly closed, the driver would open all of the doors for a moment and then re-close them.

David pulled at his foot, trying to twist it free so that the doors could close. Through the gap between the doors he could see the Mechanic's face straining as the killer tried to force the doors open. David turned his foot to the side, wrenching his ankle in the process and was able to pull his leg free. The doors sprang closer together but still did not close completely. The Mechanic's hand was trapped between the doors as he tried to prise them apart. David could see the Mechanic's fingers turning red from the pressure of the doors trying to close tight. He heard the bleeping sound signalling that the driver was about to open the doors.

David was lying on the floor of the carriage with his feet up against the doors. The bleeping sound pounded through his head. If the doors were opened David knew that he would be killed. He lifted his right leg and pulled it as far back as he could before driving his foot down on the Mechanic's fingers with all the strength he could muster. He heard the Mechanic yell out in pain as he yanked his hand from the gap. The doors slammed together, the bleeping stopped and the train began to move away. David got to this feet and caught a glimpse of the Mechanic running from the platform cradling his hand, before the train entered the tunnel.

He sloped into a vacant seat. He was exhausted. For the first time since he had dived on to the train he was aware that everyone in the carriage was staring at him. He ignored their eyes, felt the outline of the disk in his pocket and sat back in his seat.

CHAPTER 13

The Mechanic did not stand and watch the train pull away into the tunnel. He knew that the police would soon be swarming all over the airport looking for him. He had killed a police officer and the airport security net would be closing already. If escape had been his only consideration the Mechanic would have boarded the next train to depart the station and vanish. Escape however, was not the only consideration. The Mechanic did not know David's name or where he lived. If he left the airport now on the next train that pulled up at the platform, he would never find David or the disk. The only contact he had with David now was the Golf parked outside the entrance to the terminal. He had not expected to have to return to the car, but in the circumstances had no alternative.

He walked away from the platform back towards the ticket gate. Already he could see armed policemen riding the escalator down to the Underground searching for the young policewoman's killer. He had the additional problem of getting past the ticket gate without a ticket and without drawing attention to himself. The Mechanic had openly chased David across the check in lounge down into the Underground station in full view of everyone and it was likely that one of the policemen heading for the Underground might already have a description of him. Other than by train the only way out of the station was through the check in lounge. He was trapped. He turned around and walked quickly back through the subterranean arch on to the platform. There was no train at the platform and it was deserted.

He ran to the far end of the platform. When he got there he took his raincoat off, turned it inside out and tore the lining in half a dozen places. He then threw the coat to the floor and trampled on it, wiping mud from his shoes across the ripped lining and creasing the coat. He put the coat back on, this time wearing it inside out and slouched down against the wall. He spat on his hands and wiped more dirt from the soles of his shoes over his face and neck. He ruffled his hair and forced himself to break wind three times. He removed his watch and belt pulling his trousers down his waist as if they did not fit him properly.

The transformation was impressive. He looked like a tramp. He already had thick stubble around his chin, not having shaved for twenty four hours, but his beard was now smudged with dirt, his hair was a mess and he smelt bad. The torn, dirty raincoat finished the costume. He sat back with his eyes closed pretending to be asleep and waited. He did not have to wait for long.

"You. Yes you there. Are you alright?" The Mechanic slowly opened his eyes and stared up at a policeman holding a semi automatic machine gun to his chest. The Mechanic grunted disinterestedly and closed his eyes again.

"You can't sleep here old man," said the policeman. "Come on, up with you." The Mechanic mumbled his disagreement under his breath, but pushed himself up the wall to his feet and stood, slouching forward looking unsteady. He picked his nose in front of the policeman and broke wind again. "Oh my God," said the policeman, taking a step back from the sight before him. "Off with you, do you hear. There is no sleeping on this platform." The Mechanic nodded as he trundled off towards the platform exit escorted by the policeman.

When they reached the automatic ticket gate the policeman signalled to the guard to open the gate and the Mechanic walked through unchallenged. The Underground was now heaving with police officers who were randomly stopping and questioning people. Some of the people questioned pointed in the direction of the platform the Mechanic and the policeman had just left, but although the Mechanic saw this the policeman who was marching the Mechanic out of the Underground did not.

"What have you got there Stepson?" said the voice. Both the policeman and the Mechanic turned around suddenly to see a Police Sergeant standing behind then. The Mechanic dropped his head and dribbled saliva from his mouth.

"I found him asleep on one of the platforms Sarge," replied the policeman. "He's a little worse for wear. I was going to see that he left the terminal." The Sergeant studied the Mechanic for a moment.

"You know you're not allowed to sleep on the Underground laddie, better not get caught doing it again. Is that clear?" he barked. The Mechanic lifted his head a little and nodded. "See him off the premises Stepson."

"Yes Sarge," replied the policeman as the Sergeant walked off. "Come on old man, up you go," he told the Mechanic, pointing towards the escalators.

The policeman escorted the Mechanic up to the check in lounge and towards the exit doors. Uniformed police officers and security guards were patrolling the lounge. The Mechanic saw a body being carried across the lounge on a stretcher away from the Police Centre. The policeman bundled the Mechanic through the automatic exit doors and watched for a moment as his temporary charge walked off in the direction of the bus stop. As soon as the Mechanic was no longer being watched he took off his raincoat, turned it the right way around and put it back on. As he walked to the unloading bay he replaced his watch and belt and wiped what dirt he could from his face with a handkerchief. He flattened his hair as best as he could and searched for the Golf. He had been inside the terminal for over half an hour and was worried that the Golf might have been towed away. He felt around in the pocket of his coat for the car's ignition keys.

David's car was still where the Mechanic had parked it, but it had been clamped. The Mechanic cursed under his breath. He walked over to one of the luggage attendants and was directed to the Car Parks Office at the entrance to the Short Term car park. He lied to the attendant that he had lost track of time whilst saying goodbye to his wife and asked if his car could be released. The attendant was not interested in the Mechanic's excuse. She had heard every excuse imaginable. The Mechanic paid the one hundred pounds mandatory fine in cash without complaint and waited impatiently for another attendant to appear to remove the wheel clamp. As soon as the clamp was removed the Mechanic drove out of the airport, passing police cars with their sirens sounding coming the other way into the airport complex.

The Mechanic was not familiar with the roads around Heathrow. He followed the signs for London until he saw a large ESSO petrol station. He signalled and pulled into the station driving the Golf over to the corner furthest away from the road. He turned off the engine, got out of the car and removed David's suit carrier from the trunk. The Mechanic walked over to the station shop and entered the men's wash room with the suit carrier. In addition to a row of urinals the wash room was equipped with four cubicles. He washed his hands and waited for the cubicle furthest from the entrance to the wash room to become free. As soon as it did he entered the cubicle, locked the door behind him and placed David's suit carrier on the toilet seat.

The suit carrier was of conventional design. It was folded over with a large zipper style pocket on either side. The zipper handles were secured to the body of the carrier by two small padlocks. The Mechanic pulled the buckle end of his belt free of his trouser loops and using the buckle hook as a lever, snapped the tiny pad locks in turn. They broke easily. He zipped open each of the large pockets and rummaged around inside. He found a pair of shoes, blue jeans, a couple of shirts and an assortment of ties. Inside the second pocket he discovered a small fold over flap which was secured to the inside of the pocket by strips of Velcro. He pulled the flap free and removed a folded piece of thin faded yellow paper. The paper was the carbon copy of David's travel insurance policy for his trip to Miami. It gave his full name, date of birth, occupation as well as his business and private addresses. The Mechanic folded the piece of paper in half and stuffed it in the inside pocket of his jacket. He did not bother with the rest of the contents in the carrier. He had found what he was looking for. He washed the rest of the dirt from his face and hands and flattened his hair down with water from one of the taps before leaving the wash room.

The Mechanic purchased an "A to Z of London", from the station shop and walked back to the Golf. He replaced the suit carrier in the trunk of the car, studied the road map he had purchased against the addresses on the yellow sheet of paper for a few minutes then started the car's engine and pulled out of the petrol station following the signs for London.

He needed to find a telephone he could use. He had seen two public pay telephones in the station shop but they had not been private enough for the call he had to make. As he drove he watched out for a more secluded telephone booth. After a mile and a half he spotted a new style telephone box in the distance and pulled off the road, parking the Golf out of sight behind the box. The Mechanic was beginning to feel that it was time for him to change cars. The telephone box was empty. The Mechanic inspected the area around the box. There was no one around. He got out of the Golf, walked over to the box and went in. The Mechanic was not looking forward to having to speak to the Guardian. He dialled the number he had been given, gave the number of the telephone he was calling from and waited for the Guardian to call him back. He thought of David. Whatever the Guardian instructed him to do in relation to the computer disk, he did not intend to leave England until he had butchered the man he chased.

The telephone rang and the Mechanic lifted the receiver.

The Guardian had not continued his meeting after receiving the Mechanic's first call earlier that morning. Operation Domino was threatened, that much was clear. Nevertheless, no matter from which angle he considered the situation he did not think the Planner would have given the disk to a stranger he had met on an aeroplane. The Guardian was convinced that David must have accidentally stumbled upon the disk in some way and could have no idea what information it contained. However, he could not afford any loose ends. His team was in place. All preparatory steps had been concluded. It was midday in Bucharest on 24th November. The Operation was scheduled to be carried out the following day. The Planner had made it clear in his operational report that based upon the information that was available, this was the last date on which the Operation could be carried out with guaranteed success.

The Guardian could not wait for another possible opportunity. The situation in Romania concerning Protected Membership of the European Community had become a time bomb about to explode. He did not know how long he could successfully continue to blackmail the President into supporting a third application for membership. No, he thought to himself, the time is right now and it is unlikely to be right ever again.

The Guardian realised that there would be two consequences of the information on the disk falling into the wrong hands. If the information became known to the relevant authorities before 25th November, the Operation would be scuppered. Even if the Operation was carried out successfully, if the information on the disk fell into the wrong hands at any time in the future, the Guardian would be hunted for the rest of his life.

He wanted to enjoy the half a billion dollars he was going to steal from the Romanian treasury as a free man, rather than from a prison cell.

He told himself not to worry. David could not know what was on the disk and even if he might have found out eventually, that risk had almost certainly been taken care of by now by the Mechanic. He expected a call on the secure line from the assassin at any moment, confirming that the disk had been recovered and David eliminated. He looked at his watch. It was over two hours since he had last spoken to the Mechanic. Why had the assassin not called yet, he agonized? The Guardian told himself again not to worry. The Mechanic was always reliable. What could go wrong, he thought? No civilian is a match for the Mechanic's particular skills.

The Guardian's aide hurried into the room without knocking to tell his master that they had received a call from the Mechanic and were about to call him back on the secure line. The Guardian smiled to himself and followed his aide to the basement of the mansion.

"Report," was all that the Guardian said to the Mechanic over the satellite telephone. This was a time for the Guardian to listen rather than talk. There was silence on the other end of the line for a moment before the Mechanic spoke.

"I can confirm that the young man who sat next to the target on the flight from Miami has had the disk in the pocket of his jacket since the old man died earlier this morning," reported the Mechanic. "I hit him twice this morning, on both occasions in unfavourable locations. The young man is injured slightly, but he was able to get away." The Guardian's grip around the receiver of the satellite telephone tightened a he listened in disbelief to the Mechanic.

"And the disk?" he asked urgently. "Do you have the computer disk?"

"No I do not," replied the Mechanic without hesitation. He waited for the Guardian to speak, but heard nothing. Quietly he continued. "The little bastard escaped me. But I have his car and his name. I know that he is a lawyer and the name of the firm he works for and I have his home address. He will be history before the end of the day. You have my assurance on that."

The Guardian listened. Experience had taught him that it was futile to loose his temper at a time like this. He was furious however. He could not understand how a civilian could have escaped from the Mechanic, not once but twice.

"You're sure he still has the disk?" the Guardian asked after a moment.

"I'm sure," replied the Mechanic.

"Will he take it to the police?"

"He might," answered the Mechanic without any sound of concern in his voice. He did not care about the disk. He wanted David. "But he's had one hell of a fright. The last time he went to the police I almost killed him. No. I think he'll hide out somewhere for awhile at least and get himself together."

"His address in London?" asked the Guardian.

"Too obvious. He'd know I'd find him there," replied the Mechanic. The Guardian considered the situation. If the Planner had followed his instructions the information on the disk would be encoded and would not be easily accessible. The code could be broken, but only with patience if someone had cause to think the disk was sufficiently suspicious to warrant the attentions of a code breaker. Could he be sure that the Planner had followed his instructions? The Planner was dead and somehow or other the disk had ended up in the possession of a young English lawyer. He was running out of time. Nevertheless, the Guardian decided there was still time to recover the disk. He put the receiver to his mouth again.

"Can you find this lawyer before he figures out that he should go to the police?"

"Yes," replied the Mechanic. "I can be in London in less than an hour. He lives in Chelsea according to what I've been able to find out and works in the City. He'll be easy to find. As soon as he sticks his head up, I'll blow it off." The Mechanic's confidence encouraged the Guardian. The Mechanic was probably right, he thought. It was unlikely that the lawyer would rush off to the police straight away. He would soon pop back up and the Mechanic would be there to catch him. He thought of the people he had on his payroll in London and then spoke to the Mechanic.

"Alright. Find him, get the disk and then kill this meddlesome lawyer. I have people who can help find him in London. Tell me his name and the name of the law firm he works for and call me this afternoon. If I know where he is by then he's all yours, is that clear?"

"Yes. Perfectly clear." The Mechanic did not like the idea of someone else getting involved in his business, but he could see the sense of what the Guardian had said. It was unlikely that David would go back to his office or his home in London immediately. With its millions of people London was the ideal city in which to hide. Finding David might take time. He read out David's name and address and the details of Holland Chapman & Co. The line went dead.

The Guardian cut the Mechanic off as soon as he had written down David's name and addresses. He needed the secure line to make another call.

The Mechanic removed the "A to Z of London" from the passenger seat of the Golf and walked away from the telephone box leaving the car where it was parked. He needed a new car for the drive to London. Although he was anxious to resume the chase, he was not prepared to risk being spotted in the Golf which by now he expected to be listed on every police computer in the country as having been stolen from Heathrow.

He moved quickly. As he walked along the pavement away from the Golf and the telephone box he thought of David. David had been very lucky to escape him twice. The problem was that he was unarmed. Killing with just bare hands was always more difficult than killing with a weapon of some sort. Had the Mechanic been armed in the car park and in the Police Centre David would now be dead. He never armed himself when travelling by air. Electronic detection machines made that impossible. It was time he picked up a gun he decided and he knew just the place to get one.

The Mechanic walked passed a sign announcing that he was approaching Welden Comprehensive School. He strolled in through the main gates in the direction of the school car park. Three minutes later he drove out of the main gates in a dark blue Ford Sierra, pulled out on to the main road and drove off in the direction of England's famous capital city.

CHAPTER 14

David was shaking slightly although it was not cold in the train carriage. Adrenalin was still pumping around his body after the chase through the airport and his narrow escape. He took a series of deep breaths to calm himself down and closed his eyes. The swelling around his neck had become acute by now but he had almost forgotten the pain. The events of the morning were repeating themselves in his mind.

So much had happened since the 747 from Miami had touched down only hours earlier and David frantically wanted to make some sense of the confusion. He sat perfectly still trying to sort out in his mind what had occurred whilst he listened to the constant noise of the train as it hurtled through the tunnel. He found the familiar sounds of the train reassuring.

David thought of the old man whose name he still did not know, of the man with the steely eyes who had chased him relentlessly across the car park and the airport check in lounge, and about the computer disk he had in his pocket. His thoughts kept returning to the computer disk. The Planner had struggled to mention the disk on his death bed moments before his heart had given up. The man who was chasing him had asked about the disk in the car park and had attacked when he had denied knowledge of it. David tried to remember exactly what the Planner had said about the disk. He recalled something about the old man's daughter, her real name and a Romanian. What it all meant he could not work out. He had a few pieces of a jigsaw puzzle but not enough to make out the picture.

The train began to slow down. As the driver applied the brakes people in the carriage who were not sitting down stumbled forward, grabbing for hanging rails with which to steady themselves. The jolt of the train slowing down brought David out of his thoughts. He began to feel uneasy. He had seen the Mechanic pull his hand from between the doors and recoil in pain from his kick and had watched him for a moment before the train had accelerated into the tunnel out of Heathrow. The Mechanic could not be on the train David reasoned. It was not possible. The feeling of unease increased and he sat up straight in his seat. How could he have got on the train, David thought?

The train was slowing down quickly now. David watched the windows. The darkness of the tunnel prevented him from seeing out of the carriage. He knew that there was nothing to see anyway, except the ancient walls of the tunnel around the carriage. Then there was light. A burst of light as the carriage emerged from the black tunnel into the next station. The train slowed to a stop. He was afraid to move. Could the man who chased him have somehow boarded the train, he thought? His eyes searched up and down that part of the platform he could see from where he was sitting in the carriage for his attacker. People hurried on and off the carriage whilst the doors where open.

"Close. Close," David pleaded of the doors under his breath. The carriage filled with the sound of bleeping that signalled the doors were about to close and slowly the doors began to slide together. David had been holding his breath since the doors had opened and he slowly breathed out in relief as he watched the doors start to close. The doors were almost together when they were stopped by a large black boot. David saw the doors stop and looked down at the boot in horror. He jumped to his feet and ran to the far end of the carriage. A slim door that led to the next carriage along prevented him from going any further. David pulled at the door handle savagely but the door was firmly locked. He could see people in the next carriage through the thick glass of the door. He turned around, looking for something with which to smash the glass. As he turned around David saw the doors in the centre of the carriage begin to slide back.

The driver was re-opening the doors because his control panel indicated that something was blocked in the doors, preventing them from closing properly. David froze. There was nowhere for him to go. He looked down at the seated passengers on either side of the carriage in desperation. They just stared back at him, a few ignored him altogether. The doors opened as far as they could and the heavy boot stepped into the carriage followed by a thick leg and then a large torso wearing a dark raincoat. The new passenger walked into the carriage, looked around for a second and then sat down in the seat that had been occupied by David. David felt his legs go weak and he let himself slide down the door on to the floor. It was not the Mechanic.

Some of the passengers in the carriage stared at David slumped on the floor and conscious of their stares he stood up, walked to the other end of the carriage and found a vacant seat. His heart was pounding and his shoulders were tight with tension. He could feel beads of sweat on his forehead. He looked around nervously half expecting to see the steely eyes of his pursuer approaching him.

David told himself to calm down. He needed to think. He had escaped the Mechanic twice, narrowly both times it was true but he was still alive and he still had the disk. He needed to decide where to go and what to do with the Planner's disk.

He looked up at the Underground map on the wall of the carriage. He had no idea what train he was on or in which direction he was heading. At Heathrow Underground Station he had run on to the platform nearest to the escalators and had dived into the train without even considering what line it was on or where it was going. Neither had been important at the time. All that had mattered was to get away from the Mechanic. David had no delusions about his pursuer. He was convinced that if the Mechanic caught him, the assassin would kill him without hesitation.

The map above the train doors showed that the train operated on the blue line. David tried to recall what line this was. He travelled to and from the City most days on the Circle or District Lines which were marked in yellow and green respectively on maps of the Underground, but he hardly ever travelled on the blue line. He searched the map and found a key to the coloured lines which told him that he was on the Piccadilly Line. Stations from Heathrow Terminal Four to Cockfosters in north London were dotted along the blue line. David knew that he had been at one of the Heathrow terminal stations when he had boarded the train, but did not know which one. He also did not know whether the train was going west, looping around the Heathrow terminals, or east on its way to central London. David soon knew the answer.

The train began to slow down again and pulled into the next station.

From the carriage he could see signs placed intermittently along the station wall announcing the name of the station. The signs read Hatton Cross. David looked up at the map again and as the doors of the train closed and the train accelerated away from the station he found Hatton Cross on the blue line. The train was going in the direction of London. He sighed with relief. He knew where he was and the direction he was heading in.

He saw from the map that the train would eventually stop at South Kensington Station. From there it was only a ten minute walk to his flat on Godfrey Street. David considered whether it would be safe for him to go back to his flat. He was desperate to have a shower, put an ice pack on his neck and change his clothes. He looked down at himself. His jacket was ripped in several places, his trousers were covered in mud from the ride to the airport on the bumper of the bus and the soles of his shoes were cracked and torn away from the front of each shoe. He could not see his face or neck but felt thick stubble on his chin from not having shaved for such along time and could feel the swelling around his neck. He had lost all of his luggage. His flight case and overcoat were with British Airways and his suit carrier was in the trunk of his car, which he had last seen in the airport car park that morning. At his flat he had everything he needed, but was it safe to go there?

David was convinced that the Mechanic was still after him. He did not know where he was but he had no doubt about it. From what he had seen of the Mechanic, David believed that he was being chased by a professional killer. He had no heroic ideas about his two escapes. He was intelligent and realised that he had been lucky. Lucky in the car park that the Mechanic had been distracted by the screaming woman and lucky in the Police Centre at the airport that the Mechanic had slipped on the wet floor tiles. These simple everyday things were why he was still alive. He knew that he could not afford to take any unnecessary risks. Going to his flat was just too risky. The Mechanic should have little difficulty finding out where he lived. David had left his luggage behind in his car in the car park and the contents of his suit carrier would lead anyone that cared to look right to his office and his home. No, David thought to himself, the flat is out.

He next thought of going to the police. After all he had been attacked twice by a man he suspected to be a professional killer. A man who killed with his bare hands. The train would eventually stop at Victoria Station.

David knew that he could be inside Victoria Police Station within five minutes of leaving the train. He could hand over the disk, give a description of the man that had attacked him and wait in safety until the Mechanic was picked up.

At first this idea appealed to him. This was a matter for the police. He would be safe with the police. However, as he thought of the safety of Victoria Police Station he remembered how safe he had felt inside the Police Centre at Heathrow. Somehow the Mechanic had found him there and had tried to kill him. There. Right in the heart of the Police Centre surrounded by police officers. He had thought he was safe then, but he had almost been killed.

The train banked to the left as it hurtled around a bend. The familiar sounds of the train comforted David. For a second he thought it was just another day and that he was on his way to work. He thought of the police again. The more he thought about entrusting his safety to the authorities the less attractive the idea became. He wondered how he would explain the events of the day to them. He would have to tell them about the disk he realised, but what could he say. He had no idea at all what information was stored on the disk. The police might not even believe that he had been attacked. And then there was the Mechanic. David suspected that the killer would expect him to go straight to the police and that he might have men waiting for him at the larger police stations in London already. So far it seemed that only one man was after him, but David could not be certain. If his pursuer was a professional, he might have help.

He was unsure what to do or where to go. He needed time to think and he needed to find out what was on the disk. If only he could go to his flat, he thought. He had a computer on his desk at home and would be able to access whatever information was stored on the disk in a matter of minutes. He could not go home, neither could he go to his office. These were obvious places the Mechanic would look for him and David knew it. The train continued on its journey and he tossed his predicament over and over in his mind, unable to make any sense of the few concrete facts he had.

At Earls Court Station a mass of people boarded the train and for the first time during the journey from Heathrow the carriage was full and uncomfortable. David was grateful that he was sitting down, but the crowded carriage was impossible to watch. He had been scanning the carriage constantly, closely observing who got on and off at each of the stations the train had stopped at. He was still afraid that the Mechanic would appear at any moment as he had done twice before. Now, with so many people crammed into the carriage, standing up and sitting down, he could not see the entirety of the carriage. He decided he should get off the train.

He checked the map over the door once more. The first stop after Earls Court was Gloucester Road Station. David dismissed this as a place to exit the Underground. The Gloucester Road area is scattered with restaurants and bars that David had given his custom to on many occasions in the past. He had no appetite for food at that moment and thought it would be safer to stay away from places he often frequented. Next along the blue line was South Kensington Station which presented similar obstacles as an exit point for David. Knightsbridge Station was the next stop marked on the map.

Like many people who live in London, when David thought of Knightsbridge he thought of Harrods, the World famous store to the wealthy of the planet. Generally, Harrods's merchandise was too expensive for David, but before his mother had died he had always bought a Christmas present for her each year from the store. He remembered how excited she had been to receive a shinning green box with Harrods printed all over it.

Harrods sold everything from aftershave to zabaglione. David's eyes opened widely. They always did this whenever a good idea occurred to him. He considered the disk in his pocket and the police. He needed to know what was on the disk before going to the police. He could then go to them on his terms, with a guarantee of full protection, somewhere out of the way where the Mechanic would not think of looking for him. He had a few ideas about where he would be safe, but first he needed to discover what information was stored on the disk.

When the train stopped at Knightsbridge Station David got off. He waited for the platform to fill with passengers leaving the train and immersed himself in the crowd. The crowd bustled up the stairs in the direction of the ticket gates. David remembered that he did not have a ticket. He put his hand inside his jacket pocket in search of his wallet, but the pocket was empty. "Damn," he said out loud. His wallet must have fallen out of his jacket pocket at some stage during the morning, probably he thought, when he had dived from the platform at Heathrow on to the train. He slid his hand into the left side outside pocket of his jacket and rummaged around.

The lining of the pocket contained a smaller pocket, the kind that gentlemen once carried calling cards in. David used his for loose change because it tended not to fall out when he ran. His fingers found a few coins and he quickly took them out. He had three pound coins and some other change. Not a fortune, but it was enough. He walked over to the excess fare window and told the attendant that he had boarded the train at Barons Court and had not had time to get a ticket. He was afraid to say where he had actually boarded the train in case he did not have enough money for the fare. David had never taken the Underground from Heathrow to London before and was not sure how much a ticket to do so cost. The fare from Barons Court to Knightsbridge was a pound. He paid the attendant reducing his immediate wealth by almost a third and walked out of the station into Knightsbridge.

It was approaching midday and the streets of Knightsbridge were fairly busy. David had often cursed the streets of London. They were so crowded with tourists. On this day he was happy that the streets were busy. He was beginning to appreciate that crowds provide cover. On leaving the Underground station, David turned left on to Brompton Road and walked quickly, winding in and out of people who got in his way. He never stopped looking around. The image of the Mechanic was firmly printed at the front of his mind. David did not know where the Mechanic was but was sure he was either in London or on his way to the capital after him. He could not afford to be careless. He moved through the crowd away from the Underground station as quickly as possible.

This was a part of London David particularly liked. It was London at its most stylish. The shops in Knightsbridge are some of the finest in the World selling designer clothes to the very wealthy. The prices of the clothes in the shop windows are outrageous, but the people who shop at these stores are not looking for bargains. As David had once been told by the wife of one of Holland Chapman & Co.'s partners, there was no point owning a Chanel jacket unless everyone knew how much it had cost to buy.

David did not spend any time admiring the clothes displayed in the shop windows. He hurried along the wide pavement ever on the lookout for his attacker. After a few minutes of rapid walking he could see his final destination ahead of him.

Harrods is an impressive sight, dressed in its distinctive green livery. The store to the super rich fills one entire side of the street, towering up to the sky. David quickened his pace as he saw Harrods and within minutes was approaching the main entrance. He did not notice the disapproving look he received from the doorman who watched him enter the store. The doorman had hailed taxis for Harrods's customers for thirty three years and had never got used to the idea that in these modern times the store welcomed anyone, even scruffy individuals who in the doorman's opinion had no business at all traipsing over the green carpets.

David examined the store plan that hung magnificently in the main entrance lobby. Harrods is a difficult store to negotiate. It is not designed to allow customers easy access to any particular department. Most of Harrods's sales are spontaneous purchases and much like a supermarket, the department store is planned out so that the maximum number of people see the maximum number of luxury goods as they search the display halls for the particular item they thought they had come to buy. Product Placing, as the experts call it applies as much to luxury department stores as it does to local supermarkets. David studied the store plan and when he had found the department he was looking for headed in the direction of the lifts. He took a lift up to the fifth floor of the building. He walked through the Book Department and the Men's Luggage Department and eventually arrived at the Computer Goods Department.

The Computer Goods Department was packed with all sorts of computer and digital equipment. There was everything from electronic pocket diaries to large computers with colossal memories. There was a separate software desk selling all the latest programmes and a separate computer games desk. David was not interested in software or in games. He was interested in an operational computer that had a three inch floppy disk drive. He was spoilt for choice.

He walked over to the first desk mounted computer he saw that was switched on and sat down in the chair in front of the screen. The computer screen was inviting customers to play "EAGLE 3", a high tech. interactive computer game where the player was the pilot of a lone fighter jet and had to shoot down other jets flown by Russian pilots.

"May I help you Sir?" David looked around and saw a sales assistant standing next to him. The sales assistant was looking him up and down and David realised how out of place he must appear in his battered clothes.

"No thanks," he replied, "I'll just try out the game." The sales assistant hesitated for a moment before speaking again.

"I would mention Sir, that this particular game is the latest on the market and is priced at one hundred and nine pounds." David was annoyed by the assistant's suggestion that the game was beyond his resources and was about to put the assistant in his place when he remembered his scruffy appearance. He did not look as if he owned a computer and certainly not as if he could afford to pay over a hundred pounds for a computer game. He bit his tongue and smiled at the sales assistant.

"I'm thinking of getting it for my son," he replied. "I won't be very long." David regretted having said this at once. "EAGLE 3" was recommended for teenagers and he knew he did not look old enough to have a teenage son. The sales assistant looked him up and down again for a moment.

"Very well Sir," he replied. "Call me if you need any help." David smiled nervously and the sales assistant walked away.

David pushed the F7 key and the screen cleared. He removed the "EAGLE 3" disk from the floppy drive and looked around for somewhere to put it. He was aware that he was being watched from a distance by the sales assistant and did not want to leave the game disk lying out in the open in case it attracted the assistant's attention. Harrods was not in the habit of leaving expensive game disks lying around. They were either kept in the computers themselves for display purposes as this one had been, or behind one of the counters out of sight. David slipped the game disk into the pocket of his jacket being careful that he was not spotted. He removed the Planner's disk from the same pocket and inserted it into the floppy drive. He looked around to see where the sales assistant was, but could not see him.

The computer was running Word Perfect software, one of the most popular softwares in the World. David hoped that the information on the disk was compatible with this software. He waited for the cursor to appear at the top of the screen. As soon as it did he pushed the F5 key and typed "A:\", and pressed the Return key. The computer hummed softly as it switched from the hard drive to the disk in the floppy drive. Within seconds the disk had been accessed by the computer and the screen showed an index for files stored on the disk. There was only one file shown, with the letters "DIR" after the name of the file indicating that the file was a directory which, David presumed, contained subsidiary files. The directory was entitled "Operation Domino". David pressed the Return key and "A:\Operation Domino" appeared at the foot of the screen. He pressed the Return key again to call up the Operation Domino directory. The screen went blank for a moment and then the words "ENTER PASSWORD AND PRESS RETURN" appeared. David could not believe it. In order to get into the Domino directory he needed to know the Planner's password. He stared at the screen wondering if there was a way to override the password command.

He suddenly felt a heavy hand on his right shoulder and looked up. He saw two security guards and the sales assistant he had spoken to earlier. The larger of the guards had his hand on David's shoulder.

"Would you please stand up Sir?" asked the smaller of the two guards to David.

"What's this all about?" demanded David.

"Don't pretend to be so innocent. I saw you steal it," shouted the sales assistant.

"Steal what?" asked David, genuinely not having any idea what the sales assistant was talking about.

"The game disk. I saw you remove it from the computer and slip it into your pocket." David remembered the "EAGLE 3" disk in his jacket pocket.

"I've not stolen the disk," he shouted back at the sales assistant, whilst trying to pull away from the larger guard's grip. The guard held him tight.

"Why did you slip the game in your pocket if you're not going to steal it?" asked the assistant. David was stuck for a sensible answer. "You said you were thinking of buying the game for your son. Must be bloody young if you're his father."

"Look," replied David, realising that the assistant must have seen him removing the game disk from the computer after all. "I'm a solicitor and I don't steal computer games."

"What? A solicitor," laughed the assistant. "Dressed like that. I don't think so mate. You're a thief and you've been nicked." As the sales assistant said this he lent towards David and pulled the game disk from out of his pocket. He held it up triumphantly for the two guards to see. David thought fast.

"I didn't deny I had the disk in my pocket," he said. He turned to the guard who was holding him. "As I'm sure you know. You can't detain me for shoplifting unless I have walked out of the store without paying for something." The sales assistant looked at the guards for help. "So," continued David, "get your hand of me now." The larger of the guards did not let David go, but he did look over to his colleague for guidance.

"He's right," said the smaller guard to the sales assistant. "We can't bust him unless he runs out of the store with the goods or has them in his pocket and can't pay for them when challenged." The sales assistant looked at David for a moment and then held out his hand.

"That will be one hundred and nine pounds please Sir," he said, emphasising the word Sir sarcastically. David knew he was in trouble. The guard was right. Unless he could pay for the game disk they could legally detain him and call the police. He had less than four pounds in his pocket, no credit cards and no identification on him. What was worse, he looked like a thief.

"I've lost my wallet," was all that he could say. He knew this sounded pathetic. He saw the sales assistant smile and felt the larger guard take his other arm.

"You'd better come with me mate," the guard told him. David did not protest. There was nothing he could say. He had intended to go to the police later in the day anyway. As things had worked out he thought, he would be seeing them earlier that was all. He could easily explain things once the police had checked with the Security Centre at Heathrow. There was no point trying to explain to the guards. They thought he was a petty thief trying to steal from their employer.

The guards led him out of the Computer Goods Department. As he was marched through a door marked "PRIVATE" and up a flight of stairs the smaller guard asked for his name. David gave his full name and heard the guard say into his walkie talkie that he had apprehended a suspected thief and give David's name. The walkie talkie crackled back instructions that the guards should take David to a meeting room on the sixth floor where they would be met by a manager. The walkie talkie also crackled that Knightsbridge Police Station would be called immediately. As David climbed the stairs with one of the guards in front of him and the other behind him holding his arm in a half Nelson, he felt like a criminal. He hoped the police arrived quickly.

The computer screen David had been sitting in front of suddenly cleared. It was programmed to do this automatically if the keys on the keyboard were not touched for a period of five minutes. The Planner's disk remained unnoticed in the floppy drive of the computer.

CHAPTER 15

"Use the siren damn it," barked Detective O'Connor to the Constable from the back seat of the police Rover. O'Connor always sat in the back of police cars. He detested wearing seat belts and although this was required for passengers sitting in the back of cars as well as for those sitting in the front seats, few people took any notice of this relatively new safety regulation, only feeling obliged to strap themselves into the front seats. O'Connor lounged in the back of the police car without his seat belt fastened. What could any one do, he thought. He was the law.

The police car was stuck in traffic on the outskirts of Knightsbridge heading towards Brompton Road. O'Connor and the Constable were on their way to Harrods to interview and if appropriate arrest a suspected shoplifter who had been remanded by the store's security guards. Harrods had reported the shoplifting to Knightsbridge Police Station less than an hour earlier. Although Harrods were detaining the shoplifter the store could not arrest him. The correct procedure in these circumstances was for the police to attend at Harrods, interview the shoplifter and any witnesses, including the security guards and shop attendant who had discovered the theft and if the store wanted to prosecute, arrest the shoplifter and take him away to Knightsbridge Police Station if there was adequate evidence to suspect the accused was in fact guilty. It was Harrods's policy to press charges against all shoplifters no matter how petty their crimes. Any opportunity to deter thieves is always grasped by the large department stores in London. Too much merchandise was stolen each year for them to ignore shoplifting.

O'Connor was not interested in shoplifters. These days he was not interested in any aspect of police work. He was less than two years away from retirement and had given up hoping for further promotion a long time ago. Nevertheless, an order was an order. He looked down at the police report sheet he had been given by his station dispatcher. This showed the name of the shoplifter and the address of the store that was holding him. O'Connor wondered what David Bowstead had done to get himself into so such trouble.

The car began to move through the traffic again. The Constable had ignored O'Connor's instruction to sound the siren. He knew this was not allowed. The car's siren was only supposed to be used in emergencies, or if the police needed to get to the scene of a crime in hurry. The Police Handbook expressly told officers to resist the temptation to use their sirens unnecessarily. The reasoning behind this instruction was a desire not to alarm people into thinking the police were always having to rush around London in pursuit of serious villains. The Constable knew the contents of the Police Handbook inside out. He had memorised them for his final Police Academy Examinations only four months earlier. He had been a full Constable for three months. Unlike the Detective who sat behind him, he was very interested in every aspect of police work including arresting shoplifters.

The two policemen did not speak. They had nothing in common to talk about and did not know one another very well. O'Connor was forty eight years old. He was a Detective with years of service in the Force behind him. The Constable was twenty years old, fresh out of the Academy.

The traffic eased a little as the police car drove through the central Knightsbridge area. O'Connor looked out of the car window. He lit a cigarette and drew slowly on the filter. Smoking was forbidden in police cars, but this had never bothered him.

He liked Knightsbridge. He liked the women who shopped there and ate lunch in the smart bistros and cafes. They had year round designer sun tans and long, well manicured legs. O'Connor often fantasised that he had a mistress who he kept in a fashionable flat in Knightsbridge. She had a deep tan and very long legs in his imagination and existed only to please him. Instead he had an ex-wife, four children, two houses to pay for and bills. Always bills.

O'Connor liked the ladies. It was his love of legs, not necessarily restricted to long tanned ones, that had eventually caused his wife to divorce him four years earlier. She had cleaned him out in the divorce settlement. So he paid her maintenance each month as well as child support. He paid her credit card bills and the mortgage on her house in Kennington. What little money he had left for himself he spent six or seven times over on booze, prostitutes and the horses. He was flat broke. He turned his head away from the window of the car. As always when he thought about his ex-wife he thought of money.

The Constable pulled the police Rover up outside the main entrance of Harrods into a space reserved for taxis to pick up and drop of Harrods's customers. A doorman in a magnificent green livery uniform appeared out of nowhere. The Management of the super store did not like police cars parked outside the main entrance and the doormen were under instructions to ask offending police officers to park on one of the less conspicuous side roads off Brompton Road. The doorman walked around to the driver's door of the police Rover and tapped on the window with his glove covered knuckles.

"Excuse me officer," he said very politely, "would you mind parking around the corner in Hans Road?". The doorman pointed towards Hans Road. The Constable wound the car window down a little unsure what he should say. He was about to follow the doorman's instructions when he felt O'Connor's hand come down on his shoulder with some force.

"Put the hazard lights on Constable and follow me," ordered the Detective. O'Connor pushed open the car door with his left leg and turned sideways to get out of the car. He was a big, heavily set man and years of physical abuse had made his movements slow and clumsily. He planted both of his feet on the road and levered himself out of the car with his arms. He stood up. He was over six feet tall and had a huge gut that prevented his double breasted jacket from fastening. The fabric of his shirt was stretched around the buttons that held the two front pieces together by the sheer size of his gut and the flesh of his stomach could be glimpsed through the straining button holes. The doorman stared at the Detective and said nothing. O'Connor ignored the doorman and walked towards the main entrance of the store. The Constable mumbled something to the doorman about not being very long and followed the Detective into Harrods.

O'Connor stopped the first security guard he saw inside the store, presented his identification card and explained why he was there. He asked to see the Manager of the store at once and was taken up to the sixth floor of the building where the Management's offices were located. The security guard left him in the care of a junior departmental manager who explained how David had been caught by one of the sales assistants trying to steal an expensive computer game in the Computer Goods Department on the fifth floor. The Manager concluded his summary of David's crime by pointing out to O'Connor that it was Harrods's policy to prosecute all shoplifters no matter how insignificant their theft might appear to an onlooker. O'Connor asked where David was being held and the Manager took O'Connor and the Constable further along the corridor to a door that was locked from the outside. He explained that David was inside the room.

Detective O'Connor congratulated the Manager on the efficiency of the Harrods's staff in apprehending the shoplifter. He explained that before he could arrest David he would need to interview him in private. The Manager nodded, told O'Connor the number of his bleep and asked the Detective to call him from the internal telephone on the desk in the locked room when he had finished questioning David. O'Connor turned the key in the lock and put his hand on the handle ready to open the door. Before doing so, he told the Constable that perhaps he should move the police Rover after all, in case it was causing an obstruction. He told the Constable to go and park the car where the doorman had suggested and then come back and wait in the corridor until he was needed. The Constable walked off in the direction of the lifts cursing the Detective under his breath. He had wanted to move the car originally. Now he had to traipse all the way back down to the ground floor and find a parking space.

O'Connor watched the Constable walk off towards the lifts. He looked up and down the corridor. It was empty. That part of the sixth floor housed only meeting rooms and none of them, other than the one David was being detained in were in use at that moment. He turned the handle and pushed open the door. He removed the key from the outside lock as he walked into the room and closed the door behind him. He locked the door from the inside and dropped the key into his trouser pocket. The key clinked against loose change O'Connor had in his pocket as the Detective advanced towards the table in the centre of the room.

"Mr. Bowstead," said O'Connor in a matter of fact way, "I'm Detective

O'Connor of Knightsbridge Police Station. I understand you've been detained by the store's security people because you were caught shoplifting." As he spoke, O'Connor took out his identification wallet and showed it to David. David examined it carefully.

David was sitting down. He felt like a criminal and was relieved that the police had finally arrived. He intended to explain everything to the police and would ask them to check his identity with Holland Chapman & Co., if necessary. He nodded to O'Connor.

"Yes, I'm Bowstead."

O'Connor walked around to the side of David until David could not see him. David wondered where exactly he should start. He had so much to tell this man. He turned to speak to O'Connor, still sitting down. He would begin with the old man having a heart attack on the aeroplane, he decided.

David did not see the blow to his head coming. O'Connor was standing behind him when he delivered it. He hit David hard across the back of the head with his right fist. David's body went limp as he slipped into unconsciousness and fell to the floor. O'Connor pulled him away from the chair he had been sitting in and turned him over on to his back. As he got his breath back, O'Connor smiled at David lying helpless on the floor, completely still with his eyes closed.

This will solve all of my money problems, O'Connor thought to himself. He had worked for the Guardian for five years and knew how well his employer paid.

He had received a call earlier that morning from one of the Guardian's men. O'Connor had never met the Guardian and had no idea who he was or where he came from. He paid in cash for work that was successfully carried out for him. The cash arrived in the post. O'Connor had been told that a man in his late twenties or early thirties called David Bowstead was in possession of a computer disk. The messenger had gone on to say that if the disk was retrieved the Guardian would reward the retriever extremely well. O'Connor had been told to look out for Bowstead who was believed to be on his way to London, pick him up if he could, find the disk and then arrest him. He had been given a telephone number to call in the event that he came up with anything.

O'Connor knew that David would not be unconscious for long. He had hit him hard, but not hard enough to knock him out for good. The Detective's hands moved quickly across David's body. He searched every pocket of David's clothing, starting with the pockets of the lawyer's battered jacket and then penetrated deeper when he did not find what he was searching for. He felt down the legs of David trousers, checked the lining of his jacket and felt around his waist and across his chest. O'Connor had frisked hundreds of criminals over the years and knew what he was doing. When he was sure that David was not concealing the computer disk he lifted him back on to the chair he had fallen from and looked around the room for something to tie David's hands with.

He found thick masking tape in one of the table's drawers and bound David's wrists tightly to the back rest of the chair. The room contained a small discreet executive bathroom which had been built some years earlier when the owner of Harrods had complained that the meeting rooms on the sixth floor were too far away from the nearest bathrooms. Executives could not be expected to interrupt important meetings to have to walk down to the fifth floor to take a leak. He had ordered that all of the meeting rooms be equipped with bathrooms in keeping with the decor of each particular room. This had been done so that all of the meeting rooms contained a small, fully equipped bathroom.

O'Connor filled a glass he found with cold water from the bathroom. Harrods's plumbing is old and the pipes the water runs through are not well insulated. In winter the cold water is icy. David smarted as he was brought back to his senses by the ice cold water O'Connor threw over his face. It took a moment for him to focus on the room. When his sight was in focus he saw O'Connor sitting on the edge of the table in front of him, smiling and looking down at his watch every couple of seconds.

"The disk. Where's the disk Bowstead?" asked O'Connor quiet calmly. David tried to pull his arms up, but felt that they were restrained behind his back. He looked around and saw that he was strapped to the chair. He was confused. He had heard the guards on the stairs being told that the police had been called and had seen the Detective's identification himself. He was not safe anywhere. Somehow, David reasoned, the police were also involved in whatever it was he had stumbled into.

David did not know what to say. The disk. He remembered the disk in the floppy drive of the computer in the Computer Goods Department. David saw that his clothing had been disturbed. The lining of both of the side pockets of his jacket had been pulled inside out. He guessed that O'Connor must have searched him whilst he had been unconscious looking for the disk and had found nothing. He was unable to understand why the police were involved. He wished that he had been able to access the information on the disk before he had been detained by the store's guards. Operation Domino. That was all he knew and that meant nothing to him.

He looked up at O'Connor who was lighting a cigarette whilst he waited for David to answer. As O'Connor's hand came up to his mouth to light the cigarette David saw that the Detectives knuckles were bruised from where he had hit him over the head. He realised that he was on his own. He could not trust the police, at least not until he knew what was going on and his instincts told him that as soon as the disk was retrieved by the Mechanic, by O'Connor or by anyone else he would be of no further use and would be killed.

"What disk?" he finally replied. David had taken too long over the question not to know about the disk.

"Bollocks kid. My boss says you've got a computer disk that belongs to him and I want it," said O'Connor. "Now for the last time where is it?"

"Really, I don't have it," replied David in all sincerity. "You've apparently searched me so that must be clear even to you."

"Yes, I've searched you," replied O'Connor, "and I didn't find the disk. Where've you stashed it?" David thought for a moment.

"What's on the disk?" he asked.

"I haven't got a clue kid, and I don't give a damn. Now where is it?" David said nothing. O'Connor stood up and drew aggressively on his cigarette. He walked around to David's side as he had done before he had hit him on the back of his head. David braced himself for another blow. "You're beginning to get on my nerves kid. I haven't got time to play games with you." O'Connor was aware that shortly the young Constable would return and would wonder what was going on inside the locked room. "Last chance. Where've you hidden the disk?" David remained silent.

O'Connor bent down behind David and grabbed a handful of his hair in his left hand. He drew on his cigarette again before pressing the red hot tip against the back of David's swollen neck. The pain was considerable and David screamed as O'Connor held the tip of the cigarette firmly against David's neck. After five seconds he pulled the cigarette away. David was still in pain. He clenched his teeth together to prevent himself from yelling out again, but could feel his eyes watering.

"The disk. Where is it?" demanded O'Connor.

"I don't know," replied David as he struggled to get free. O'Connor was still holding his hair firmly and David could not move. O'Connor walked around to David's other side and pressed the burning tip of his cigarette against David's neck again. David pulled his neck forward and again cried out from the pain. This time O'Connor held the cigarette in place for longer than before, but still David did not reveal where the disk was. O'Connor pulled the cigarette away. David's muscles relaxed and he slouched forward in the chair.

"You're a pretty tough customer kid," said O'Connor, "but you'll tell me. Maybe not here and now, but soon." He let go of David's hair and stood up. He had smudged ash from the crushed cigarette over the left sleeve of his shirt. "Shit," he said. "We're going to go to a quiet little place I know Bowstead and talk about this computer disk some more." David did not respond. His head had dropped forward and his hair had fallen about his face.

O'Connor looked at his watch. He had been there too long already. He would cuff the kid he decided and march right out of the store. O'Connor knew a small hotel by King's Cross Station where he could take David and work on him in peace. He took prostitutes there usually. The manager of the hotel would not ask any questions and he would have plenty of time to make David talk. O'Connor was sure that if David knew where the Guardian's disk was he would tell him eventually. He would have to get rid of the Constable he realised, but that should not be too difficult. He looked at the smudge marks on his sleeve and then over at David. He can wait for a few minutes, O'Connor decided. He walked into the small bathroom and turned on the cold tap. He wanted to rinse the ash stains off his shirt sleeve before walking through the store with his prisoner.

David waited until he heard the sound of water running from the tap into the basin. He could feel blisters beginning to form on either side of his neck where O'Connor had burnt him. Although his wrists were securely taped to the back of the chair his leg movement was not as restricted. Under the cover of the sound of the open tap, David tried to stand up. He found that by leaning forward he could lift the chair off the ground and walk. With the chair on his back his movement was limited at first, but as he rapidly became accustomed to walking with his back hunched over like the infamous bell ringer, he was able to move faster.

The chair he had been sitting in was one of ten around a conference table in the centre of the room. David managed to pull one of the other chairs from under the table with his feet, just far enough to allow him to step upon it and then on to the table itself. Once he was on the table David walked to the far end nearest the bathroom door. He estimated that the end of the table he was perched on was about ten feet from the bathroom door. A long way, but he had the advantage of altitude. The table stood about three and a half feet off the floor. David moved his feet over the end of the table so that about half of each shoe hung over the table's edge. He had to be careful not to lose his balance. This was a one shot deal, he realised and if he stumbled there would not be another opportunity.

The sound of running water from the bathroom stopped gradually as O'Connor shut off the cold tap. He walked out of the bathroom still drying his hands and wiping his face on a green towel with the familiar Harrods's logo across it. As he walked out of the bathroom he did not notice David perched on the end of the table.

As soon as David saw O'Connor, he leaped forward into the air, twisting his body so that the chair to which he was strapped turned towards the Detective.

Had O'Connor been a smaller man he might have been able to dodge David and the chair. As it was he could not. The chair with David attached to it crashed into O'Connor knocking him against the wall and then to the ground. The chair smashed and David tumbled free as the back rest of the chair shattered on impact.

David got to his feet as quickly as he could. O'Connor was dazed but not unconscious. Moving swiftly, trying to ignore the pain in his neck and the bruises he had gained from his collision with O'Connor, David undid the thick masking tape that held two straight pieces of wood that had been part of the chair back to his wrists and bent down over the fat Detective. He squeezed his hand into O'Connor's trouser pocket and rummaged around for the door key. The fat of O'Connor's thigh was pressed against his trouser leg and David had to force his hand deep into the pocket before he felt the key. As he pulled the door key from O'Connor's pocket he felt the Detective stir as he began to recover from the fall.

David ran to the door and pushed the key into the lock. His hands were shaking and he made slow work of unlocking the door. As soon as the door opened he burst out of the room into the corridor and ran in the direction of the lift shaft.

O'Connor recovered his senses just in time to see his meal ticket swing the door open and dash out of the room. O'Connor staggered to his feet. He was not a fast man, but the thought of the Guardian's money spurred him on. He ran out of the room and down the corridor after David, panting from the exertion.

David was at the lift door in a matter of seconds. He was on the sixth floor and saw that the lift was on its way up from the fourth floor. He banged on the lift door impatiently and looked over his shoulder. He could not see O'Connor yet. The lift passed the fifth floor and David got ready to jump on as soon as the doors opened on the sixth floor. He looked around again as O'Connor came into sight at the other end of the corridor. The lift bell rang and the doors slid apart. David turned to face the open lift and hurried in. He walked right into the lift's only passenger, a young policeman. The policeman was surprised to be pushed back inside the lift by David and at first did not see his superior running down the corridor towards the lift.

"Stop him, stop him," shouted O'Connor to the Constable. "He's getting away." It took a few seconds for the Constable to understand what was happening. In those seconds David turned around and ran out of the lift towards a door marked "STAIRS". He pulled the door back and practically dived down the first flight of stairs. The Constable reached the stairs in time to see the door to the fifth floor close on its spring loaded hinge below him.

"Sir. He's on the fifth," shouted the Constable to O'Connor who still had not reached the lift. O'Connor waved his hand to indicate that the Constable should follow David. The fat Detective was too out of breath to give the order orally. He slowed down, grabbed the receiver of a wall mounted internal telephone and dialled the number the Manager had given him. The Manger answered his bleep almost immediately. He was on the second floor, close to a wall mounted telephone.

"Bowstead has escaped," panted O'Connor down the telephone.

"Escaped?" replied the Manager sounding a little bemused.

"He's on foot on the fifth floor, probably heading for the street. One of my men is after him. Can you get your guards to watch out by all the exits on the ground floor?" The Manager was taken a little by surprise, but understood what the Detective was trying to do. It would take David sometime to work his way down five floors.

"No problem," he replied. "All the security guards have walkie talkies.

I'll put the word out at once."

"Good," said O'Connor before hanging up the receiver. The Manager dialled a number on the internal telephone and within seconds was in direct contact with all of the store's security guards. He gave instructions and mentioned that they were assisting the police. The security guards on the ground floor ran in the direction of the various exit points, whilst the guards on the other floors made their way towards the stairs and the lifts. O'Connor got in the lift on the sixth floor and pushed the button for the ground floor.

David did not have much of a head start on the Constable, but once he was on the fifth floor it became more difficult for the Constable to spot him. At first the Constable was not able to see David as he ran out of the stairwell. Then he spotted him, running in the direction of the Computer Goods Department. David should have walked. Any hope he had of losing the Constable amongst the Harrods's shoppers was wrecked as soon as he was spotted dashing across the green carpet. David realised this, but he did not have time to walk. He knew that to leave the store he had to get down to the ground floor and had no time to waste. He guessed that O'Connor would try and secure the exits before he reached the ground floor so he ran as fast as he could, knocking shoppers out of his way.

His escape was further complicated because he had to return to the Computer Goods Department. He needed the computer disk and as he ran he prayed that it was still in the floppy disk drive of the computer he had used earlier. As he ran into the Computer Goods Department the sales assistant who had called the security guards to detain David, spotted him and shouted. David wasted no time turning around to see if the sales assistant was after him. He ran up to the computer, found the lever on the base of the machine that ejected the floppy disk drive and retrieved the Sony computer disk and stuffed it into his right hand jacket pocket, turning the lining back the right way in as he did so.

David looked up and saw the main floor exit that led to the escalators in the centre of the store. The escalators elegantly wound their way down to the ground floor. It was the quickest way out of Harrods, David knew. He ran towards the main floor exit and was spotted by the Constable who cut across the Ladies Gifts Department to narrow the distance between himself and David. David ran out into the hall way and jumped on board the down escalator. The escalator was crowded with people, but as they saw David running towards them they moved over to the right hand side creating a path way along the left side of the moving stairs. He took the escalator steps two at a time. It was a long way to the ground floor and time was of the essence. At the bottom of each escalator David ran the short distance along the landing until he reached the next escalator. He was on the escalator that linked the second floor to the first before he saw guards waiting for him on the first floor landing. David turned to run back up the escalator against its flow, but the Constable had by now reached the top of the escalator and was walking down it, also taking two steps at a time. David was trapped. The guards saw that he had nowhere to go, and began to walk up the escalator against its flow. There progress was slow but they gradually closed in on David who was about a third of the way from the bottom of the escalator. David walked backwards holding his position.

He looked over the handrail. He could see the first floor landing some twenty feet below him. He turned and looked up the escalator. The Constable was seconds away from him and his route down was blocked by the guards who had managed to climb half the distance from the bottom of the escalator to where David was holding his position.

He knew that he must not be caught. The police had already demonstrated what they were prepared to do to get hold of the disk and O'Connor had told David that there would be more torture as soon as they were alone again. Now that he had retrieved the disk, David was afraid that he would be killed by the fat Detective as soon as it was discovered. Mustering his courage he gripped the moving handrail and hurled himself over. He crashed down on to the first floor landing and lay still for a moment.

The Constable and the guards stopped moving and stared over the handrail in disbelief. It was too far to jump without injury.

David was injured, slightly. He had twisted his right ankle on impact. He got to his feet and began to limp towards the doors which led to the first floor. He could not risk the lifts any more. Running was incredibly painful. Every time he put weight on his right leg the pain from his ankle shot up through his body. He had no alternative however. He had to run.

The Constable pushed past the guards and ran from the landing on to the first floor. He saw David hobbling ahead of him, moving towards the fire escape stairs. The Constable radioed O'Connor who by now had reached the ground floor and reported David's position. O'Connor grabbed the nearest sales assistant and demanded to know where the fire escape stairs from the first floor came out on the ground floor. He was pointed in the direction of the far side of the building, past the Food Hall. O'Connor began to run, indiscriminately knocking people out of the way as he carried his large frame past the food counters which displayed dressed turkeys in anticipation of Christmas, colossal sides of ham and the famous Harrods's Christmas Hampers.

O'Connor was free of the Food Hall and only ten or twelve feet away from the fire escape door when it was flung open and David limped out, his face distorted from the pain of running on his twisted ankle. He saw O'Connor and did not stop running. The two men ran along the perimeter of the Food Hall. If David had not been injured he would have easily accelerated away from O'Connor. As it was the overweight Detective struggled to keep up with the younger man even with David's injury. However, David was tiring and his ankle was becoming worse. He was starting to slow down and was aware that O'Connor was gaining on him.

David turned a corner and could see large glass doors ahead of him on the far side of the Perfume Department which led out to the street. It was too far. O'Connor would catch him before he reached the doors. He slowed down and looked around. O'Connor had not rounded the corner yet, but could only be moments from doing so. To David's left were a set of swing doors with the words "DRY STORE" written across them. He pushed up against the doors and hurried through them, looking over his shoulder for O'Connor as he entered the store room. He did not see the young woman until he was lying on the floor of the store room on top of her.

O'Connor came around the corner expecting to see David a few meters ahead of him, but he did not. He slowed down and then stopped running altogether, turning his head from side to side so he could view the vast area around him. He could see scores of designer perfume booths pandering to women he would ordinarily have ogled, but he could not see David. David had not been very far ahead of him and judging the distance from where he was standing to the doors that led on to the street, O'Connor was certain that David could not have made it to the doors and escaped out of the building. Not with that limp, he thought. Nevertheless, David had vanished. O'Connor turned around and saw the swing doors that led to the dry store area. He approached them slowly.

David had crashed through the store room doors and knocked over a young woman who had been walking through the store room on her way out of Harrods. The two of them had fallen to the floor. David looked at the woman as they both got to their feet then he looked around the room he found himself in. He had nowhere left to run and no strength left with which to run.

"Please," he said to the woman in desperation "help me."

The woman looked at David. His clothes were battered and torn, he was unshaven and his neck was heavily bruised and swollen. Yet she was instantly struck by how handsome he was. Her instincts told her to run away as fast as she could, but there was something in the young man's eyes, something she could not quite make out.

"Please," repeated David. "Is there somewhere I can hide?" David's eyes searched the store room for a hiding place, but he could see nothing. There was no point hiding anyway. The young woman would only tell the Detective where he was. He looked at the woman.

There it was again the woman thought to herself as she reached down to the floor to pick up her coat, which she had dropped when David had crashed into her. In his eyes. In his beautiful blue eyes. At first she had not recognised it, but then she saw it clearly. Fear. Absolute fear that few people ever experience. She had seen this look only once before, many years ago and she was seeing it now in the face of the man standing in front of her asking for her help. David looked at her and she found it hard to look away. She reacted instantly without thinking what she was doing.

"Over there," she said, pointing David in the direction of a large pallet loaded with boxes of perfumes that were waiting to be stacked on to shelves on the other side of the store room door. David was surprised to hear her voice. He had expected her to scream or at least tell him to get lost, and walk off. She gently pushed him towards the pallet and behind the first large box of perfume. The box was only three feet tall, but with the added hight of the pallet it stood almost three and a half feet from the floor. David crouched down behind the box as the doors to the store room were pushed open by O'Connor.

"Have you seen anyone Miss?" asked O'Connor after a moment. He had expected to find David in the store room and was disappointed to find only a young woman taking perfume packets out of a large box.

"No," replied the woman. "Who are you? What are you doing in here? This room is not open to customers." O'Connor was not in uniform and the woman genuinely did not know who he was. He was sweating from the chase. His shirt flaps had worked free from his trousers and hung below his jacket. O'Connor yanked his identification wallet from his pocket and flashed it at the young woman. He did not have time for this.

"I'm Detective O'Connor," he said quickly. "I'm chasing a shoplifter and I think he came in here a few moments ago. Have you seen anyone?" David held his breath afraid that now she knew he was being chased by the police for shoplifting, she would turn him in. He looked around the room from his hiding place and got ready to make a run for it.

"No officer," replied the woman as she stopped what she was doing. "I haven't seen a sole for the last ten minutes." O'Connor approached her. She was young and pretty and he wished he had time to flirt with her.

"Are you sure you've not seen anyone?" he asked.

"I can assure you," she replied taking a firm tone "that no shoplifters have been through here." O'Connor looked around the store room as the young woman spoke. He could not see David. The room had two fire doors at either end of it that were illegally propped open by fire extinguishers. He could see someway down both of the passages and saw nothing.

"OK Miss," he said, turning back to the woman. "If you do see anyone strange report it at once. The man I'm looking for is very dangerous. We wouldn't want a pretty little thing like you to come a cropper now would we?" The woman looked at the Detective and said nothing. O'Connor turned and walked back out of the room.

"What an arrogant, male chauvinistic pig," said the woman as soon as the doors had swung shut behind O'Connor. "Pretty little thing indeed," she repeated. David stood up cautiously, watching the doors. They remained closed.

"Thank you," he said once he was satisfied that O'Connor had gone. "I think you might have saved my life." The woman half smiled at David.

"Are you very dangerous?" she asked.

"I'm in a lot of trouble," David replied slowly, as if this fact was only just beginning to ring true in his own mind, "but I'm not dangerous. Do you often lie to the police?" he asked, still surprised that his hiding place had not been given away when O'Connor had produced his credentials.

"Are you a shoplifter?"

"No," said David firmly.

"Then I didn't lie," she replied. "I told him that I had not seen any shoplifters in here, which from what you have to say is true." This time David smiled.

"My name is David Bowstead and I'm extremely grateful to you no matter what you said. Is there some way out of here other than through those doors?" David pointed to the store room doors that led to the Perfume Department.

"Rebecca Adams," she replied. "Yes, there's a staff exit along the corridor there, but it's patrolled by a doorman." She pointed towards the corridor. David realised that he did not have much time. Soon O'Connor would figure out that he could only have escaped into the store room and would come back to search the room properly. He had to get out of Harrods.

Rebecca was intrigued by David. Although she had only just met him there was something about him that told her he was not dangerous. In spite of his crumpled appearance she did not think David was a shoplifter, or that she had anything to fear from him. He looked so lost and confused. She hesitated for a moment, unsure of what she was about to do.

"Come with me," she said taking David gently by the hand. She led the way down the corridor towards the staff exit followed by David. When they got to the exit doors she smiled at the doorman.

"Hi Pete. Any improvement in the weather since this morning?"

"I'm afraid not Miss Adams," the doorman replied. "Still bloody cold out there. I think we're in for one hell of a winter this year." The doorman gave David a curious look. Rebecca smiled at him and he opened the door and they left Harrods. They exited on to Basil Street at the back of the store. Rebecca, still holding David's hand led him down the road until they got to the corner of the building where she let his hand go.

"There. You're out in one piece," she said.

"Thank you again," David replied.

The doorman had been right. It was cold. David turned the collar of his jacket up around his neck to lessen the effect of the wind. He watched Rebecca pull her coat on. She was quite petite, no more than five foot two, with shoulder length blond hair that fell loosely around her face. She had large bright green eyes. Rebecca smiled at David as she put her coat on. David thought how beautiful she was.

"Where will you go now?" she asked. She saw the fear in David's eyes return as he was forced to consider his immediate position.

"I don't really know," he said, "but I'd better get going before the police discover I've got away. Thank you again. You've been so very kind to me." He smiled at Rebecca and turned to walk away.

"I only live ten minutes from here by taxi," she shouted after him. "Would you like tea and maybe something to eat?" David stopped.

"I can't, but thank you."

"Why not?" asked Rebecca. "You look like you need a good rest. Are you hungry?" David was tired, very tired and he could use some food.

"I can't let you get involved," he said. "It's not safe, believe me." It started to rain and David and Rebecca both stepped back against the building to shelter.

"Just until it stops raining. How about that?" David was getting soaked and found himself nodding. Rebecca stood out on the pavement and hailed a taxi. They both got in. She told the driver to take them to Abbeyville Road in Clapham. David knew her address was more than ten minutes away. They sat in the back of the taxi in silence.

David watched Harrods disappear behind him. He heard police sirens and saw a police car pass the taxi in the direction of the store. It pulled up outside the main entrance.

David wiped the rain from his forehead with the sleeve of his jacket. "Thank you Rebecca," he said quietly. Rebecca smiled at him but said nothing.

CHAPTER 16

O'Connor was furious. He sat at his desk in Knightsbridge Police Station clenching his fists. He did this whenever he was nervous. Somehow he had lost David and with him the chance to collect a considerable sum of money from the Guardian. O'Connor could not work out where David had vanished to. One minute he had been ahead of him, limping badly through the store the next he had vanished.

O'Connor had driven himself back from Harrods. He ran three red lights and had sounded the police Rover's siren all the way to the station.

The Constable had been left at Harrods in charge of the sweep up enquiry. Whenever a shoplifter escapes it is routine for the police to question shoppers and anyone else who might have seen the thief leave the store in question. O'Connor did not think the Constable would turn anything up, but procedure had to be followed. He had sent two additional officers to Harrods to help the Constable with the questioning.

He glanced at the number he had scribbled on his blotter pad earlier that morning. It was an odd number and he did not recognise the code prefix at all. It was the telephone number the Guardian's messenger had given to him. He was supposed to call the messenger if he found David, or if he came across any information concerning the whereabouts of David or the computer disk. O'Connor did not have David any longer, but he certainly had information concerning him. He could confirm that David was in central London and he knew that David did not have the disk on him, or at least had not had it when he had been searched at Harrods.

What O'Connor did not know and what he was trying to decide was how much this information was worth to the Guardian. He was sure it was worth something, although he had no idea why and did not really care. He looked at the number on the blotter pad again and pondered. The only problem he could anticipate in contacting the Guardian's messenger was that he would have to explain how he had trapped and then lost David. He was afraid that the Guardian would consider him incompetent and would not only refuse to pay him anything, but would never use his services again. In the last five years he had been paid over twenty thousand pounds by the Guardian for one job or another. He did not want to jeopardise future earnings by having to admit that David had managed to slip through his fingers.

The telephone on his desk rang sharply. He had an ancient telephone and the bell had become a little painful in its old age. It was police policy to only replace office equipment when it no longer worked at all. O'Connor hoped that the painful ringing signalled the imminent demise of his telephone. He lifted the receiver and the horrible sound stopped. He was not in the mood to talk to anyone.

"Detective O'Connor?" asked the voice.

"Yes."

"We've found him Sir." It was the young Constable. He sounded excited.

"What? Are you sure?" asked O'Connor sitting up in his chair and forgetting about getting a new telephone. "Where is he?"

"Well, Sir I mean that we know, that is we think we know where he is," replied the Constable.

"What?" Have you got him or not man?" asked O'Connor, who could not make much sense of what the Constable was saying.

"Sir," replied the Constable, trying to calm himself down, "I followed procedure and interviewed each of the guards and everyone else I found at the store's exits. At the staff exit on Basil Street I spoke to a Mr. Peter Sherwin, the doorman. He confirmed that a man fitting Bowstead's description left the store about an hour and a half ago by the staff exit."

"Great," barked O'Connor, who was becoming increasingly agitated. "So we know which door he left Harrods by. I'm not interested in that. I know he's not there any more. I want to know where he is."

"But Sir," pleaded the Constable, Mr. Sherwin remembered who Bowstead left with."

"He left with someone?" said O'Connor. "Who?"

"A Miss Adams, Sir. A Miss Rebecca Adams" replied the Constable triumphantly.

"Adams," repeated O'Connor.

"Yes Sir."

"Who is she?" asked O'Connor.

"Apparently she's one of Harrods's cooks Sir." The Constable had anticipated these questions and had interviewed Mr. Sherwin thoroughly, according to procedure.

"You think he's still with her Constable?" asked O'Connor.

"Why not Sir? Where else would he go?"

"Worth a try," said O'Connor out loud without realising he had spoken.

"Yes Sir, I think so," said the Constable who thought the Detective was speaking to him.

"Constable, get Miss Adams's full address from the Harrods's Personnel Office and call me back."

"I have it already Sir," replied the Constable quickly.

"Good, go ahead then." The Constable read out Rebecca's address. O'Connor recognised part of the address as he noted it on his blotter pad. She lived in Clapham in south London. He smiled and looked at his watch. It was a little before 3:30 pm. Ideal he thought. "Constable I want you to take the other officers and go to the girl's address. Don't park too near her house. I don't want Bowstead or the girl to spot you, is that clear?"

"Yes Sir," replied the Constable. He felt a little insulted. After all it was standard procedure not to park a marked police car in front of a staked out address. O'Connor continued.

"Keep an eye out. If either the girl or Bowstead leave the building call it into me, it must be me, understand. If they leave the girl's place together leave one of the officers observing the address and the rest of you follow them. If they leave separately, or if only one of them leaves follow each of them and call me at once." Again this was standard procedure for a tailing operation. "I'll meet you at the girl's place as soon as I can get over there."

"Yes Sir," replied the Constable, but O'Connor had already hung the receiver up. He got up from his chair and walked around to the other side of his small desk. This was good he thought, very good. He had a second chance to get paid in full. He wondered about the girl. The Constable had said that Rebecca Adams was a cook at Harrods. Was she Bowstead's accomplice? He had no idea. He wondered who she was and recalled the pretty girl he had encountered in the store room at Harrods. If it was her, he thought to himself, she had lied and therefore owed him in his book.

He thought of the Guardian's money and sat back down at his desk. His hands were sweating and he wiped them across the front of his shirt leaving brown smudge marks on the creased fabric. He wanted to call the number on his pad and warm the Guardian up. If he was clever, he thought, he might be able to get a lot of money out of the Guardian on this occasion.

O'Connor checked that he was alone. There were a few other officers at the far end of the room, but they were uninterested in him and well out of ear shot. Few people bothered much about O'Connor any more. He lifted the receiver of his telephone and carefully dialled the numbers on his blotting pad. Twice his excitement made him dial incorrectly and he had to start again. Eventually he completed the numbers and waited. It seemed like a long time before he heard the familiar voice of the Guardian's messenger on the other end of the line. He wondered where the voice was coming from. He had no idea. The voice said "Yes," and O'Connor gave his name as he had been instructed to do. He was asked for the number of the telephone he was ringing from and gave it. He was told to wait and the line went dead. He waited impatiently.

Two minutes later his telephone rang out sharply. He grabbed the receiver to his ear and cupped his hand around the mouth piece.

"Hello." He sounded nervous and a little scared.

"What do you have for us my friend?" O'Connor did not recognise the voice on the other end of the line. It was not the voice of the Guardian's usual messenger. That did not matter. He hesitated for a moment before quietly replying.

"Bowstead, I've found Bowstead." There was silence on the other end of the line for a second or two.

"Where is he?" asked the voice.

"In London, shacked up with some girl," replied O'Connor. He was not in fact sure of this, but was on a roll and just hoped that Bowstead was still with the girl.

"And the computer disk?"

"I have every reason to believe that he has hidden the disk somewhere in the girl's flat." Again, O'Connor had no idea if this was correct, but he needed to dangle a carrot in front of the Guardian before mentioning money.

"I see my friend," replied the voice. "Can you pick him up and retrieve the disk?"

"I already have men watching the flat and I'll go to the girl's address myself to supervise the arrest as soon as I get off the 'phone with you," he answered. Again he lied. His men were on the way to Rebecca's address but had not called in yet to say that they had arrived and he could not be certain that the Constable's hunch that David was with the girl was even right. O'Connor was not thinking of these details. He was deciding how much money to ask for.

"Very good, my friend," said the voice. "What is the girl's address?" David read out Rebecca's address in Clapham. "Once you have him and the disk call in again on this number." O'Connor paused for a second before speaking.

"This job is a little different from the other jobs I've done in the past. I assume that my remuneration will reflect the considerable risk I'm taking."

"Be assured my friend, if you pick Bowstead up and retrieve the computer disk you'll be rewarded beyond your wildest dreams," replied the voice. "Call again when you have the disk." The Guardian hung up. O'Connor slowly replaced the receiver on the telephone. He could not help smiling. Rewarded beyond his wildest dreams. Soon he would be rich, he thought to himself and his financial problems resolved.

O'Connor scribbled a note on a yellow Post-It which said he was following up a lead on the Harrods's shoplifter and expected to be out for the rest of the afternoon. He stuck it to the back of his chair. He made one call to the manager of the hotel he sometimes took prostitutes to and reserved a room on the top floor. If he did not find the disk in the girl's flat he would need a discreet place to work on David. He picked up his radio and walked off in the direction of the main entrance to the station, where he had parked the police Rover.

CHAPTER 17

The Mechanic held the hand gun flat in his right hand checking the weapon's balance. It felt good. More importantly it was untraceable. The serial number on the side of the gun had been patiently filed away and the handle, trigger and barrel of the gun were taped to prevent finger prints being left. The gun was small but could take a magazine of six bullets at a time. It was ideal for the Mechanic's needs.

"I'll also need five additional magazines, all taped and an effective silencer," he told the old Chinese man. The Chinese man nodded and went off towards a doorway at the far end of the small room that had a silk screen for a door.

The Mechanic was in the basement of a restaurant in China Town. A small restaurant that was not popular with the thousands of tourists who visit Soho and China Town each day or with the Londoners who venture into China Town for good sushi. The restaurant's clientele comprised the local Chinese who worked in and around China Town, drug dealers and the local Chinese pimps. It was grotty in appearance but the food was good. As well as catering to the local Chinese population the owner of the restaurant sold guns.

In England, unlike North America, it is actually quite difficult to get hold of untraceable weapons.

The Mechanic never travelled with a gun. If he was ever stopped it would certainly give him away. If he needed a weapon he would pick one up. He had made a point over the years of knowing where he could get hold of untraceable weapons in the major cities of the World. It was over five years since the last time he had visited the Chinese restaurant, but the old Chinese man had recognised him at once. It was in the gun dealer's best interests to remember his professional customers.

The old man reappeared from behind the silk screen with a box containing the additional items the Mechanic had asked for. The killer inspected the five magazines and the silencer. Again, the magazines had been taped and the central part of the silencer was also taped where it would have to be handled to be fitted to the gun. He nodded his approval as he tested the fit of the silencer to the hand gun. He had missed the opportunity to kill David twice already and he did not intend to miss again.

The Mechanic removed the silencer from the barrel of the gun and slipped it inside the breast pocket of his raincoat. He put the silencer and the magazines into each of the coat's side pockets. The gun and accessories were light and unnoticeable in his pockets. He nodded his approval again and took a bulging money clip from the back pocket of his trousers. This was not the kind of store that accepted credit cards. The hand gun, silencer and magazines cost five hundred pounds. The Mechanic paid in cash without comment.

He had to leave the restaurant by the same door he had used to enter it. He walked back up the stairs accompanied by the old man into the small restaurant area. There were a few Chinese men sitting around a table eating noodles and rice talking quickly at one another in Cantonese. They paid no attention to the Mechanic who slipped out of the restaurant.

The Mechanic had dumped the school teacher's Ford Sierra in an underground public car park behind Covent Garden. The chances were that it would not be discovered for days. London was not a city where a car was essential and in central London a car could be a positive disadvantage due to the heavily congested roads. The Mechanic headed back towards Covent Garden on foot. China Town is not far from Covent Garden. He needed a change of clothes and a shave. David had seen him at close quarters twice and would certainly recognise the Mechanic the next time the killer approached him.

At Leicester Square Underground Station the Mechanic spotted a small chemist's shop. The chemist's best selling item was film. Tourists poured in and out of the shop all day buying film for their cameras and postcards of the Royal Family. The Mechanic purchased a sachet of blond hair dye, a pair of plastic gloves and a pair of light reactive sunglasses. He asked for light reactive sunglasses in particular. The chemist had to fetch these from his store room. It was late November and there was little demand for sunglasses. The Mechanic also purchased a disposable razor and a canister of shaving foam. He paid in cash for the items then left the shop.

Next he went into Hackett men's wear on the outskirts of Covent Garden and purchased underwear, a white shirt with a button down collar, a blue tie and a new grey woollen suit. He also purchased a black cashmere overcoat. The suit the Mechanic preferred was, in the shop attendant's opinion, a little too large, but the Mechanic had insisted that he liked room to move in his suits and the attendant had said no more.

The Mechanic walked through the centre of Covent Garden carrying his purchases looking like any other shopper on a week day afternoon. He walked down on to the Strand in the direction of Charing Cross Station. He was oblivious to the beggars in the shop doorways who asked for his loose change. It had been some time since the Mechanic had been in this part of London and he was not sure if what he was looking for still existed. He did not have to walk far down the Strand before he saw that it did.

The Strand Palace Hotel is nicely nestled between theatres that open out on to the Strand. The doorman politely opened the door for the Mechanic and he walked into the old hotel. He stopped for a moment once he was inside the lobby. This place was ideal, he thought to himself. He walked up to the desk and made enquiries about a room. He was in luck. There were some single rooms available. He took one, paying in advance in cash for the one night he told the desk clerk he would be staying. He took the lift to the third floor and walked along the passage until he found room 318. He let himself into the hotel room and locked the door behind him as soon as he was inside.

The Strand Palace Hotel was ideal in the Mechanic's opinion. He needed somewhere to telephone the Guardian from and somewhere to change. He had no intention of spending the night at the hotel, but was confident that the desk clerk would not remember him if she was asked to describe the man who had checked in. The lobby of the hotel was chaotic. People of many different nationalities were in the lobby surrounded by suitcases, either waiting for tour buses to pick them up, or for tour guides to allocate them rooms. Amongst this confusion it was extremely unlikely that the desk clerk would remember a rather ordinary looking man who had checked into a single room.

The Mechanic looked at his watch. It was about time he called the Guardian. He did not know whether the Guardian would have been able to come up with anything since the last time he had spoken to him. He suspected that David had gone into hiding and that finding him again would not be easy. The Mechanic intended to track down what leads he had as soon as he had spoken to the Guardian. He was going to break into David's flat in Chelsea and turn the place over in the hope that he would be able to ascertain where David was most likely to go to hide. If he found nothing he would break into David's office during the night for the same reason. The second course of action was more perilous than the first, the Mechanic realised. He suspected that the law firm David worked for would have some kind of security system that he would have to overcome and might possibly be patrolled at night by guards. Nevertheless, he had few alternatives.

After showering and shaving he spent the next ten minutes working the blond dye into his dark hair with his fingers, bent over the small hand basin in the bathroom. The dye was the strongest the chemist had and the Mechanic wore the plastic gloves he had purchased to protect his hands and nails. The dye was not as effective on his dark hair as he would have liked. His hair did not turn blond. Instead it went a lighter shade of brown and became blotchy in places. His hair was cut conservatively short and he brushed it back from his forehead as much as he could, in a different style than before.

Next he put on the sunglasses. Because they were light reactive and there was not much light in the room the lenses were clear. They looked like spectacles. The Mechanic went back into the bedroom and looked at himself in the room's dress mirror. Although his hair looked a bit of a mess, with the glasses on he looked quite different from before. He smiled. David would not easily be able to recognise him.

The Mechanic checked his watch again. It was time to call the Guardian. He went over to the telephone and sat down on the bed. It was not comfortable but the Mechanic did not plan to sleep on it. Although it was over twenty four hours since he had last slept he was not tired. He had conditioned himself over the years to function effectively without much sleep.

He picked up the receiver of the telephone and read the instructions on the card by the side of the telephone which told the hotel's guests how to get an outside line. He dialled "9" for a line and then the Guardian's number. Since the last occasion on which he had called the satellite telephone the Mechanic had memorised the number and destroyed the piece of paper the number had been written on. He told the voice that came on the other end of the line the telephone number of the hotel which was printed on the instruction card and gave his room number, then the line went dead. He replaced the receiver and waited for the Guardian to call him back. A few minutes passed and the telephone in the room rang.

"Yes," said the Guardian over the satellite line to the Mechanic.

"I'm in a hotel in central London. You told me to call you," he replied. The Guardian had forgotten that the Mechanic had been told to call in. He had been distracted by the news that O'Connor had found David and the disk and was in the process of picking the young lawyer up. He wondered if he still needed the assassin, but knew better than to dismiss him before David was dead and the disk retrieved. He thought for a moment.

"We've located Bowstead," replied the Guardian. "A policeman who works for me knows where he's hiding out and is on his way to pick him up now." The Mechanic was annoyed that someone else had found David. This was one person he wanted to kill personally.

"I see," he said slowly. He waited to hear what the Guardian would say next.

The Guardian did not know how reliable O'Connor was. He had provided information in the past, but had never been entrusted with anything as important as this before. On the other hand the Mechanic had always been reliable.

"I want you to go to the house where Bowstead is hiding out," ordered the Guardian. "Watch the police pick him up. Follow the Detective to wherever he takes Bowstead. He will call me when he has Bowstead to himself. You can then take over. Get the disk and bring the damn thing to me here in Bucharest as arranged."

"And Bowstead?" asked the Mechanic.

"Kill the bastard," replied the Guardian. He did not know whether David had decoded the disk and read the Domino file but he could not afford to take any chances. He repeated his order slowly. "Kill him."

The Mechanic did not reply. His instructions were clear. Had the Guardian told him to spare David he would have killed him anyway and waived his fee for the hit. The Guardian wanted David dead and so did

166

the Mechanic. The Guardian gave the Mechanic Rebecca's address in Clapham and mentioned that David was with a girl. He was told to kill her as well if he had the opportunity to do so, but not to waste time if he did not. The Guardian thought that it was unlikely that she would know anything, but one more killing did not bother him and he could not be absolutely sure that David had not already told her everything. The Mechanic made a note of Rebecca's address on a small pad that was by the telephone in his room. As he put the receiver of the telephone down he pulled the copy of the "A to Z of London" he had with him from inside the large pocket of his raincoat. It took him a few minutes to locate Abbeyville Road where Rebecca's flat was situated. He ran his finger over the relevant page of the "A to Z" and found Clapham South Underground Station which was shown as the nearest Underground station, to Abbeyville Road. It was a little after 4:00 pm and the Mechanic knew that the traffic in central London would be starting to get heavy as the rush hour began. The Underground would be the fastest way of getting to David.

The Mechanic wasted no time at all. Quickly he took off the hotel gown he was wearing and threw it on to the bed. He put on the new socks and underwear he had bought from Hackett and ripped the new shirt from its packaging. The shirt was buttoned up. He undid the top three buttons and pulled the shirt over his head as if it were a sweater. He took the new grey suit from the Hackett's bag and put it on. Next, he pushed his feet back into his shoes and did up the laces. He stood in front of the mirror and tied his tie. He put the sunglasses back on and then stuffed his discarded clothes into the larger of the empty Hackett's bags. He emptied the contents of the pockets of his coat on to the bed, including the hand gun, spare magazines and silencer and placed the discarded coat in the Hackett's bag as well. He pulled the new black overcoat on and filled its pockets with the various items he had removed from his discarded coat.

In the bathroom he put the used razor and the canister of shaving cream in a small bin under the sink and flushed the empty hair dye sachet down the toilet. He collected the Hackett's bag from the bed and left the room, closing the door behind him as he departed. He walked quickly towards the lifts.

As he left the hotel he checked to make sure that the desk clerk who had checked him in did not notice him leaving. She did not. The Mechanic could see her at the check in desk struggling to deal with half a dozen or so Japanese tourists who had accidentally been double booked in the same rooms.

The Mechanic turned right out of the Strand Palace Hotel and walked down the Strand in the direction of Charing Cross Station. Just before the station he passed a McDonald's restaurant and turned left into Villiers Street. At the end of Villiers Street is Embankment Underground Station. There he could pick up the Northern Line to Clapham South Station. It was twenty minutes by Underground to Clapham from the Embankment

At the end of Villiers Street the Mechanic saw a dry cleaning shop on the opposite side of the road. He crossed the road and entered the dry cleaners. He emptied the contents of the Hackett's bag on to the counter and asked the attendant to have the items cleaned for him. The Mechanic was given a ticket and told that his clothes would be ready in three days time. He nodded and walked towards the door of the shop. Above the door a sign informed customers that if items of clothing were not collected within three months they would be disposed of. That suited the Mechanic. He would not be coming back.

He walked into Embankment Underground Station, purchased a ticket for Clapham South and passed through an automatic ticket barrier. As he walked down the stairs that led to the south bound Northern Line platform, he thought about how he would kill David.

CHAPTER 18

Detective Inspector Packard sat at his desk at Scotland Yard and studied the photographs in his left hand. There could be no doubt about it he decided, the man in the photographs was the Mechanic.

The photographs had been made from frames of film taken by an automatic surveillance camera situated in the Police Centre at Heathrow's Terminal Two. They showed the Mechanic running along the corridor of the Police Centre after another man and in two of the photographs the Mechanic had been captured snapping the neck of a young policewoman.

Packard had worked for Scotland Yard's Assassination Division for twelve years. The police simply refer to the division as the AD. It was a small, specialised division and Packard was the longest serving detective in the squad. The AD hunts down professional assassins who operate in the United Kingdom and investigates murders whenever it is suspected that the killer is a hired professional. Professional killers do not usually leave many clues at the scene of a murder and tracking them down is extremely difficult. Actually preventing them from carrying out their trade is rare. Although the AD is only small, its officers are well respected throughout Scotland Yard.

The photographs had been routinely passed to the AD because the police at Heathrow, after watching the video play back of the incident in the corridor of the Police Centre, suspected that the man who had killed the policewoman so quickly and effortlessly might be either a gang killer or a professional assassin. Packard knew that their suspicions were correct. Although he was older and his hair shorter than in other photographs the AD had, Packard recognised the man in the photographs as the assassin simply known as the Mechanic.

Packard had never personally met the Mechanic and had heard nothing of him for over five years, but it was his job to be familiar with killers of the Mechanic's calibre. The AD had files on hundreds of known or suspected professional assassins. The file on the Mechanic dated back some ten years. It contained a mixture of photographs that had been acquired over the years from various international agencies that do in other countries what the AD does in the United Kingdom. Not much was known about the Mechanic other than he was believed to be a South American, was extremely good at what he did and had never been caught.

Packard looked at the Mechanic's picture again and wondered what he was doing in England and why he had been inside the Police Centre at Heathrow. The only clue he had was the man in the photograph who the Mechanic appeared to be chasing. The police report which accompanied the photographs identified the other man as Mr. David Bowstead, a solicitor who had been attacked in the airport's car park, who had been in the Police Centre waiting to give a statement. The report went on to say that the Mechanic had been seen chasing David through the terminal building in the direction of the Underground where both men had been lost. David's flat in Chelsea had been checked but no sign of him had been found there. Packard could not think of a sensible explanation for the Mechanic being at the airport other than to kill Bowstead in these circumstance, but why he had no idea.

He had already checked the police computers to see if anyone called Bowstead or anyone matching David's description had turned up dead anywhere. No one had. He knew that this did not mean a great deal. If the Mechanic had already killed David and did not want the body to be discovered for months or at all, he was skilled enough to know how to ensure that the police did not find the body. For the time being at least, Packard had decided to treat the enquiry as a murder prevention operation on the basis that David was still alive, rather than a murder investigation which it would become if David turned up dead.

He had checked a legal directory Scotland Yard kept in its library and soon established that David was employed by Holland Chapman & Co. Although Packard had not come across Holland Chapman & Co., in his professional capacity, because the firm did not practice crime or murder, he was aware that the firm was one of the oldest and most successful of the City litigation practices. He had telephoned the firm's Senior Partner a few minutes earlier and had briefly explained that he suspected that David was in hiding and that potentially his life was in danger. The Senior Partner had been reluctant to discuss David's whereabouts or his business in Miami over the telephone and had asked Packard if he would go to Holland Chapman & Co's offices to discuss things with him face to face. This had been fine with Packard. Other than David, he had no leads.

Packard slipped the new photographs of the Mechanic into the file on the assassin and stuffed it inside his briefcase. As he walked out of his office through the building down towards the car park behind Scotland Yard, he thought of the dead policewoman. The report said she had been in the Police Force for less than four months.

Packard drove himself. He was a senior officer and was entitled to be driven when on duty but rarely took advantage of this. He was forty five years old, had a wife and two sons, the eldest of which had started at university studying modern languages two months earlier. Packard had originally been in the Army. As a sergeant he served for a year in Northern Island at a time when hostilities were rife. He was cited twice for bravery and won his battalion's Marksman Trophy four years in a row. He was shot whilst on patrol in Belfast. He had dismissed the shooting as an occupational hazard of being a solider, even joking about the bullet wound in his right side. His wife however, could not come to terms with the possibility that her husband might be killed either in Northern Island or elsewhere whilst on active service. She put him under considerable pressure to leave the Army and pursue a safer career. Eventually, she succeeded and Packard retired from the Army without a pension. He was still a young man.

Although his wife had been able to persuade him to leave the Army, she was unable to persuade him to become a bookkeeper or a manager. Three months after leaving the Army Packard joined the Police Force. At first his wife was worried for his safety and wanted him to leave. He would hear nothing of this and in time she learnt to accept the fact that her husband was a policeman. Packard was as very good policeman. The same down to earth manner that had made him an effective soldier made him a reliable, impressive police constable. He was quickly promoted and after five years in uniform was invited to take the Detective's examinations. He did so and passed with honours.

He was applauded by his superiors for being a thorough investigator. He solved a number of murder cases as a young detective which more experienced officers had given up on. Before long he was invited to apply for a job with the AD at Scotland Yard. This was a great opportunity for Packard. The typical period a detective is assigned to the AD for is five years. The work is difficult and most of the time not very exciting. Within the Police Force however, it is accepted that officers who have spent time with the AD are of the best in the Force. After five years at the AD most detectives are rapidly promoted, some to the very top of their profession.

After five years at the AD Packard had not applied for reassignment or for promotion. After seven years there his superiors invited him to leave and take on a murder squad elsewhere. Still Packard stayed. The following year he was promoted and left the AD for three weeks. After three weeks in charge of an division of officers at Special Branch he applied to be reinstated as a Detective Inspector at the AD. This required a technical demotion. The AD welcomed him back and he was once again a Detective Inspector. However, the AD continued to match the higher salary he had enjoyed for the three weeks of his promotion.

Since Packard's reinstatement at the AD he had not been invited to apply for other jobs outside the AD. He was regularly offered promotion within the AD at Scotland Yard which would take him out of the area of detective work. He turned all positions down. He was where he wanted to be. He had become the most experienced assassination detective in the Force and the police brass knew it. Officers assigned to work for him emerged from the AD as considerably better detectives than when they joined. He had created a unique position for himself and intended to stay at the AD until he retired in five years time.

As he drove along the embankment into the City, Packard tried to figure out what David could be involved in that had resulted in someone hiring the Mechanic to kill him. The Mechanic was a professional killer. As far as the AD knew killing was his sole occupation. He was after David and that could mean only one thing. Someone with a great deal of money and power wanted the young lawyer dead. Packard needed to establish why and he hoped that the man he was going to see would be able to help.

Forty five minutes after speaking to the Senior Partner of Holland Chapman & Co. on the telephone, Packard pulled into the law firm's private car park. He was expected and a security guard opened the door of his car, directed him inside the building and explained that his car would be parked for him.

Packard rode one of the lifts to the fourth floor of the building and stepped out into the firm's main reception area. He gave his name to one of the immaculately dressed receptionists and explained that he had an appointment to see the Senior Partner. He was not kept waiting for long.

Robert Metcalf had been the firm's Senior Partner for three years. He was regarded as one of the finest solicitors in London and was well respected by his peers in the other City firms. He greeted Packard with a firm handshake and escorted the Detective Inspector to his office which was near reception. Metcalf offered Packard tea which he politely declined before asking how he could help Scotland Yard and David.

"That's not exactly clear yet," replied Packard. "As I explained earlier today, the AD has been provided with a series of photographs of an incident that took place at Heathrow Airport this morning. Mr. Bowstead is seen in the photographs being chased by a man." He handed the photographs to Metcalf.

"That's David alright," said Metcalf as he studied the photographs. "Who's the other man?"

"A professional assassin known as the Mechanic, I'm afraid to say," answered Packard. Metcalf was visibly shocked by this revelation.

"A professional assassin chasing David through Heathrow Airport," said Metcalf in disbelief. "Are you sure Detective, that David is being chased in these pictures?"

"Absolutely certain," replied Packard. "These pictures are extracts from a film that was made by a surveillance camera at the airport. From the film it is clear that Mr. Bowstead is being chased by the man we know as the Mechanic. Do you know where Mr. Bowstead currently is? You mentioned on the 'phone that he was expected back today but had not shown up yet."

"He was expected back from a business trip this morning, so his secretary tells me, but he has not come into the office yet. But there is nothing unusual about that Detective. David is a senior assistant here and we don't keep tabs on him. He could be at his home?"

"Unfortunately he isn't," replied Packard. "The police checked his flat this morning as soon as he was identified from the photographs. His neighbours have confirmed that he has not been seen all day."

"I see," said Metcalf. Packard continued.

"We have no doubt that Mr. Bowstead is being pursued by the

Mechanic, who will kill him if he has an opportunity to do so." Packard wanted to add, "if he has not done so already," but decided this would be unnecessarily dramatic. "Can you tell me what he was doing in Miami? It's possible that his business there might in some way be connected to the Mechanic."

Metcalf sat up in his chair. "I very much doubt that Detective. We don't come across the type of litigants who hire killers to bump off either their own lawyers or the opposition's lawyers."

"Nevertheless Sir, what was Mr. Bowstead up to in Miami?" asked Packard. Prior to Packard's call, Metcalf had not even known that David was travelling on business. His firm was large and the lawyers who worked there travelled frequently. In anticipation of his meeting with Packard, Metcalf had spoken with Mike Henderson who had sent David to Miami. Henderson explained that David was taking a fairly routine witness statement from a client called Garces and hopefully would be collecting a cheque in respect of unpaid fees. Metcalf passed this information on to Packard.

"Doesn't sound very exciting," said Packard after Metcalf had finished.

"I agree."

"Is Mr. Bowstead involved in any other case which might shed some light on why a professional killer is trying to kill him?" asked Packard bluntly.

"He's got a pretty conventional practice," replied Metcalf. "Shipping, insurance, commodity trading and some oil work I believe. As far as I'm aware Detective, none of my lawyers are involved in cases that are likely to get them killed." Packard looked up from his note pad and politely nodded to Metcalf.

"Could you let me have details of Mr. Garces. He might have information that is helpful."

"Of course," said Metcalf. He picked up the receiver of one of the two telephones on his desk and dialled his secretary's extension. He asked her to get Mr. Garces's address from Henderson and bring it into him as soon as she had it.

"Thank you," said Packard when Metcalf had put the receiver down. "What can you tell me about Mr. Bowstead? It might help me find him if I know something more about him." Metcalf gave Packard a potted history of David's life, so far as he could. He explained that both of David's parents were dead, that David was not married and had no children. Metcalf described David with some pride as being one of the best litigation solicitors of his generation in the City. He could not imagine David getting involved in anything perilous either deliberately or inadvertently. In Metcalf's opinion he was just too sensible.

Metcalf's secretary lightly knocked at the door and came in interrupting him. She handed her boss a single piece of paper and then left without saying a word. Metcalf inspected the details on the sheet of paper before handing it to Packard.

"Garces's address and 'phone numbers in Miami," he said.

"Thanks," replied Packard as he took the sheet of paper from Metcalf. "If Mr. Bowstead calls you or any of his colleagues, it is crucial that he is told to stay where he is and call my office at once. We'll pick him up straight away. I can't stress how much danger he will be in if the man who is looking for him discovers where he is."

"I understand Detective," replied Metcalf. I'll arrange for him to be put through to me personally if he calls the office irrespective of who he asks to speak to."

"Good," said Packard. He handed Metcalf his card. "If he does contact you tell him to call me on the number on the card. He'll be able to reach me twenty four hours a day."

"Of course," replied Metcalf. "If there is anything else we can do at all let me know will you."

"I'll keep in touch," replied Packard. "Just tell him to call me if you speak to him." Metcalf nodded as he stood up to escort the Detective Inspector back to reception. The two men shook hands and Packard got into one of the lifts. Once the lift was on its way, Metcalf hurried back to his office and closed the door behind him. He made two calls. The first to Mike Henderson who he asked to come and see him straight away and the second to his secretary. He told her to arrange an emergency Partners' meeting at once.

Packard drove back to Scotland Yard. He had hit the start of the rush hour coming out of the City and his progress was slow. On balance he was fairly confident that whatever David was involved in was probably unrelated to Holland Chapman & Co. However, the young lawyer was involved in something. Something that could get him killed if he did not get to David before the Mechanic did. Packard needed to speak to David to fit what pieces of the jigsaw puzzle he had together. He looked at the stationary traffic around his car and hit the top of the car's steering wheel with his hand in frustration.

"Where the hell are you David Bowstead?"

CHAPTER 19

David stood slightly behind Rebecca as she opened the door to her flat. She lived in a flat in an old town house on Abbeyville Road in Clapham that had been converted into three separate flats years earlier. David knew the area. When he first moved to London he had shared a flat in a house not unlike this one with three other trainee lawyers. Rebecca's flat was in a nicer part of Clapham than the flat he had once rented. Her flat was on the ground floor of the house.

The vast majority of the smart 1920s built London houses have been modernised and converted into flats over the years, as the demand for more affordable, but comfortable accommodation has increased. Rebecca's flat was the result of such a house conversion. Accommodation in London is limited. Generally, whether a person chooses to buy a property or rent the position is the same. He can live in a flat in a converted town house like Rebecca, a flat in a mansion block like David, a new flat in Docklands or he can live further out of town in somewhere like Blackheath, mortgage himself to the hilt and buy a three or four bedroom house ready for when he starts a family. Which of these options a person chooses does not solely depend upon how much money he has at his disposal. Younger people tend to prefer to live as close as possible to central London. Fulham, Chelsea, Battersea and Clapham have become particular favourites for the young professional set and the price of property in these areas reflects this trend.

David followed Rebecca into her flat. He closed the door behind the two of them and hesitated over the bolt. He wanted to lock the door but was concerned that this might frighten her. Reluctantly, he decided against bolting the door and followed Rebecca along the small corridor into the sitting-room. The two had hardly spoken since David had thanked Rebecca in the taxi for helping him escape from Harrods. David was wet from the rain and his black hair was matted to his forehead. The room was a little cold.

"Why don't you take your jacket off David," suggested Rebecca, as she went over to the gas fire on the other side of the room and lit it. David saw the flames leap up the chimney and instinctively moved closer to the fire to warm himself. He took his jacket off and noticed how torn and battered it had become by the events of the day. "I'll make some tea," continued Rebecca. "Are you hungry David?" David was very hungry. He was beginning to relax for the first time since he had been approached by the Mechanic in the airport car park that morning and as he relaxed he felt his stomach ache for sustenance. He had not eaten all day.

"Actually, I'm starving," he replied smiling at Rebecca. She smiled back at him.

"Let me see what I can rustle up." Rebecca walked out of the room. She shouted from the kitchen. "Whilst you're waiting you might want to dry off. There are towels in the bathroom at the far end of the hall." David did want to dry himself. He followed Rebecca's directions and found the bathroom. As he walked through the flat he noticed how stylishly the hall way and rooms were decorated. Assuming Rebecca rented the flat, he thought that whoever owned the flat had good taste and some money.

David dried himself off with a towel he found in the bathroom. He looked at his reflection in the bathroom mirror. He looked terrible. His hair was a mess, he was unshaven and dark stubble was prominent across his chin and neck. His eyes were a little bloodshot from lack of sleep and his lower neck was visibly bruised. As he considered the sight before him in the mirror he was surprised that Rebecca had even bothered to help him in the store room let alone bring him back to her flat to shelter from the rain. He looked like a tramp. David thought Rebecca was not only beautiful, but also very kind.

He replaced the towel on the bathroom rail and went back to the sitting-room. On the table in the centre of the room was a large silver tea pot with steam slowly winding its way towards the ceiling from the opening of the spout. He saw cups, sugar, milk and croissants that David knew were piping hot from their delicious smell. There was also honey, jam, butter scones and cream. Rebecca was sitting on the settee. When she saw David she picked up the pot and poured two cups of steaming hot tea. The pot was so huge in her small hands that David was concerned it might slip and she would be scalded, but she manoeuvred the tea pot around the table with considerable skill and without spilling a drop of tea. David sat down in the armchair opposite her.

"Thank you," he said as Rebecca handed him a cup of tea. "You have a beautiful flat. Do you share it with anyone?"

"No I live here by myself," she replied as she offered David a plate with two croissants on it. He took the plate and tucked in. "To tell you the truth," she continued, "after years of girls dormitories I love coming home to the privacy of my own place."

"I know what you mean," said David. "I was at boarding school for years myself. How long have you rented this place?" he asked.

"I thought you British considered it bad manners to ask questions like that of strangers." David cringed.

"Yes we do," he said. "I didn't mean to pry, I'm sorry." Rebecca laughed.

"Don't worry, I'm always asking questions that I shouldn't be," she said. "Actually I own the place. I bought it just under two years ago."

"It's lovely."

"Thanks. I am rather proud of it," Rebecca replied. David took a moment to properly look around the room he was in. It was lovely. The settee and armchairs were covered in a luxurious fabric that toned in perfectly with the curtains and carpet. At one end of the room was a small antique writing desk and a sideboard with some photographs on it that David was not able to make out from where he was sitting. At the other end of the room there was a large television and a hi-fi system, bookshelves crammed with books and an elegant tall lamp. The centre piece of the room however, was a large mirror that hung over the fireplace. The frame of the mirror was a yellow and gold colour that twisted like a rose bush at each corner. It was quite magnificent.

Since he had first heard her speak, David had been aware of something unusual in Rebecca's accent. He heard it again as she offered him more tea and told him to help himself to the food on the table. He remembered what she had just said.

"You said, you British just then. Are you not a native of this great country of ours?"

"No. I'm from that even greater country over there," Rebecca replied, pointing to her left and smiling at David again. David looked confused. "You know the one, it's called America. I'm a second generation yank," she explained. "My father's clan escaped to the States just before the war when he was a boy."

"You're an American?" David was truly surprised.

"That's right. You know, we don't all live in Oklahoma," she joked.

"Of course," said David. "It's just that you sound, well so English." Rebecca grinned triumphantly.

"I should hope so after all the money my father spent educating me over hear. Other than school holidays when I was a child and a few trips home during the last few years, I haven't really lived in the States since I was nine years old." David saw a sadness momentarily overcome Rebecca's face as she told him this. She pushed her blond hair back behind her ears and sipped from her cup. "But I love London," she said a moment later.

"Your family are still over there?" asked David.

"Just my father. My grandparents died before I was born and my mother's dead."

"I'm sorry."

"Oh that's OK, she died when I was a child." David was a little embarrassed. He was sitting in Rebecca's flat asking her personal questions about her family when she was being so kind to him. David's own parents were both dead and he would not like it much if a total stranger started asking him questions about his deceased mother. He wanted to change the subject.

"What is it that you do at Harrods?" he asked.

"I have a small catering company," she replied. "Sometimes I do lunches for their executives."

"You have your own business," he said. "Well if you're ever in need of a lawyer my services are at your disposal. I have a considerable debt to repay you."

"You're a lawyer?" said Rebecca, trying not to sound as surprised as she was.

"Yes, I'm a solicitor with a firm in the City."

"Then neither of us are what we first appear to be," said Rebecca.

David grinned. She was absolutely right. He looked anything but a City solicitor at that moment. There was a pause in the conversation before Rebecca spoke.

"What are you running from David?" she asked in a gentle voice. Talking to Rebecca, David had temporarily been able to ignore the predicament he was in. Her question brought reality crashing back down on top of him. He looked across at his jacket which was hanging over the back of a chair in front of Rebecca's writing desk and thought of the computer disk and remembered the Mechanic and O'Connor. The feeling of safety he had slipped into as he talked to Rebecca was gone. He put the cup he was drinking from back on the table and stood up.

"Rebecca. You've been very kind to me, but I think I should go," he said.

Rebecca saw the look of fear in David's eyes again. She stood up.

"David, don't go, I want to help you," she said in a hurry as he walked over towards his jacket. She looked at him. Her look was full of sympathy and compassion and her face was beautiful. The two of them had not known one another for very long, but David felt something when he looked at Rebecca that he could not rationalise. A feeling he had almost forgotten.

"No," said David. "I'm in serious trouble. Men are trying to kill me and I don't know why. Even the police are trying to kill me. It's a miracle that I'm still in one piece. I won't let you expose yourself to that kind of danger Rebecca. I can't." To Rebecca, David appeared vulnerable and scared. She didn't want him to leave, but did not know why exactly. Somehow she wanted to help him.

"Where will you go David?" Rebecca said firmly. "You look so tired. Please, at least rest for awhile before you leave." David stopped and looked at her again.

"I am tired," he said as if he was admitting this to himself. "But Rebecca, if the men who are after me find me here they might hurt you as well."

"How will they find you here, David?" she asked. "We've only just met, by accident really. No one knows where you are, how could they? Get some sleep and leave in the morning when you have rested." David could see the sense of what Rebecca suggested although he was surprised that she was so insistent that he stay. She was right. He had nowhere to go and the afternoon was wearing on. He had not slept for over twenty four hours and was exhausted. Surely she was right, he thought to himself, no one could possibly know where he was. He took a step back and sat down in the armchair again.

"Thank you Rebecca," he said. "I'll leave first thing in the morning."

"You're welcome," she replied. Rebecca could not take her eyes from David's eyes. For a moment the two of them looked at one another. They did not speak. They did not need to at that moment.

Rebecca was the first to break the silence. "I have to pop out. I have some errands that I need to run. I won't be long. Why don't you get some sleep and I'll wake you when I get back and we can have dinner. You can tell me whether I have a future in the catering business or not."

"I could use some sleep, if that's OK," he replied. Rebecca showed David to the spare room. He was ready to collapse and sat down on the bed. It was still light outside and Rebecca drew the curtains.

"I'll be as quick as I can," she said. "Promise me you'll be here when I get back."

"I'll be here. Asleep most likely, but here," he replied. Rebecca pulled the door of the bedroom closed behind her as she left. Five minutes later she was walking up Abbeyville Road towards Clapham Common. The rain had stopped but it was still cold.

David lay on the bed and closed his eyes. Although Rebecca had drawn the curtains the room was not completely dark. Chinks of light could be seen through gaps in the curtains which partly lit the bedroom. David was not disturbed by this though. He turned over on to his left side to make himself more comfortable. Next to the bed David saw a small bedside table. On it was a lamp and a telephone. He stared at the telephone for a few seconds then looked at his wrist watch. The hands were slightly illuminated. It was 4:45 pm. Holland Chapman & Co. would be bursting with activity until well after 9:00 pm. Even after nine, there would inevitably still be lawyers there preparing for Court applications the following morning or dealing with clients who eat breakfast when the British are eating lunch.

David had been thinking of calling someone at his office for help since he had escaped from Harrods. His employers were influential men whom he trusted completely. He needed to discuss the mess he was in with someone who could help. He thought of Mike Henderson. After all, if Garces had not made him miss his original flight David reasoned, he would never have met the Planner and would never have come across the computer disk.

David sat up and swung his legs over the side of the bed so that he was facing the telephone. He lifted the receiver and dialled the number of Holland Chapman & Co. The line rang. David hesitated for a moment then replaced the receiver in a hurry. He needed to decide what he was going to say. He considered that Mike Henderson would know that he had not made it into the office that day, but would think nothing of this. David would have to recount all of the events of the day, starting with the Planner's heart attack on the aeroplane. He decided that he would start there. The Planner and his computer disk, as far as he could see were the keys to the entire puzzle.

He re-dialled the number of the firm and waited for a telephone operator to answer.

"Good afternoon, Holland Chapman & Co.," said one of the operators after a few seconds.

"Mike Henderson please," asked David. He did not expect the receptionist who answered his call to recognise his voice. The firm was too large for that.

"Who may I say is calling?" asked the receptionist.

"David Bowstead."

"One moment please, I'll connect you." David waited what he suspected was more than the usual amount of time clients of the firm were expected to wait.

"Come on," he murmured impatiently under his breath.

"David, its Robert Metcalf. Are you alright?" David had expected to hear the familiar voice of Mike Henderson. Instead he had somehow been put through to the firm's Senior Partner.

"Robert?" asked David. "I wanted Mike Henderson."

"I arranged for your call to be put through direct to me David," replied Metcalf. Now, are you in one piece?"

"Yes." David was confused.

Metcalf continued.

"David, where are you? I know all about it. Tell me and I'll have the police pick you up immediately." David did not answer. He did not understand what was going on. What did Metcalf know and how? He felt uneasy with Metcalf's questions.

"David, can you hear me? Where are you? I need the address of where you're calling from." Still David did not say anything. "I've spoken to the police, a Detective called...." David had hung up the receiver of the telephone before he heard the rest of the sentence. He jumped out of bed and ran into the sitting-room. Oh God, he thought, O'Connor has got to the firm.

As he calmed down he realised how stupid he had been to call Holland Chapman & Co. He had escaped from Detective O'Connor in Harrods, but O'Connor knew his name and it would be simple to find out where he lived and worked. O'Connor could have told the firm anything. His call might even have been traced. David estimated how long he had been on the telephone. Not long. He had some experience of telephone call tracing and did not think he had been on the line long enough for a trace to have been completed. Nevertheless, he had made a mistake. He cursed himself out loud. He would have to be more careful than that if he was going to stay alive.

He drew the curtains in the sitting-room and went to the door of the flat and slammed the bolt into place. He felt trapped. Not just in Rebecca's flat, but in London. David realised that he was now truly on his own. Whoever it was who wanted the disk had powerful friends and had the police, or at least some of them in his pocket. The partners of the firm had been got to as well. David had only one friend in all of this. Rebecca. She was the last person he wanted to expose to any danger.

He sat down in the armchair. His tiredness had passed. He was too on edge now to sleep. He could not be sure if he was safe in Rebecca's flat. Part of him wanted to leave at once, but he had promised Rebecca that he would be there when she got back from wherever it was she had gone. He was also worried about Rebecca and wished she would hurry up and return to the flat.

David had some good friends in London, mainly other solicitors and barristers and a few friends left over from his university days. He was reluctant to call any of them in case he exposed them to danger. In any event, he was not sure how they could help him.

He needed a safe place to hide. Somewhere he knew well, but as far away from London as possible, where neither the police nor the Mechanic would be able to find him. He also needed answers to the questions he had. The answers were on the disk. David was sure of that.

He considered his options and then decided. First a safe place to hide for a few days and then the disk.

It was five o'clock. The remains of the food Rebecca had prepared earlier were still on the table in the centre of the room. David was hungry and picked up the last scone. For the first time he noticed that the table was actually an old wooden sea chest. A square piece of glass had been placed over the top of the chest so that it could be used as a table. The effect worked well in the sitting-room. As he leant over the table to reach for the last of the cream to spread over the scone, he noticed something on the top of the old sea chest. An engraving at the front of the lid of the chest that could be seen through the glass. It was an ornate carving which David was not able to make out at first. As his eyes became accustomed to the style of the letters he saw that it was a word. The engraving read "Bobinski".

David's attention was diverted by the sound of a key in the door to the flat. He got up and ran to the door.

"David open up quickly, it's me Rebecca." He undid the bolt and opened the door. Rebecca hurried in. "Lock the door," she said.

"What is it?" asked David.

"There are police cars parked outside," replied Rebecca. David went to the curtains in the sitting-room and looked from the side of one of the curtains out of the window. It was getting dark already outside, but the street lights made it possible to see the road and the pavements clearly. David looked up and down Abbeyville Road, but could not see any police cars.

"I can't see anything out there." Rebecca came to the window and looked herself.

"No," she said. "Around the corner out of sight. I walked passed them on the opposite side of the road on my way back."

"How many cars and men?" asked David.

"One car to start with," she said, "but a second car, a Rover I think pulled up just as I was walking past."

"Around the corner," said David. "Then they might not be after me." He looked at Rebecca unsure what he should do.

"I recognised the man in the back of the second car, the Rover," she said. "It was the fat Detective who was looking for you in Harrods."

"Are you sure?" asked David.

"Yes," she replied. "He turned sideways to get out of the car and I had a clear view of his face."

"O'Connor," said David as he collapsed into the armchair.

O'Connor was smoking a cigarette. It was the eighth he had lit since leaving Knightsbridge Police Station. November days in England are short and although it was just approaching 5:00 pm it was already getting dark. O'Connor had arrived by himself. He was anxious to restrict the number of officers who became involved in the arrest and on this occasion had driven himself to Clapham. He joined the Constable who had chased David through Harrods and two other policemen who had been sent to Harrods after David had escaped to help with the questioning of the security guards. The young Constable had assumed control of the situation in the absence of O'Connor. He was enjoying himself and was getting on the other policemen's nerves. His authority came to an end with the arrival of Detective O'Connor.

"Is he in there?" O'Connor asked the Constable.

"We're not sure Sir," he replied. "As you ordered, we've been keeping pretty much out of sight. I walked passed the girl's flat ten minutes ago and saw someone close the curtains in the front window. It looked like a man."

"He's in there alright," said O'Connor confidently. O'Connor pictured himself on a Caribbean beach with a young woman with very long legs. He decided he deserved a holiday.

"Shall I radio for back up Sir?" asked the Constable enthusiastically. He was surprised that O'Connor had not arrived with half a dozen officers in view of the fact that David had already escaped from them once.

"No," said O'Connor firmly. "The four of us will be able to take him." The last thing he needed was more policemen to get rid of once David had been picked up. O'Connor looked up and down the street. The location was perfect. A quiet area off a main road.

He told the constables to follow him. They walked to the end of the road and rounded the corner into Abbeyville Road. O'Connor hesitated and looked at the young Constable to point the right house out to him. Rebecca's flat was in a house not very far along Abbeyville Road and O'Connor was able to see the window with the drawn curtains that the Constable had referred to. Although it was getting dark most of the curtains in the other windows in the houses along the road were not drawn yet. Their occupants for the most part were either still at work or were beginning to make their way home.

Rebecca had been correct, thought David, it was O'Connor. He could see the overweight Detective through a gap in the curtains from the sitting-room. He could also see the black and yellow all weather jackets of three other policemen. This time O'Connor had more men with him. David hurried over to the writing desk and pulled his jacket from the back of the chair and began to put it on.

"David, what are you doing?" shouted Rebecca.

"I have to get out of here fast," he replied.

"Don't be stupid," said Rebecca taking the firm sensible tone she had taken with David when he had wanted to leave the flat earlier that afternoon. "The whole area is probably crawling with policemen by now. You won't make it past the garden gate." David knew that she was right, but he could not just sit in the flat and wait for O'Connor to kick the door down. He turned sharply to face Rebecca.

"What else can I do Rebecca, but run?" Rebecca thought for a moment. She went to the curtains and peeped out of the window herself. She could see O'Connor crouching behind a bush to the right of the house. He was trying to keep out of view but the small bush was not able to mask his vast bulk.

"Come with me," she said to David. She took him by the hand and led him along the corridor to the bathroom he had dried himself off in earlier. She pulled a cord and the room filled with light. Rebecca opened the mirrored cabinet that hung above the sink and took out a canister of shaving foam and a packet of disposable razors. David watched bemused. Rebecca noticed the expression on his face.

"I keep them for when my father visits," she said not looking at David. "Shave you beard."

"What?" said David in a tone that betrayed his surprise at her command. "Rebecca this is no time for you to worry about my appearance." Rebecca put her hands on David's shoulders.

"Trust me, please," she said in a soft tone. She ran out of the room shouting "Shave, shave David."

He looked at the shaving tools Rebecca had placed on the edge of the sink and picked then up. He turned on the cold water tap, smeared shaving foam across his chin and neck and began to shave.

By the time David had finished shaving Rebecca had returned to the bathroom. She took David by the hand and practically dragged him into the spare bedroom. On the bed was an assorted heap of clothes.

"Take you jacket, shirt and trousers off," insisted Rebecca. David's mouth fell open. "David, you're right. You must run. But not as David

Bowstead. As a woman." David looked at the clothes on the bed and realised what Rebecca was saying. They were women's clothes. He started to undress.

"Will your clothes fit me?" he asked. Rebecca was substantially smaller than David.

"These aren't mine. I found them here when I moved in. Whoever they belonged to was a big girl, a lot bigger than me. I think they'll fit you just about."

Rebecca was right. The clothes did fit David. Rebecca left the room and David pulled an old tweed skirt over his legs. He found a pair of thick hockey socks amongst the pile on the bed and put them on. Rebecca returned carrying a bra and a roll of cotton wool.

"You won't pass as a woman without breasts," she said. Rebecca stuffed the cups of the bra with the cotton wool and helped David put the bra in place across his chest. Unfortunately, the straps were not long enough to fasten across his back. Rebecca fetched a ball of string and a pair of scissors from the kitchen and using the string secured the bra in place. David put a white frilly blouse on over the bra and buttoned it up. The blouse was too small for him but he was able to do up all but the top three buttons. The stretched blouse exaggerated his artificial bosom considerably.

The previous occupant of Rebecca's flat had not left any shoes behind and Rebecca's shoes were far too small for David's size ten feet. He made do with his own black brogues.

Rebecca led David into the bathroom again and sat him down on the toilet seat. She produced a bag of make up and dabbed blusher on his cheeks and smeared bright red lipstick over his lips. She stood back to inspect her handy work.

"Not bad," she said, "but one thing is missing." She rummaged around in one of the storage cupboards in the bathroom and found what she was looking for. A wig of curly blond hair.

"I always knew this thing would come in useful one day," she said. "I bought it years ago for a fancy dress party, but it was so big for me that in the end I didn't wear it." She positioned the wig on David's head and checked to make sure that no strands of his black hair could be seen.

"Well, you're certainly not the prettiest woman I've ever seen," said Rebecca when she had finished, "but I think you might just fool them in the dark." David stood up and looked at himself in the mirror. She was right he thought, in the dark he might just be able to slip past O'Connor and the other policemen without them seeing through his disguise.

"You'll need a shawl and a bag for your own clothes unless you intend staying dressed like that," said Rebecca half smiling.

"No," said David. "I'll take a bag if you can spare one." Rebecca fetched a tartan shawl from her bedroom and draped it over David's shoulders. David felt that it was made of cashmere.

"I can't take this Rebecca," he said.

"David you need to cover your face. The make up helps, but if anyone looks too closely they'll see that you're a man. Pull the shawl up around you head as you go out." David nodded and thanked her.

Whilst David collected his own clothes from the floor of the spare bedroom Rebecca searched for a bag.

"I'm not much of a bag person myself," she said as she walked back into the bedroom. "This is all I have that's big enough". She handed David a yellow and green duffel bag with "SOUTH BEACH" and a picture of a dolphin printed across it. "I know, it's horrid. My father got it for me the last time I was in the States. I've tossed some fruit in the bottom in case you get hungry again."

"It's fine," replied David as he stuffed his jacket and other clothes inside the bag and pulled the cord that closed the mouth of the duffel bag tight. He walked ahead of Rebecca into the sitting-room and looked around the side of one of the curtains out of the window. He could see O'Connor talking to another officer half hidden by a bush and saw a third policeman on the pavement opposite Rebecca's flat, squatting down behind a parked car. It was time he left.

David turned to Rebecca. "I must leave," he said softly.

"I know," she replied. "Where will you go?"

"I have to get out of London. My parents' place in Shropshire I think." David paused for a moment.

"Rebecca, I can never thank you enough for everything you've done for me. You've been so kind." Rebecca smiled, but was unable to answer him. She put her hand in the pocket of her trousers and pulled out a twenty pound note.

"Take this," she said offering the money to David, "it's all I've got on me."

"I can't," said David instinctively. Rebecca pressed the bank note into David's hand.

"You can pay me back the next time I see you." He took the money and stuffed it in the top of one of the hockey socks. Rebecca followed him to the front door of the flat.

"Turn left out of the house and you'll eventually come to the common," she said.

"I will, thanks."

David went to turn the door knob but stopped. He looked down at Rebecca and she looked up at him. They both took a small step closer to one another. Rebecca's face was full of expectation. David thought again how beautiful she was. Without saying anything he bent forward and gently kissed her on her lips.

The door opened and he was gone.

"Take care," whispered Rebecca, as the door closed behind him.

O'Connor was instructing his men where to take up position. He had sent one of the constables around to the back of the house in case David tried to make a run for it when Rebecca's flat was entered and another was in position on the other side of the road should David get past O'Connor and the remaining constable and emerge from the front door of the old converted house.

O'Connor did not know the layout of Rebecca's flat and was briefing the young Constable who would accompany him into the house on how he wanted the flat to be secured once the two of them were inside. He told the Constable that once they were inside he would deal with David and that the Constable was to take care of Rebecca. Suddenly, O'Connor stopped talking and withdrew further behind the bush that was partially hiding his body. O'Connor and the Constable were twenty feet away from the front door of the house but had a clear view of the steps up to the entrance and of the large black door itself.

O'Connor saw a heavily built lady in a long thick skirt walk from the doorway on to the top step. She was wearing a thick scarf around her face and other than for a mess of curly blond hair he could not see her features clearly. O'Connor noticed her thick legs and the hockey socks she was wearing and turned back to the Constable to complete his instructions. He was not interested in looking at a woman with bad legs.

David walked down the steps as daintily as he could. Once, when he had been at school he played a woman in a school pantomime and he tried to recreate the female walk he had practised for weeks before the opening night. He remembered what Rebecca had said and kept the shawl up around his head as he walked down the steps and turned left when he was on the pavement. His heart was pounding as he walked away from the house. He wanted to break into a sprint, but knew that would alert O'Connor to his disguise. He walked as slowly as he could without turning around, expecting to feel O'Connor's hand on his shoulder with every step that he took.

He had walked about thirty yards when he heard the sound of rapid footsteps somewhere behind him. He looked around and saw too men running up the steps to the front door he had moments earlier closed behind him. David quickened his pace as he approached a turning off Abbeyville Road. Once he was around the corner and out of sight of Rebecca's flat he ran as fast as he could to the end of the road, his heart beating furiously and adrenalin pumping through his body as he ran. At the end of the road he saw a taxi dropping off an elderly man. As he approached, the taxi began to pull away. David shouted for the driver to wait and he heard the screech of the taxi's brakes. He got into the taxi and told the driver to get going. David looked out of the back of the taxi as the driver followed his fare's instructions and saw that he was not being followed. The pounding of his heart began to slow and he slumped forward in the seat. He thought of Rebecca and hoped that she was alright.

"Where to Miss?" asked the taxi driver.

"Euston," replied David.

As soon as David was gone Rebecca went into the sitting-room and over to her writing desk. She rummaged around in a drawer until she found a key ring with two keys on it. She took the key ring and let herself out of her flat, pulling the door firmly shut behind her. Quickly, Rebecca ran up the stairs in the hall way to the second floor of the house and fumbled to get the keys into the locks of the second floor flat. Once the door to the flat opened Rebecca went in and quietly closed and bolted the door behind her. It was dark in the flat, but she did not turn the lights in the corridor on. Instead she waited for her eyes to become accustomed to the dark and then gradually walked away from the door.

The man who owned the second floor flat worked as a broker in a bank in the City. He often came home late in the evenings having been out after work for drinks with colleagues. He had a habit of losing his keys and had asked Rebecca if she would keep a set of keys to his flat just in case he came back a little drunk one evening and was unable to let himself in. Rebecca liked her neighbour and had agreed.

O'Connor considered that surprise was crucial. He had already lost David once and could not afford to risk losing him again. The Constable forced the lock on the main door of the house with a police standard issue crow bar he had brought with him from the trunk of one of the police cars. The door lock came free easily. O'Connor had been told that Rebecca lived in the ground floor flat and he and the Constable proceeded to the door of the flat. The Constable expected O'Connor to knock on the door or produce a warrant, but he did not. Instead he ordered the Constable to force the door to Rebecca's flat.

As the door came free of the bolt, O'Connor ran inside shouting "police," at the top of his voice. He was followed by the Constable. O'Connor inspected each of the rooms in turn, but found no one. He cursed loudly and kicked over a chair in the sitting-room. He could hardly believe that David was not their. Both he and the Constable climbed the first flight of stairs to the next floor and knocked at the door of the first floor flat. The door was opened by a woman in her mid thirties. O'Connor brandished his identification card and demanded to know if the woman had seen Rebecca or a man fitting David's description that afternoon. She said she had not. O'Connor asked if he could take a look in her flat and in spite of being slightly afraid of the large Detective the woman invited him in. He inspected her flat with only a little more caution than he had displayed in Rebecca's flat, but again found nothing. He walked out without thanking the woman for her cooperation.

O'Connor was furious. Where could David be hiding, he thought to himself as he climbed the final flight of stairs to the second floor of the house? O'Connor knocked loudly at the door of the second floor flat and waited for the door to open. It did not. He knocked again and shouted that he was the police. Still the door remained closed. He knelt down and pushed the letter box flap back with a finger and looked through the hole. The flat was dark and he could not see much.

He thought of forcing the door, but knew that the Constable would become highly suspicious if he did. He did not have a warrant and there were clearly no lawful grounds for him to forcibly enter the second floor flat. He bashed the door with his fists and shouted that he was the police one last time before giving up, pushing past that Constable and hurrying down the stairs. He had lost David again and he knew it.

O'Connor called the other constables into Rebecca's flat and they searched for the computer disk that O'Connor told them had been stolen from Harrods. The constables were surprised that O'Connor was expending so much energy to recover a computer game, but they could all see how angry the Detective was and no one said anything or asked any questions. The search turned nothing up. Not only had O'Connor lost David, he had failed to recover the Planner's disk.

After the search of Rebecca's flat had been exhausted, O'Connor lead the constables out of the flat back to the police cars. His vision of himself on a Caribbean beach with a long legged woman had dissolved. All that he could think of was the Guardian.

CHAPTER 20

The Mechanic was thinking about the peculiar looking woman he had seen leaving the converted town house minutes before the police had forced open the main door.

He had been hiding in the back seat of a parked car thirty yards along from the house that Rebecca's flat was in. His hiding place was ideal. He could not be seen, but had an excellent view of the road and the front of the house. The Mechanic had watched O'Connor and the constables leave the house without either David or Rebecca. From the way in which O'Connor had furiously marched out of the house, the Mechanic was certain that the Detective had not found the computer disc either.

The curtains in the ground floor windows had twitched a few times since the Mechanic had been observing the house as if someone was occasionally peeping out of the windows. He had reasoned that either David or Rebecca were in the flat and had been confident that O'Connor and his men would pick up at least one of them during the raid. As the fat Detective emerged from the house empty handed the Mechanic thought of the woman who had left the flat fifteen minutes earlier. He recalled her size and how awkwardly she had walked down the steps from the front door of the house. There had been something else about her. The Mechanic remembered that she had been wearing what had looked like a pair of men's black shoes. At the time he had not thought this suspicious. Now the truth struck him. He realised that he had watched David walk out of the house disguised as a woman. He clenched his fists tightly. He had missed David again.

The Mechanic waited in the parked car for ten minutes after O'Connor and the constables were out of sight before emerging from his hiding place. He walked quickly towards the front door of the house. The door was closed but the lock had been ripped from the door frame by the Constable's wrench. He was able to push the door open and walk inside the house. He knew which of the flats belonged to Rebecca and without hesitating silently approached the door of the ground floor flat. The door to Rebecca's flat was closed but the Mechanic could see a thin line of light around the door where it was slightly ajar. O'Connor's rough entry tactics had broken the door latch and bolt with the result that the door would not close completely.

The Mechanic carefully pushed the door open and stepped into the small hall way. He opened the door just enough for him to walk through the gap. Once he was inside, he pushed the door closed behind him. Other than the faint sound of the draught excluder at the foot of the door rubbing along the carpet in the hall way as the door was opened and then closed, the Mechanic made absolutely no sound as he entered Rebecca's flat.

He walked along the corridor inspecting each room he passed in turn, but saw no one. At the end of the corridor he looked into the sitting-room. Rebecca was at her writing desk at the far end of the room with her back to the Mechanic. She had returned to her own flat once she had seen O'Connor and his colleagues walking back to their cars. She had not heard the Mechanic enter her flat.

The Mechanic silently approached Rebecca. As he walked towards her he pulled his hand gun from the inside pocket of his overcoat and holding it in his right hand pointed it towards Rebecca's head. When he was only a few feet away from Rebecca he grabbed her hair with his other hand and dragged her back off the chair she was sitting on down to the floor, so that her face was firmly pressed against the carpet.

Rebecca was momentarily disorientated then felt the pain across her scalp. She was about to scream when the cold metal of the hand gun pressed against the back of her neck and she froze.

"Make a sound and it'll be your last bitch," whispered the Mechanic into Rebecca's ear. Rebecca was too scared now to even cry. She made no sound at all. "Good," said the Mechanic. "Now, where did David Bowstead go?" She remained silent. The Mechanic slid his left hand across Rebecca's small head and with hardly any effort at all suddenly turned her over on to her back by sharply twisting her head as easily as if she were a doll. He grabbed her by the neck and put his thumb on her throat and applied some pressure. The barrel of the hand gun remained pressed against her head.

Rebecca looked into the Mechanic's eyes as he repeated his question and was terrified. She said nothing.

The Mechanic pressed down on her throat and Rebecca struggled a little but realised that it was no use. The Mechanic was much bigger than she was and the more she tried to move the more difficult it was for her to breath.

"Last chance bitch. Tell me where he's gone and I'll kill you quickly. If you don't tell me, I'll hurt you real bad and then kill you slowly." The Mechanic's face showed no emotion as he threatened Rebecca. She knew that he meant what he said. Still she said nothing.

The Mechanic waited for a few seconds and then pulled Rebecca to her feet. He hit her hard across the face with the back of his right hand and Rebecca's body went limp. Her lips exploded and she saw blood splash across the room on to one of the walls. She would have fallen to the floor from the blow had the Mechanic not stopped her from doing so. As her body went limp he took hold of the top of the denim shirt she was wearing and violently ripped the front of the shirt open, exposing her naked breasts and stomach. He ran the barrel of the hand gun over her left breast before hitting her across the face again. This time he let her fall to the floor.

Rebecca could feel her face throbbing from the blows and her right eye was beginning to close. She wanted to scream for help, but was too afraid. She lay on the floor coughing a little and pulled her ripped shirt over her breasts. She could not bring herself to look at the Mechanic's face.

He walked around to Rebecca's side. Some of her blood had got on his cashmere overcoat and he methodically wiped it off with a handkerchief. As Rebecca started to pant less and breath more easily the Mechanic kicked her in the stomach. The blow caused Rebecca to double up in pain. The Mechanic bent down and placed the tip of the hand gun on Rebecca's forehead.

"Where's Bowstead?" he demanded. She said nothing. The Mechanic ran his left hand down over Rebecca's breasts and stomach whilst he held the hand gun to her forehead with his other hand. Her body tensed as he touched her and he twisted the end of the hand gun hard into Rebecca's forehead to remind her that if she moved too much he would shoot. He slid his hand inside the top of her trousers, turned his hand over so that the back of it was pressed against her groin, and yanked open the top of her trousers. The Mechanic ripped the material open beyond the restraints of the zipper and rubbed the palm of his hand aggressively over her underwear. "Where is Bowstead?" he demanded again without looking at Rebecca's face.

Rebecca was in tremendous pain. Her stomach and head were hurting from the Mechanic's blows. She trembled as the Mechanic ran his hand over her body. She realised with horror that her attacker was going to rape her. Her eyes filled with water as she tried not to cry, afraid that if she did the Mechanic would shoot her in the head. She thought of David and said nothing.

The Mechanic turned Rebecca over on to her stomach and violently ripped her underwear off. She began to cry. He took hold of her hair and hit her across the side of the head with the barrel of the hand gun.

"First you'll feel my cock inside you bitch, then you'll feel a bullet in your head." The Mechanic put his hand under Rebecca's bottom and yanked her on to her knees whilst the top half of her body remained bent over by the force of the Mechanic's arm.

He roughly moved his hand over Rebecca's bottom and around her groin. With each touch she felt sicker and became more afraid. It had become more than she could bear. She did not want the Mechanic inside her. He was hurting her and was going to violently rape her. Knowing that terrified Rebecca even more. She heard the sound of a zipper being pulled and closed her eyes. She thought of David and wanted to be brave, but this was just too much for her to bear. She felt the Mechanic's penis moving across her groin as it was guided by the Mechanic towards her vagina.

"His parents' house," sobbed Rebecca. "He's going to his parents' house." Although she had only spoken softly the Mechanic had heard her. He had been listening should she decide to talk. Rape was just another weapon in his arsenal.

"Where?" was all that he said in response. Rebecca could feel the Mechanic's penis still moving across her bottom towards her vagina and realised that this disclosure alone was not going to stop him.

"Shropshire," she said. "He said Shropshire."

"Where in Shropshire?" demanded the Mechanic. Rebecca had

started to cry. She tried to stop her tears and speak.

"He didn't say. All he said was that he was going to his parents' house in Shropshire," she sobbed.

The Mechanic stopped, then moved back off Rebecca. She heard his clothes rustle and she collapsed on to the floor in tears. She was relieved for a moment that she was not going to be raped, until she appreciated that she would now be killed. She saw the Mechanic's shoes appear in front of her and she looked up. He stood over her holding the hand gun in one hand and the silencer in the other.

He saw that Rebecca was looking up at him and kicked her in the jaw as if he was kicking a football. The blow knocked her back and more blood spurted from her face. Both of her eyes were swollen and her vision was quite blurred, but she could see the Mechanic slowly screwing the silencer to the barrel of the gun. Despite the pain she was in, she was unable to take her eye's from the gun and the silencer. The Mechanic seemed to move in slow motion. She lay on the floor waiting to be killed.

"Beccy are you in there? What's happened to your door?" The voice came loudly from the landing of Rebecca's flat and the Mechanic and Rebecca heard the door open and footsteps approach the sitting-room. "Sorry Beccy, but I've locked myself out again," continued the voice from the landing.

The Mechanic was startled by the voice in the hall way. Furiously he screwed the silencer to the end of the hand gun. Rebecca's neighbour walked into the sitting-room just as the Mechanic got the silencer in place. He saw Rebecca lying half naked on the floor, her face resting in a pool of her own blood. He saw the Mechanic lift the gun towards him and heard the faint sound of the gun as a bullet was fired from it through the silencer. Rebecca's neighbour managed to move before the bullet hit him with the result that the bullet, which was destined for his head, clipped his ear instead.

He charged the Mechanic as the second bullet pierced his skin. This time the bullet went into his stomach but as he fell he crashed on to the glass top of the table in the centre of the room, catapulting the large tea pot that Rebecca had served David tea from earlier into the air. The lid came off the pot and cold tea sprayed around the room as the tea pot spun through the air. The Mechanic's aim was disrupted by the liquid that splashed across his face, so that his third bullet hit Rebecca in the leg and his fourth bullet buried itself in the wall behind her. He cursed in a language that Rebecca did not recognise.

The crash had been loud and unnerved the Mechanic. He had been in the flat far too long. He decided that it was time to leave before the crash of the table and the tea pot brought more of Rebecca's neighbours out of their flats. Indiscriminately he fired the last two shots of the magazine in Rebecca's direction as he ran from the sitting-room out of the flat. The first of the two shots broke a window, the second missed Rebecca entirely. It hit her neighbour in the back of the head, killing him instantly.

CHAPTER 21

David regretted that he had taken a taxi from Rebecca's flat to Euston Station as he paid the driver. The eleven pounds fare seriously depleted his already modest financial resources. He was still dressed as a woman and was given a few odd looks as he walked into the station.

The first thing he did when he got to the station was go to the Men's toilet and take off the woman's clothes he was wearing and wash Rebecca's make-up from his face. He emerged from the toilet a man again, but carried his disguise in the duffel bag in case he had need of it again. The computer disk was still in his jacket pocket.

David could not be certain that he was safe and as he walked through the station towards the ticket office he looked around for the Mechanic or O'Connor.

It had been a long time since he had taken the train to his parents' house in Shropshire. When he had first moved to London before he had a car, he often travelled to visit his parents by train. He had not made the journey by train for over five years.

David needed a ticket to Shrewsbury. From there he would have to catch a bus to Chesterton, the village in which his parents' house was situated. He queued for a ticket and when it was his turn to be served discovered with horror that he did not have enough cash on him to buy a one way ticket. The price had increased considerably in the last five years, but even on the basis of the price he used to pay he was over ten pounds short. He apologised to the attendant and walked away from the ticket window. He looked at the large computerised timetable board that hung above the entrance to the platforms and searched for the departure time of the next train for Shrewsbury. There was a train leaving at 7:15 pm. David checked his watch. It was 6:50 pm. He looked at his watch again and then ran out of the station.

He ran along Evershot Street away from Euston Station looking for a vaguely familiar turning. He stopped at the corner of Doric Way and surveyed the scene. It looked familiar. He turned and ran quickly down Doric Way. Almost at the far end of the road David saw what he was looking for.

Years before he had been to a small shop near to Euston with a friend from university. The friend had asked David to help him carry a double bass to the shop, which did not have a case. The friend had pawned the double bass to the shopkeeper and with some of the proceeds had bought David a few pints of beers at the pub at the end of the road to thank him for helping to carry the large, cumbersome instrument halfway across London.

A bell rang as David pushed open the door of the shop and the shopkeeper appeared behind the counter. He was eating something wrapped in paper and David saw steam rising from the indistinguishable meal. This was the kind of shop that stayed open all hours.

David pulled back the sleeve of his jacket and un-clipped the strap that held his watch in place on his left wrist. He slid it off without saying a word. The shopkeeper watched David slide the watch from his wrist as he chewed. He lifted his head to indicate that David should put the watch down on the wooden counter. David understood and placed the watch on the counter in front of the shopkeeper. It was a Swiss made, solid silver Longines. His parents had given it to him the day he had qualified as a solicitor. It had cost them over a thousand pounds.

"Fifty quid," said the shopkeeper in between stuffing more steaming food into his mouth. David was surprised. Not having bought the watch himself he did not know exactly what it had cost, but he had a pretty good idea of its value.

"Fifty pounds," he repeated, sounding surprised. "It's a handmade Swiss watch. Totally water resistant with a life time guarantee. It would cost five hundred pounds at least in any Bond Street jewellers." The shopkeeper stuffed the last morsel of food into his mouth, screwed the paper it had been wrapped in into a ball and tossed it on the floor behind the counter as he chewed and then swallowed.

"It might be worth five hundred pounds in Bond Street," he replied, "but here it's worth fifty quid. Take it or leave it." Crumbs spilled from his mouth as he spoke. David noticed the time showing on his watch. It was almost 7:00 pm.

"I'll take it," he said.

The shopkeeper handed David five battered ten pound notes and he hurried out of the shop. He ran all the way back to Euston Station as quickly as he could. The duffel bag on his back slowed him down a little and twice he almost discarded it. He was back in the ticket office by 7:10 pm and purchased an Economy Class single ticket to Shrewsbury. It cost him twenty four pounds. He took the ticket and ran out of the ticket office. His train was departing from platform fifteen and David saw people showing their tickets to an inspector as they walked on to the platform. He did the same and boarded the train by the first door he came to, only moments before a whistle blew and the train began to pull out of the station.

He had boarded by a door in the First Class section of the train and had to walk through six carriages before he reached an Economy Class carriage. He collapsed into the first empty seat he found and stuffed the duffel bag down between his legs, on to the floor. The carriage was only half full and the seats next to and opposite his were empty.

Through the window he saw the station disappear as the train gained speed. He relaxed a little. He felt safer leaving London and was confident that no one would find him in Chesterton.

As a child, whenever David had not been at boarding school he had been in Chesterton. It was the only home of his parents he could remember, although he had already been three years old when his father had bought the old country house. The house stood in three acres of land in the centre of a small village about eleven miles outside of Shrewsbury. Appropriately, the house was named Chesterton House after the village. There were only four other houses in the village.

David had loved Chesterton House and the surrounding countryside when he had been growing up. He had learnt to horse ride in one of the fields behind the house at the age of seven, first learnt to drive a car in the same field at the age of twelve and had made love for the first time one summer in the field when he was seventeen years old. His sister had been born in the house and eight months after his father had died in hospital, his mother had passed away quietly one night in the same room in which she had given birth to his sister years earlier. Over the years, before his parents had died, David had enjoyed many very happy times at Chesterton House. Since his parents had died however, he had only been back to Chesterton on a few occasions, the last time being at the end of the summer.

David no longer enjoyed staying at Chesterton. The old house reminded him of his mother and father and of happier times in his life. He knew that he should really sell the place. That was certainly what his sister wanted to do, but for some reason every time he got around to speaking with local property agents about selling, he could not bring himself to put the house on the market. The time would come when the house would have to be sold, but as much as David no longer liked spending time at Chesterton, the house was all he had left of his parents and so far he had not been able to bring himself to sell it. As the train hurtled along the tracks out of London, he was relieved that he still had the house.

The journey to Shrewsbury would take almost three hours. David was tired but unable to sleep. Every time he closed his eyes he imagined the Mechanic creeping up on him and slitting his throat whilst he slept. He went over the events of the day in his mind again trying to make some sense of the situation he was in. He knew that the disk was important to someone, but did not know why. Even if he was able to get to a computer that had a disk drive he realised that he would not be able to access whatever information was stored on the disk without knowing the Planner's password. This frustrated David. Although he was caught up in the middle of something dangerous and his main concern was to stay alive, he knew that he would not be able to run and hide forever and was certain that the key to the mystery was the disk. Somehow he would have to decode the disk and access whatever was on it. That was a tall order. David was proficient with a computer, but he was not in the code breaking league.

The train slowed to a stop at Northampton Station and three people in David's carriage prepared to get off. Soon the train was off again. David felt safer when the train was moving.

He thought of Rebecca and wondered if he would ever see her again. She had been so kind to him. He smiled as he thought of himself in her wig dressed as a woman. She had been right. Without her disguise O'Connor would have caught him at her flat and by now he would probably be dead. Under his breath David prayed that she was alright and that he would see her again.

He was getting hungry. Thinking of Rebecca he remembered the fruit she had put in the duffel bag for him. David took the bag from under his feet and pulled it open. He searched around inside with his hands but could not feel any fruit. He emptied the contents of the bag on to the table in front of him and searched through the clothes. Entangled in the tweed skirt he discovered two apples and an orange. David bit into an apple immediately and felt some of it's moisture drip down his chin. He put the other apple and the orange to one side and holding the apple he was eating between his teeth, started to stuff the clothes back into the bag.

As he stuffed the tweed skirt inside the bag he caught sight of something at the bottom of the bag. David was curious. He pulled the skirt out again and turned the bag upside down. Nothing dropped out. He turned the canvas bag inside out and discovered a photograph stuck to the inside bottom of the bag. It was a polaroid, the kind which develops automatically in the camera within moments of a photograph having been taken. David guessed that the front of the photograph must have still been damp and sticky when it had been dropped in the bag and had become stuck to the base and forgotten about. Carefully, he peeled the photograph from the bag and turned it over to see the picture. What he saw surprised him.

It was a picture of Rebecca with her arms around a man. The photograph was grubby around the area of the man's face and David could not make out his features. Rebecca was wearing a swimming suit and by her feet was the duffel bag she had given to him with "SOUTH BEACH" and a picture of a dolphin printed across it. David wiped the photograph clean on his sleeve to reveal the man's face. He could not believe what he saw as the picture he was looking at became clear. In the photograph Rebecca had her arms around the waist of the Planner.

He stared at the photograph for a long time trying to understand what it meant. At first he could only fathom that it was some kind of trick, but soon realised that was impossible. As David thought, it became clear to him that there could be only one explanation. Rebecca was the daughter the Planner had proudly boasted about on the flight from Miami. It all fitted he realised. The Planner had told him that his daughter had a catering company and lived in south London. That she was pretty and full of life. Rebecca had told him she cooked at Harrods and had mentioned that she sometimes visited her father in Florida. And now there was the photograph. Rebecca was the Planner's daughter.

David tried to recall exactly what the Planner mumbled to him before he had died. He had been worried for his daughter David remembered and had said she should use the disk to protect herself. There was something else that the Planner had said, but try as he did David was unable to recall what it was.

By pure coincidence David had literally bumped into the Planner's daughter in Harrods and had had no idea.

He felt sorry for her. Rebecca's father was dead and she did not even know.

He wondered if she was in danger. He had so many questions and hardly any answers.

David looked at the photograph of Rebecca and her father again. They were both smiling in the picture. He guessed that the photograph must have been taken by someone else on South Beach in Miami. He slipped the photograph into the inside breast pocket of his jacket and sat back in his seat. He so desperately wanted to talk to Rebecca. He wanted to tell her that she would be alright and that he would protect her. But he was stuck on a train rushing away from London and did not even know Rebecca's telephone number or full address. David closed his eyes and saw Rebecca.

The train finally pulled into Shrewsbury Station five minutes behind schedule at 10:10 pm. David got off quickly and hurried to the exit. He went to the first telephone he saw and dialled the number for Directory Enquiries in London. He asked the operator for the telephone number of Rebecca Adams and gave her address as Abbeyville Road, Clapham, London. The operator told David that the number he wanted was listed as ex-directory and that she could not give it to him. He pleaded that it was a matter of life and death, but the operator was firm. She could not divulge Rebecca's telephone number to him. Angrily, David hung up the receiver and cursed British Telecom for its efficiency.

He walked out of the station. It was cold and a light drizzle was falling in Shrewsbury. David crossed over the road and made his way towards the bus station. There he waited for a bus going to Bridgenorth via Chesterton. He had to wait for half an hour in the cold before a bus he could take pulled into the bus station. He sat at the back of the bus. He wanted to be able to see everyone who got on and off. The bus pulled out of the station with him as the only passenger. The driver drove through Shrewsbury town centre stopping it seemed to David every hundred yards or so to pick people up. By the time the bus had cleared the town it was over three quarters full. It was 11:00 pm and people were beginning to make their way home from the pubs. David was careful not to catch anyone's eye. He did not want to see someone who might recognise him. He did not want anyone to know that he had left London.

Most of the passengers who had boarded the bus in Shrewsbury got off at the various stops on the outskirts of town. By the time the bus pulled over at the stop nearest to Chesterton Village, there were only a handful of people still left on the bus on their way to Bridgenorth. No one got off the bus with David. He stood on the side of the road and watched the bus pull away. He watched until the bus's lights were out of sight.

David looked around. There were no street lights along the road which ran through acres of fields, but the moon was quite bright despite the drizzle and he could see well enough. He picked up Rebecca's duffel bag and started to walk. After three or four minutes he turned off the main road on to a narrow road that had no markings. The road was just wide enough for a car to drive along. It was the only road into Chesterton. David knew this road well. He had walked and driven along it many times. On this occasion he walked the mile and a half to the village. It was a little after 11:40 pm as David approached Chesterton House. He could not see any lights in any of the houses in the village.

He opened the gates that led into the driveway of his parents' house and walked up to the kitchen door. The front door was actually at the back of the house and could not be accessed easily from the village road. When David got to the kitchen door he put his hand up and felt around the rim of the door frame. He touched a long thick key and pulled it off the frame. He caught it as it fell to the ground. He unlocked the kitchen door and entered the house. Security had never been a problem in the village. David's father had always said that if a burglar was determined enough to find the village and negotiate the track in the dark no lock in the World would keep him from the family silver. In fact in all the years that David's parents lived there they had never once been burgled.

The kitchen was dark and cold. He felt along the wall until he came to a drawer. He pulled the drawer open and felt inside for candles and matches. He lit a large candle and the room instantly filled with a dim light. David did not want to turn the lights on in the kitchen in case a neighbour noticed that someone was in the house. He took a saucer from the sideboard and pressed the base of the candle to the centre of the saucer until it stuck firmly.

The kitchen was clean and tidy. David paid a lady who lived in the next village to come into the house once a week and make sure it was clean. She also generally kept an eye on the house for him when he was not there, which was most of the time.

David sat down in a large wooded high backed chair which stood at the head of a long kitchen table. He was shattered and for the first time since he had been at Rebecca's flat that afternoon felt he could sleep. His eye lids began to close and before he could stop himself he was asleep.

He dreamt of Rebecca.

CHAPTER 22

The Mechanic worked quickly and quietly inside David's flat. After Rebecca had divulged that David was on his way to his parents' house in Shropshire, the Mechanic had made his way by taxi to David's flat. On the way he had purchased a pocket torch at a petrol station. David's flat was in a mansion block not far from the King's Road in Chelsea. It had taken the Mechanic less than a minute to pick the two locks that secured the main door of the building and the door to David's flat and let himself in. Like many Londoners, David had never got around to fitting an alarm inside his flat.

The Mechanic searched for the address of David's parents' house in Shropshire. First he reviewed the layout of the flat. It was a typical smart Chelsea two double bedroom flat, with a separate dinning room and a smaller single bedroom which David used as a study. The Mechanic had started his search in the study. He had been through David's desk thoroughly, but had found no address book or details of the house in Shropshire. The Mechanic suspected that David kept most of his private papers at his office.

He searched both of the double bedrooms and again found nothing. The dinning room was searched next but the Mechanic came across no clues as to where David might have gone. Finally, he walked into the kitchen and looked around the room. The flat's kitchen was quite large with a bench that peeled from one of the walls into the centre of the room. It was an impressive feature, but did not interest the Mechanic.

At the far end of the kitchen, built into the wall was a huge fridge freezer. The doors of the fridge were littered with decorative magnets which secured a range of bills, taxi cards and other scraps of paper. The Mechanic carefully inspected each of the bills in turn. He paused for a moment over an electricity bill stuck under a magnet in the shape of the West Ham Football Club insignia, before ripping it from the fridge, sending the magnet to the floor.

The bill was from the Shropshire Electricity Board. It was addressed to David Bowstead at his London address, but was stated to be in respect of electricity used at Chesterton House. The full address of Chesterton House was given on the bill including the post code. The Mechanic smiled to himself and folded the bill in half and placed it in the inside breast pocket of his suit. It was time he called the Guardian again.

The Guardian had been too worried to eat dinner and was not in the habit of sleeping when things were going wrong. The events of the day had not gone to plan and he was concerned. He had been contacted by O'Connor earlier in the evening and had been told that neither David nor the disk had been found at Rebecca's flat in Clapham. It seemed to the Guardian that David, the girl and the disk had all disappeared without trace.

He sipped again from the large balloon of cognac he cupped in his hand. He pondered his options in the circumstances. He had to decide whether or not to give the order to his people to abort Operation Domino whilst it could still be aborted. It was not an easy decision. Operation Domino, if executed properly, and the Guardian did not doubt the Planner's scheme, would reap approximately half a billion dollars for him in no more than six months. The Operation's success would secure the Guardian's retirement once he left Romania, in the style he craved. He would be accepted as a tycoon throughout the World with wealth and power beyond his wildest imagination. He had spent months preparing for Operation Domino and the Planner had made it clear in his report that if the Operation was not executed on one of the three specified dates, the opportunity to virtually guarantee Romania's membership of the European Community would not exist again for some time and possibly never again.

The Guardian had no fall back or contingency plan in case Operation Domino was aborted. He had not anticipated any complications. The

Planner was dead and the Guardian knew of nobody else who had the appropriate skills who he could trust to put together a fool proof alternative plan. Even if he was able to find a replacement for the Planner, the Guardian realised that it could take months for an alternative operation to be devised. The position he was facing in Romania was getting worse. The President was becoming more unpopular every day and the Guardian was not certain that he would be able to keep the President in office for very much longer in the face of overwhelming criticism of his economic record. If he was replaced as leader of Romania before the country was admitted into the European Community, his successor might not support a renewed application for Protected Membership and the Guardian's ambitions would be scuppered completely.

Against this the Mechanic considered the danger to the Operation and to himself if David had already managed to access the information on the disk. If David passed the information to the right authorities the Guardian knew that the Operation would be defeated. So far however, it appeared that David had either not accessed the information on the disk, or if he had, had not given it to the authorities. The Guardian's international sources assured him that details of Operation Domino had not been passed to any of the appropriate European agencies. If details of the Operation ever got out, either before or after the Operation was executed the Guardian knew that he would be hunted throughout the World for the rest of his life and would be unable to enjoy the money he intended to steal from the Romanian treasury. For the Guardian to get away with his plan, no one could ever find out that he was behind what was about to happen.

The Guardian considered David. The young lawyer had stumbled into his affairs. He had the disk and was on the run that much the Guardian knew, but did David know what information the disk contained? The Guardian struggled with this question. The more he thought things through the more he became convinced that he could risk David being in possession of the disk and on the run whilst there was still time to track him down and kill the lawyer, but could not afford to take this risk in circumstances where David had vanished with the disk without trace on the very eve of the Operation. His main concern was that David could stay hidden until after the Operation had been executed long enough to figure out what had actually happened and then pass the disk to someone who would be able to decode it and gain access to the details of Operation Domino. The information on the disk would then read as the Guardian's epitaph.

Grudgingly, relying on the survival instincts that had kept him alive for so long, the Mechanic decided that he had no alternative but to abort Operation Domino.

As he slurped back the rest of the cognac in frustration his aide hurried into the room and told him that the Mechanic was waiting on the satellite telephone.

The Guardian took the receiver from the telephone operator in the basement of his mansion and placed it to his ear.

"What news?" was all that he said. The line remained silent for longer than usual. Then the Guardian heard the familiar voice of his hired assassin.

"Our David Bowstead is smart," said the Mechanic slowly. "I watched him slip right passed your tame policeman this afternoon."

"You saw him get away?" replied the Guardian in a startled tone.

"He's only escaped temporarily," said the Mechanic. "I know where he's gone to hide." The Guardian was momentarily speechless.

"Are you sure my friend?" he asked, not wanting to sound too relieved.

"He's on his way to his father's house in a place called Chesterton in Shropshire," replied the Mechanic. "And I'm right behind him." A wide smile appeared across the Guardian's face. There was still time to retrieve the disk before the Operation had to be carried out. He regained his composure.

"Excellent," he said confidently. "Then we are still on schedule. Kill him. No more games. Is that clear?"

"He's as good as dead," replied the Mechanic.

As soon as the line went dead the Mechanic slipped out of David's flat as quietly as he had entered it. It was approaching midnight and the inhabitants of the mansion block were asleep. Before leaving the flat, the Mechanic had consulted a copy of the Yellow Pages he had found in David's study and had noted the addresses of three all night executive car hire companies in the Chelsea area. Within minutes of leaving David's flat the Mechanic was in the back of a taxi heading towards the offices of the nearest company. He had no time to sleep if he was going to catch up with David before daybreak.

He estimated that it would take him less than three hours to get to Chesterton if the car hire company had a fast car available.

Packard looked at Rebecca. She did not look very pretty. He was in South Western General Hospital, in south London. After the Mechanic had left her flat, Rebecca had crawled over to her neighbour, only to find that he was dead. She had hardly been able to get to her feet. She had managed to pull the telephone in her sitting-room off her desk on to the floor by it's cord and had dialled 999 and asked for the police and for an ambulance. She had explained that her friend had been shot. The police and an ambulance arrived within ten minutes of her call. Rebecca waited motionlessly for them to arrive. She was holding the telephone receiver in her hand and was still trembling with fear when the police eventually burst into her flat.

She had calmed down a little by the time the medics were ready to zip her neighbour into a black body bag. Rebecca watched them carry his body passed her out of the flat and knew that if he had not entered the flat when he had done, she would have been killed. She described every detail of her attacker to the police and they listened intently.

The Mechanic's description was fed into the country's National Police Computer within twenty minutes. Detective Inspector Packard's current assistant detective was comparing Rebecca's description to the photographs of the Mechanic taken at Heathrow that morning, less than an hour later. Other than Rebecca's description of the Mechanic's hair colour, her description matched the photographs. Rebecca's statement that her attacker had fixed a silencer to his gun before using it, told Packard that he was a professional and all of the Detective Inspector's instincts told him that the man who had attacked Rebecca Adams was the Mechanic.

Rebecca was in considerable pain when she had first been admitted to hospital. She had two broken ribs, a bullet wound in her left leg, a broken cheek bone and a badly bruised right eye. She had been given strong pain killers by the duty doctor which had made her fall asleep. Packard sat next to her bed waiting for her to wake up. It was a little before midnight and although he was anxious to talk to Rebecca, he did not try and wake her. In his opinion she had been through a lot and deserved to rest.

Packard waited at Rebecca's bedside for over an hour before he heard her groan and watched her gradually wake up as the effects of the pain killers began to wear off. He stood up so that she could see him without having to move her head.

"How do you feel Rebecca?" he eventually asked when he saw that she was awake.

"How do you know my name?" she replied as her eyes focused on the middle aged man standing at the side of her bed. Packard produced his identification card and carefully displayed it in front of Rebecca's face. "Oh," she continued, "you're with the police."

"Sort of," he answered.

"I've already given a full statement to you guys as well as a description of the maniac who attacked me," she said turning her head to one side as she tried to make herself more comfortable. Her body ached and she felt sick.

"I know," replied Packard. "I'm here about David Bowstead." Rebecca turned her head around suddenly to face Packard on hearing David's name.

"What about David?" she asked. "Is he OK?"

"I don't know Rebecca," replied Packard honestly. He's caught up in the middle of something bad, really bad, but I'm not sure what it is or even if he's still alive." The frankness of Packard's words shocked Rebecca. She had realised that David was in some kind of trouble and after she had been attacked that some pretty serious people were after him, but the rational way in which Packard summarised David's predicament made her even more scared for him.

"I was hoping that you might be able to help me find him Rebecca," continued Packard. "You did see him today didn't you? That's why you were attacked?" Packard was half guessing and half detecting. The only thing that had linked David to Rebecca before Packard had spoken to her was the Mechanic. However, Packard had deliberately mentioned David's name to gauge Rebecca's reaction. Her reaction had confirmed that she knew David. Packard was guessing though that she had seen David earlier in the day.

Rebecca considered Packard. David had not trusted the police. She had helped him slip past O'Connor and the other police constables. If David had a reason to be afraid of the police, Rebecca had no intention of disclosing his whereabouts to a Detective Inspector, no matter how polite he might be.

"I know David," she said finally. "We've been friends for years, but I haven't seen him for a few weeks." Rebecca moved awkwardly in the hospital bed. Packard had been lied to hundreds of times before and could not recall having heard a less convincing story than this. He took a small flip pad and a pen from one of the pockets of his jacket as if he was going to take routine notes.

"How long exactly have you known Mr. Bowstead?" he asked.

"Three years more or less," answered Rebecca quickly.

"I see."

"Yes," continued Rebecca, "we have some mutual friends from our respective college days."

"You know Mr. Bowstead from college, is that right?" asked Packard.

"Well, not exactly."

"Where did he go to university?" he asked. "Can you tell me that at least?" Rebecca paused. She had no idea where David had gone to university. All she knew was that he was a lawyer and had figured that he must have been to some kind of college to study law.

"Er, I think he went to one up north somewhere," she said, being careful to avoid Packard's eyes.

"Well surely you know his brother Jason then?" asked Packard. "They went to Manchester together."

"Jason!" exclaimed Rebecca. "Of course I know him. Yes that was it, he went to Manchester University with Jason."

Packard's enquiries had revealed that David did not have a brother and had not studied at Manchester University. Rebecca was clearly lying to him, but he could not understand why. He had assumed that Rebecca knew David, that she was a friend of his. As she answered his questions he realised that she did not know him very well, but nevertheless was prepared to lie to the police about her relationship with him for some reason. He closed the pad.

"Rebecca. David Bowstead doesn't have a brother and he never attended Manchester University. How long have you really known him?" Rebecca went a little red. She was not a very good liar. She never had been and she knew it. She felt defensive.

"Look Detective," she answered. "I'm in this hospital bed, bust up. You should be asking me about the man who did this to me and then go and catch the bastard, rather than play games with me."

"I want to catch the man who beat you up Rebecca," said Packard, "but the only leads I have are Mr. Bowstead and you. I believe that the man who attacked you is a professional killer, well known to us at the

Yard. If I'm right and he is after Mr. Bowstead, your friend is in more danger than you can possibly imagine. I must get to David before the killer does Rebecca, do you understand that?" Rebecca suddenly felt guilty. She had divulged to the Mechanic, David's destination in order to prevent him from raping her, but she was now scared that she might have signed David's death certificate by doing so. But could she trust Packard, she wondered?

"Rebecca." Packard interrupted her thoughts. "Did David tell you where he was going when he left your flat this evening?" She said nothing. She wanted to answer, but remembered the fear she had seen in David's eyes when he had fled into the store room at Harrods to escape O'Connor and the police. It had been the same look she had seen in her father's eyes after her mother had died.

"Why were the police chasing David earlier today?" she asked, this time looking Packard straight in the eye. Packard was taken aback by her question. He had been pursuing leads in relation to David for most of the day. The lawyer's description had been entered into the National Police Computer, but as far as Packard was aware there had been no reports of David having been sighted.

"I'm not aware that we've been chasing him," he replied honestly. "Where was this exactly?" Rebecca did not answer. She was studying Packard's face carefully to see if she could detect whether he was lying to her. He did not seem to be, she decided. Still, she was surprised that a Detective Inspector from Scotland Yard was not aware that the police had already tried to pick David up on two separate occasions that day.

Rebecca had no one else to trust. If Packard was right, the information she had given the Mechanic might lead the killer to David. She hated the idea of David being attacked by the man Packard had described as a professional killer. Her instincts were telling her to trust the Detective Inspector. David needed help, Rebecca realised that. Who else could help him she thought, if he was really in as much danger as Packard said he was, which she did not doubt.

She looked up at Packard. The effects of the pain killers had almost completely worn off and her body ached considerably. "Can you really help him Detective?" she asked softly, as tears began to well in her eyes. Packard moved closer to the bed.

"Yes, I can help him Rebecca. I can save his life."

"He's gone to his parents' house in Shropshire," she said after a moment.

Rebecca was unable to tell Packard exactly where in Shropshire David had gone. He had only told her that his parents' house was in Shropshire, but it was enough for Packard. He made a call to his office from a pay telephone outside the ward. It was the middle of the night but his assistant was still on duty. Packard told him to call the Senior Partner of Holland Chapman & Co. at his home and get David's address in Shropshire from him. Packard guessed that David like most City lawyers was required to give all of his possible contact details to his firm. He was right. Metcalf was not able to provide David's address in Shropshire immediately when he was woken up at home, but Packard's office had it thirty minutes later.

Whilst Packard was waiting for his assistant to track down David's address he interviewed Rebecca. She was forthcoming with what other information she had. Rebecca explained how David had literally bumped into her in Harrods and how she had taken him back to her flat. She mentioned the police having chased David through Harrods. Rebecca explained how David had slipped passed the police outside her flat and had escaped, before she was attacked by the Mechanic in her sitting-room. When she finished her account of her afternoon with David, Packard had only one question. He wanted to know the name of the policeman who had chased David through Harrods. Rebecca told him that David had referred to the man as O'Connor. Rebecca's story made sense to Packard, other than the involvement of Detective O'Connor who he did not know.

CHAPTER 23

Chesterton Village. 25th November 1994.

David awoke with a start. The early morning cold of the unheated kitchen in Chesterton House had woken him. He shivered and wrapped his arms tightly around his chest in an attempt to warm himself up. The sky through the kitchen windows suddenly exploded in the distance and David heard a loud crack, as a bolt of lightning left its mark on the morning.

He had been dreaming about Rebecca. At first David had been alone with her, but the Planner had eventually appeared in his dream. The Planner had been hugging Rebecca on a beach as the two of them had posed endlessly for a photograph that David had been taking. The Planner had looked old and tired and in contrast Rebecca was bright, young and beautiful.

David had been dreaming about the photograph he had found in Rebecca's bag. He removed it from his jacket pocket and placed it on the table in front of him. There was just enough light to be able to see. He could still hardly believe that Rebecca was the Planner's daughter. He wanted to talk to her so badly, but could not. Even if he had her telephone number, Chesterton House did not have a telephone. David had the telephone line disconnected after his mother had died. Usually when he stayed at the house he had a cellular telephone with him.

Looking at the photograph it was hard to see any resemblance between the Planner and Rebecca. David assumed that she must take after her mother rather than her father. Rebecca was blonde with a fair complexion and delicate features. The Planner was darker, with heavy set features. He looked Eastern European to David who remembered that Rebecca had told him she was a second generation American. She had explained to David that her father's family had escaped to the States just before the war. David's mind was beginning to work faster. He had managed to get some sleep and did not feel as tired as he had done on the train. He rubbed his eyes as he tried to concentrate.

The Planner must have escaped from Europe just before the Nazi's began their invasion of Europe, thought David. He wondered where Rebecca's ancestors had originated from in Europe. The Planner had told him during the flight from Miami that he had been on his way to Romania to see a friend who was ill, David remembered. Perhaps they came from Romania, he considered.

David had studied the outbreak of the Second World War at school and recalled that what exodus there was from Europe just before the War was from Poland, mainly by Jews. First as some of them realised what Hitler had in store for them and the country they lived in and later for awhile at least, during the confusion that immediately followed the German invasion of Poland.

Could the Planner have escaped from Poland on the eve of the War? David thought this was possible in the circumstances. He had known a few Poles at university and had even done work for the Polish Steam Ship Company. The Planner could have been a Pole, he concluded. David knew from his history lessons that most of the Jews who had escaped from Poland had done so in small boats, from villages down the coast from Gdansk, by crossing the Baltic Sea to Sweden. From there many of them had found passage to the United States and had been allowed to stay on the outbreak of war in Europe.

He remembered the old wooden sea chest he had noticed in Rebecca's flat. Some of the pieces of the puzzle were for the first time beginning to fit together in his mind. He wondered if the chest Rebecca used as a coffee table had once carried her ancestors' possessions across the Atlantic Ocean to the safety of the United States.

Suddenly he remembered something the Planner had struggled to say to him moments before he had died and he sat bolt upright, forgetting how cold it was in the kitchen. He dropped his right hand to his side and felt the familiar outline of the Planner's disk in the pocket of his jacket. He knew that somehow, he had to access the information on the disk.

He wondered what time it was and instinctively looked at his left wrist for his watch forgetting for a moment that it was no longer there. Instead he looked up at the one item in the kitchen that always worked. An old ship's clock that hung on the wall over the Aga. It told him that the time was 3:45 am.

David got up from the chair. There was just enough light in the kitchen for him to be able to see, the candle he had lit earlier having burnt itself out. He went over to a cupboard on the opposite side of the kitchen and hunted around until he found a torch. It had been in the cupboard David could recall ever since he had been a boy and he was not sure it would work. It did not. David flicked the "On" switch several times but nothing happened. Eventually he gave the torch two solid blows with the palm of his hand and a tepid light appeared from the lamp. It was a tired beam, but good enough for David's needs.

He opened the door of the kitchen and walked out into the night. It was raining hard and the wind howled and whipped around his collar as if it was surprised that anyone would venture out in such cruel conditions. David wished he had a coat to keep the Shropshire weather at bay. He shone the torch's beam at the ground and made his way as quickly as he could to the bottom of the drive. He turned left out of the gates and walked along the hedgerow away from the house of his childhood trying to keep out of the rain as much as possible. The moon provided a dim light, but David was glad he had the torch. Twice he thought he heard someone following him from behind and spun around, only to glimpse the fluffy tail of a rabbit or a fox dart into the base of the hedgerow escaping the weather.

He walked for about ten minutes until he reached his parents' neighbours' house. Mr. and Mrs. Walker had a small dried flower company which they ran from a converted barn behind their house. The flower company only employed three people in addition to the Walkers, but it was a successful business, particularly during the summer months when Mrs. Walker's dried flower arrangements were in demand throughout the parish to decorate churches for weddings. Mr. Walker had been a good friend of David's father and had kept an eye on David's mother for him after his father had died. The previous summer, after three bottles of wine one afternoon Mr. Walker had given David the grand tour of his flower company. David had been shown the drying room built in a converted stable, the dying room which had once been the house's outside toilet and the small makeshift office at the back of the barn, which Mr. Walker had sarcastically described as the heart of his empire.

David had not been particularly interested in the flower business, but had politely followed Mr. Walker on the tour. As he crouched in the hedgerow outside the house, he hoped that the computer he remembered having seen the previous summer was still in the office at the back of the barn.

As well as dried flowers the Walkers' had dogs, lots of dogs. David could not afford for them to start barking and wake Mr. Walker. He did not want anyone to know that he was in the village and had no idea how he would explain to his father's old neighbour why he needed to use a computer at four o'clock in the morning. Out of nowhere lightning filled the sky again and David prayed that the dogs kept quiet.

He opened the gate and ran up the driveway towards the barn at the back of the house. To get to the barn, David had to pass quite close to the house. As he did so he walked as quietly as he could, aware that the wet gravel of the driveway was crunching under his feet. His heart pounded as he walked past the house and although it was bitterly cold he could feel sweat gathering on the back of his neck.

He managed to get past the house without either the sound of his footsteps or the weather waking the dogs. He was thankful that Mrs. Walker fed the giant Irish Wolf Hounds well in the evenings causing them to sleep soundly.

David approached the barn door and let himself in, closing the door to keep out the rain as soon as he was inside. He was relieved to be out of the wind and rain. He shone the torch ahead of him. He saw trestle tables covered with a vast assortment of dried flowers and baskets, with coloured ribbons and bows and saw large industrial pots of transparent glue strategically placed at the end of each of the work benches. David walked through the barn as lightning broke in the sky once more. The sky filled with a bright light for a few seconds as the bolt of lightning made its mark in the distance. The rain pelted the barn and as David walked towards the office at the back of the building he was occasionally splattered by rain water which dripped through small holes in the barn's ancient roof.

Ahead of him David saw a narrow door with the word "OFFICE" painted across it. The paint was semi-fluorescent and glowed when David shone his torch at the door. The door was closed but unlocked as the barn door had been. He quietly let himself into the office and shone his torch around the small room searching for the Walkers' computer. It was there on a desk against the far wall surrounded by piles of paper and used polystyrene coffee cups. Next to the computer was an old fashioned bubble jet printer which the Walkers used for printing proforma bills. David breathed a sigh of relief and sat down in a wooden captain's chair in front of the screen. The computer was an old Amstrad PC 2286/40, which was very outdated. Nevertheless, it was a computer and it had a three inch floppy disk drive which was all that David needed to load the Planner's disk into the machine.

David felt around behind the machine for the "On" switches for the computer and the screen. He found them and flicked the computer and screen to life. The computer hummed as it warmed up and David watched and waited for the screen to flash and for characters to appear.

Lightning cracked again. The storm was getting closer. Slowly the black screen cleared and characters appeared. The screen prompted David to type in the code of the system he wanted the computer to run. He knew from loading the disk into the computer at Harrods that the disk was compatible with Word Perfect, and typed "WP" then pressed the Return key. The screen flashed blue for a moment and David was confronted with the familiar Word Perfect banner list. The Walkers' computer was old and slow, but the software was up to date David was pleased to discover. He moved the cursor on to the Word Perfect 5.1 label and pressed the Return key again. The screen cleared and David knew that the computer was ready to take the disk.

He removed the disk from the pocket of his sodden jacket and inspected it for a moment to make sure it had not got wet on the journey from Chesterton House, before sliding it into the computer's floppy disk drive. He pressed the F5 key and entered "A:\", then pushed the Return key. The old computer groaned as the disk was loaded. Within a few seconds David saw on the screen the index of the files stored on the disk that he had seen in the Computer Goods Department of Harrods the previous morning. There was only one directory entitled "Operation Domino". He moved the cursor down to the Domino Directory and pressed the Return key. As before the screen went blank before the words

"ENTER PASSWORD AND PRESS RETURN" appeared. David paused and sat up nervously in the captain's chair. He carefully typed "Bobinski", pushed the Return key and waited.

"Bobinski" was the word David had noticed elaborately carved along the top of the sea chest in Rebecca's flat. Before he had died, the Planner told David to tell his daughter to use her real name. At the time this had meant nothing to David. He had not even been sure that he had heard the old man properly, but as he pieced what he could of the puzzle together it had struck him that the word on the chest might be the Polish name of Rebecca's grandparents, who he guessed had fled to the United States on the outbreak of World War Two, with what possessions they had managed to take with them crammed inside the old sea chest. If he was right, Rebecca's original Polish family name was the key to Operation Domino.

The computer screen flashed as the password was considered and then went black for a second before a new index appeared simply labelled "Operation Domino File Index". "Bobinski" was the code. David was in at last.

The index listed so many files that the entire screen was full. David used the cursor control keys to scroll the screen down until the list of files finished. In all, the Operation Domino directory contained sixty seven files. David reviewed the names of the files. They were abbreviated because it was only possible to use a few letters to describe any file in the index. This was usual. The abbreviated names appeared to give no clues as to the contents of the files and David did not waste time reading each of the abbreviated file names in turn. They were listed alphabetically. David decided to go through each of the files in turn in alphabetical order. He had not been expecting so many files.

He moved the cursor on to the first file name which read "A.Pal" and brought the file up on the screen. The file contained drawings which David was unable to make out at first. He scrolled the document down and discovered page after page of drawings. They were architects plans of some sort of huge hotel or mansion with hundreds of rooms. The plans were considerably detailed, showing all of the rooms clearly and in scale and even included the contents of some of the larger rooms. The stairwells and lift shafts were also marked on the plans. The alarm points of the building were marked by a star which could be identified on each of the plans from a key guide. David looked briefly at each of the plans in turn, but could not ascertain the building or where it was located. No names appeared anywhere on the plans.

After fifteen minutes of carefully inspecting each of the plans, David exited the file and moved on to the second file. This was entitled "A.X-ray". It contained X-ray prints of a human body. Again there were hundreds of X-ray copies. David assumed that like the plans, the computerised images on the screen had been copied on to the Planner's disk by a sophisticated laser computer copier. He had not seen such a machine and was impressed by the quality of the computerised reproductions. David reviewed each of the X-ray copies in turn which took some time. It was not until he got to an X-ray of the human's knees that he found any notations. At the foot of the X-ray, was typed:

"Knee joints weak as a result of several riding accidents over the last ten years. The subject is unable to sustain any serious blows to his knees. If struck, his knees invariably give way and could break".

David was intrigued. The X-rays were of a man that much he could be sure of, who had weak knees from years of horse riding. He moved on through the X-rays. Every now and then one of the X-rays had commentary below it pointing out where bones had been broken or where the man had a minor physical defect such as a crooked finger or slightly short vertebrae. The detail was remarkable in David's opinion, but the X-rays did not tell him who the man was or give even a hint of the significance of the computerised documents. David reviewed all of the X-ray copies on the file before moving on.

The third file he called up was entitled "E.Meds". It contained copies of medical records beginning with the records of a male baby immediately after his birth and progressed, page after page through the boy's childhood, his adolescence, his teenage years into manhood. David was growing impatient and scrolled through the childhood records quickly. In the last of the medical records the age of the man was given as thirty nine years old. Throughout the records the male's name had been blocked out. Other than assume that the medical records were of the same man as the X-rays had been, David could make little of them. The records indicated that the man had mild asthma as a child, had broken his left wrist playing rugby at the age of eleven and again at the age of sixteen, had fractured his jaw at the age of twenty three, had his first Aids test at the age of thirty four and had weak knees. He had medicals every year without fail according to the records.

David exited the "E:Meds" file. All he knew was that the man whose anatomy he was learning about had a fairly normal medical history and was at least thirty nine years old. He wondered if the Planner had been some kind of doctor, but dismissed this idea as he scrolled through the fourth file in the Domino directory. This file was entitled "F:Cars". It contained the blue prints of several luxury cars. For each car there were over fifty blue prints, beginning in each case with a master blue print of the entire vehicle and continuing with more detailed prints as David proceeded through the file, right down to complicated plans of each car's fuel and electrical systems.

Following a blue print of a car's fuel tank, was a long notation:

"The vehicle's fuel tank has a subtle design fault that potentially could cause an explosion. The fuel entry funnel is set at too acute an angle. If the width of the flow line is reduced by only fifteen per cent, by a blockage of some sort, when petrol is pumped into the tank the flow line will become clogged around the neck of the entry funnel, as petrol is not able to drain down inside the tank quickly enough. If the vehicle is driven before the blocked fuel has had a chance to run into the fuel tank, the overflow system will automatically operate and pump the blocked fuel out of the fuel flow line into the right hand side of the trunk. It is calculated that in view of the way the trunk is built, at least fifty per cent of the fuel pumped from the flow line will gather to form a pool at the base of the rear driver's side light unit, rather than drip through tiny holes in the base of the trunk as intended by the designers. The light unit should become sufficiently hot to ignite the pool of fuel after it has been in operation for about thirty three minutes, in average temperatures. The fuel will burn and the trail of fuel will lead the flame into the fuel tank, causing an explosion. It is estimated that neither the car nor its occupants would survive the explosion".

David was shocked by the graphic account of the car exploding, but was still not sure what any of the information he was discovering meant.

The next forty files in the directory that David reviewed were similar to the first four. They contained all sorts of detailed plans, copies of personal records, copies of bank accounts and scores of timetables for everything from train journeys to church services. David even came across a copy of the Oxford University Union's debating and lecturing time table for the year. His eyes were beginning to get sore and he was starting to think that the disk contained nothing but a bizarre collection of irrelevancies when lightning struck again not far from the barn. The fierce crack made David jump. The rain had become worse and David could hear it beating down on the roof relentlessly. He thought of the walk back to Chesterton House and turned the collar of his jacket up as the wind made itself known inside the barn.

The next file David called up was simply entitled "Plan". He had not noticed it when he had initially reviewed the abbreviated names of the files on the Directory's index. He began reading the text of the file on the screen in horror:

"Operation Domino"

"The assignment I have been set is to plan an operation to kill His Royal Highness Prince Richard, Prince of Wales, without detection and without any possibility of the assassination, once it has been carried out, being associated or connected in any way to yourself or to any aspect or area of your business.

The operation to assassinate the Prince is, I am informed, to be referred to simply as Operation Domino".

David stared at the screen in disbelief. Someone, without doubt the same person who was after the Planner's disk, was going to assassinate the Prince of Wales and the Planner, it was now obvious, was the architect of the intended murder. David was shocked by the businesslike manner of the text on the computer screen.

He used the cursor keys to scroll the text forwards and continued to read:

"In planning an operation, I have been set various practical perimeters, which I have strictly complied with. The most significant of which is that the Prince must be killed by no later than 31st May 1995. Although this date would appear to allow considerable time in which to assassinate the Prince, for reasons explained below, in fact the opportunities I have identified to kill the Prince mean that time is in fact limited before the stated deadline.

In devising this Plan, I have given full consideration to all of the material supplied to me by your associates. Most of the material, with the exception of video tapes and audio recordings is stored on this computer disk as usual and reference should be made to the material as necessary when familiarising yourself with this Operation.

The Prince of Wales is one of the most effectively guarded people in the World. Since the Duke of Kent was shot dead by IRA terrorists outside the Houses of Parliament two years ago, the level of security surrounding the Royal family has expanded considerably. The Prince is without doubt now the most closely guarded member of his family. He is a widower, his wife having died during childbirth last year. He is active in European Politics, but other than this can fairly be described as something of a recluse, considering his social position.

The combination of the Prince's very limited social activities and the twenty four hour security he is required to maintain, makes assassinating him extremely difficult.

The Prince resides in London for most of the year. During the winter he takes up residence at Sandringham, the Queen's Estate in Scotland. The Estate is better guarded than Buckingham Palace and the Prince spends most of his time when he is there painting in a studio on the Estate. At all times he is guarded.

He has three principal full time bodyguards who accompany him everywhere. They are employed by the Royal Protection Division of Scotland Yard and are beyond reproach. The selection procedure to become one of the Prince's personal bodyguards is extremely rigorous. On balance it is my opinion that none of the Prince's current guards could be blackmailed, bribed or threatened into either killing the Prince or participating in his death. This is regrettable so far as Operation Domino is concerned, as the Prince's bodyguards certainly offer the easiest way of killing the Prince in view of their close proximity to him at all times.

When in London the Prince resides in rooms at Buckingham Palace. Since the death of his wife, the Prince has given up Highgrove House. His quarters are on the top floor of the east wing of the Palace. His rooms are entirely self sufficient from the rest of the Palace. His domestic servants are employed for him through the main Palace household. For the right price, one of the Prince's junior footmen might be induced to assist with the assassination of the Prince. Two of the footmen have financial problems according to their bank records. One of the two is a regular gambler and has considerably abused his credit line over the last ten months and is desperately in need of cash. Whilst the footman has easy access to the Prince and could certainly kill him, or assist in an operation to get an assassin into the Prince's quarters, he would be an obvious suspect in the inevitable police investigation following the Prince's death and would almost certainly lead the police back to you eventually. My opinion is that an operation to kill the Prince *using his own employees would work, but that the police would have little difficulty tracing the assassination back to you. Therefore, I have rejected any opportunities to assassinate the Prince that would require the involvement of any of his or the Palace's staff".*

David wondered who the "you" was the Planner referred to as he read the introduction to Operation Domino in amazement.

"During the summer months the Prince regularly takes afternoon tea in the private garden on the roof patio of Buckingham Palace. The garden is open to attack from the air. However, the air space around the Palace is continuously monitored by the Royal Air Force and it is unlikely that a helicopter, even flying at low level, would be able to enter this air space, attack the Prince and retreat before it was detected. If it was detected it could be tracked by radar anywhere".

David read on. For the next thirty five pages the Planner considered in turn various options for killing Prince Richard. Each of the options were disregarded by the Planner, generally because he was not satisfied that an assassin would be able to murder the Prince without being detected or caught. The Planner was clearly of the opinion that if the assassin was ever caught, the authorities would one way or the other be able to trace the killing to the Guardian. David continued to read:

"The Prince is at his most vulnerable to attack when he is taking part in a public event of some sort. Unfortunately, so far as the Operation is concerned, his public engagements are limited in the immediate future. Since the death of his wife, the Prince has restricted his public duties to attending State openings of the British Parliament, appearances connected with his support of the European Community Protected Membership scheme and attending a very few charitable functions and the occasional ad hoc reception. Whilst your sources confirm that the Palace is putting the Prince under considerable pressure to adopt a more rigorous schedule, it is unlikely that he will do this for some time, and not before the cut off date for the Operation has passed.

The Prince's limited public schedule is published by the Palace six months in advance, for the benefit of Court reporters. I have been provided with a copy of this and with a copy of the Prince's private, unpublished schedule for the second half of this year. During the next six months the Prince will attend three "public" functions where it will be possible for an assassin to kill the Prince and escape without detection and without you being connected to the murder. These are in turn, a charity concert at the Royal Opera House on Monday 24th August 1994, a Polo match in aid of the Prince's Trust on Sunday 4th September 1994 where the Prince is due to hand out the trophies, and a lecture at the Oxford Union on Friday 25th November 1994, where the Prince will give a lecture on Protected Membership of the European Community.

Because the Prince's diary is only ever published twice a year, on each occasion only six months in advance, I am unable to plan the Operation to take place beyond 31st December 1994, in any event. The Prince's diary for the first half of 1995, will become available at the beginning of January 1995. It is possible that he might be scheduled to attend public functions during the first half of 1995, that would be suitable venues for his assassination. This can be reviewed if necessary, once reliable details of the Prince's engagements for 1995 have been obtained.

I have devised plans to assassinate the Prince on each of these three days on the basis that he attends each of the events mentioned as precisely scheduled, giving you three separate opportunities to assassinate him before the stated deadline. It is possible that he might miss one or even two of the events for reasons that cannot be anticipated now, but statistically, bearing in mind his attendance at public events over the last ten years, I consider that the prospect of him missing all three of the events is highly remote.

Each of the dates and events identified are equally attractive for the intended assassination. The precise details of the three assassination operations I have devised are set out below in turn, as follows:".

Lightning broke the sky above the barn and thunder boomed as the storm arrived in the village. The computer made an sudden fizzing sound and the screen went blank.

"Damn it!" exclaimed David. He shone his torch around the back of the computer and found the switches that operated the screen and computer base. Desperately he flicked them backwards and forwards several times as he watched the screen, hoping the introduction to Operation Domino would reappear. It did not. He tried the "On" switch for the printer next to the computer, but that did not work either.

David realised that the last bolt of lightning must have knocked out the electricity in the village. The electricity cables were suspended from tall posts and had blown out before in bad weather. The village was considered too small by Shropshire County Council to justify the expense of underground electricity cables. David knew it was no good. He could not read the Planner's three options for killing Prince Richard, but he had read enough before the computer went down for him to know what he had stumbled into. Most importantly he knew the dates of the proposed alternative assassinations and their locations. He thought what day it was. The dates for the first two assassination attempts had passed and Prince Richard was still alive. David had seen a picture of him alive and well in the Times Newspaper arriving back from Brussels, only a few days earlier. He thought of the third date proposed by the Planner on which the Prince could be killed without detection. 25th November 1994. David's heart sank as he double checked in his mind what day it was.

"Oh my God," he said to himself quietly as he realised what day it was. "It's today."

The third date proposed by the Planner in his report to the Guardian on which to kill the Prince was that very day. The storm had knocked out the village's electricity before David had been able to read the details of the three alternative assassination plans, but the report had summarised the dates and locations of the assassination attempts with reference to public functions the Prince was scheduled to attend. The third option for the assassination was to be carried out that day, in Oxford, where Prince Richard was due to deliver a lecture to the Oxford Union on his favourite subject, Protected Membership of the European Community.

David did not know the time of the lecture or the actual details of the Operation. The section of the Planner's report he had read did not say how the Prince was going to be assassinated, at what time or precisely where, but David had no doubt that it was going to happen. He realised that he was probably the only person who could warn the authorities. He also understood for the first time exactly why he was being hunted.

He could think of many organisations who would like to kill a senior member of the Royal family. The IRA had killed the Duke of Kent only two years earlier as the Planner had correctly mentioned in his report. Operation Domino could be the idea of anyone from the Iraqis to an anti Royalist faction group that bore a serious grudge.

David removed the disk from the computer's floppy disk drive and returned it to his jacket pocket. The information on the disk would not have been lost as a result of the power failure, he knew. He only wished that he had been able to read more of the detail of Operation Domino.

He left the converted barn and hurried to the end of the Walkers' drive. It was still raining and the wind was strong. The sky, in spite of the storm, was light and David realised that it was almost daybreak. He wished he still had his watch as he wanted to know exactly what time it was. He tried to estimate how long he had been inside the Walkers' barn. He had reviewed page after page of computerised documents on the flower company's computer before he had come across the Plan and figured that he must have been at it for at least two hours. He guessed that it was about 6:00 am.

David's mind raced. During his time at Oxford University he had attended many lectures and debates organised by the Oxford Union. The lecture hall would be packed to capacity for the lecture by the Prince, and David knew that it would be difficult to police the chaotic audience of students and press men. He understood why the Planner had identified this particular public event as being ideal for the Prince's assassination.

He decided that in spite of his suspicions that in someway the police in London were involved with Operation Domino, he had to pass on to the authorities what he had discovered. David turned left out of the Walkers' drive and broke into jog. A mile and a half down the road was an old red telephone box. He did not stop running until he reached it. The telephone was the old fashioned type that only takes coins. He lifted the receiver and dialled 999.

When the operator asked what service he required he said the police. He waited to be connected and when he was finally put through, told the police operator that he had come across details of a plot to assassinate the Prince of Wales during a lecture he was due to give at the Oxford Union sometime that day. He spoke quickly, trying to cram in as much information as he could.

The police operator waited until David had finished and calmly asked for his name. He hesitated for a moment before telling her that he preferred not to say. He was asked how he had come across details of a plot to kill the Prince of Wales and again after a moments hesitation told the operator that it was too complicated to explain over the telephone. She asked him if he knew how or by whom the Prince would be killed. David desperately tried to explain what he knew, without divulging who he was or how it was that he came to have the Planner's disk, but realised that his explanation was hardly convincing. At the end of the conversation the operator thanked David for the information and assured him that it would be passed to the appropriate authorities. She then hung up before he was able to say anything else.

As he walked back from the telephone box to Chesterton House, he was not at all confident that the police operator had believed him or even taken him seriously. He could not blame her. Even knowing everything that he did, David hardly believed what he was caught up in himself.

The police operator followed the procedure for logging anonymous information she received concerning a public figure. She recorded the time of the call on the station computer and made a note for the computer operator, when he began his shift, to enter details of the call on to the National Police Computer, where they would automatically be passed to the Royal Protection Unit at Scotland Yard. The unit receives on average details of over one hundred anonymous death threats to members of the Royal family each week. Invariably, they are bogus and such calls are understandably not taken too seriously by the busy unit.

CHAPTER 24

By the time David was back in the kitchen at Chesterton House he was convinced that his warning would not be taken seriously by the police. He looked out of the kitchen window. The sun was coming up as daybreak arrived. David was frustrated. He knew of a plot to assassinate the heir to the British throne and his efforts to warn the authorities had almost certainly failed. He cursed under his breath that the Walkers' computer had crashed before he had been able to discover the exact details of the assassination plot. It was the only computer in the village.

If he turned himself into the police in Shrewsbury, he was concerned that by the time he had explained the existence of the disk, its contents, the Planner and the Mechanic and the police had verified his story, it would be too late to prevent the assassination or get a message to the Prince's bodyguards that the Prince should not deliver his lecture. Even if a message was passed to the Royal Protection Unit in time, David feared that the officers and the police might not regard the information as reliable. Without knowing what else was on the disk David could not be sure that the police would take him or Operation Domino seriously. He imagined that the Prince would not easily be persuaded to cancel his lecture and disappoint almost a thousand students, particularly when dozens of death threats were made against him each week.

He stood in the icy kitchen and decided that he had no alternative. He would have to go to Oxford himself, to the Prince's lecture and warn the Prince's bodyguards and the police protecting him in person. If he was actually there, able to explain what he knew of Operation Domino and showed them the information on the disk, David was sure he would be able to persuade the authorities to cancel the lecture and take steps to protect the Prince from whatever it was the Planner had devised to kill him.

He looked up at the clock in the kitchen. It was 6:30 am. He wondered what time the Prince was scheduled to give his lecture. Oxford Union lectures are not restricted to the evenings. David knew that for a speaker as eminent as Prince Richard, the university would timetable the speech to accommodate the Prince. It was possible that the Prince could be scheduled to deliver his speech that morning. This realisation made David decide that there was just not enough time for him to explain everything to the police or find another computer and learn the details of Operation Domino. He had to get to Oxford as quickly as he could.

As a student, David had been able to drive to Oxford from Chesterton in a little over two and a half hours. He looked at the clock again. Since David had lived in London a new motorway, the M40 had been built which links the Midlands to Oxfordshire. David considered that the M40 route would probably be faster than the route he had taken as a student. He should be able to reduce the journey time. He calculated that even if it took him two hours to get to Oxford, and allowing for the early morning traffic he would run into once he got to the university town, if he left almost immediately he should be at the Oxford Union's lecture theatre where he guessed the Prince would give his speech, by no later than 9:30 am. Even if the lecture was scheduled to take place in the morning, David did not think it would begin before 10:00 am, when the working day at the university started.

He hurried into his father's old study at the far end of the house and hunted through the bookshelves until he found a copy of the Reader's Digest Touring Guide To Britain. It was a relatively new book that David had brought for his father as a birthday present the year before he had died. David knew it would show the new M40 motorway.

He took a pad of paper from his father's desk and returned with the map book and the pad to the kitchen. He still did not want to turn on any of the lights in the house and the kitchen had the best natural lighting. Using the map, David worked out the shortest route from Chesterton Village to Oxford. He scribbled the route down on the pad, noting where he needed to get got on and off the M40 motorway in particular. He would not need to take the book with him. The route was pretty straightforward. He tore the top page with the route written on it from the pad, folded it in half and stuffed it into his jacket pocket. He left the map book open on the kitchen table and went to the kitchen door. Before leaving Chesterton House, David looked around the kitchen and remembered his parents. He wondered what his father would had done if he had stumbled across a plot to assassinate the Prince of Wales. He hoped he was doing the right thing.

He walked to the stables on the other side of the driveway. David's father had not wanted to spoil the pretty country village by building a modern garage, so he had converted the existing stables into a double garage. The only things which signalled that the stables no longer housed horses were the large double wooden doors that had been needed to accommodate the width of a car, instead of the narrower traditional doors that had once kept horses inside the stables.

The key to the padlock on the double doors was under a stone at the side of the stables. David's father had not been a security conscious man and David was reluctant to abandon his father's habits. He unlocked the old padlock and pulled open the double doors in turn. The last time the doors had been opened had been at the end of the summer when David had parked his Mercedes in the garage for the winter months. He only hoped the car started. Usually, he arranged for a local mechanic to service the car a few days before he was due to return to Chesterton to collect it at the beginning of the spring.

The old Mercedes was protected by a cover which David pulled off and stuffed into the car's boot. SL model Mercedes come with a soft top and a bolt on hard top. Because David had only ever driven the Mercedes during the spring and summer months he had never used the hard top, which was resting up against the wall at the back of the garage under a tarpaulin. The weather outside was terrible, but fitting the hard top was a two man job and David did not have time to waste trying to fit it by himself. He would have to make do with the car's soft top, he decided.

David pulled up the soft top from the specialised storage compartment behind the back seats and quickly secured it in place. He got inside the car and fumbled around under the foot mat for the ignition key. Keeping the key under the mat was a habit he had picked up at university. He inserted the key and turned the ignition to the first position. The generator light came on signalling that the battery was not flat. David turned the key to the next position and the engine murmured, but did not start. He tried again. This time the engine strained as it tried to start. David began to worry that the car had been sitting there for too long to start without a jump from another vehicle. However, on the third attempt the three and a half litre engine roared into life. David could not help but admire Mercedes' engineering. The car was over twenty years old and the engine had not been turned over for more than two months, yet it started on only the third attempt.

He revved the engine and fumes filled the rear of the garage. He turned on the car's headlights. It was getting light outside but David knew the country lanes around Chesterton Village well enough to know not to try and drive in the early morning in bad weather without headlights. He checked the petrol level indicator. The tank was only a quarter full. He would need more petrol to get to Oxford and was grateful that he had at least got fifty pounds for his watch.

He dropped the automatic gear shift selector from Parked into Drive and felt the familiar jolt of the car as first gear engaged. He pressed down gently on the accelerator pedal and drove the Mercedes out of the garage. Rain fell on the windscreen as soon as the car was clear of the old stable roof and David switched the car's wipers on. He turned right out of the driveway without bothering to stop to close the garage doors. He was very aware of how little time he had to get to Oxford and warn Prince Richard's bodyguards and the police of Operation Domino.

He drove down the narrow road he had the previous evening walked into the village along. It was almost 7:00 am. No one was about. David turned on to the main road and drove towards Bridgenorth. He pressed down hard on the accelerator pedal once the Mercedes was on the main road and the powerful engine roared as the car's speed increased. He was going to have to drive through Stourbridge to get to the M40 motorway and wanted to clear the town if he could before the morning traffic became heavy.

David drove along the main Bridgenorth Road for ten minutes before he started to slow the car down. He indicated to turn left out of habit even though his was the only car on the road and pulled into a petrol station and up to a pump. The Mercedes took old fashioned four star petrol and drank a lot of it.

David got out of the car and checked how much money he had left.

He had exactly thirty seven pounds and fifty pence in his pocket. He removed the petrol cap and pumped petrol into the tank. He carefully watched the indicator on the pump that told him how much money he was spending and stopped when the amount shown on the pump was exactly the same as the amount he had counted in his pocket. He knew that the tank would not be full, but estimated that he should have enough fuel to comfortably get him to Oxford.

He walked over to the station shop and at the desk paid for the petrol. As he was leaving he noticed the morning newspapers piled up on the floor of the shop. He picked up a copy of the Times and flicked through it. The attendant watched him, annoyed that David was reading a newspaper without appearing to be going to buy it. He did not know that after paying for the petrol, his first customer of the day had no money left, not even twenty pence to pay for the Times.

David found what he was searching for on page eighteen. The Court Circular is a small daily feature in the Times, which does not interest many readers. It had never interested David before. It sets out the official engagements of members of the Royal family each day, in minute type. David looked down the small print until he saw the listing for Prince Richard. According to the Times, the Prince was delivering a lecture to the Oxford Union that morning at 10:00 am.

He replaced the newspaper on the pile and hurried out of the station shop. He had no time to lose if the Prince's speech started at 10:00 am. He got back into the Mercedes and turned the ignition key. This time the old car started immediately. David drove up to the garage exit and looked left and right before pulling out and turning left. As he pulled out a black Ford Escort drove past him on the other side of the road. The Escort was travelling at just under one hundred miles an hour and David was only able to glance at the car as it hurtled passed him.

Within seconds David's Mercedes was moving away from the petrol station. The road ahead was empty and David pressed the accelerator pedal down as the old car sped up to seventy miles an hour.

CHAPTER 25

The Mechanic broke hard as soon as his car passed the Mercedes. The Mechanic's rented Ford Escort swerved across the road as he applied the brakes heavily. He had got a good look at the driver of the Mercedes as he had driven past in the Escort. There could be no doubt about it. The driver was Bowstead.

The Mechanic had tried three different car hire companies in London, before he eventually found a car. Whilst the first two companies he tried were open for business twenty four hours a day, all of their cars had been either out or booked for the following morning. Eventually he had hired the Ford Escort, on the strength of a forged German driving license. The Mechanic had paid for the car in cash. He had driven out of London in the early morning and had sped along the motorway towards Shropshire at an average speed of over one hundred miles an hour most of the way. He had been pulled over by a police patrol once during his journey for speeding, about twenty miles south of Birmingham, and had been forced to slow down to seventy miles an hour for the following fifteen miles whilst the police followed him. He could not risk being arrested. As soon as the police car had turned off the motorway, the Mechanic had accelerated away up to one hundred miles an hour again. He was desperate to catch up with David.

The further north the Mechanic had driven the worse the weather became. By the time he was in Shropshire it was raining heavily and the wind was strong. Driving became more difficult, but still the Mechanic had not driven at a more sensible speed.

He regained control as the brakes slowed the car down and steered the Escort back over to the left hand side of the road. As soon as the car had slowed sufficiently, the Mechanic swung the steering wheel hard over to the right and pulled on the hand break. The car skidded across the road moving sideways at it did so. The car came out of the skid facing in exactly the opposite direction. He had performed a text book one hundred and eighty degrees turn. He dropped the gear stick into first gear and pressed the accelerator pedal flat to the floor. The Escort's front wheels spun for a moment and the tyres screeched on the wet tarmac. The car leaped forward and the Mechanic accelerated up through the gears quickly in pursuit of the Mercedes.

Packard's unmarked police car pulled into Chesterton Village at a little after 7:00 am. The Detective Inspector was accompanied by two other officers from Scotland Yard's Assassination Division.

After Packard had learnt from Rebecca where David had gone to hide out, he had returned to his office. It had been three thirty in the morning and Packard should have been at home in bed with his wife. However, in between her tears, Rebecca had explained that she had told the Mechanic that David was going to his parents' house in Shropshire, in order to stop the killer from raping her. Packard had no difficulty finding out the address of David's family home in Shropshire and was certain that the Mechanic would be able discover the address almost as easily. He did not have time to sleep.

He had considered contacting the local CID office that covered Chesterton and having the police there pick David up for his own safety. Packard could not be sure that he would be able to get to David before the Mechanic did. Nevertheless, he decided against involving the local police in Shropshire. Rebecca had explained how Detective O'Connor and his men had been chasing David and how David had slipped out of her flat past the police, disguised as a woman. Packard recognised that David did not trust the police which explained why he had not simply walked into a police station already and asked for protection. He also recognised that David was fairly resourceful. Whilst Packard did not rate David's chances against the Mechanic, he had to accept that if the local Shropshire police turned up at his parents' house with the inevitable uniformed officers and blazing sirens, even if they were instructed to approach David with subtlety, the young lawyer might slip past the police and Packard would lose the only lead he had to the Mechanic.

He had rounded up two junior AU Detectives who were on the night shift and the three of them had set off in Packard's car for Chesterton.

The unmarked police car parked fifty feet from Chesterton House and the driver turned off the vehicle's lights. The three Detectives got out of the car and walked in the rain towards the house. Packard could not see a light in the house and hoped that he would find David asleep. One of the Detectives went around to the back of the house to watch for David should he try and make a run for it. Packard and the other Detective approached the back door from the driveway. Packard saw the garage doors swinging open in the wind and spotted tyre marks in the gravel across the drive. He became worried that perhaps David was not in the house after all.

The two men entered the house quietly through the back door, which was unlocked. They searched the ground floor and the cellar in minutes. David was not there. The two policemen climbed the stairs to the first floor landing and searched each of the bedrooms off the landing in turn. David was not in any of the rooms and none of the beds had been slept in. Finally, Packard searched the attic, which had been converted years before into a bedroom and study. Again he found nothing.

He shouted out to David to show himself if he was hiding, explaining that he was with the AU and knew that a professional killer was chasing him. He even shouted out that he had spoken with Rebecca who had told him where to find David. No one replied. Packard was satisfied that David was not in the house. He returned to the kitchen and turned on the lights.

On the kitchen table he saw the saucer with melted wax stuck to it, the open Reader's Digest Touring Guide To Britain, a blank pad and the photograph of the Planner and Rebecca. David had been in the house recently, concluded Packard. He sent the other Detective outside and told him to check the garage. Packard then sat down in the wooden chair at the end of the kitchen table. He recognised Rebecca in the photograph, but not the Planner who he had never seen. He noticed that the map book was open at a page which showed part of the M40 motorway. Oxford was also shown on the map. Packard pulled the map book closer to him and looked at the open pages in more detail. Nothing was marked in manuscript on the map. Damn, he thought to himself. Where have you vanished to David?

Packard was sure that David was running from the Mechanic, but still had no idea why any one would want to kill the young solicitor. He was feeling tired and rubbed his hands over his eyes. It would be a long drive back to London. As he took his hands away from his face and started to get up from the chair he noticed something on the blank pad of paper. He sat down again, but it was gone. Packard picked up the pad and held it to the light. When held at a certain angle, indentation marks could be seen across the top page of the pad. They were words which Packard guessed must have been written on the previous top page of the pad, before it had been torn from the pad by the writer. The indentation marks were difficult to read.

He took a pencil from his jacket pocket and very lightly rubbed lead over the top page of the pad as a child might do as part of a nursery school lesson. As he rubbed, the lead revealed David's route from Chesterton to Oxford.

Packard jumped to his feet and ran outside with the pad. He called the two Detectives and the three men hurried back to their parked car. Packard told the Detectives they were going to Oxford and handed the officer who was navigating the pad of paper. He told the driver to take the route shown. The driver wasted no time. He reversed the car around and accelerated back along the narrow village track towards the main road. As he did the second Detective who had a map and the imprint of David's route to Oxford quickly worked out directions.

Packard picked up the cellular telephone from the car's back shelf and dialled the number of Scotland Yard's Vehicle Tracing Division. He needed to know what make of car David was driving.

CHAPTER 26

The Guardian had not bothered with breakfast that morning. It was 9:15 am in Bucharest and if everything went according to plan, Prince Richard would be dead within a matter of hours.

Although the Planner had worked out exactly how to kill the Prince, Operation Domino had been dreamt up by the Guardian. Whilst all of the European political commentators knew that the Prince was opposed to Romania becoming a Protected Member of the European Community, none of them knew why. The Guardian did.

The Prince had never been active at all in British politics. The heir to the British throne was not even entitled to vote. Parliament would never tolerate a member of the Royal family openly using his or her position to influence national opinion in relation to a domestic issue. Europe however, was different. Prince Richard had always been a supporter of European union. He believed in European political and economic union passionately. Because of his title he was prevented from holding a European Community position, but during the previous ten years he had been quietly involved in the development of the Community at the highest levels.

The Prince had not bullied his way into influence in Brussels, the seat of the Community's government. Neither had he taken advantage of the fact that he was the heir to the British throne, although it would be unrealistic to suggest that initially this fact had not opened doors for the Prince that would otherwise have been closed to him. Prince Richard had gained considerable influence in Brussels because he was highly respected when it came to European affairs. He was an expert on European history and knew more about the European Community than practically anyone else alive. His judgement on European matters was generally considered to be extremely sound.

Protected Membership of the European Community had been Prince Richard's own answer to the problems caused by the disintegration of the Soviet Union. He had put together a working committee which he had personally financed. The committee had formulated the Prince's ideas on Protected Membership. At all times he had been behind the scenes as an unofficial voice in the debate. Most of the European leaders knew that the Prince was indirectly responsible for Protected Membership.

In the United Kingdom, his involvement in European matters had become concentrated around the Protected Membership scheme. Politicians, the press and the ordinary man in the street did not complain that the Prince was too influential in this arena. The less serious elements of the press had even elevated the Prince to the status of the country's champion in Europe. No one denied that Britain appeared to be getting a better deal in Europe since the Prince had become involved in European politics.

The British Prime Minister was basically pro European, but his stance on European affairs changed frequently. He had suffered considerably for this in the press and Europe had become something of a difficult topic for him. He was unpopular as well and this was really the root of the Guardian's problem so far as getting Romania admitted into the European Community was concerned.

Prince Richard was very popular in the United Kingdom. Most British people sympathised with the Prince over the death of his wife. The Prime Minister never missed an opportunity to associate himself with the Prince, or with the Prince's ideas. On matters relating to Europe, the Prime Minister always followed the Prince's private recommendations. In return the Prince did not distance himself from the Prime Minister whenever the British leader sought to strengthen his own position in the polls by taking advantage of the Prince's popularity in some way. This suited both of them. The Prime Minister was a politician interested in re-election. The Prince was a statesman interested above all else in a strong Europe.

This meant that in effect when the Prime Minister had used the British veto twice in the past to prevent Romania becoming a Protected Member of the European Community, he had really been exercising the veto on behalf of the Prince. The Prime Minister had been criticised on both occasions in the House of Commons by the leader of the Labour Party for vetoing the Romanians, but the criticism had not been sustained for long. Protected Membership was considered by the British press to be a foreign matter. The press and therefore the opposition to the government were far more interested in the Prime Minister's domestic policies than in squabbles over which former Soviet satellite countries should benefit from Protected Membership of the Community. As far as the Prime Minister was concerned, temporary criticism for vetoing Romania was a small price to pay for the Prince's unofficial support on difficult domestic issues.

The Guardian's sources in Whitehall had repeatedly informed him that whilst the British Prime Minister had followed the Prince's recommendation last time by vetoing Romanian membership, privately the Prime Minister was not opposed to Romania entering the Community. The Guardian was convinced that if the Prince was not around to influence the British leader, on the third vote, in the face of every other Member State voting to include Romania in the Community the British would not exercise their veto again. Romania would be allowed to join the European Community as a Protected Member.

The Guardian was also convinced that the Prince's opinion on Romania's eligibility for Protected Membership would never change.

It was over two years until the next general election in the United Kingdom and whilst the Conservatives were currently behind Labour in the polls, and their leader unpopular, history showed that the Conservative Party had a habit of winning elections when it mattered. It was possible that the current British Prime Minister would be re-elected in two years time. Even if he was not and Labour got in, the Guardian feared that Prince Richard might be able to influence the Labour leader on European affairs to the same degree that he influenced the Conservative leader. These considerations coupled with the fact that the Guardian did not know how much longer the Romanian President would be able to hold on to power and therefore, for how long the Guardian could guarantee that Romania would continue to apply for Protected Membership in the face of repeated failure, had lead him to the decision that Prince Richard had to be assassinated before the Community voted on the next round of Protected Membership applications on 31st May the following year.

With the Prince out of the way the British Prime Minister would no longer be influenced against Romania. There was little doubt that then the British leader would vote in favour of Romania joining the European Community the following summer.

As a child, one of the few pleasures the Guardian had enjoyed was playing dominos with his mother. At the end of a game the Guardian's mother would let her young son stand the dominos in a line on their ends, topple over the domino at the far end of the line and watch all of the others fall in turn. The Guardian's plan was to topple Prince Richard and watch opposition to Romanian Protected Membership fall away. Protected Membership, which had been the Prince's creation, was to bring about his death.

The Guardian had not heard from the Mechanic since the early hours of the morning when the killer had telephoned him from David's flat. He was certain that the Mechanic's silence meant that the killer was in the process of doing away with David and retrieving the computer disk. Everything needed for Operation Domino to be carried out was in place. Even if the Guardian had wanted to stop the assassination, it was now too late to do so.

CHAPTER 27

Telephoning the Guardian was the last thing on the Mechanic's mind. He had gone beyond the point of wanting to kill David because he was being paid to do so. He just wanted to kill him. First, he wanted to hurt David and then he wanted to watch him die, slowly.

The journey from London to Shropshire had been the final straw for the Mechanic. He was breaking all of his own rules to catch David: rules that had kept him alive for over fifteen years in a business which few survived in for long.

He was no longer interested in impressing his best customer or in preserving his reputation as one of the most reliable assassins in the World. For the first time in his life he hated his target and killing David had become everything to him.

The Mechanic drove fast. The hired Ford Escort rarely dropped below seventy miles an hour as he drove along the winding Bridgenorth Road in pursuit of David's Mercedes. He was still too far behind to be able to spot the old red car. The Escort screeched around the bends as the Mechanic gripped the steering wheel tightly. He was functioning now fuelled on pure rage.

He drove as fast as he was able to for ten miles before he saw David's car in the distance ahead of him. The Mechanic had gained on the Mercedes, but was still about a quarter of a mile behind. David was in a hurry as well and on the straight sections of the Bridgenorth Road, the powerful 3.5 litre engine of the Mercedes ate up the tarmac.

The Mechanic watched the Mercedes turn left at an island and accelerate in the direction of Stourbridge. It was still early and other than the Mercedes the Mechanic could not see any cars on the road.

He threw the Escort around to the left when he reached the island and almost lost control of the car. He spun the car's steering wheel hard over in the opposite direction and the Escort corrected. The car darted back on to the left hand side of the road. Smoke blew out of the exhaust pipe as the Mechanic rushed up through the gears.

The Mercedes disappeared over a slight hump in the road. Less than three minutes later the Escort left the road as it literally flew over the same hump. As the car's tyres came back into contact with the tarmac the Mechanic pressed down hard on the brake pedal and grappled with the steering wheel as the car slowed down, skidding on the wet road surface as the brakes bit in. He had narrowly missed driving into the rear of a tractor which had pulled out of a field just after the hump in the road. The tractor filled more than half of the narrow road and the first time the Mechanic pulled out blind to overtake, the Escort nearly ended up in the hedgerow along the side of the road.

He bashed the car's horn on the steering wheel repeatedly and shouted through the windscreen to the driver of the tractor to pull over and let him pass. The tractor engine was loud and the driver was wearing ear protectors to muffle the sound. He could see the brand new Escort in his wing mirror, but was not going to move over for the driver.

Again the Mechanic pulled out from behind the tractor to try and overtake the painfully slow vehicle. Headlights suddenly flashed at the Mechanic and he turned the steering wheel to the left. The Escort swerved back behind the tractor as the only car other than the Mercedes that the Mechanic had seen for over a hour, drove passed on the other side of the road.

The tractor was moving at no more than ten miles an hour along the country road. The Mechanic knew that every minute he was stuck behind the tractor David was getting further away.

The tractor approached the bottom of a steep hill and the driver changed down to a lower gear. The tractor jerked a little as its gears were changed then slowed down even more as it began the climb. The Mechanic positioned the Escort as close to the rear of the tractor as he could. As soon as the tractor began its long, slow slog up the hill, he dropped the car into second gear, turned the steering wheel sharply to the right and pressed the accelerator pedal flat to the floor.

The Escort leaped from behind the tractor, the engine revving loudly and shot past the slow vehicle. The Mechanic was lucky. This time nothing was coming in the opposite direction.

Once again the Mechanic accelerated up through the car's gears chasing the Mercedes. The road was clear ahead of him, but he had lost sight of David's car. He drove even faster than he had done before in an effort to catch his prey. He finally caught sight of the Mercedes again some way ahead of him as David approached the outskirts of Stourbridge. David's route took him through Stourbridge town centre and then on to the M40 motorway. The morning was wearing on and as the two cars approached the town centre traffic was starting to build up.

David was forced to stop at traffic lights that were showing red on the approach to the centre of town. In the time it took the lights to change from red to green the Escort had reached the back of the queue waiting to drive over the junction. There were only five cars between the Mercedes and the Escort.

In spite of the rain, the Mechanic was able to clearly see the distinctive shape of the red sports car ahead of him. The cars moved past the lights one by one. As the Escort approached the junction the lights turned amber signalling that the next car should slow down and stop. Ignoring the lights, the Mechanic pressed down quickly on the accelerator and the Escort shot across the junction as the lights changed to red.

The line of cars drove through Stourbridge town centre and on to the duel carriageway that leads to the M40 motorway. The Mechanic was able to overtake two of the five cars that separated the Escort from the Mercedes once the cars were on the wider road.

He saw David's Mercedes indicate to move over to the right to join the motorway two cars ahead of him. The Mercedes moved to the right and joined the motorway traffic. The Escort followed.

The Mechanic was startled as the motorway came into view. The three lanes were crowded with traffic, moving at no more than fifty miles an hour. He had expected the motorway to be empty as it had been during his drive from London in the early hours of the morning. Instead it was congested with cars carrying their occupants to work at the start of the rush hour. He looked around for David's car and at first was unable to see it amongst the mass of traffic across the three lanes. Then he caught sight of the Mercedes moving to the right across two lanes as David drove the car into the outside lane. The Mechanic had fallen back and was now seven cars behind David. He followed the Mercedes into the outside lane.

The traffic on the motorway became less congested as the Mercedes and the Escort drove further away from the Stourbridge junction. The rain also began to ease off the further out of Shropshire the two men travelled. Nevertheless, the motorway was still too crowded for the Mechanic to risk approaching David's car and he fell in three cars behind the Mercedes, tracking David's every move.

Packard was not far behind. The unmarked police car joined the motorway at the Stourbridge junction ten minutes after the Mercedes and the Escort had done so. Packard had telephoned Scotland Yard and within minutes of his call had been informed that two cars were registered to David Bowstead, a Golf GTI and a red 1971, SL Mercedes.

The police car had joined the motorway at the Stourbridge junction. The junction identified by the imprint of David's selected route to Oxford.

None of the Detectives in the car knew exactly how far behind David they were. The Detective who had inspected the garage at Chesterton had reported to Packard that he could smell fumes at the rear of the garage, as if a car engine had recently been revved whilst it was still in the garage. This and the fresh tyre tracks in the gravel of the driveway had lead Packard to conclude that David was not very far ahead of them.

The driver of the police car moved the car as best as he could in and out of the traffic, trying to make up time on David. Ordinarily he would have used the car's magnetic roof siren to get through the traffic, but Packard was concerned that the sound of the siren might alert David that he was being pursued and force him off the motorway. If David deviated from his route before they spotted his car, Packard would lose him and the Mechanic for good. Packard and the Detectives looked out for a Golf GTI or a red SL Mercedes.

David had no idea that he was being followed. He was not aware of the Ford Escort a few cars behind. He was watching the road ahead, driving faster as the motorway became increasingly less congested the further south he went. He had no way of knowing that as well as the Mechanic biting at his heels, Packard was only five miles behind him.

The Mechanic followed David, staying either two or three cars behind the Mercedes at all times for fifty miles.

As the traffic had begun to thin out, David had accelerated and had been maintaining a constant ninety miles an hour for the last twenty five miles. The Mechanic did not lose sight of the Mercedes.

By the time the Mercedes and the Escort were less than fifteen miles away from the exit ramp for Oxford, the motorway was almost empty. It was 9:10 am and David was on schedule. He knew that he had been pushing the old car hard for some time and slowed down from ninety miles an hour to seventy five. The Mercedes fuel gage showed that the tank was still a quarter full. He had more than enough fuel to get him to Oxford. He began to work out in his mind what he would say to the police. He knew that it would be no use blurting out that he was aware of a plot to kill the Prince of Wales. He would have to show the police the information on the Planner's disk and persuade them to take it seriously. He was good at persuading people. It was his job after all. David was confident that if he could get to speak to the policemen who were actually assigned to protect the Prince, with the aid of the disk he would be able to persuade them to stop the lecture.

It had stopped raining some time ago and David could see the empty road ahead of him clearly. He checked the car's rear view mirror. The view from the plastic screen in the hood was not so good. The screen was old and a little yellow in places. David thought he could see a car moving closer to the Mercedes. His eyes moved down to the right hand side of the car and he looked at the reflection in the Mercedes's wing mirror. He caught a glimpse of a car which he could not make out as it pulled left out of the lane behind him. David turned his head quickly to the left and looked at the opposite wing mirror. He could see the reflection of a Ford Escort accelerating towards his car. He assumed the driver of the Escort was trying to overtake him on the inside. He was surprised by this because he was not driving slowly and the driver of the Escort had not flashed his headlights to signal David to move over and let him pass.

David waited for the car to come into view alongside his passenger window. The front of the Escort gradually appeared. David checked the speed of the Mercedes. He had crept over eighty miles an hour. The Escort was doing close to ninety miles an hour. More of the car appeared across from David. Slowly the inside of the Escort came level with the Mercedes's passenger window and David looked across again to see the driver. He did not recognise him at first. The driver had a peculiar hair colour and was wearing glasses. David looked again. The driver of the

Escort turned and examined the Mercedes. David recognised the Mechanic and froze in astonishment.

The Mechanic looked up at David and the two men's eyes met. The killer turned away and leant over to his left, keeping the Escort positioned alongside the Mercedes as he did so. David was unable to take his eyes off the Mechanic. He could not believe that the killer was right there, across from him. His mind was rushing. How had he found him? Where had he come from? Had he been tailing him since he left Chesterton?

The Mechanic turned and looked over at the Mercedes again. The driver's window of the Escort slid down under the steady control of the power unit. All David could do was stare at his pursuer. The killer swung his right arm out of the open window and aimed his hand gun at the bonnet of the Mercedes.

David saw the gun and instinctively slouched down in his seat to try and avoid the barrel. The Mercedes swerved from side to side as David momentarily lost control of the steering wheel causing the Mechanic's first two shots to miss the car's radiator. The Mechanic wanted to force David to stop. He did not want him to crash and be killed in his car.

The sound of the bullets embedding themselves in the body of his car sent a shiver through David. He grabbed the steering wheel with both hands and managed to straighten out the Mercedes. David stayed slouched in his seat and without being able to see out of the windscreen, flattened the accelerator pedal to the floor. The powerful engine roared and the Mercedes pulled away quickly from the Escort. David sat up as he saw the Mechanic's car disappear from view. He checked his wing mirrors and saw the Escort behind him.

The Mechanic stuck his right arm out of the window again and fired two more bullets at the car. The first missed completely. The second tore through the back of the car's fabric hood and shattered the left side of the windscreen. The Mechanic could not control the Escort and shoot accurately at this speed. He brought the gun back inside the car and floored the accelerator pedal.

The Mercedes was flat out at one hundred and twenty four miles an hour. The rev counter needle flickered into the red area of the dial and David prayed that the old engine would not blow up. He could see the Escort behind him in his wing mirrors. The Mechanic was not gaining on the Mercedes. The Escort's top speed was one hundred and twenty two miles an hour. It was travelling at this speed, but could not gain on the

Mercedes whilst David drove flat out.

The two cars hurtled along the road. David had never driven the Mercedes so fast before. Whilst the owner's manual identified a top speed of one hundred and twenty four miles an hour, this had been achieved when the car had been new, back in 1971. David was not certain whether his beloved old sports car could hammer along at such a speed for very long. The Ford Escort was less than six months old and whilst its top speed was less than that of the Mercedes, it could maintain one hundred and twenty two miles an hour for as long as it had fuel to do so.

David caught a glimpse of road signs along the central reservoir of the motorway. He was travelling so quickly, however, that he was unable to read what the signs said. Within seconds he knew.

Up ahead David saw that the outside lane of the motorway in which the Mercedes was travelling, suddenly tapered off. The Mercedes would be forced over to the left as the outside carriageway vanished into a forest of cones and road surface repair machinery. He knew he would have to slow down to manoeuvre across the carriageway. To turn the steering wheel even slightly at almost one hundred and twenty five miles an hour would be suicide. David checked his mirrors very quickly, reluctant to take his eyes off the road in front of him at the speed the Mercedes was travelling. He saw the Escort still behind him to his left.

The lane the Mercedes was in was just running out as David took his foot off the accelerator pedal and manoeuvred the car over to the inside lane. The Mercedes slowed down instantly and David was able to turn the steering wheel without losing control of the car. The Escort was immediately behind him now, the Mechanic not having had to change lanes.

As the two cars entered the area of the road surface repairs the motorway lanes became narrower causing David and the Mechanic to reduce their speeds. The Mechanic did not waste the opportunity. Both cars had slowed down to just over fifty miles an hour. Again the Mechanic shot at the back of the Mercedes. He fired two bullets into the trunk and a third in through the back of the fabric hood. This bullet easily pierced the flimsy hood and narrowly missed David's left shoulder blade. David however, was more concerned by the bullets that had been fired at the trunk. The Mercedes's fuel tank was stored at the front of the trunk. He watched the fuel gauge on the instrument panel closely to see if he could detect if the tank was loosing fuel. It did not appear to be.

Out of nowhere the outside lane of the motorway appeared again. The cars had passed the end of the road works. The Mechanic took advantage of the extra space before David was able to. The Escort screeched loudly as the Mechanic dropped the car down into third gear and accelerated past the Mercedes into the outside lane. The Escort was now alongside the Mercedes and before David had a chance to escape by using the old car's marginally superior speed, the Mechanic yanked the steering wheel of the Escort hard over to the left and rammed his car against the driver's door of the Mercedes.

David felt the door panelling of his car crumple in against his right thigh. He moved the Mercedes to the left and straddled the first and second lanes. The Mechanic was positioning the Escort for a second attack, but this time David was ready for him. As the Escort was about to hit the right hand side of the Mercedes for the second time, David turned the steering wheel of the old German made car firmly to the right and pressed down on the accelerator. The front right hand side of the Mercedes collided with the left hand side of the Escort, knocking the Escort across the road. David straightened the Mercedes and floored the accelerator pedal. He could see the Escort following, about twenty yards behind him.

The passenger side of the Escort was crumpled, the headlights were smashed and part of the car's front under spoiler had been knocked off in the collision. The Escort was no match for the Mercedes in a street fight.

Packard's unmarked police car travelled for most of its journey along the M40 motorway at speeds of between eighty and ninety miles an hour. For thirty five miles, ever time the Detectives passed a Golf GTI, the police car slowed down to allow Packard to inspect the occupants. Packard did not see anyone who even remotely looked like David and none of the Detectives saw an SL Mercedes. After they had driven thirty five miles, the car's cellular telephone rang and Packard was informed by his office that David's Golf GTI had been discovered apparently abandoned by the side of a telephone box on the outskirts of London. Packard told the two Detectives to ignore Golfs and concentrate on looking out for a red Mercedes sports car.

Five miles before the exit junction for Oxford, which David had noted on his route, the driver of the police car suddenly swerved the car in order to avoid a redundant spoiler that was laying in the middle of the carriageway. The second Detective consulted the map and David's route, then instructed the driver to take the next exit ramp.

David was able to keep the Mercedes ahead of the Escort for the few miles that remained before the exit ramp for Oxford was signposted. The Escort was constantly in David's wing mirrors, but did not get any closer to the Mercedes. As soon as he saw the sign announcing that the next exit ramp was for Oxford, David moved the Mercedes into the left hand lane of the motorway, making sure that the car's speed did not drop significantly. The Mechanic followed him.

The Mercedes left the motorway for Oxford at exit nine and was followed by the Escort. The two cars approached a junction at the end of the "off" ramp and were forced to slow down. David had no intention of stopping. If he did, he was sure the Mechanic would pull up next to his car and shoot him. As the Mercedes approached the junction David did not stop, or check for on coming traffic. Instead he drove straight over the junction following the signs for Oxford, trying to get his bearings. He heard car horns sound behind him and looked in his rear view mirror. Through the torn hood behind him he saw the Escort dart over the junction after him, narrowly missing two cars which had right of way over the Escort. Once again the Mechanic's determination terrified David.

It was 9:35 am according to the clock in the Mercedes. David was running out of time. The Prince's lecture was scheduled to begin in twenty five minutes time and David was not at the university yet.

David's directions stopped at the exit ramp for Oxford. Packard and the two Detectives drove towards the town centre not knowing where to look next. Packard told the driver to drive into the centre of town and lookout for David's car. This was an unscientific approach to police work and all three of them knew it. Packard picked up the car telephone and set about organising a scientific approach to locating David's Mercedes.

By the time the police car had reached the centre of Oxford the police helicopter Packard had requested was airborne. The pilot's instructions were clear. Search the centre of Oxford for a red SL Mercedes until the helicopter runs low on fuel, then land, re-fuel and search some more. It was not every day that a Detective Inspector from Scotland Yard's Assassination Division asked for help and the Oxford CID were happy to provide what assistance they could.

The helicopter pilot had a police map that divided the City of Oxford into grids. He flew low over each of the girds in turn searching for David's car.

The last time David had been in the centre of Oxford he had been having lunch at Bangkok House, without doubt the best oriental restaurant in the city, with his mother and father after collecting his degree certificate from Merton College. His mother had been proud and his father had for first time talked to his son as a fellow professional. David had enjoyed that day, but he suspected that his father had enjoyed it even more.

Oxford can be a delightful place in the summer. The city is crowded with tourists, but still the summer months to David had always been enjoyable.

Oxford University has thirty five colleges, each has its own character and distinct flavour. St John's College has the most money, Wadham and Balliol Colleges are the most left wing and Christ Church College is traditionally the most public school dominated. The university buildings include some of the country's greatest architecture. David had loved his years at Oxford.

As he tried to overtake a Mini Metro that was cautiously crawling along in front of him, the November wind whipped into the Mercedes through the ripped roof and made David's face smart. The Mercedes pulled on to the other side of the road and managed to find room along the old cobbled street to pass the Mini Metro. David was running out of time and he knew it.

He could still see the Mechanic's car behind him. For every daring manoeuvre David carried out to make up time the Mechanic made two such moves. The Mercedes worked its way through the winding streets of Oxford in the direction of the Oxford Union building where the Prince would deliver his lecture. David was followed by the Mechanic.

He knew he had to lose the Mechanic some how. He drove the Mercedes faster along the roads, occasionally bumping a dustbin or a parked car when the road he was on narrowed suddenly, which the Oxford roads have a habit of unexpectedly doing. Although he had not driven through Oxford for years, David remembered his university town well.

He suddenly turned the Mercedes sharp right, drove through a shallow pool of water in the middle of the road and accelerated away. Hopefully, he checked his mirrors. The bruised Escort was still behind him.

He drove the Mercedes hard, turning as often as he could to try and lose the Mechanic. It was no use. Whilst David had the advantage of knowing Oxford well, the Mercedes had not been designed for quick manoeuvrability around town and every time he thought he had lost the Mechanic, he would check his rear view mirror and see the Escort still behind him.

It was by now almost 9:50 am and David knew that he had no choice. He pulled the Mercedes out on to Woodstock Road which leads to the university and pressed hard on the car's accelerator.

The police helicopter had been in the air for less than fifteen minutes when the pilot spotted the Mercedes moving towards the main university buildings. The helicopter hovered low so that the pilot could check the number plate of the car. Shoppers looked up at the helicopter whilst it hovered above them. It did not hover for long. As soon as the pilot had confirmed the registration number of David's car he flew to a higher altitude and radioed in.

Packard was contacted three minutes later. The Detectives had had no luck driving around Oxford looking for David's car. None of them had been to the famous city before and even using the map they had purchased, the driver had lost his way once already. Packard was told over the car telephone that the Mercedes was moving quickly along Woodstock Road into the heart of the university. The second Detective consulted the map, located the road that David was on and gave the driver directions. Packard wondered why David was heading towards the university.

The Mercedes had a clear run from the north of Oxford along St. Giles and on to Magdalen Street. At the turning for St. Michael's Street, David turned right.

The Oxford Union building is situated at the far end of St. Michael's Street. David checked his mirrors again and saw the Mechanic's car behind him. He drove right passed the Oxford Union building. He saw police cars and a BBC Television outdoor production van. Having the Prince lecture to the students was a rare treat for the Oxford Union and it intended to publicise the event.

David drove to the end of the road and without stopping at the junction pulled out, turning the Mercedes quickly to the left, on to New Inn Hall Street. As soon as the car had rounded the corner, David slammed on the brakes, pointed the car towards the far left hand side of the road and leaped out, before it had completely come to a stop. He passed the Mechanic's car on foot just as the Ford Escort turned left out of St. Michael's Street. The Mercedes's sudden left turn at the junction had taken the Mechanic by surprise. He had hesitated and checked the road before pulling the Escort out into New Inn Hall Street. David had been counting on the Mechanic doing exactly that.

As soon as the Mechanic saw David run past him back up St. Michael's Street, he brought his right foot down hard on the Escort's brake pedal. He even used the hand brake to reduce the car's speed more quickly. The Escort eventually stopped when it smashed into the back of David's Mercedes. The Mechanic was no longer in the car by then. He was running after David waving his hand gun in the air.

By the time the Mechanic realised what David was doing and had rounded the corner back on to St. Michael's Street, David was running up the steps towards the Oxford Union. There were people filing into the Union building and the Mechanic was unable to get a shot off. He stuffed the hand gun in his overcoat pocket and ran along the road towards the crowd.

David stood amongst the throng of students and professors as they walked into the Union building. He was thankful that there were so many people for him to hide amongst.

As a student, David had attended numerous lectures and debates hosted by the Oxford Union. Many budding politicians from Edward Heath to Tony Benn have tuned their oratory skills in the famous arena. The Debating Chamber can hold up to a thousand people if the galleries around the room are used. As David was bustled inside the Debating Chamber he saw that the room was bursting with people. More that he could remember having ever seen in the Oxford Union before. Students were crowded into the famous room waiting for the Prince. It was 9:55 am.

David looked around for a policeman. He could see several strategically placed throughout the Chamber, but the crowd of people was so dense that the nearest officer was at least fifty feet away from him. He remembered the policemen he had seen sitting on the bonnets of their cars outside.

David could see why the Planner had selected this place for the Prince to be assassinated. No one was being searched as they entered the room, the galleries around the Chamber were crowded and people were pushing this way and that shouting for Prince Richard. The assassin could kill the Prince and vanish into the mass of bodies in a moment. It was organised chaos.

David did not know exactly how the Prince was to be killed. The electricity in Chesterton had failed before the Planner's disk had divulged that information. He had assumed that a gunman with a high velocity rifle would shoot the Prince from a hidden place on one of the galleries, but the galleries were all in use, crowded with students. He looked around desperately trying to see from where the fateful bullet might be shot. The more he looked around the crowded Chamber the more he realised that even if he told the police what he knew, they would not be able to protect the Prince if he insisted on delivering his lecture in spite of an alleged threat to his life. David needed to be able to tell them exactly how the Prince was to be assassinated.

There was not enough time before the Prince walked out on to the podium for David to tell his story to the police and persuade them to read the details of Operation Domino from the Planner's disk. David was unshaven, his clothes were torn and he had blood stains on his shirt. If he approached the police screaming assassination, they were certain to drag him out of the Chamber believing him to be a crazed student who did not like the Royal family. He knew that he would at the very least have to be able to tell them straight away exactly how the Prince was going to be killed.

As he twisted his head looking up at the galleries, David was sure that the Prince was not going to be shot. An assassin would be spotted. The details he had seen of Operation Domino were clear. The assassin had to be able to escape undetected. Rebecca's father had planned some other way to kill the Prince, David was certain.

He elbowed his way back towards the entrance to the room. He needed to get to a computer as quickly as possible and would have to risk being spotted by the Mechanic if the killer was outside.

The courtyard in front of the Oxford Union building was deserted. Every one was now inside the Chamber. Chanting had broken out. The audience was calling for the Prince.

David could not see the Mechanic. He ran from the building across the courtyard and in through an open door, his heart pounding. He was inside the Oxford Union Administration Office.

CHAPTER 28

His Royal Highness The Prince of Wales sat in a deep arm chair going over his lecture notes one last time. He was waiting in an ante room behind the podium area of the Debating Chamber. He could hear the crowd in the main room chanting his name.

The Prince had delivered many lectures on Protected Membership of the European Community and was an accomplished speaker. Nevertheless, this was his first lecture on the topic since returning from Brussels where Britain had exercised its veto to prevent Romania from joining the Community. His lecture would last exactly forty five minutes and he had agreed to take fifteen minutes of questions from the floor at the end of his speech. Inevitably some of the questions would concern his own involvement in blocking Romanian membership. He was prepared for these. He would answer truthfully that the decision to use the veto had been taken by the Prime Minister with the advice of the Foreign Secretary and other appropriate government aides. He wished he could be frank and explain why he was so against Romania being allowed to join the European Community, but he could not.

The Prince knew that the Romanian President had fixed the vote in the Banat region of his country during Romania's first democratic elections in May 1990. He knew that on the President's orders government aides had conspired to falsify the ballot count and that as a result, the President had come to power with a majority in each of the country's regions. The Prince knew these things for certain, but was unable to prove them.

Without proof, to make such allegations would cause an international incident and would damage his own reputation and more importantly, the reputation of the United Kingdom.

The Prince could not explain his motives for preventing Romania from joining the Community to his audience, as much as he would like to. He had not even discussed the matter with the British Prime Minister. There was no point. Without proof, he would not be interested. All that the Prince could do was prevent Romania from joining the European Community until the Romanian President was either overthrown, voted out of office or resigned.

The Prince looked at his watch. I was almost 10:00 am. He stood up and went over to the mirror that hung on the wall by the door to the room. He straightened his tie, pulled out his cuffs and waited to be called to speak.

Packard flashed his identification card in front of the police constable's face and asked where the entrance to the Union building was. He had been informed over the telephone in his car that Prince Richard was delivering a lecture at the university that morning. He told the two Detectives to investigate the Union building.

Packard showed the police at the bottom of the steps leading up to the Oxford Union courtyard, photographs of David and the Mechanic and asked the officers if they had seen either of the men in the last hour or so. One of the policemen explained that for the last hour the entire courtyard and the area around the steps had been packed with hundreds of students waiting to go into the Chamber. They had seen too many people to be able to remember specifically two faces. Packard accepted this and ran up the steps towards the entrance to the Chamber.

David sat down behind the President of the Oxford Union's desk and typed Rebecca's original Polish family name into his computer. Within moments he was in the Operation Domino Directory and had found the file entitled "Plan".

He quickly scrolled through the pages, stopping the text every few seconds to read. It was taking too long. He pressed the F2 key and the screen prompted him to identify the phrase he wanted to search for. David typed "Oxford Union", and the computer automatically searched the text of the document for these words. Three seconds later the cursor flashed at the end of a sentence that read:

"Option three: Assassinate the Prince during his lecture at the Oxford Union".

David read how the Prince was to be assassinated.

When he knew, he got to his feet and dashed back towards the courtyard. He did not bother with the disk. He now knew everything.

He was rushing through the door of the Administration Office when he felt the butt of the Mechanic's hand gun in his ribs. At that moment a deafening cheer came from inside the Chamber.

David's heart sank.

Prince Richard walked on to the lecture platform and up to the podium to the cheers and applause of the Oxford students.

"We meet again Bowstead," whispered the Mechanic in David's ear. He pushed the barrel of the gun further into David's rib-cage and David moved forward. As they walked across the courtyard, David heard the audience in the Chamber laugh as the Prince cracked a joke before beginning his lecture.

David looked down the steps for the policemen he had seen earlier, but they had gone. They had only been there to keep the crowds in order as the students had waited and then filed inside the Chamber. Now that the lecture had started and all the students were inside the Chamber, the policemen had left to get a late breakfast before having to return to be on hand again when the lecture finished. The courtyard was deserted. The Mechanic guided David in the direction of the steps with the end of the gun.

David and the Mechanic were walking down the steps when they both heard the sound of a heavy door slam behind them. The Mechanic spun around quickly when he heard the noise and saw Packard walk out of the Chamber and look across at them.

Packard did not recognised David at first. He recognised the Mechanic instantly.

The Mechanic pushed David to the ground and swung his hand gun around towards Packard. He took aim and began to squeeze the trigger of the gun. The sound of a single bullet being fired disturbed the silence of the courtyard.

The Mechanic's head was knocked back slightly as the bullet struck him squarely between the eyes. He dropped down on the steps by the side of David and rolled on to his back. He was dead.

David looked up from the Mechanic's body at Packard as he walked towards him. The Detective Inspector held a small gun in his left hand. Packard always carried a gun when he was in the field although he was rarely required to use it. Privately, he still thought he could win his former battalion's Marksman Trophy.

Packard had pulled his gun from its holster as the Mechanic had swung away from David towards him. Packard had taken aim the moment his gun sight had come into line with the Mechanic. It had taken the Mechanic only a few seconds to aim his own gun at Packard, but those few seconds had killed him.

David was motionless. It had all happened so quickly and he was slightly shocked. He had never seen Packard before and was apprehensive as the middle aged Detective Inspector slowly walked towards him still holding the gun he had killed the Mechanic with.

"You must be David Bowstead," said Packard as he nudged the Mechanic's lifeless body with the toe of his shoe. "Don't worry. He's dead." David slowly got to his feet as it became clear that Packard was not going to shoot him as well.

"Thanks," was all that he could saw.

A loud round of applause erupted from the Chamber bringing David's attention back to the Prince.

"He's still alive," mumbled David. "There's still time." He pushed passed Packard and started to run towards the Oxford Union Chamber.

"Who's still alive?" shouted Packard after him. "What's going on?"

"The Prince," replied David as he ran towards the entrance of the Chamber. "They're going to kill Prince Richard during his lecture." Packard was taken aback by this, but reacted quickly. He ran after David.

The Chamber was full. David pushed his way in amongst the crowd trying to look over the audience's heads at the Prince. Some of the students at the back of the room where David was standing, were quietly discussing what the Prince had just been saying. At the front of the Chamber the students listened intently.

Prince Richard was explaining why it was essential for Western Europe to secure the economic cooperation of those former soviet satellite countries in Europe that had properly embraced democracy, and that in order to achieve this, those countries had to be reassured that if they joined the European Community, at a time when there own economies were vulnerable, the existing Member States would not take advantage of their resources.

David was not listening. He was elbowing people out of the way trying to get a clear look at the lecture podium the Prince was standing at. At first he was unable to see the podium at all. There were too many students in front of him. He strained his neck to try and look over the crowd, but the podium was only slightly elevated and he could still not see it clearly. David pushed at the mass of bodies around him. It was impossible to get through.

Suddenly he began to shout at the top of his voice.

"Your Royal Highness, Your Royal Highness."

He waved his arms in the air and people around him turned to see who was shouting at the Prince. As they did David was able to move forward a little, in the direction of the podium. He continued to shout and more of the audience diverted their attention from the Prince as they searched amongst the crowd for the heckler. Oxford Union stewards and police constables who were stationed around the room also noticed the disturbance and began moving through the crowd towards David.

The people in front of him moved out of his way when they realised that the heckler was behind them. David kept pushing forward getting closer to the podium. Eventually, he reached the centre of the room and could see the podium clearly.

Prince Richard became aware of the disturbance as the commotion in the crowd moved nearer to the front of the room. He looked up from his lecture notes and momentarily paused. He could not hear above all of the noise exactly what was being shouted, but he had been heckled before and was not phased by the disturbance. He continued to talk.

David was desperate. He shouted and shouted, trying to attract the Prince's attention. However, although he was now close enough to see the Prince standing at the podium he was still some way back and the noise that had broken out around him made it difficult for him to hear even his own voice.

The Prince looked up again from his lecture notes and stopped talking. He could see a section of the crowd in the centre of the Chamber pushing and shoving one another. He could also see policemen moving towards the disruptive section of the crowd. The Prince decided to wait until the police had reached the hecklers and were removing them from the room before continuing. He took advantage of the interruption to have a drink of water.

David watched as the Prince stopped talking, picked up a tall clear tumbler full to the brim with water from the podium, and drank the glass dry.

Two police constables reached David first and pushed him to the floor. One of them held his head down and twisted his left arm hard up behind his back. Stewards arrived followed by three more policemen who made a human barricade around David. They half escorted him towards the back of the Chamber and half dragged him. People cheered as David was removed from the room. He tried to protest. The constable who had hold of David's arm heard him say something about the Prince but could not understand what his prisoner was saying due to the noise inside the Chamber.

The Prince replaced the empty glass on the podium and regained the audience's attention by joking that hecklers at Oxford University had more perseverance than Cambridge University undergraduates. He looked down at his lecture notes trying to find his place. The Prince felt dizzy and could not see the typed words on the page clearly. He looked up at the crowd and started to talk. His speech was slurred and his words confused. The Prince again looked at his lecture notes and then out into the crowd. He tried to talk, but could not. His eye lids began to close and his balance deserted him. He fell to the floor. The crowd went silent.

The Prince's bodyguard was at his side as the Prince hit the floor. He was followed on to the platform by half a dozen of the Prince's staff who made a human shield around the unconscious body.

The stewards and the policemen dragged David out of the Chamber just as the Prince fell to the floor. The constable who had hold of David's arm loosened his grip as they left the Chamber and David was able to straighten up. The noise that had surrounded the group as they had escorted David from the building suddenly subsided. For the first time they could hear what David was saying.

"Prince Richard has been poisoned," he shouted at them.

CHAPTER 29

Pandemonium broke out in the Oxford Union Debating Chamber as word spread through the crowd that Prince Richard was not moving. People yelled and pushed, unsure what was happening exactly. Some of the women in the crowd cried whilst others at the front nearest to the podium, just stood and stared at the Prince lying motionless on the platform.

A stretcher was brought to the podium and the Prince was lifted on to it and carried out of the Chamber. A police Range Rover was waiting at the rear entrance with its tail gate open. The stretcher was placed in the back of the Range Rover and the doors were slammed shut. Sirens sounded and lights flashed as the Range Rover, accompanied by police motorcycles and police cars, hurried towards John Radcliffe Hospital.

Packard had followed David into the Chamber, but had lost sight of him in the crowd. Eventually, he spotted him being manhandled out of the room by a group of police constables and stewards. He had pushed his way back to the main door of the Chamber and had still been inside when the Prince had collapsed and the crowd had fallen silent. He had then understood what David had mumbled about someone killing the Prince and ran outside after him.

Detective Inspector Packard produced his identification card and pulled David free of the police constable's grip. The constable gave David up without argument as soon as he saw Packard's senior Scotland Yard credentials. Packard took David by the arm and led him in the direction of his car. David followed without complaint relieved to have his arm back. The two men got into Packard's car forgetting the Detectives who had arrived with Packard who were stuck inside the Chamber. Packard started the engine and turned to David.

"Prince Richard has collapsed. I think the police are taking him to hospital," he said.

David's heart sank.

"The water he drank from was poisoned," he replied.

"Poisoned?" Packard was surprised. "I thought the Mechanic was after you not the Prince."

"The Mechanic?" questioned David.

"The man who's been chasing you. The one I shot," Packard explained.

David understood.

"He was, I think," said David. "I stumbled upon a plot to kill the Prince. But they were going to poison him."

Packard put the car into first gear and pressed hard on the accelerator pedal.

"Where will they take him David?"

"The John Radcliffe Hospital in Headington is the nearest fully equipped hospital," he replied without hesitation. "They'll take him there, if he's still alive. Turn left at the end of the road."

The police Range Rover screeched to a halt outside the Emergencies entrance of John Radcliffe Hospital. The hospital had been notified that the Prince was on his way. Four doctors, three orderlies and two nurses were waiting outside as the Range Rover came to a halt.

The orderlies opened the back of the Range Rover and with the assistance of the Prince's bodyguard, carefully lifted the stretcher out of the vehicle and placed the Prince on a hospital trolley.

As the trolley was wheeled quickly along the hospital corridors towards the Cardio Vascular Unit, the doctors began their examination. The nurses undressed the Prince removing his jacket, shirt and trousers. One of the doctors checked the Prince's breathing whilst another checked his heartbeat and blood pressure.

The senior doctor, a Consultant, turned to the Prince's bodyguard. "What happened?" he asked.

"I'm not sure. His speech went funny and then he collapsed."

"Had he eaten or drunk anything shortly before he passed out?" demanded the Consultant as he took the Prince's pulse.

"No," replied the bodyguard. "He just had a glass of water whilst his speech was interrupted."

"Water. What, just before he collapsed?" asked the Consultant.

"That's right. A few minutes before."

"And he passed out immediately after that?"

"Yes," replied he bodyguard.

"Damn it. I think he's been poisoned," shouted the Consultant to his medical team. He turned to one of the nurses. "Call the Pharmacist and find out which fast acting lethal poisons are dissolvable in water." The Consultant turned to the bodyguard. "Without knowing which poison he's been given we won't know which antidote to give him even if we can stop him from going into cardiac arrest." The orderlies crashed through a set of rubber doors into the Cardio Vascular Unit's operating theatre.

As soon as the trolley came to a stop one of the doctors inserted a clear plastic tube into the Prince's mouth to ensure that he did not swallow his tongue and to keep his air way clear. An oxygen mask was placed over the Prince's nose and mouth. A nurse began pumping a rubber bag every four seconds that controlled the air flow to the mask. She pumped steadily and consistently counting to four each time in her head. Oxygen flooded into the Prince's lungs.

The nurse who had contacted the hospital's Pharmacist ran into the operating theatre and told the Consultant that there were over fifty fast acting poisons that were lethal which could be dissolved easily in water.

The Consultant put an ear to the Prince's bare chest, but could still not hear a heartbeat. He signalled to a nurse who rubbed paste on two sections of the Prince's chest. Another nurse placed small electronic disks on the paste. The disks were connected by thin wires to a heart monitoring machine on a trolley behind the Prince. Everyone except the nurse who was methodically pumping oxygen into the Prince's lungs looked at the monitor. The fine line that ran across the monitor which indicated the Prince's heartbeat produced a weak flicker. The Prince was alive. Just.

Then without warning the machine sounded loudly. The flicker on the monitor vanished. The thin line was completely flat. The Prince had gone into cardiac arrest.

Packard's car pulled up next to the police Range Rover and David and Packard leaped out. Packard waved his identification card in the air and explained to the policemen who surrounded the two of them that he was with Scotland Yard's Assassination Division. David and Packard were allowed inside the hospital.

Packard grabbed the first doctor he came across and again waving his credentials in the air asked what the Prince's condition was. The doctor did not know, but directed them to the Cardio Vascular Unit. When they arrived they found the entrance blocked by three officers from the Royal Protection Unit who would not let them in, even on sight of Packard's credentials. The two men stood impatiently outside the Cardio Vascular Unit blocking the entrance.

The rubber doors to the unit opened and a nurse and a doctor rushed out. Packard tried to ask them what was going on, but they could not stop and talk. The two men could hear voices and snippets of a conversation coming from behind the rubber doors. Again Packard tried to get inside the unit, but was firmly refused entrance.

The Consultant placed the base of his hands over the Prince's chest as soon as the line on the monitor flattened. He gently pressed down on the Prince's chest trying to resuscitate the heir to the British throne. It did not work.

Another doctor held two large electric pads in his hands and waited for the Consultant to get clear. He placed the pads on the Prince's chest. The Consultant looked over at the nurse who was operating the Defibrillator and shouted "two hundred joules." An electric shock was sent through the Prince which caused his body to bounce slightly on the trolley. The Consultant looked up at the monitor. The line was still flat.

"Three hundred joules," ordered the Consultant. Again the Prince's body shuddered on the trolley as the electricity ran through him. Again the line on the monitor refused to even flicker.

"Three hundred and twenty five joules," demanded the Consultant. The nurse operating the Defibrillator turned the dial to the level ordered. She blinked back tears as she did so. She knew that the Prince was already dead.

"Stand clear," shouted the Consultant. Three hundred and twenty five joules of electricity ran through the Prince. His body shook dramatically from the force of the shock.

The operating room was silent. Everyone prayed for the monitor to respond.

Nothing, but then, to the Consultant's amazement the line flickered very slightly.

"We've got weak fibrillation," announced the Consultant. "He's back with us." The Consultant gently massaged the Prince's chest trying to strengthen his heartbeat.

The line on the monitor was flickering, but irregularly. The Prince was alive for the moment but everyone in the theatre knew that unless the antidote for the poison was introduced into his blood stream very quickly, he would go into cardiac arrest again and would be dead within minutes.

"The poison," shouted the Consultant desperately at one of the younger doctors, "ask the policemen who brought him in. Ask anyone. He can't hang on for much longer."

The doctor hurried out of the operating theatre. He pushed through the doors and spoke to the Prince's bodyguard.

"The Prince has been poisoned. We can't save him unless we know exactly what poison he's been given."

"I know," said the bodyguard as he ran his fingers through his hair in desperation. "It must have been in the water he drank. I should have checked. I should have checked, but we never check the water. We never have."

David and Packard were standing in the waiting area by the swing doors and heard everything the young doctor said. Packard knew that it was no use. The Prince could have taken one of many poisons that are dissolvable in water. It was impossible to guess which antidote he needed and the wrong antidote would be as fatal as the poison. The policemen in the waiting room stared silently at the doctor. There was nothing any of them could do.

"I think I might know which poison the Prince has taken," said David, breaking the silence. "I saw it written down." They all looked at him.

"What?" asked the doctor. David tried to remember what he had seen on the computer screen in the Oxford Union Administration Office.

"It began with a E," he replied, desperately trying to remember. Packard looked across at David and then spoke to the doctor.

"He knows. Don't ask how, he just knows. Come on David, remember the name."

The doctor could not recognise the poison. There are too many that begin with the letter E. He took David by the arm and quickly led him through the swing doors. Packard and the Prince's bodyguard followed.

They were taken into the operating theatre. David had never been in an operating room before and the sight that met his eyes as he was pushed inside took him by surprise. The surroundings were unfamiliar, but he could see the heartbeat monitor resting on a trolley behind the Prince's head showing a very weak heartbeat. David understood that the Prince was dying.

"This man claims he knows what poison the Prince has taken," the young doctor told the Consultant who was gently massaging the Prince's sternum. The Consultant removed his hands from his patient's body and turned to face David.

"Thank God. What was he given young man?"

David had left the Planner's disk in the computer in the Oxford Union Administration Office. He tried to remember exactly what poison the Planner had chosen for the third option of Operation Domino. He had not paid particular attention to the name of the poison. It had not seemed important.

The Planner had studied television and video footage of the hundred most recent occasions on which the Prince had delivered lectures or given speeches. Whenever the Prince agreed to take questions from the floor at the end of a lecture, the Planner had observed that he always drank water from a clear tumbler as the questions were asked, putting the tumbler down whenever he answered. It was as if he needed something to do with his hands whilst he listened to a question. The Planner noted that the Prince had adopted this routine consistently on every occasion he had taken question after giving a lecture in the last five years. The Planner's recommendation to the Guardian for assassinating the Prince at the Oxford Union had not been to shoot him, or blow him up. It had been to poison the mineral water he would drink from as he listened to questions from the floor at the end of his lecture.

"I can't remember," said David eventually.

"Think man, think," shouted the Consultant.

David looked at the Prince lying on the trolley and then at the monitor behind his head. The signal which indicated that the Prince's heart was still beating was getting visibly weaker. David desperately tried to remember the name of the poison. He could not.

"It was a scientific name. I didn't pay attention to it," he said. "All I remember is that the document recommended it as being reliable because it's used by Mossad."

"Ergot alkaloid," said Packard instantly from behind David's shoulder. "It's used by Mossad, the Israeli secret service all the time."

"Are you sure?" asked the Consultant.

"Absolutely sure," replied Packard. "It's one of the most effective methods of killing a man quickly and quietly."

The Consultant turned to one of the nurses. He had no time to waste. "The antidote is GKN." The nurse went straight to the poisons cabinet in the operating theatre and took out a vial of glyceryl trinitrate. She handed the vial to the Consultant. He sucked the blue liquid from the vial into a syringe and without waiting to test that the liquid was free flowing by squirting some into the air, pumped the antidote into a vein in the Prince's left arm, which had been located by one of the other doctors.

David, Packard and the Consultant watched the heart rate monitor and waited. Within seconds the line flickered more constantly.

The Prince would live.

CHAPTER 30

London. Ten days later.

David stood next to Rebecca in Putney Crematorium. He held her glove covered hand and could hear her sobbing faintly. The priest said a prayer before the Planner's coffin was rolled behind a purple velvet curtain, out of sight. The small room was empty other than for the three of them.

The Planner had no friends in London and Rebecca had been his only family. Her father had wanted to be cremated and Rebecca had decided not to send his body back to the States. He had hated his adopted country so much towards the end of his life, that Rebecca had arranged for him to be cremated in England, her new home. She had no intention of returning to the States. There was nothing there for her any longer.

The bruising on the side of her face had not completely healed and her broken ribs and the bullet wound to her left leg made walking painful. She leant on David as they left the chapel.

Prince Richard had been discharged from hospital the previous afternoon. Every newspaper in the country and most across the World had carried pictures of the Prince walking out of John Radcliffe Hospital, smiling and waving to the crowd of reporters and well wishers that had gathered to see him. The Palace had explained that the Prince had been suffering from a common iron deficiency, which had caused him to collapse during his lecture. He was reported to be completely recovered, but under doctor's orders to rest for two weeks.

David had spent two days being thoroughly interviewed and de-briefed by Detective Inspector Packard and the Royal Protection Unit at Scotland Yard, before he had finally been taken to South Western Hospital to see Rebecca. He had told them all about the computer disk, which had been retrieved from the Oxford Union Administration Office by Packard's men. David had accessed the information on the disk for the police and a team of experts had studied each of the files. Everyone had wanted to know how David had come into possession of the disk. He explained that he had found the disk in the pocket of his jacket, inside an envelope with the password scribbled on it, after the Mechanic had attacked him in the car park at Heathrow.

He had lied to protect Rebecca. She had no idea what her father had been involved in and David had no intention of exposing her to the inevitable harassment that would ensue if the police learnt the identity of the architect of Operation Domino. The Planner was dead and David did not think that Rebecca deserved to spend the rest of her life paying for her father's mistakes.

The Royal Protection Unit concluded that the Mechanic had slipped the disk into David's pocket on the flight from Miami, to avoid having to carry it through customs at the airport, intending to recover the disk from David after he had cleared Heathrow. David suspected that Packard did not believe this, but the Detective Inspector had not let on if he saw the flaws in David's account. The Mechanic, one of the most illusive assassins in the World was dead and the Prince had been saved. Packard was satisfied, even though he was convinced that David had not told the authorities everything he knew.

The information the Planner had included on the disk about the Guardian quickly led Interpol and the AU to the Romanian. The Guardian fled Romania two days after the failed assassination attempt, as soon as it became obvious that Operation Domino had been scuppered. He was picked up three days later in Bonn, in Germany. The United Kingdom Government asked for him to be extradited to England and the German Court had granted the extradition immediately. He would be tried for plotting to murder the Prince. Technically, this was treason and if found guilty he could face the electric chair. However, the United

Kingdom has not executed a convicted criminal for decades. The reality was that the Guardian would spend his precious retirement in solitary confinement in a maximum security prison, serving out a life sentence, without any possibility of parole. At his age, he would almost certainly spend the rest of his life there.

A few days after the Prince collapsed, the Times carried a short report that in the face of two previous rejections the Romanian Government had no plans to re-apply for Protected Membership of the European Community in the immediate future.

After interviewing David, it had not taken Packard very long to understand Detective O'Connor's association with the Guardian and his involvement in the hunt for David and the computer disk. Packard arrested him after he dropped David off at the hospital to visit Rebecca. He was in bed naked, with a prostitute in a seedy hotel near King's Cross Station, when Packard and his men arrived with a warrant for his arrest. He protested again and again that he had never heard of Operation Domino, but no one believed him.

David helped Rebecca into the passenger seat of his Golf. His Mercedes was being repaired. It was dented and smashed in places from the journey to Oxford and he was having new panelling all round and a full respray. The old car had got him to Oxford in one piece and David considered that she deserved some pampering.

Rebecca had stopped crying. She was sad and happy at the same time. Her father had died unexpectedly of a heart attack whilst travelling to pay her a surprise visit. She would miss him. But David was alive. Somehow he had escaped the man who had almost killed her and she was thankful for that. She leant across, put her arms around David and gently kissed him.

David returned Rebecca's kiss. The horror of Operation Domino was over and something wonderful was beginning.

THE END

ABOUT THE AUTHOR

Andrew Iyer is a solicitor practising law in the City of London. He grew up in the Midlands and in Shropshire, before moving to London on finishing university to pursue a legal career. He has travelled extensively, particularly through North America, and is a keen musician. He lives in London with his girlfriend.

He has written a number of articles on aspects of international trade and shipping law, as well as a play entitled *"The Big Game"* and a revue entitled *"Living in America"*. Domino Run is his first novel.